TRACK
HER
DOWN

ALSO BY MELINDA LEIGH

Echo Road

BREE TAGGERT NOVELS

Cross Her Heart

See Her Die

Drown Her Sorrows

Right Behind Her

"Her Second Death" (A Prequel Short Story)

Dead Against Her

Lie to Her

Catch Her Death

On Her Watch

MORGAN DANE NOVELS

Say You're Sorry

Her Last Goodbye

Bones Don't Lie

What I've Done

Secrets Never Die

Save Your Breath

SCARLET FALLS NOVELS

Hour of Need

Minutes to Kill

Seconds to Live

SHE CAN SERIES

She Can Run

She Can Tell

She Can Scream

She Can Hide

"He Can Fall" (A Short Story)

She Can Kill

MIDNIGHT NOVELS

Midnight Exposure

Midnight Sacrifice

Midnight Betrayal

Midnight Obsession

THE ROGUE SERIES NOVELLAS

Gone to Her Grave (Rogue River)

Walking on Her Grave (Rogue River)

Tracks of Her Tears (Rogue Winter)

Burned by Her Devotion (Rogue Vows)

Twisted Truth (Rogue Justice)

THE WIDOW'S ISLAND NOVELLA SERIES

TRACK HER DOWN

MELINDA LEIGH

Published by Montlake, Seattle

www.apub.com

Amazon, the Amazon logo, and Montlake are trademarks of Amazon.com, Inc., or its affiliates.

ISBN-13: 9781662516931 (hardcover)
ISBN-13: 9781662516948 (paperback)
ISBN-13: 9781662516955 (digital)

Cover design by Shasti O'Leary Soudant
Cover images: © Mohamad Itani / ArcAngel; © lzf / Shutterstock; © sutipong / Shutterstock; © Smileus / Shutterstock

Printed in the United States of America

First edition

For Ladybug
Miss you every day

CHAPTER ONE

Juggling a take-out tray and her house key, Claire hesitated in the dark foyer. The AC blasted, and cool air rushed over her hot skin. Even with the movement of air, the house felt too still. Goose bumps rose on her arms. A prickly sensation enveloped her, almost like static electricity, as if she'd rubbed a balloon on the carpet and suspended it over her skin.

It was well past ten thirty. It wasn't unusual for them both to be asleep by now. But tonight, the quiet wasn't normal. The stillness turned over and over in her belly, unsettled.

Anticipating.

In the kitchen, she dumped her mom's key fob and the milkshakes she'd bought on her way home from work and went up the stairs. The landing creaked, as usual, but tonight, Claire startled at the sound. Light glowed at the end of the hall, from her parents' open door. Passing her own bedroom, she continued down the corridor. The carpet cushioned her steps. Her heartbeat cranked before she stepped into the doorway.

Claire froze as she took in the scene.

It didn't seem real.

Didn't seem as if it *could* be real.

She squeezed her eyes closed, then opened them wide again.

Nothing had changed.

The first thing that commanded her attention was the blood, what seemed like gallons of it, soaking the pristine white sheets. Both of her parents were in bed, as she'd expected. Her father stared at the ceiling, his eyes blank, his face nearly as white as the pillowcase behind his head. *Dead*, Claire knew instantly with a certainty that chilled her heart. Blood saturated his T-shirt, but his face was untouched. Perfect.

She shifted her gaze to her mother. The gaping hole in her face was so grotesque that Claire wanted to turn away, and yet she couldn't. She stared, transfixed by the horror. A flash of bone showed in the torn flesh. Bits of—*face?*—splattered the headboard. More blood pooled . . .

Everywhere.

Still, Claire didn't move, as if her feet were glued to the carpet, shock locking the joints of her legs into position, keeping her upright. If not for her terrified rigidity, her body would have folded like the legs of a camera tripod.

So much blood.

How could two people bleed this much?

Claire stared, not willing to accept what she was seeing.

"Yeow!" The cat ran into the room and jumped onto the bed. With another yowl, it leaped to the floor, arched its back, and hissed.

The cat's reaction jolted Claire out of her shocked stupor. She stumbled to her mother's bedside. Was she dead? Claire crouched and touched her mother's neck. She didn't feel a pulse, but then again, she wasn't a doctor. She'd never checked to see whether someone was dead before. How could she know for sure? What should she do? Panicked thoughts raced through her mind.

Something. Do something. Do something.

Claire's feet tangled. She tripped, falling to her hands and knees. Her phone dropped out of her pocket onto the red-stained carpet with a wet thud. She stumbled to her feet, grabbed her mother's shoulder, and shook. Her mom's body jiggled with a limpness that suggested it had given up.

"Mom!" Claire shook her again, then crouched and got a good look at her mother's eyes in the middle of her ruined face.

Vacant.

No one was there.

Probably.

Definitely?

Unsure, Claire stacked her hands and pressed them into her mother's chest, the way she'd learned CPR in health class. Her mom's body bounced on the mattress. Claire knew it was futile. *Right?* But she did it anyway. For how long should she continue? She saw in her mind the words from the slideshow: *Continue chest compressions until help arrives.*

Fifteen, sixteen, seventeen.

Except she hadn't called for help. Abandoning first aid, she fumbled for her phone, but her pocket was empty. She spotted it on the stained carpet and grabbed it. Her fingers were slippery with blood and shaking so hard that she was barely able to stab 911 before the phone slid from her hand. It fell back to the carpet, landing face up. She touched the speakerphone icon.

"My parents are dead," she sobbed.

The person on the other end of the line said something, but Claire barely heard anything over the sound of her own pulse pounding inside her head. She shouted her name and address. "I think they're dead. I think someone shot them or something. Send someone. Please." The last word came out as a choking plea.

A woman's voice suddenly clarified, coming into focus like a camera lens. "Is the person who killed them still in the house?"

CHAPTER TWO

Sheriff Bree Taggert shined her flashlight over the swift-moving dark waters of Grey Lake. Temper heated her blood. The 911 call had to be a prank, and she didn't have time for fake callouts. At the tail end of summer, she had one deputy out with a concussion from a bike accident and another recovering after being shot by a serial killer. With a limited staff, Bree filled in as needed. She was already stretched as thin as fishing line.

She walked to the other side of the dock, leaned over the railing, and pointed the beam into the shadows. A frog croaked from its perch on a log, the sound reverberating in the humid night. A mosquito the size of a blue jay buzzed past her face, and she swatted it away.

Shoes slapped on the wooden dock behind her, and Bree spun, shining her light in the direction of the sound. A man of about forty approached. He wore a T-shirt emblazoned with a trout and wrinkled cargo shorts smeared with a rusty-looking substance. From ten feet away, he carried a beer can and the unmistakable smell of fish.

"I'm Boyd Harrison. I operate the bait shop." He jiggled his can in the direction of a shack near the parking lot at the public boat launch. "I called 911."

"Can you tell me what you saw again?"

"An alligator." He pointed to a spot about fifteen feet from the dock they currently occupied. "It was right there. Floating. Red eyes staring at me." He shook himself. "It was creepy."

Bree lifted the light to point at his face.

Harrison shielded his eyes. "Hey!"

Bree turned back to the lake. "Could it have been rubber?"

"That's what I thought at first too, that maybe it was a toy and somebody was yanking my chain." Harrison shook his head. "But the way it moved . . . No, it was definitely alive. Scared the crap out of me."

Maybe he'd seen a fish or a snake.

"How big was it?" she asked.

He spread his hands wide. "About three feet long. It bolted into the water and swam away, so unless it was remote-controlled, it definitely wasn't a toy."

"There's nothing else it could have been? Maybe a snake?"

Harrison's head shook once. "It had legs. Could have been a croc, I guess."

"What's the difference?" Bree regretted the question the second it left her lips.

"A gator has a flat snout. A croc has a pointier one. Crocs are more aggressive too." Harrison shoved his free hand into the pocket of his cargo shorts. "I like documentaries," he said, as if he felt the need to explain possessing this tidbit of knowledge.

Bree made a noncommittal noise. "I don't see a gator here now."

"You don't believe me," Harrison said without animosity. "It's OK. I wouldn't believe me either."

Given Morrison's beer goggles, a snake was still a possibility, or a hellbender. Bree hadn't even heard of one in this area. But the endangered salamanders grew quite large and lived in the nearby Susquehanna River Basin. They had legs and long dark bodies. Or he could have imagined the whole thing.

"Who knows?" She swept her light over the water one last time. "If you see it again, call us."

"Will do." Harrison nodded.

She turned back to him. "You're not driving home, are you?"

"No, ma'am." Harrison jerked a thumb at the street. "I live down the road."

"Good night, then." Bree turned and headed for her vehicle. On her duty belt, her radio crackled. "All units, multiple 12-89s at 27 Wheeler Road."

A 12-89 was code for a dead body.

Deputy Renata Zucco's voice came over the radio. "Unit Twelve, responding. ETA eight minutes."

Bree slid behind the wheel, starting the engine with one hand and reaching for the mic with the other. "Sheriff Taggert responding. ETA seven minutes. Details?"

"Female caller, Claire Mason, says she lives at the address, reported coming home from work and finding her parents deceased and a lot of blood."

"Ten-four." Bree ended the call, pulled out of the parking spot, and gunned the engine, sending gravel flying from her tires. Her heart rapped against her sternum as she raced away from the dock, two-wheeling her vehicle around a bend in the road. Two dead bodies and a bloody scene indicated violence. The first possibility that flashed in Bree's mind was domestic violence, potentially a murder-suicide, like Bree's own parents.

Shuddering, she blocked the images that flooded her mind. Without facts, there was no point in torturing herself with the comparison.

Now was not the time for a trip down her personal nightmare lane.

Because another possibility was murder. *Did Claire end the call willingly?*

Or . . .

Is the killer still in the house?

Did he get Claire?

Seven minutes could be a very long time, but rural living meant help wasn't always nearby. Bree drove faster. The radio crackled, and

Deputy Zucco announced her arrival on scene. "Unit Twelve, code eleven."

Bree responded, "Sheriff Taggert, ETA one minute." Then she added, "Wait for me, Zucco."

"Ten-four," Zucco responded.

Randolph County's newest deputy had joined the sheriff's department several months before. She came from the NYPD, with plenty of patrol and vice experience. She was no rookie and had recently proven herself extraordinarily capable in the hunt for a serial killer. But Zucco could be bold and wouldn't want the caller to wait any longer for help. Bree didn't want her deputy going into a dangerous situation alone.

Bree braked hard, then made a sharp left into a neighborhood of large newish homes. An ache in her wrist reminded her that she'd recently had the cast removed after breaking a bone apprehending the same serial killer. She'd been worried the break would affect her aim. Thankfully, while shooting hurt, she could hit her target just fine.

The SUV leaned precariously. She straightened the wheel, leveled out the vehicle, and stomped on the gas pedal. Her SUV roared forward. Down the block, lights from a patrol car swirled in the darkness.

As she slid the SUV to the curb behind Zucco's vehicle, Bree reached for the mic to report that she'd also arrived on scene. Then she slammed the gearshift into park and jumped out of her vehicle. Sweat instantly beaded on her forehead. The approaching end of August had brought no relief from a brutally hot and dry summer.

Zucco met her in the street. "No movement or noise from the house. Backup is eleven minutes away."

"Too long." Bree pulled her weapon as she sized up the house. Landscaping lights blazed outside the McMansion, and interior lights glowed in several windows. Bree and Zucco crept up the driveway.

As they approached the house, the front door swung open and a figure raced out. Female, young, eyes wide in panic, and screaming. "Oh, my God! Oh, my God! *Ohmygod.*"

Zucco angled left and raised her handgun. "Stop! Police!"

Bree stepped right to make herself and her deputy separate targets. She leveled her weapon at the approaching figure. "Sheriff! Show me your hands."

The female stopped in the pool of light from the lamppost, and Bree got a better look at her. An older teen, small and slender. Dark stains saturated the knees of her khaki pants and streaked the front of her red polo shirt. *Blood?* The girl blinked, looking confused as she raised her hands into a natural surrender position.

Killer or victim?

Bree's instincts said victim, but she wouldn't compromise her own safety or that of her deputy by making assumptions.

"Watch the house," Bree said to Zucco, then crossed to the girl. "What's your name?"

The girl looked up.

I know her.

She went to high school with Bree's nephew, Luke. Both kids had worked on the yearbook committee the year before. "Claire?"

The girl didn't respond, and Bree prompted her again. "Claire? Look at me."

Brown eyes shifted to meet Bree's, but the girl's gaze wasn't fixed. Her eyes were lost and vague-looking. Shock.

"Are you injured, Claire?" Bree holstered her weapon.

She whispered in a voice filled with disbelief, "No."

Bree patted her down, simultaneously checking Claire's pockets—which were empty—and looking for injuries. "Does anything hurt?"

Claire shook her head, then spoke in a detached tone. "They're dead."

"Who's dead?" Bree asked, hoping to confirm the details provided by dispatch.

"My parents." Claire's voice drifted. "This can't be happening. Has to be a nightmare," she murmured.

"Claire, is there anyone else in the house?" Bree couldn't remember if Claire had siblings.

Terror filled Claire's gaze. "I don't know."

"Does anyone else live here?" Bree specified. "Did your parents have company this evening?"

Claire shook her head.

"Where are they?" Bree glanced at Zucco, who was scanning the front of the house.

"In their bedroom," Claire sobbed. She raised her hands toward her face as if to cover it, then stopped and stared at her blood-coated palms. She made a feral, whimpering noise and began to shake violently.

Bree steadied her, cupping her elbow. "I'm going to put you in the car to keep you safe while we check the house."

Bree and Zucco led the girl toward the patrol car. The night was warm, but Claire shivered. Zucco removed a blanket from her trunk and draped it over Claire's shoulders before guiding her into the back seat and locking the vehicle doors.

As much as she hated leaving the girl, Bree needed to get into the house. The odds that the killer was still inside were small—especially after her and Zucco's sirens-and-swirling-lights arrival. But the chances weren't zero.

And Claire could be wrong. Her parents could still be alive. Bree needed to make sure medical assistance wasn't required.

Bree and Zucco returned to the front door, which now stood open from Claire's exit. The rush of Bree's blood echoed in her ears as she drew her gun again. She and Zucco moved across the threshold as a team. The house had a basic center-hall design, with a staircase facing the foyer, living and dining rooms on either side. They cleared the front rooms and moved down the hallway toward the back of the house, into a large kitchen and attached family room. The open floor plan didn't allow for many hiding spaces. The counters were model-home clean, except for a take-out tray. Condensation dripped down the sides of two cardboard cups.

Ignoring her heart banging against her sternum, Bree reached for a door handle, yanked it open, and aimed her weapon into a walk-in pantry. Empty. A security system pad on the wall was dark, signaling the alarm wasn't engaged. "Clear."

A doorway on the other side of the kitchen led to a hallway, which teed off into two directions. Zucco went right. Bree slipped left, into a laundry and mudroom. She swept her gun from corner to corner. Nothing.

"Home office is trashed, but clear," Zucco said.

Bree eased up to a closed door and pressed her shoulder against the wall. She pulled open the door to find a closet filled with coats long enough for someone to hide behind. She swept them aside, found nothing but a few pairs of winter boots, and blew out a hard breath. "Clear."

She looked in the attached garage, which was thankfully very clean. A small BMW sedan and an Audi Q7 SUV sat side by side. The hood of the BMW was still slightly warm.

She met Zucco back in the kitchen. The deputy pointed to a set of french doors. A hole had been neatly cut in a glass pane, making it easy for an intruder to reach through and turn the dead bolt. Beyond the door, landscaping lights outlined the flower beds and illuminated a large patio and pool. The yard beyond was dark. Bree scanned the exterior but saw no movement.

She made a mental note of the potential point of entry and kept moving. She and Zucco eased toward a rear staircase. Bree stepped onto the bottom tread. A board squeaked and she paused, listening over the thrum of her own pulse.

Something crashed. Bree startled, putting her back to the wall. Zucco dropped into a crouch, and they both froze, weapons extended.

Light thuds approached. A small gray body streaked down the stairs and past their ankles. It emitted a howl as it disappeared into the living room.

Cat.

Zucco exhaled. Bree did the same. The release of tension left her lightheaded for a second. She took one more deep breath, holding it for a few seconds before letting out the air with deliberate control.

With a shake, she refocused and started up the steps. Tiny red paw prints on the cream-colored Berber led the way. Dread gathered in Bree's belly as she and Zucco ascended the steps. On the second-floor landing, she paused. More paw prints disappeared down the hall.

Ignoring the cat's path, Bree kept left, checking a guest room and hall bathroom. Zucco turned right into another bedroom. The light was already on, showing lavender-colored walls.

Claire's room?

The next bedroom held a treadmill, some dumbbells, and a TV. Bree approached the last room with Zucco at her flank. The lights were on in the primary suite, giving them a clear view of two bodies in the king-size bed. Zucco ducked into the en suite bath. Bree checked a huge walk-in closet, vaguely noticing it was in disarray, before meeting Zucco at the foot of the bed.

The sight looked like a scene from a horror movie. It made Bree ill to think of Claire coming home to the nightmare in front of them. Her parents had been shot in their bed. The volume of blood alone was gruesome, but the mother had been shot in the face.

Bree thought of her own sister's death and shuddered. She hadn't viewed the scene in person, only the crime scene photos, but she knew Claire would have the image of her parents' brutal murders in her head until her own death. Because if Bree lived to be a hundred, she would never stop seeing her sister's dead body.

Years ago, before Bree had assumed guardianship of her sister's two kids and moved back home to upstate New York, compartmentalizing her emotions had been easier. Now, suppressing her emotions took work. As if she'd been numb before, but the happier she became, the more horrific murder seemed. How long would she be able to cope?

"Sometimes I really hate people." Zucco's voice was cold with anger.

Bree breathed deeply to suppress her own rage and disgust, but her control felt brittle. The smells of blood and death flooding her nostrils didn't help. The bowels and bladder sometimes released upon death. "Call it in. We need the ME and a forensics unit."

While Zucco communicated with dispatch, Bree approached the bodies. Though vacant eyes and pale, pale skin said both victims were likely dead, she needed to confirm. The nightstand drawer hung open, and a lamp had been knocked to the floor. She stepped around the shards of ceramic and a few small personal items scattered on the carpet on the woman's side of the bed, where blood had been tracked away by the cat. A cell phone lay on the carpet. From the bejeweled purple Taylor Swift case, Bree thought it belonged to Claire. Blood smeared the screen. It had a wallet attachment on the back.

Avoiding the debris on the carpet, Bree reached for the woman's neck but stopped before touching her flesh. *Too close to the wound.* She chose the woman's wrist. No life beat against her fingertips. Then she stretched over the bed to press two fingers to the man's neck. He didn't have a pulse either, but both bodies were still warm to the touch. They hadn't been dead very long.

Bree stepped back. "Let's go outside and talk to Claire."

She needed air, and she needed to call Matt, her part-time criminal investigator and full-time live-in boyfriend. A former sheriff's deputy and K-9 handler, he'd been shot in the line of duty years ago. Nerve damage in his right hand kept him off the force, but he was still a damned fine detective. As much as she wanted his expertise, she also just wanted to hear his voice. He grounded her.

She dialed his number on the way downstairs.

He answered in a rough voice. "What's up?"

Bree checked the time. It was 10:57. "Sorry if I woke you."

"I was watching TV. Must have dozed off." Fabric rustled over the connection. He cleared his throat. "You need me?"

Always.

Instead, she said, "Yes. Just arrived at a double homicide." She gave him the address.

He paused, likely mapping the route to the crime scene from her farm. "Be there in twenty." He ended the call.

Sirens sounded outside. By the time Bree and Zucco exited the house, a second patrol vehicle was parking at the curb and a third was approaching. A few neighbors clustered on the sidewalk across the street.

Bree assigned the two new deputies to search the perimeter of the property and secure the crime scene.

Zucco opened the back door of her vehicle, but Claire didn't move for a few seconds. She huddled under the blanket, looking lost.

Bree crouched and kept her voice low. "I need to ask you some questions."

Clutching the edges of the blanket over her chest, Claire sobbed, her tone panicked. "At first, I tried to stop the bleeding but . . ." She looked up, her gaze searching. "They're dead, right? I couldn't have saved them?"

Did the poor girl think she was somehow responsible for their deaths?

Her grief would be crushing without the added guilt.

Pity gathered in Bree. She placed her hand on the girl's forearm. "You could *not* have saved them. I'm so sorry for your loss." As always, the words felt inadequate in the worst way, a Band-Aid for a severed limb.

Claire released one fist from its grip on the blanket and stared at it. The blood had dried into a crusty mess. "I'd like to wash my hands."

"Soon," Bree promised. "How old are you, Claire?"

"Seventeen," she whispered.

Damn. Still a minor, which meant family services needed to be involved. "Where were you tonight?"

Claire named a big-box retailer. "I clocked out at ten." She burst into giant, soul-destroying, whole-body sobs that ripped at Bree's heart like claws.

"Do you have any family we can call?" Bree asked.

Claire managed to shake her head.

Bree backed off. She turned to Zucco. "Take her to the station. Swab her hands for GSR and DNA, then let her clean up. Scrounge up something for her to wear. Take her soiled clothes into evidence."

"Yes, ma'am," Zucco said. "I think I have gym clothes in my locker." Zucco was petite, like Claire.

"Good." Bree lowered her voice. "I need to ask her some questions, but she's already fragile. Seeing the medical examiner and forensics unit roll in won't help. If we get her away from the scene, she might be calmer."

Zucco nodded. "On it."

Bree eyed the neighbors. They needed to be questioned as well, and someone had to canvass the rest of the houses on the block, but that would have to wait until morning. She didn't have enough deputies to do everything at once. Doorbell and security cameras for the surrounding residences needed to be checked. She pulled out her phone and called her chief deputy at home. She would need all her resources for a double homicide.

CHAPTER THREE

Matt followed the swirling emergency lights and parked at the curb behind a row of patrol vehicles. His boots crunched on sun-scorched grass as he crossed the strip of ground between the sidewalk and street. Drought conditions had been unrelenting, and water restrictions meant brown lawns for the region. Matt walked past a group of neighbors gathered on the sidewalk. Outside the front door, he checked in with the deputy manning the crime scene log, where every person who entered the house would be listed.

The deputy slid his pen into the clasp at the top of the clipboard. "Top of the stairs, end of the hall."

Matt donned gloves and booties and stepped over the threshold. He spotted deputies—also suited up—at the back of the house. Evidence markers stood on the stairway next to small, dark-red paw prints. Matt carefully avoided them on his way up. At the end of the hall, he stopped just inside the primary bedroom.

Bree faced a king-size bed, studying the two dead people sprawled on it. She was of medium height with brown hair and hazel eyes, but there was nothing else average about her. She commanded respect from every cell in her being. It wasn't the uniform, which bulked up her slim frame, or the badge she wore with pride. It was her. He respected the hell out of her, and there wasn't a single deputy in her department who didn't.

He stepped up next to her. "Hey."

Bree glanced at him. Her gaze softened. "Hey, yourself. I'm glad you're here."

"No offense, but I'd rather be home in bed."

"No offense taken. So would I, but here we are." Bree pointed to the bodies. "Josh and Shelly Mason. They've lived at this address for twelve years. Neither has a criminal record. They were found by their teenage daughter, Claire."

Claire Mason.

"I know that name," he said.

Bree cleared her throat. "She worked on the yearbook committee with Luke last year."

"Shit. That Claire." A deep sigh squeezed Matt's chest as he pictured the girl. Now Claire was an orphan.

"Yeah," Bree agreed with a bone-rattling sigh.

Crimes involving children cut him to the core, especially since he'd moved in with Bree. Matt had grown close to her niece and nephew, nine-year-old Kayla and seventeen-year-old Luke.

Together he and Bree turned back to the bed. The blood seemed amplified by the bright-white sheets. Mr. Mason slumped sideways on doubled pillows. Red saturated his gray T-shirt in two distinct blotches. The stain near his shoulder was quarter-size. The second stain, larger than a dinner plate, was in the dead center over his heart. From the chest wound, blood had spread down both sides of the victim's ribs to the mattress beneath him. A hardcover book still sat open on his lap, the pages smeared with red.

Mrs. Mason had flung the covers off her legs. Her body was twisted sideways, as if she'd started to get out of bed before she was killed. Her hand reached toward the nightstand. An obvious gunshot in the side of her face had blown her cheek wide open. Blood and gore splattered the pillowcase and white leather headboard. A second shot below her armpit had bled copiously, leaving a shiny puddle of red that had dripped down the side of the mattress onto the carpet. Brachial artery, Matt guessed.

"Looks like two shots each," he said.

Double tap.

"Execution?" Bree asked.

"They weren't head shots, but it was quick and efficient."

"They killed him first," Bree said as they continued to theorize.

"Makes sense," Matt agreed. "He was the bigger threat, self-defense wise. Take him out of the equation. She'd be easier to manage."

Bree paused. "She saw it coming."

"Yeah. She did." Matt pictured the husband, startling as someone charged into the bedroom, his book falling to his lap. "What would most people do if a stranger walked into their bedroom?"

"Some people might freeze," Bree said. "Fear can be paralyzing. But once he started shooting, survival instinct should have kicked in. Fight option: grab a weapon if you have one and are thinking clearly enough to use it. Flight option: get out of bed. Try to escape."

"The intruder either shot them straightaway or had the gun pointed at them while they exchanged words."

Most people didn't have the skills to fight and instinctively fled. Had his wife screamed or been silenced from panic?

Matt heard the shots in his imagination, saw the husband's body jerk, the wife flinch. "The shots spurred her into motion. She tried to get free of the covers and run. But she didn't have a chance. He shot her before she could even get out of bed."

The woman's face was turned awkwardly back toward her husband. She hadn't died instantly. She'd seen her husband's fate.

Matt hoped death had come quickly for them both because lying there, unable to move, bleeding, watching the life drain from a loved one, would be worse.

It took effort for him to not reach for Bree's hand. Their cohabitation wasn't a secret. Everyone knew he'd moved in with her, but they agreed that on-duty PDAs weren't professional. Being together helped, though. Even without touching her, he felt stronger standing next to her. Their relationship didn't have a legal status—yet—but his heart belonged to her just the same.

Considering the inherent danger in their work, it wasn't hard to imagine them in that bed . . . His stomach rolled over, and he fought the image.

Can't happen to us. We have top-of-the-line security. We have dogs, including a former K-9. We're armed.

But the scenario where a killer beat their alarm system wasn't impossible, and he knew it. So, instead of dwelling on the risk that came with Bree's job, he focused on the crime in front of him—and on locating and stopping a vicious killer or killers before they could destroy more lives.

"Find any stray bullets?" He scanned the wall behind the bed but saw nothing except for a few individual blood droplets.

"Not yet. Forensics is on the way. As soon as the medical examiner is finished, we'll get to work on this room."

The ME had jurisdiction over the body. No one would disturb the remains until she gave the order.

Matt pivoted in a circle, scanning the room. The nightstand drawer hung open. A few small items—a pen, a pad of sticky notes, a book—had fallen to the floor. The primary bedroom was large, with a sitting area in front of a wide window. He could see into a roomy walk-in closet with a built-in organization system that looked like furniture. Clothes, shoes, and bags were strewn on the floor. Matt crossed the room and stared into the closet. "Her handbags are all open. Coat pockets have been turned out. Is the rest of the house neat or messy?"

"Very neat and organized, except for this room and the home office, which were both tossed."

"Maybe the killer was looking for something specific." With a gloved finger, Matt opened a skinny top drawer on the woman's side of the closet. Inside, small, felt-lined compartments held jewelry. He gave the man's drawers on the opposite side a cursory look and found expensive-looking cuff links. "They left valuables in the closet. This probably isn't a burglary gone wrong."

"Agreed." Bree pointed to the corpses. "If the Masons surprised a burglar, they wouldn't have already been in bed, and most burglars would have run when they realized someone was home."

"Do we know how they got in?" he asked.

"They cut a neat hole in the patio glass door. They scoped out the place. Planned the entry. Knew what time the Masons went to bed."

"Yep." Matt stepped away from the closets and faced the bed again. Mr. Mason wore plaid pajama bottoms with a gray T-shirt. His mostly gray hair was thinning and cut short. He had a runner's body, lean and wiry. His wife was dressed in a matching pajama set in a silky material. A floral robe in shades of red was draped over the foot of the bed. She was slim and had good muscle tone for her age.

A commotion in the hall caught Matt's attention. He turned to see the ME carrying her kit through the doorway, her assistant following in her wake. Dr. Serena Jones was a tall African American woman. She wore blue scrubs and rubber clogs under protective booties.

"You're quick to respond," Bree said.

Dr. Jones stopped, set down her kit, and tugged on gloves. "I was working late, catching up on paperwork from that multivehicle collision the other day." She approached the man's side of the bed. Leaning over him, she prodded his face and manipulated his jaw. Rigor mortis, the stiffening of the muscles after death, began in roughly two hours and affected the small muscles of the face first. She lifted his shirt hem and examined his torso, paying particular attention to the skin of the back. The chest wound gaped like a screaming mouth. She used a scalpel to make a tiny slit in the torso, well away from the gunshot wound. She inserted a thermometer into the incision and took a core body temperature via the liver. Then she moved to the female's side of the bed and repeated her examination. "They haven't been dead very long. Facial muscles are beginning to stiffen. Lividity is also just starting to show. A body loses about 1.5 degrees every hour after death in normal conditions, but normal temperature does vary a bit between people, so considering that"—Dr. Jones tipped her head—"my initial takeaway is they've been dead two to three hours. And unless the autopsies reveal a big surprise, cause of death is fairly obvious: multiple gunshot wounds. Manner of death is homicide."

Matt checked his watch—11:30 p.m. "The victims were killed between eight thirty and nine thirty p.m."

"The sun set about seven thirty. It would have been dark by eight or so," Bree said.

Criminals generally preferred darkness for breaking and entering.

And murdering.

CHAPTER FOUR

Matt followed Bree down the hallway, leaving Dr. Jones and her assistant to finish taking pictures and remove the bodies. He spotted Bree's chief deputy, Todd Harvey, at the bottom of the steps issuing orders to several new deputies.

Todd was in his thirties. He'd earned his exceptionally lean physique training for triathlons. He was also currently living with Matt's sister. The deputies dispersed, and Todd turned to Matt and Bree as they descended the staircase. "What did the ME have to say?"

"Time of death is between eight thirty and nine thirty p.m.," Bree said.

"Where do you want to start?" Matt asked as they skirted a deputy taking pictures of the bloody paw prints on the steps. "Cat or dog?"

"We saw a cat," Bree said. "We should look for it."

Matt crouched and found a very well-fed gray tabby perched on a dining room chair. "It's here."

"Hold on. I saw a pet carrier in the closet when Zucco and I cleared the place." Bree went down a hallway and returned with a blue nylon case.

Matt held out a hand. The cat jumped down and rubbed on his fingers. Matt scooped it into his arms. It purred as he rubbed its head. "Friendly."

Bree opened the pet carrier. "Sounds dumb, but I don't want Claire to lose her cat on top of everything else."

"Not dumb at all." Matt scooted the cat inside and left the carrier in the corner. "Where do you want to start?"

"Let's do the home office while Dr. Jones finishes upstairs." Bree headed down the hallway.

With its white cabinets, sleek counters, and modern lines, the kitchen looked like a home magazine spread. A fancy espresso machine and a pricey juicer shared space in the butler's pantry between the kitchen and dining room. The foods in the fridge were mostly organic. Greens and other fresh vegetables filled the crisper bins to bursting.

Matt gestured to the healthy food. "I guess this is why they both looked so good for their ages."

Bree shrugged. "And yet they both died relatively young."

"No argument from me. I'm taking one of Dana's scones to my grave." Matt appreciated the baking skills of Bree's retired former partner, Dana Romano, who'd moved upstate with Bree to help with the kids.

"Same."

They walked past an island the length of a bowling lane and turned into a short corridor that led to the home office. Matt surveyed the chaos while Bree used her phone to take a video of the room.

Floor-to-ceiling bookcases lined the back wall. The desk was made of some exotic grained wood that had been varnished to a mirror sheen. Money was always a great motive for murder, and the Masons clearly had some. Drawers had been removed and turned over, their contents spilled onto the floor and desktop. Books had been pulled off the shelves. He bent to examine an overturned drawer. "The lock is broken."

Bree lowered her phone, leaned closer, and snapped a picture of the busted lock.

Matt eyed two smashed bookends on the floor. "Whoever did this didn't do it quietly, so the house was searched after the parents were killed."

Bree moved behind the desk and went down on one knee to look at the underside. "He, she, or they were moving fast too."

"The search was methodical and quick." Matt went to a pair of filing cabinets in the corner. One drawer gaped. He tugged it open, turned his head, and read the file tabs, all names of companies. He eyed an empty space in the middle. "These look like business records, and it appears as if some files could be missing." Though they'd have to find someone familiar with the business records to know for sure.

Bree frowned. "We need to find out what the Masons did for a living."

"Yes." Matt scanned the books littering the wood floor and cream-colored area rug. "Did the intruders find what they came for? Or did Claire interrupt the search?"

"They already killed two people in cold blood. Why would they stop at killing her too?"

"Maybe they drew the line at killing a kid?" Matt hoped some people were unable to kill a child. "Maybe they had a personal grudge with the adults but not Claire. Maybe they didn't know *who* was arriving."

"All good theories." Bree stood and brushed a paper clip off the knee of her uniform trousers. "Whatever the reason, this room has been thoroughly turned over. We need to find out what—if anything—was taken."

Matt eyed a square on the desktop with no debris. A cord snaked from the desk to the floor, where a charging brick plugged into an outlet. "Seems like there might have been a computer here." He checked the desk drawers and scanned the bookshelves for more charging ports. "I don't see any personal electronics either."

"Most people keep phones and tablets near them. I didn't see any in the bedroom, but we'll check more thoroughly after the ME is finished."

Bree propped her hands on her duty belt. "Worst-case scenario, I can have Rory search for an iCloud account. We can access some of their personal information that way."

County tech Rory MacIniss was a forensic jack-of-all-trades, but he had a special knack with digital information. Electronics contained the detailed trail of a person's life, from their calendar and contacts to bank accounts, prescription renewals, and store purchases. Most providers stored certain data for only a short period of time. So obtaining cell phone data from the cloud wasn't optimal. Plus, not everyone remembered to back up their devices regularly.

A deputy appeared in the doorway. "Ma'am? We found a footprint outside."

Bree and Matt followed him out of the office. On the back patio, a yellow evidence marker sat on the teak table next to a perfect rectangle of glass. Beyond the pavers, the rear lawn was suspiciously green and lush. Flowers overflowed their beds. The yard was large and ringed with full trees and shrubs that provided impressive seclusion in the middle of suburbia.

Matt waved a hand toward the grass. "Looks like someone has been watering regularly back here."

Bree shook her head. Disobeying watering restrictions wasn't likely related to the murders, but it did provide insight to the homeowners' personalities. The lawn out front—in plain view of the neighbors—had plenty of brown spots, but the Masons had watered where no one could see.

The deputy led them to the paver walkway that wound around the side of the property and connected the rear hardscape to the driveway. Low lights in the shrubs illuminated the entire path like a miniature runway.

"How did you get footprints?" Matt asked. "It hasn't rained in at least a week."

The deputy pointed to a partial footprint in mud on the gray pavers. "The flower beds are damp. There's an automatic sprinkler system."

Matt was suddenly grateful the homeowners had disobeyed water restrictions. He crouched next to one of the prints. "I can't tell the exact size of the shoe, but it's big enough to likely be from a man."

"The tread is visible," Bree said. "Looks like an athletic shoe. Maybe forensics can find the shoe brand and model."

The forensics department had access to databases and software for footwear-tread analysis. A match could be useful if they identified a suspect.

Matt turned in a circle. Trees blocked the neighbors' views on both sides, and the property backed to woods. "They probably waited until dark, but there's plenty of privacy here."

"Agreed. You could cut the glass with no one seeing you. Let's get photos." Bree walked toward the house. She and Matt toured the rest of the residence, where there were no overt signs of disturbance.

After Dr. Jones and her assistant wheeled the black-bagged bodies out, Matt followed Bree back to the primary bedroom.

Bree headed for Mrs. Mason's nightstand. "Let's check for electronics. Most people at this income level have—at minimum—a phone and a tablet or laptop." Crouching over the bejeweled phone on the floor, Bree used a gloved finger to slide a credit card and a driver's license out of the wallet attachment on the case. "This is Claire's phone." She bagged and tagged it.

Matt checked the husband's side of the bed. "Nothing." His gaze dropped to the floor. A thin wire snaked along the carpet. "There's a phone charger plugged in behind the nightstand."

"Same here." Bree straightened from peering into the open nightstand drawer. "Forensics will do a deeper search throughout the whole house, but I would bet whoever did this"—she gestured toward the bed—"also took their devices."

"But why?" Matt scanned the bed. Without the bodies, the only thing in it was a huge puddle of blood.

CHAPTER FIVE

At two in the morning, Bree led the way into the rear door of the sheriff's station. She'd left Todd in charge of the scene. Her chief deputy's investigative skills had come a long way since she'd taken over as sheriff.

"Coffee?" Matt veered off toward the break room, hefting the cat carrier.

"Oh, yes." Bree followed him.

Matt started a fresh pot while Bree pulled mugs from the cabinet. She went to the vending machine and chose two packs of Peanut M&M's. Nuts contained protein, but it was the sugar she craved.

She handed a bag to Matt.

"You always know what I want." He took it with a tired sigh. With short reddish-brown hair and a trimmed beard, he always reminded her of a Viking. His six-foot-three-inch broad-shouldered frame seemed born to swing a battle-ax.

Zucco walked into the room, carrying an empty glass.

"How is Claire?" Bree asked.

"Quiet." Zucco filled the glass at the tap. "I don't think she's processed what happened yet."

Bree watched the coffee drip. "Unfortunately, there's no getting around asking her questions."

"She asked for her phone."

"It was in the bedroom." Bree reached for her own phone and sent a text to Rory in forensics. "I'll have them process it ASAP. She'll feel even more isolated without it."

"What will happen to her?" Zucco asked.

Bree shrugged. "I was hoping to run across a will when we searched the house that would declare a guardian. So far, we haven't had any luck, but we still have business files in the home office to go through. Hopefully, they have a will in a safe-deposit box or with a local attorney. Maybe Claire will know. I'm waiting for a call back from family services about a temporary placement."

Zucco nodded. "She's in the conference room. I offered her a cot, but she said she couldn't sleep."

Poor kid. Probably doesn't want to close her eyes for fear of what she'll see.

"I can't imagine." But Bree *could* imagine Claire's terror all too well. When Bree was eight, her father killed her mother and then himself. Bree had hidden her siblings under the porch. He'd been violent and abusive her entire life. She knew in her heart that if he'd found them, he would have killed them all. Bree had heard the shots that ended her parents' lives over and over, like a boomerang video clip.

An image of her mother flashed into her mind. Her father pinning her to the wall by the neck. Her mother's eyes pleading to Bree—not for help but for Bree to take her siblings and run. Her mother had sacrificed her own life to save her children.

Too little, too late? Afterward, people said that her mom should have left him before the situation escalated to the point of murder-suicide, but Bree knew better. Her father would never have let her get away. She belonged to him, and if he couldn't have her, then no one would. There was nowhere her mother could have run that he wouldn't have found her eventually. If he'd been put in jail, the reprieve would have been temporary. No restraining order would have stopped him. The violence had only one possible end: his death. While he'd remained alive, Bree's mother hadn't had a chance.

Ironically, the same people who'd criticized her mother for not leaving had never offered to help—because they'd also been afraid of him.

Claire would carry this trauma for the rest of her life.

Bree dumped M&M's into her mouth, finishing the bag in two minutes. Then she and Matt filled their mugs and went down the hall. She knocked on the door before opening it. Claire sat at the table, resting her head on her folded arms. As Bree and Matt entered, Claire straightened. Her eyes were swollen, the expression on her face still locked in disbelief.

The girl had cleaned up and dressed in Zucco's yoga pants, T-shirt, and sneakers. Her hands were clear of blood, but the skin was almost raw looking, as if she'd scrubbed and scrubbed to remove all traces of the night. She chewed a thumbnail while eyeing them warily, as if afraid of their questions—or of what they were going to tell her.

Matt set the cat carrier on the table. "Is this your only pet?"

Claire reached out, sobbing. "Chunk!"

Bree closed the conference room door, and Matt opened the carrier. Chunk strolled out and sauntered across the table, straight into Claire's lap. The girl hugged the cat close, and it began to purr like a lawn mower while Claire cried into its fur.

Misty-eyed, Matt sat on the other side of the table.

Bree eased into a chair catercorner to her. "Hey, Claire."

Claire sniffed and drew in a shaky breath. Her shoulders were curled inward, like she was trying to make herself as small as possible. She bent her head toward the cat's.

"I need to ask you a few questions," Bree began.

Claire shuddered and said, "OK," in a weak voice.

"Were your parents nervous about anything recently?" Bree asked.

Claire shook her head. "No."

"Did they get any troubling mail or messages?"

"Not that they told me." Claire hugged her cat harder.

"Did they normally set the alarm at night?"

Claire rubbed her cheek on Chunk's. "We turn it on when the last of us gets home. If we're all home, then when everyone goes to bed."

So it was probably off when the intruder broke in.

"You said you were at work this evening," Bree said. "What time did you go in?"

"I worked from six to ten."

"Did you see anyone near the house when you got home?"

"No."

"Any strange cars on the street?"

"I don't think so." Claire lifted her head and rhythmically stroked the cat's head. Chunk turned up the volume.

"Do you know the doorbell-camera password?"

"No, my parents controlled it from their phones." A tear slipped down Claire's face. "I don't know anything. I'm useless. Who would do this?"

Bree knew better than to make promises she might not be able to keep. If Claire was going to trust her, Bree needed to be honest, even if the truth hurt. "We don't know yet, but we will do our best to find out. What time do your parents usually go to bed?"

"Usually, they go upstairs at nine o'clock, but they don't go to sleep for an hour or two. They like to read."

"What about their work schedules?"

Claire tucked the cat's head under her chin. "They work from home. They're lawyers."

"What kind of law did they practice?" Bree asked.

"Small-business stuff." Claire shrugged. "They didn't talk about work much, and when they did, it was boring. I didn't pay attention."

"That's understandable." Bree checked her notes. "Where did they see clients?"

Claire lifted another thin shoulder. "They use Zoom, phone calls, email . . . They meet people at a coffee shop or go to the place of business."

"No one comes to the house?"

"No." Claire shook her head, not as a response, but as if to clear it. "What's going to happen to me?"

"Family services will find a place for you to stay temporarily while we sort that out. Where did your parents keep their important papers?" Bree asked.

"Work stuff is in the office. They have a safe in their closet for personal papers."

"We found that." Bree paused. "This is a hard question, but do you know if they had a will? It wasn't in the personal safe." They'd found the key to the retail fire safe in Josh's drawer.

Claire shook her head. "I don't know."

"You said they had phones. What about electronic tablets or computers?"

"Yeah. They both have their own phones and iPads. There's a laptop in the office, but they use it mostly for business stuff." Claire grabbed a tissue from the box on the table and blotted her eyes.

So the electronics are all gone.

"Do your parents have close friends, distant family members, even business associates they were especially close to? Anyone who comes over to the house?"

"Not really," Claire said. "They're not very social. It's always been the three of us."

"Did you spend holidays with anyone special?" Matt asked.

Claire's head swiveled back and forth. "Like I said, it's only the three of us. Sometimes, we go skiing over winter break." Her voice took on a whiny edge.

"Have you had any workmen in the house recently?" Bree asked.

"I don't think so," Claire said. "We have a house cleaner. The owner is Amanda something."

"How long have you used her?" Matt asked.

"I don't know," Claire said. "A long time. Years."

"When was the house last cleaned?" Bree asked.

"This morning." Claire's gaze drifted to the ceiling for a few seconds as if she were thinking, then her gaze dropped back to Bree's. "No. It's tomorrow. So yesterday."

The day of the murder.

"Did you see the cleaners that morning?" Bree asked.

Claire shook her head. "Mom and I went to Starbucks."

"And your father?"

"He went running. He's training for a marathon."

Bree leaned a forearm on the table. "Can you tell me what happened tonight after you finished work?"

"I clocked out at ten. On the way home, I stopped at Smoothies 4 All to get milkshakes. Mom had a tough week." Claire broke eye contact and stared down at her cat. *What was she not saying?*

Bree pictured two take-out cups on the kitchen counter. "How many did you buy?"

"Two. Dad doesn't eat sugar. He only eats like, clean and organic." Every time Claire used the present tense was an ice pick to Bree's heart.

"What did you drive home?" she asked.

"Mom's BMW." Claire burrowed her fingers into the cat's fur.

"Does she always let you drive her car?"

Claire sniffed. "Sometimes she takes me to work, but she was busy and didn't have to go anywhere, so she let me take the car."

"What was tough about your mom's week?" Bree asked.

"Some client yelled at her."

"Yelled?"

"Yeah. She said it was no big deal. He was just mad 'cause she told him something he didn't want to hear, even though it was the truth."

"Did she feel threatened?"

Claire tilted her head, considering. "Maybe? I don't know if *threatened* is the right word, but she was definitely upset."

"Do you remember the client's name?"

31

Claire rested her forehead on her cat. "Mom never said."

Bree made a note to find the unhappy client.

"You work at the store near the interstate?" Matt asked.

Without looking up, Claire nodded.

"The drive is only fifteen minutes from the store to your house," Matt said. "Did you stop anywhere else?"

"There's a boy who works at the smoothie place. I wanted to see him." Claire lifted her gaze. "If I had come right home, could I have saved them?"

"No," Bree said firmly, momentarily debating how much information to share. "They were gone before you even left work. There's nothing you could have done to prevent this." Bree did not want Claire to feel responsible in any way. Her life was already destroyed. She didn't need guilt on top of her grief. "What happened next?"

A sob broke through Claire's resolve. "I'm sorry." Hiccups and sniffs interrupted her words. "I want to help . . . help find . . . them."

"Take a breath," Bree said in a soothing voice. "You're doing fine."

Claire inhaled through her nose, clearly trying to pull herself together. She clasped her hands tightly enough to whiten her knuckles, as if she could hold in her emotions through the pressure of her palms. "I drove home. Everything looked normal. I left the milkshakes in the kitchen and went upstairs to tell Mom. Their bedroom light was on, so I went in. Dad usually falls asleep first. Sometimes Mom waits up until I get home. She might come down to the kitchen to hang out with me for a while." She closed her eyes. Her body trembled.

Not tonight. Not ever again.

Bree gave her a minute.

Claire opened her eyes. "I'm sorry."

"Take your time," Bree assured her.

Claire's head tilted as her gaze turned inward. "I went into their room—and I saw—" She pressed her lips into a tight, flat line, but a sob leaked out. "There was so much blood . . . I went to Mom, tried

CPR like we learned at school, then realized it didn't matter. Not with all that blood." She hiccuped. "I called 911, and the woman asked if whoever shot them might still be in the house. Then I started thinking they might hear me on the phone, so I hung up. I didn't know what to do. I kind of froze until I saw your lights in the street outside."

For the longest seven minutes of her life.

Bree's phone vibrated. She glanced at the screen, recognizing the phone number of the social worker she'd spoken with earlier. "Excuse me. I have to answer this."

She stepped out. In the hallway, she took a cleansing breath before answering the call. "Sheriff Taggert."

"Hi, Sheriff," a female voice said. "This is Lindsay Bell. I've found a temporary placement for Claire Mason."

"What about the cat?" Bree asked.

"Sorry," Lindsay said with sadness. "No cats. The family has another foster child who's allergic. Can someone hold on to the cat for a few days?"

"I'll figure out something." Bree could not take Chunk home. Her own cat was territorial. Vader hadn't even accepted Matt yet. There was no way he'd allow another feline—especially a male—into his house.

"Great," Lindsay said. "I'll come by the station to pick up Claire within the hour."

"OK. I'll have a deputy collect some clothes for her as soon as possible, but it might be end of day tomorrow."

"You get me copies of whatever paperwork you have for her?" Lindsay asked.

"Claire has a driver's license. If we run across other paperwork, I'll forward you copies." Bree ended the call.

Zucco stood in the hallway. "I didn't mean to eavesdrop."

Bree waved off her comment.

Zucco glanced at the closed conference room door. "I could take the cat for now."

"That would be helpful," Bree said.

"Seems like the least I can do. I don't want to take it to the animal shelter." Zucco sighed.

And Claire's going to miss her cat. She just lost her parents and now she'll be forced to leave behind the one thing that gave her comfort.

"Thank you, Zucco. You can go home and catch some sleep."

"A shower and breakfast should be enough. I'd rather keep working."

"All right." Bree understood wanting to work a disturbing case. "Then drop off the cat, freshen up, and check in with Chief Deputy Harvey. The neighborhood around the Mason residence needs to be canvassed."

"Yes, ma'am." Zucco retreated down the hallway.

As if Claire hadn't already had the worst day of her life, Bree headed back into the conference room to tell her she couldn't take her cat with her to the foster home.

Feeling awful in a hundred different ways, Bree retreated to her office. Then she issued a formal statement for the press. She'd hold off on a press conference until she had more information, but it would have to happen today. People were going to panic. Bree hoped she could soon tell them that the murder was personal. That this killer posed no threat to the general public.

For now, she could make no such promises.

CHAPTER SIX

At seven a.m., Bree followed Matt into the farmhouse kitchen. They would have barely enough time to eat breakfast with the kids, shower, and change into fresh clothes before heading back to work. But the time—however short—was worth it to recharge. When she came home, whatever weight she was carrying always felt instantly lighter.

They were greeted politely by Brody the German shepherd, Matt's former K-9 partner. Bree's dog, a big chunky rescue named Ladybug, leaned on Bree's knees hard enough to buckle them. Bree rubbed her soft ears while the dog grunted.

Bree's black tomcat, Vader, disapproved of the crowd from the top of the refrigerator, casting glares at the dogs and Matt. Bree left her boots by the door. To prevent Vader from gifting him with a hair ball in his own footwear, Matt carried his boots to the laundry room and carefully shut the door. The cat watched with slitted eyes. *Is he plotting? Probably.*

Luke and Kayla sat at the table. Luke was plowing through a plate of pancakes, using his fork like a shovel. Kayla drew a syrup smiley face on her much smaller stack. Greetings finished, Ladybug took a position next to Kayla, always ready to catch a dropped bite of food or lick a sticky hand.

At the stove, Dana ladled batter onto a griddle. "Sit down. I'll get you some caffeine."

When Bree had moved north, Dana, on the brink of retiring with no post-retirement plans, had joined her. She now served as an honorary aunt and nanny to the kids, for which Bree would be forever grateful. She trusted no one more.

Dana brought two more plates of pancakes to the table. Then she added a cappuccino for Bree and a black coffee for Matt before sitting down to join them.

Bree used as much syrup as Kayla. "What's on the schedule for today?"

"School shopping," Kayla said with a happy smile.

"Shopping," Luke echoed, groaning.

Dana laughed. "I can't help that you grew several inches over the summer. Your pants are all too short. If you want, you can drive separately to the mall. We'll do your shopping first, then you can leave."

Luke brightened. "Really?"

"Really," Dana said.

"Cool." Luke finished his pancakes. "I'll go turn out the horses."

"I'll help," Matt said.

They took their empty plates to the sink. Matt carried his coffee out the back door. Since he'd moved in, he tried to take some of the physical work off Luke's shoulders. Bree turned to watch them cross the backyard. Luke was only a few inches shorter than Matt's six three. No kidding he'd grown over the summer.

"We're going to pick out school supplies." Kayla was practically giddy. "I'm getting new colored pencils and everything."

Bree pushed back her plate and took a long drink of her cappuccino. "That sounds fun."

Dana snorted.

Kayla ate two bites of pancake. "I can't wait until school starts. Mallory and Emma are in my class, but Harper got Mrs. Snow."

Kayla's social circle was ever evolving. She seemed to make a new friend every month. Bree marveled at the change in the little girl. When their mother had first died, both kids—and Bree—had grieved hard. Those first months were a horrible blur of pain. They still had moments, but they were happy more often than they were sad. And raw grief had transformed into bittersweet memories. As a family, they were moving forward.

"I'm going to go get dressed." Kayla carried her plate to the sink.

"The stores don't open for hours," Dana said. "There's no rush."

"I want to be ready." Kayla skipped out of the kitchen.

"Never saw anyone so excited over pencils and notebooks." Dana scrutinized Bree's face. "Rough night?"

For a few minutes, Bree had forgotten about the murder. "Very. Double homicide." She gave Dana a quick summary. "Luke knows the girl."

"Ugh. Are you going to tell him?"

"I have to. Better he hear it from me than from his friends." Bree stood. "I'll do it now. I hate to ruin his day, though. This is bound to bring back memories for him, and he's been doing so well."

"He's resilient, and he has plenty of support." Dana started on the dishes.

"He does." But it didn't sound as if Claire had anyone. She seemed more isolated, like Bree after her own parents' deaths.

Bree went out the back door. The air smelled of manure, a scent she oddly equated with hearth, home, and happiness. After the age of eight, she'd been raised in the city—and her life before that had been anything but ideal. But it seemed as if the country were bred into her.

Four horses grazed near the gate in the pasture. Bree's paint gelding, Cowboy, had belonged to her sister. When she called his name, he ambled over for scratches before heading for the hay Matt had tossed into the pasture. There wasn't much grass left after the summer drought.

Bree found Luke and Matt in the barn. Luke was raking the aisle.

One horse—her brother Adam's standardbred—remained, his head hanging over his stall door. Bree scratched under his mane. The former

Amish buggy horse never complained. His current life must feel like a vacation after being a working beast. "Bullseye isn't going out?"

"Uncle Adam texted me, asking me to keep him in. He's on his way over to ride."

Matt hung a lead rope on a nail. "I'm going to shower."

"I'm next," Bree said as Matt left the barn. She turned toward her nephew. "Can I talk to you for a minute, Luke?"

He set aside the rake. "Sure. I'm done anyway."

"Last night, your classmate's parents were killed in a double homicide. I'm going to hold a press conference this morning, but I wanted you to have the correct information in case you heard it from your friends."

His eyes saucered, then he frowned. "Who?"

"Claire Mason."

"Oh, man. That's . . . terrible." He turned and paced a few steps, then pivoted. "Should I reach out to her? Or do you think that would make it worse for her? We're not exactly close."

"Maybe give her a day to collect herself, but she might appreciate knowing you're thinking of her." Hopefully, Bree could return the girl's phone later today.

"I'll do it tomorrow, then." With a nod, he left the barn and headed for the house.

Pride bloomed in Bree's belly. He was a good-hearted kid. Talking to Claire would bring up his own terrible memories, but he'd face them to do the right thing.

Bree's phone beeped with a reminder. She glanced at the screen. She'd forgotten about her virtual therapy appointment. She quickly sent her therapist a message that she would need to reschedule. The relief that initially flooded her faded in a moment, leaving her with a vague sense of discomfort, like she was a coward for not wanting to face her own issues. Sometimes, she felt less emotionally evolved than her niece and nephew.

She'd begun speaking with a counselor after long-suppressed memories of her mother began resurfacing. She didn't feel like she was making progress. The therapist warned her that it would take time, and that progress couldn't be measured linearly. But the therapy itself focused on terrible memories. Bree always felt drained afterward.

She brushed aside her inner debate. She couldn't spare the hour—or the mental energy—this morning. She had to focus on Claire.

But there was no denying that watching Claire deal with her trauma had stirred up Bree's own pain, and that the case reminded her of both her sister's murder and her parents' deaths.

"Hey," Adam said as he walked into the barn. Bree smiled at the sight of her younger brother. He looked like the artist he was, a rangy body, shaggy hair, and the tragic hazel eyes all the Taggerts possessed. Did he own any clothing that wasn't speckled with paint? He might be extremely successful—his paintings sold for eye-popping amounts—but he often looked homeless.

He stopped next to her and greeted his horse with a forehead rub.

Still facing Bullseye, Bree gave her brother a one-armed hug. "Hey, yourself."

He pushed back. "You look upset."

Bree reorganized her face. "Is that better?"

"Yeah, no one else will know, but I do." He scanned her face. His artist eyes saw things other people did not.

"Are you OK?"

"Working a hard case," she said.

"The home invasion murders?" Adam asked. At her raised brow, he added, "I saw it on the news."

"Is that what the media is calling it?"

Could be worse.

"Yes."

Bree sighed. "Their teenage daughter found the bodies."

"Oh, no." Adam's hand stilled, flattening on Bullseye's forehead. The horse appeared to sense his owner's shift in mood and rested his head on Adam's shoulder. Adam wrapped an arm around the long neck. "I never knew horses could be so . . . empathetic."

"They're like giant dogs." *Giant, expensive dogs.* Adam didn't care much about money, though.

Adam ducked out from under his horse's head. Snapping a lead rope to Bullseye's halter, he led him into the aisle and secured him on the cross ties. Not that Bullseye needed to be tied. He loved to be groomed and would gladly stand there all day. Adam plucked a soft brush from the grooming bucket and began sweeping it over the horse's back.

Bree turned to lean backward on the stall door. "You know, I wasn't thrilled to move back home. All my life I avoided this place and all its memories. But now, I couldn't imagine going back to the city. I couldn't give up the kids, the farm—or our relationship." Bree and Adam hadn't known each other very well until recently. Adam had been a baby when they'd been separated. He'd helped Erin financially, but he'd been an aloof introvert, consumed by art that reflected his tumultuous emotional state. But since their sister's death, he'd stepped up for Bree and the kids. He'd worked hard to be available and responsive. He might not have the horrible memories of their parents' deaths that Bree carried, but his life hadn't been easy either. "I want you to know how much I appreciate you."

Adam paused and met Bree's gaze. "Thanks. I appreciate you too. Is everything OK?"

Bree realized that it was, despite her rough night. "Work is what it is, but life? Yeah. That's coming along nicely."

He smiled at her. "We've come a long way."

"We've run a freaking emotional marathon."

"It's hard, but worth it."

"So worth it." Growth was work, but the rewards were better than she had ever imagined.

They shared a moment of contented silence.

Adam swept a brush along the horse's shoulder, pausing to lighten the pressure over a hairless patch where years of harness wear had left their mark.

Bree frowned. "Poor Bullseye saw too many years of hard use."

"Yes, but he's getting a nice semiretirement. He seems to enjoy our rides." Adam touched the scar. The horse didn't even flicker an ear. "The scars bother us, but he doesn't dwell on them."

"I need to learn something from your horse." Bree half laughed.

"We could all use the reminder to live in the moment," Adam said in a serious tone. "His past led him to the here and now, and that is where he exists."

"So Bullseye doesn't have regrets?"

"You shouldn't regret things you had no control over. Regrets are for decisions *we* made, not the things that happened *to* us."

"That's powerful." *And freeing?*

Adam exchanged the brush for a hoof pick. "Don't think of scars as wounds. Think of them as badges, tally marks of survival. After all, the dead can't heal. Therefore, they don't scar."

CHAPTER SEVEN

Matt was back in the sheriff's station by eight thirty. He carried a container of fresh scones and a stainless-steel mug of Dana's supercharged coffee. Bree veered off toward her office door, where her admin, Marge, waited with a stack of messages and a frown. Not much rattled Marge, so her troubled expression was not a good sign. She was dressed in black slacks and reading glasses on a chain. In deference to the heat outside, she wore her trademark cardigan unbuttoned.

Matt offered Marge a scone. "They're fresh."

She raised her drawn-on eyebrows and took one. "Thanks. I fear it's going to be a long day. Reporters are waiting for you," she said to Bree.

Bree grimaced. "I issued a statement last night. I need some time before I can answer questions." She and Marge disappeared into Bree's office.

Matt went into the empty conference room and started the murder board by pinning photos of the victims to the top center. He added a picture of Claire off to the side. Todd appeared in the doorway with his own mug in one hand and a manila folder piled on a laptop in the other.

Without speaking, Matt nudged the scones toward the chief deputy.

"Thanks." Todd inhaled two scones and washed them down with coffee. Sugar and caffeine were a sad substitute for sleep, but when working a big case, they would all take what they could get.

"How's Cady?" Matt asked. His sister and Todd lived together, and Cady was six months pregnant. She'd had a slew of routine tests the previous week.

"Worried." Todd held up crossed fingers. "The results from the scans and blood work should be in today. I wish she could relax a little and enjoy the rest of the pregnancy now that we're past the critical point."

"She's not going to breathe easy until that baby is here and healthy." Years ago, Matt's sister had experienced a late miscarriage. Though the doctors had told her she couldn't have prevented it, Cady's ex-husband had blamed her. *The ass.* Matt tamped down the anger that always surfaced when he thought of his sister's ex. If Matt lived to be a hundred, he was still going to want to bash the ex's face.

Again.

Todd nodded. "Three more months. Then we'll all feel better. Maybe she'll even marry me."

"She loves you."

"I know that. I know I'm being old-fashioned, but I was hoping we'd be married before the baby was born. I would never pressure her, but I can't help feeling the way I do."

"I get it," Matt commiserated.

"I don't understand how us getting married could jinx the pregnancy."

"If there's one thing I've learned about parenting, it's that it makes you less than rational at times. If Luke doesn't text me back in fifteen minutes, I picture him in every terrible accident I responded to in my patrol days. When the baby comes, you'll probably worry in ways that don't make sense too."

"The more I read about pregnancy, the more I freak out." Todd shook his head. "There's so much that can go wrong. I wish I could help her."

"You are," Matt assured him. "By letting her call the shots and being there for her."

Matt understood Todd's dilemma better than he would admit. He would marry Bree tomorrow, but she wasn't ready. Her past made personal relationships difficult. She didn't trust or commit easily. He knew she loved him all the same.

Bree entered a minute later. "I need to give a press conference. Home invasions are terrifying. The press and public want information."

Todd wiped his hands on a napkin. "Forensics should be finished with the scene this afternoon. Juarez will be in shortly. I'll start him on gathering background information on the Masons."

Deputy Juarez had been shot in the leg by a serial killer over the summer. Though he wasn't recovered enough to return to patrol duties, he had begged Bree to let him come back to work. He was so bored he'd even volunteered to man a desk and type reports.

"Good," Bree said. "What did we learn from questioning the neighbors?"

"Not much. We're still working on the neighborhood canvass." Todd removed a photo from his folder, a close-up of the hole in the Masons' glass door. "As you know, entry was gained through the patio doors. Whoever came didn't break the glass but entered quietly, as if they knew the Masons were home."

Bree stared at the photo. "Dr. Jones established time of death as between eight thirty and nine thirty that evening, but Claire said her parents went to bed at nine. They looked to be settled and reading when they were shot. So, I'd bet they died closer to nine fifteen or nine thirty."

Matt paced, the movement spurring his brain into gear. "Chances are good the killer or killers knew the Masons' routine. Possibly also knew the layout of the house."

"On that note, we need the name and number of the cleaning service," Bree said. "Claire said they were in the house the day of the murders."

Matt pictured the couple in their bed. "The killer broke in, went upstairs, and killed the Masons, then searched the bedroom and home office. The only things we know were taken were electronics and likely a few business files."

"If we knew which files, that might point us to a lead," Bree said.

"We can ask Claire to look at photos of the house and see if she can identify anything that's missing," Todd suggested.

"She didn't seem to know much about their legal work, but she might identify other items that were taken." Bree nodded. "It's a big ask, but we don't have many options. Without other family members or close friends, there's no one else to do it."

"The fact that they had no family or friends seems odd," Matt said. "I mean, some people don't have family they're close to, but most people have at least one distant relative floating around somewhere. An aunt, a second cousin twice removed, *someone.*"

"And people without family sometimes fill that space in their lives with friends," Todd added. "But according to your interview with Claire, her parents didn't socialize."

"Maybe they're introverts?" Bree stared at their photos.

"Aren't lawyers extroverts?" Todd asked. "They have to connect with clients and court personnel."

"We don't know what kind of small-business law they practiced," Matt said. "They might write contracts all day."

"Yes, but they still have to deal with clients." Todd pulled two business cards from his folder. "I found these in the desk. It appears they were partners in their own firm, Mason and Mason."

Each business card bore the firm's logo, two *M*s connected by a fancy ampersand. Underneath, text read LEGAL SERVICES FOR YOUR SMALL BUSINESS. Their individual names, ATTORNEY-AT-LAW, a phone number, and an email address were printed in the corner.

Todd pointed to the phone numbers. "These numbers are registered to Josh and Shelly Mason personally."

"Maybe they were killed by a client," Bree suggested. "Maybe the one Claire said was giving her mother a hard time."

"The killings did have an execution vibe." Matt wrote *client?* on the board.

"The murders were efficient," Bree agreed. "And lawyers can be privy to sensitive client information."

Todd typed on his keyboard. "We have business records to read." He gestured toward a stack of boxes in the corner.

"They might do some of their work digitally," Bree said in a doubtful voice.

"Which might explain why the personal electronics were taken." Matt wrote more notes under the word *client?*: *location of records, business contacts.*

"Did you review everything in the home safe?" Bree asked Todd.

"Yes," Todd said. "Did you know Claire isn't the Masons' biological child? They adopted her twelve years ago. We found her adoption order, along with Shelly's and Josh's birth certificates, all their passports, and social security cards. They also kept their home and life insurance policies in there."

"So Claire has lost two sets of parents," Bree said, her voice full of sorrow.

"We don't know that her biological parents are dead," Todd said.

"Claire would have been five when she was adopted. I wonder how much she remembers about her bio family." Matt noted her adoptive status on the board. At this point, they had no idea what information might result in an investigative lead. Better to include everything they found and sort the threads later.

"She was adopted at age five, but that doesn't mean that's when she lost, was taken from, or relinquished by her biological parents. She could have spent time in the foster care system."

"We'll have to ask her," Bree said. "Erin was four when our parents died. She had snatches of memory. Maybe Claire does too."

"How much did they carry in life insurance?" Matt asked.

"Two hundred thousand each," Todd said. "Primary beneficiaries were each other. Secondary beneficiary is Claire on both policies." At least Claire wouldn't be penniless, like so many orphans. She could go to college, have a life.

"Nothing excessive then, and no other beneficiaries that might want a payout. What about tax returns?" Bree asked. "Or the name of an accounting firm."

Todd lifted a hand. "I'm still sifting through the papers in the office. I spotted tax returns but I haven't had a chance to review them."

"Still no will?" Bree asked.

"Nothing that we found at the house," Todd said. "We're requesting cell and financial records. Maybe we'll find an attorney in their phone contacts or an appointment with one on their calendars."

"Considering they were attorneys themselves, maybe not." Bree turned to Todd. "Let's see the adoption paperwork. I'll need to forward copies to the social worker."

Todd sifted through the papers in his folder and slid several pages across the table toward Bree. "Here."

Bree looked over the documents. "There must be a will somewhere. They're lawyers."

"Maybe it's the same as the contractor who doesn't fix his own house," Matt suggested. "Also, some people can't face the thought of their own death."

Todd went back to his computer. "I called Claire's manager first thing this morning. He confirmed her hours last night." Dotting i's and crossing t's was a boring but critical part of the job. He closed his computer and gathered his papers. "I'll get Juarez working on those warrants and background checks. Deputies will be knocking on doors this morning. Maybe we'll get lucky and someone saw a stranger last night."

Matt considered the murder scene. A stranger crime didn't feel right, but all investigative avenues needed to be pursued at this point in the case. Procedure existed for a very good reason.

Bree ran a hand across the top of her head. "I'm grateful my sister left a clear will naming me as guardian. I had no legal issues assuming care of the kids. They never had to go into the foster system. Dealing with the death of their mother was hard enough without the added uncertainties of where they were going to live and who would care for them. I can't imagine how Claire is coping. She has the trauma of finding them on top of the grief of losing them."

"And they left her with no one to reach out to." A burst of anger speared him. How could a parent neglect such an important detail?

"Maybe they have digital copies of their wills in their cloud account or physical copies in a safe-deposit box," Bree suggested. "Safe-deposit box keys are small. One of those might still turn up." She checked the time on her phone screen. "I have to prepare for the press conference." She got up and headed for the door.

After she left the room, Matt stared at the murder board. "I can start reviewing those business records." He reached for the top box.

"I'll go give Juarez his instructions." Todd stood. "Then I'll come back and help you."

Matt opened the box. As Bree had noted, lawyers were privy to sensitive information. Maybe something the Masons knew got them killed.

CHAPTER EIGHT

Renata Zucco stopped at the supermarket for a cat box, litter, and the brand of food she'd seen in the Masons' pantry. Then she drove home and carried everything into the foyer of her mother's house. A real estate agent would call the small bungalow *cozy*, but the house sat on a nice, large lot, and her mom—before she'd gotten sick—had tended her garden like a pro.

Renata opened the pet carrier, and Chunk strolled out, seemingly unconcerned with his change of venue. He wound around Renata's legs, then sniffed. His nose wrinkled with curiosity.

How would her mother take to the cat? Would she trip over him? She was already unsteady. Anxiety knotted in Renata's belly.

"Mom?" Renata called.

"In the kitchen," her mom replied.

Renata scooped up the cat. "I see how you got your name. I could use you to do weighted squats."

Chunk purred.

Renata walked to the back of the house. The morning sun poured in the windows. Her mom sat at the table, a steaming mug in front of her. Her fancy big-wheeled walker with a seat and brakes was parked at her side. The scent of coffee and toast made Renata's stomach rumble.

Her mom's eyes perked up at the sight of the cat. "Who is this?"

"This is Chunk." Renata leaned forward so her mom could pet him.

Her mom reached out a hand to stroke the cat's side. Chunk cranked up his motor in approval. Her mom smiled. "Isn't he sweet? Where did he come from?"

"A crime victim." Renata explained about Claire. "I didn't want her to lose her cat. She's been through enough. So, I volunteered to babysit him for a while. Is that OK?"

"It's lovely." Her mom pushed back her chair and motioned to her lap. "Let me have him so you can get some coffee. It's fresh."

"Prepare yourself. He's not a small boy." Renata carefully lowered the cat into her mother's arms. She'd seen no sign that the cat would scratch, but any animal could try to bolt if frightened. Chunk settled in, continuing his contented purring. Her mom's face brightened into a soft smile.

Renata should have gotten her a pet months ago.

"That's a good boy. How long can we keep him?" Her mom bent over Chunk and planted a kiss on his big noggin. Chunk bumped his head against her chin.

"I don't know." Renata went to the coffeepot and poured a cup. She shook the pot at her mother. "More?"

Her mom didn't look up. She was busy loving on the cat. "No, thank you."

"I'm in the mood for some eggs. Can I make you some?"

"Yes, please." Her mom sighed. "I wish *I* could make *you* breakfast."

"I'm not changing my name to Julia, but I can manage a few poached eggs." Renata pulled out a pan and added an inch of water from the tap. She turned on the burner, then took a few seconds to check her mother's pill dispenser. The A.M. compartment was empty. She hadn't forgotten.

So many pills.

Still, they were both grateful the meds were available, and her mom's cancer was treatable. Renata poached four eggs and served them on avocado toast. Renata scarfed hers down. Her mom picked at her food.

Renata eyed her mom's thin arms, paper-white skin, and prominent veins. Her mom was sixty, but the disease had aged her. She looked ten years older. Renata crossed her fingers the treatment would work, and her mom's life could return to some semblance of normal.

"I'm going to shower and change. Then I'm going back to work. Will you be OK here with the cat?"

"We'll be fine, won't we," her mom crooned. "I'm going to enjoy his company."

Renata rinsed plates and washed the pot with the efficiency of someone accustomed to squeezing daily chores into every spare moment. Then she filled bowls with cat food and water and set up the litter box in the laundry room. She carried Chunk to the box. He climbed in, used it, then trotted right back to the kitchen, found the kibble, and crunched away.

Very chill.

Renata's mother got up and carried her mug to the sink. She kept one hand on the walker but seemed steady today. Chunk moved out of the way, giving her space, as if he instinctively knew what she needed. Her mom went into the tiny sunroom that adjoined the kitchen. Her book and the afghan she was knitting sat on the wicker table. As she settled on the couch, Chunk leaped up next to her and curled against her legs.

"Oh, my." Her mom laughed. "I guess I'll have to knit around him." But her eyes sparkled as she stroked his tubby side.

"Well, Chunk is content." Renata went to her room, showered, and dressed in a fresh uniform. Back in the kitchen, she kissed her mom on the cheek. "You have your cell phone?"

Her mom patted her pocket. "I do."

"Text me if you want anything on my way home. I can run by the grocery store."

"I will." Smiling, her mom opened an app on her phone, and a true crime podcast played from a nearby speaker. She picked up her knitting, and the needles began to clack. The knitting was supposed to be therapeutic. Her mother had been NYPD, same as Renata, until she'd retired and moved upstate. How did she not lose her mind being stuck in the house?

Renata would rather stick one of those needles in her own eye than sit and knit all day. "You know, after Chunk returns to his owner, why don't we adopt a cat from the shelter?"

"I would love that." Her mom paused to give the cat a pat. Chunk closed his eyes.

"Be careful not to trip over him."

"I will. Don't you worry. We'll be fine. I'm going to enjoy having him here."

Then it was decided. Renata had been worried a cat would be too much to manage. She worked as many hours as she could get. Luckily for her, the sheriff's department was always shorthanded. She could usually grab an extra shift or two per pay period. The additional money was helpful—her mom's treatment meds didn't come cheaply, even with insurance—but she felt guilty leaving her mother alone. She couldn't drive right now. The ladies from her bridge club collected her for a weekly outing, but other than that, her mom was mostly homebound.

Renata filled an insulated bottle with ice water, locked up, and set the alarm on her way out. She'd brought her patrol vehicle home so she could drive directly to the Masons' neighborhood. She was right on time— nine thirty—when she parked at the curb behind another patrol car and reported her location to dispatch. Then she climbed out of the vehicle.

The morning sun already felt hot on her face. By lunchtime, she'd be cooking inside her body armor and uniform. At the Masons' house, crime scene tape fluttered across the front entrance and between saw- horses at the end of the driveway. Renata shuddered. The Masons hadn't been the first dead bodies she'd seen. In her experience with the NYPD, she'd worked patrol and vice. She'd gone undercover. She'd seen dead people, murdered working girls, women she'd known. But the scene in the Masons' bedroom had been jarring in a way she couldn't explain. The deaths she'd seen before had been in a different context, people who engaged in high-risk activities: hookers, pimps, addicts, dealers. But the Masons' perfect bedroom, saturated by liters of their blood, had shaken her. If death could find them in the perfection of their suburban neighborhood, then no one was safe.

No one.

Nowhere.

Another deputy emerged from his car and met her on the sidewalk. "These are the houses we need to visit this morning." He handed her a list, then pointed across the street. "You take that side. I'll work this one."

"Got it." Renata strode up the walk and rang the first doorbell. No one answered. She noted the address on the list and moved on. They'd have to come back in the evening and try again. At the second house, an elderly woman answered the door. She was about seventy years old, in psychedelic-print yoga pants and a pink zip-up jacket. Her pink sneakers would no doubt glow in the dark. She rocked short, spiky gray hair with a purple streak and held a ridiculously small dog in one arm. The bow holding back the dog's hair matched its owner's hair.

Renata smiled. "I'm Deputy Zucco. I'd like to ask you a few questions."

"I'm Helen Haverford. Is this about last night?" The woman's eyes gleamed with macabre interest.

"Yes, ma'am."

Mrs. Haverford stepped back. "Please come in so I can set down Squidward."

"Squidward?" Renata couldn't hold back a short laugh as she walked into the house. If ever there was a name that did not fit an animal's appearance . . . The little poof ball should be called Princess or Fluffy.

Mrs. Haverford closed the door. "My grandson named him because he's so grumpy." She set down the dog, who gave Renata the stink eye and growled. "Hush." Mrs. Haverford gave him a gentle nudge. Squidward retreated down the hallway, looking over his shoulder and grumbling. "Now then, what did you want to know?"

"Did you see anything unusual last evening? Anyone out and about? Strange cars?" Air-conditioning, an instant relief from the heat outside, wafted over Renata.

Mrs. Haverford clasped her hands together. "I did. I saw a car parked down the street. There was a man sitting behind the wheel. He was there for at least fifteen minutes."

"What time was this, ma'am?" Renata pulled a notepad and pen out of her pocket.

"About eight fifteen. I know because I always walk the dog from eight to eight thirty, and we were halfway through our walk." Mrs. Haverford's eyes sparkled. She was clearly enjoying the interview.

Renata sighed. People were morbid. "Can you describe the vehicle?"

"I can do better than that." Mrs. Haverford raised her chin with pride. "I took a picture." She produced a phone from the pocket of her jacket. "I always take pictures when I see strange vehicles, so I can send them to the head of our neighborhood watch. So much crime these days, you know. One can't be too careful." She turned the phone screen toward Renata, showing her an image of a dark SUV parked at the curb under a tree. Details were murky in the darkness, but it looked like a Ford Explorer.

"You can't see the license plate because of the dark, but I wrote it down." Mrs. Haverford turned to a small hall chest. On it, a silver tray held keys, a purse, and a notepad. She ripped the top page from the notepad. "Here you are."

"You take pictures of every car you don't recognize in the neighborhood?"

"Always." Mrs. Haverford tapped the notepad. "I keep them all in here."

Seriously? Who does that?

She answered her own question. *People with a lot of free time on their hands.*

Renata took the paper. "Thank you, ma'am. Did you get a look at the driver?"

"No. He was wearing a baseball cap." Mrs. Haverford toyed with the spiral binding of the notepad. "Do you think he was in a gang?" She lowered her voice to a whisper. "I hear there are gangs everywhere now. It's terrible. I hate the thought of violent gangs roaming the streets of Grey's Hollow. Have you seen any?"

Renata blinked. "No, ma'am. Can you describe the hat?"

Mrs. Haverford shook her head. "It was dark. Black or navy blue? I can't see colors that well anymore."

"OK." Renata pulled out a business card. "Would you please email the photograph of the car to this address?"

Mrs. Haverford took the card, her face drawn in a doubtful frown. "I don't know how to do that. I'm pretty good at texting, but email . . . My computer never works right. My grandson says I click on the wrong things and get viruses and things called *mall ware*."

"Malware." Renata gestured toward the phone. "You can send it right from your phone. May I?"

Nodding, Mrs. Haverford handed it over, but her email wasn't set up on the phone.

"Is it OK if I text the picture to myself?" Renata asked.

"Of course."

Renata texted the photo to herself and gave back the phone. "Thank you for your help, ma'am."

Mrs. Haverford beamed. "Always happy to do my civic duty." Her face sobered. "Plus, the Masons seemed like nice people. I can't believe this happened to them right here." She hugged herself, rubbing her biceps.

"How well do you know the Masons?"

Mrs. Haverford's lips pursed and wrinkled with concentration. "Not that well. They always waved when we saw them, but they didn't attend the neighborhood parties. They were good neighbors, though. Kept up their property. Never a bit of trouble."

"Thanks for your help," Renata repeated. "Call us if you think of anything else."

"I will." Mrs. Haverford nodded and lifted her phone. "I have your number since you texted yourself from my phone."

She's sharper than she looks.

"Yes, ma'am." Regret flashed through Renata, and she wondered how many calls she would be getting from Mrs. Haverford in the near future. Small-town living, she supposed.

The second deputy was called away, leaving Renata to finish. She had less luck at the other twelve houses she visited. No one answered the door at five addresses. She spoke to seven additional neighbors who didn't remember anything odd about the previous evening. By eleven thirty, Renata returned to her vehicle. The interior was an oven. She started the engine and lowered the windows to let out the hot air. Sweating, she used her cell phone to report back to Chief Deputy Harvey.

"Any luck?" he asked.

Renata filled him in on what Mrs. Haverford had seen. "It feels too easy."

"Run the plate. You never know," Harvey said. "Mrs. Haverford could have caught the killer on camera. I've seen stranger things."

"That's the truth." Renata checked the picture information.

Mrs. Haverford had snapped the photo at 8:16. The Masons had died between eight thirty and nine thirty. What if Mrs. Haverford had caught the killer in her photo?

Cool air began to flow from the dashboard. Renata sipped water from her insulated bottle. She adjusted her air vents and reached for the button to close the windows. Renata froze. The hairs on the back of her neck quivered. Something—no—someone moved in the window of the Masons' house. The shadow shifted again. Something pale flashed from behind a sheer curtain. A face? Definitely a person.

Renata's ice water flip-flopped in her belly.

The crime scene had not been released. No one was supposed to be inside the house.

CHAPTER NINE

Bree stepped away from the crowd of reporters. The press con had been uneventful for a change. The last time she'd handled a major murder case, she had been attacked by the media, the public, *and* the county board of supervisors. But they'd all had to eat their attitudes when she was proven right about the killer's identity. Today, everyone had acted respectful and subdued. She'd gotten accustomed to a combative environment. The change was almost unsettling.

She had reports to type and a mound of paperwork to tackle. The county sheriff was responsible for everything from law enforcement to managing the jail to running the animal shelter. An endless sea of forms, requests, and complaints crossed her desk and computer. She walked through the station. In the squad room, Deputy Collins typed on a computer. At her feet, the Randolph County K-9, Greta, reclined.

Bree's fear of dogs had greatly abated, but Greta's intensity still made her nervous. She purposefully approached. "Can I give her a treat?" she asked Collins.

"Of course." Collins reached into her desk and pulled out a bag of dog treats. Bree took one from the bag and presented it to the dog.

The black German shepherd thumped her tail on the floor as she gently accepted the treat.

"Good girl." Bree held out a hand, then stroked the dog's head.

"It's best if she recognizes the rest of the department as part of her team." Collins tossed the bag back into her drawer.

Juarez limped through the doorway. Greta's tail thumped harder. Juarez was the dog's favorite person to wear the bite sleeve for K-9 practice sessions.

Collins grinned. "Sorry, girl. He's not up to playing bad guy yet."

He stopped and scratched the dog's head. "We'll get back to fun and games soon. I promise."

Bree retreated to her office. Her butt had barely touched her chair when someone knocked on her door. "Come in."

Todd entered. "Got a minute? I have some interesting information."

"Of course." Bree turned away from her computer.

Todd dropped into one of the chairs facing her desk. "I spoke with Rory in forensics. He obtained access to the Masons' business email accounts. We'll want to go through the emails in detail, but I skimmed the most recent ones and found one from a disgruntled client." Todd looked at a sticky-note pad in his hand. "Mrs. Mason had a combative exchange with Peter Vitale. He owns a small real estate company. He hired the Masons to represent him in a sexual discrimination dispute with a female job applicant. Mrs. Mason reviewed the case, informed him that he wasn't likely to win the suit, and advised him to settle. Mr. Vitale's response, in an email, was 'I didn't hire you for advice. I hired you to make this go away. Do your job.'"

"He sounds angry," Bree said.

"Mrs. Mason told him to find a new attorney if he wasn't satisfied with her counsel. That angered him even more." Todd lifted a piece of paper and read from it. "'What kind of attorney are you? Did you even go to law school?'" Todd looked up. "Mrs. Mason told him he was free to ignore her advice. Then she sent him a final invoice, and he said there was no way in hell he was paying her another nickel. He ended the email with 'I want my retainer back or you'll regret it.'"

"Sounds like a threat." Bree rubbed her palms together. "Copy me on that email chain."

Todd handed her a sheaf of papers. "I printed them for you."

"Do we have a background check on Mr. Vitale?"

"We do." Todd referred to his paperwork. "He has no criminal record. He has a few speeding and parking tickets. Nothing more serious."

Glad to have a lead, Bree rose. "Matt and I will pay him a visit."

"He has a premises license for a Glock 19," Todd warned.

A premises license meant he could have the gun at his home or place of business. It was not the same as a concealed carry permit.

"Thanks." Bree called Vitale's office. The woman who answered the phone told her that Mr. Vitale was out showing a home, but he would be returning to the office in a half hour. Perfect timing.

She walked out of her office and down the hall. Ducking into the conference room, she waved for Matt. "Want to interview one of the Masons' clients?"

Matt jumped up, excitement in his eyes. "Yes! If I stare at tax returns any longer, I won't be able to keep my eyes open."

"In that case, we'll make a run to the coffee shop for a shot of serious caffeine."

They left through the back door. At the coffee shop drive-through, Bree ordered her usual cappuccino but with a double shot. Matt went with straight espresso, which he downed like a college kid with a shot of tequila.

Bree parked at Vitale Real Estate. The company maintained a small storefront, with a larger space in the rear of the building. Pickled oak furniture with mauve cushions called to the 1990s, but the space was clean and smelled of lemon furniture polish. A pod-style coffee maker and a tin of cookies welcomed visitors. Four chairs clustered around an oval coffee table.

They went inside. Peter Vitale ran an old-school business, with a fortyish-year-old receptionist sitting behind a computer. She stopped typing as Bree and Matt entered.

Bree showed her badge. "I called about speaking with Mr. Vitale."

The woman turned her head. She frowned at Bree. "Why do you want to see him?"

Bree said, "I'll discuss that with Mr. Vitale."

The woman crossed her arms. "He's not here."

Bree smiled. "You can answer some questions while we wait for him. What's your name?"

She huffed. "Jennifer."

Jennifer did not look happy. Her gaze darted to Bree's badge to the sheriff's department logo on Matt's polo shirt and back to Bree.

"Are you familiar with Shelly Mason?" Bree asked.

Jennifer rolled her eyes. "I am. Peter paid her good money for legal services, and she didn't do what he asked. Then she had the nerve to want *more* money."

The door opened behind Bree, and a tall, broad-shouldered man in his early forties walked in. He was square-jawed and walked with the swagger of a man who knew he was attractive. He wore tailored dark-gray slacks and a white button-down shirt with the sleeves rolled to the elbows, exposing tanned forearms. He handed Jennifer a folder as he passed her desk. "I outlined an offer for the Holland Road property. Would you take care of the paperwork, please?"

"Of course." She took the folder, opened it, and skimmed a page of handwritten notes.

The man turned to Bree and extended a hand. "I'm Peter Vitale. Can I help you?"

Bree introduced herself and Matt. "We're here to talk to you about Shelly Mason."

His jaw sawed back and forth, and he gestured toward an open door. "Let's go into my office."

Bree and Matt followed Peter into a cramped space. He closed the door behind them. Two chairs faced a metal desk with barely enough room to walk around them. Peter sidled behind the desk into his chair. Unlike most people when approached by law enforcement, he said nothing. *A cool one.* He folded his hands on the blotter and waited. Bree faced him over the desk. Matt's chair squeaked as he sat.

"You hired Shelly Mason for legal counsel," Bree began.

Peter's body remained still, but his brows knit in confusion. "That's privileged information. Why do you want to know?"

"Please answer the question."

Peter's thumbs rubbed together. "Actually, I hired *Josh* Mason, and he pawned me off on his wife." The corner of his mouth turned down.

"Was Shelly not a good attorney?" Matt asked.

"Obviously not, though I didn't know that at the time." Peter's nostrils flared.

Bree asked, "Had you worked with their firm before?"

"No." Peter shook his head. "The only attorneys I usually deal with specialize in real estate and contracts. I needed someone . . ." He paused, his mouth flattening. "Someone with a different skill set."

"What kind of skill set did you need?" Bree pressed. She knew the general answer, but she wanted more details and his perspective. She found it interesting that he didn't want to tell her. *If the case was bogus, he should be indignant, not secretive, right?*

"Employment law," he said vaguely.

Bree let it go for the moment. She'd circle back to the reason Peter had hired Shelly Mason. "You sent Mrs. Mason some emails that could be interpreted as threatening."

"I never threatened her." He shifted his position in a classic butt scoot, a typical display of discomfort during an interview.

Liar.

"You said"—Bree pulled her notepad from her pocket and read from it—"'I want my retainer back or I'll make you regret it.'" She looked up. "Sounds like a threat to me."

Peter's face flushed. "I shouldn't have written that."

Bree noticed he didn't say *I didn't mean that* or *I shouldn't have said that to her*. He specifically used the word *written*, which meant he probably only regretted leaving digital evidence of the threat.

When neither Bree nor Matt responded, Peter said, "I thought about suing her or complaining to the state bar. That was all." He leaned back in his chair, putting some distance between them. "Did Shelly Mason send you here because of my email?" His tone was incredulous.

"No," Bree said.

Peter looked more confused. "Then who did? I admit I sent a regretful email, but I was angry. She took my money knowing the details of the case. Then she said I should settle. And invoiced me for a thousand bucks."

Bree dropped her bomb. "Shelly Mason is dead."

Peter froze. His mouth opened as if he were going to speak, then he smashed his lips together. "I don't have to answer these questions. I have rights."

"You do." Matt's smile was feral, not friendly.

Peter licked his lips. Clearly, he hadn't seen the news, and curiosity lifted his tone. "How did she die?"

"She was murdered." Bree repeated the basic information she'd given at the press con earlier. "So was her husband, Josh. They were shot in their own bed."

Peter paled. "Fuck," he said with shock but no heat.

"Yeah," Matt agreed.

Bree went for it. "Where do you keep your gun, Peter?"

"At my house." Sweat rings broke out in Peter's armpits.

While he was nervous, Bree circled back to her earlier question. "Why did you hire Shelly Mason?"

"A person named Taylor McKnight applied for a job opening I posted for an agent. When he got here, *he* was a *she*. I didn't want to hire a woman. It's too dangerous for them to sit alone at open houses. It's asking for trouble. She's liable to get raped or flirt with a prospective buyer or mistake something I say and sue me. I told her that I didn't think she was right for the job. Two weeks later, she fucking sued me for discrimination. That's why chivalry is dead. Women killed it."

"Was she qualified for the job?" Matt asked.

Peter's eyes shifted. "She had some experience," he admitted.

Bree interpreted that as a *yes*. She didn't roll her eyes, but it took effort. Peter knew what he'd done was illegal. She could see it in his eyes.

"Did you fill the position with someone more qualified?" Matt asked.

Peter looked away.

Bree asked, "You filled the position with someone less qualified?"

Peter sniffed. "He's young but eager."

Bree made a note. "What did Shelly Mason say?"

"She spoke with Taylor's lawyer and said I would be better off settling out of court. That defending myself was going to cost a lot of money, and that I was probably going to lose the case anyway, which would add court costs, et cetera, to the total."

"You disagreed?" Matt asked.

"Yes! Isn't this an employment-at-will state?" Anger flared in Peter's eyes.

"Yes, but you still can't discriminate," Bree pointed out.

Peter's face went deep red.

"Have you ever been sued for discrimination in the past?" Matt asked.

"None of your business." Peter's silent stare was an unspoken *yes*.

Bree continued. "So, Shelly Mason gave you legal advice, and you didn't want to pay for her services."

"Damned straight. I wanted my retainer back, and there was no fucking way I was giving them another cent of my hard-earned money." His flush darkened to impending-stroke red. "Then she said she would send my bill to collections. Can you believe that?"

Yes. People liked to be paid for their time. But Bree said, "I assume you signed a legal contract to engage their services."

Peter's eyes went small and mean. "She didn't live up to their end of the contract. She didn't *do* anything."

Bree wasn't going to argue the merits of the legal bill with him. "Did you think if they were dead, you wouldn't have to worry about paying the thousand dollars?"

Peter's eyes bulged. A vein on the side of his temple throbbed. "You think I would kill two people for a thousand bucks?"

"I've seen people kill over twenty bucks," Matt said dryly.

"And you threatened Shelly," Bree pointed out. "Maybe it wasn't about the money. Maybe you lost your temper. Do you get angry often?"

"I was going to *sue* her, not kill her." Sweat beaded on Peter's upper lip.

"Where were you last night between eight thirty and nine thirty p.m.?" Bree asked.

Peter shifted forward. His palms hit the desktop, rattling his computer. "I was here, working."

"Was anyone here with you?" Bree asked.

"No. I was alone." Peter's fingers curled into fists.

Bree glanced at a pad for an alarm mounted on the wall. "Do you have a security system or surveillance cameras?"

Peter followed her gaze. "That hasn't worked in years, and we don't have cameras. There's nothing of value here." He waved a hand in a circle.

Matt asked, "Did you make any phone calls or see anyone?"

"No. I was catching up on paperwork." He froze. "Wait. Are you asking me for an alibi? You think I killed the Masons?"

Bree didn't respond.

Peter lowered his voice. "This interview is over. I won't answer any more questions without a lawyer."

"Suit yourself." Bree rose and offered him her business card. He ignored it. She dropped it on his desk before leaving. They didn't say anything until they were in her vehicle.

Matt slammed his door. "What an asshole."

Bree pressed the heel of her hand to an ache in her forehead. "People can be exhausting."

"What now?"

"We hope Dr. Jones recovered bullets from the bodies, then we get a warrant for his gun for ballistic testing."

"He doesn't seem like a complete idiot. If he killed them, he wouldn't have used his own gun."

"We'll dive more deeply into his background." Bree didn't trust Peter Vitale, not one bit.

Matt fastened his seat belt. "If he was being sued for discrimination now, maybe he has a history of the behavior."

Bree thought of his attitude about Josh handing the case to his wife and his refusal to hire a female real estate agent. "Or a history of hostility toward women."

"He acted like he didn't know they were dead. Maybe he's a good actor."

"Maybe." Bree reported to dispatch and started the engine. Her phone buzzed. "That's the ME." She answered the call. "Go ahead, Dr. Jones."

"I finished the autopsies on the double homicide from last night," Dr. Jones began. "Time of death remains the same, and there were no unexpected conclusions. Both victims were in good health and died from traumatic injuries and blood loss from gunshot wounds. Bullet trajectories are consistent with a single shooter standing at the foot of the bed. All four bullets were extracted and sent to ballistics. I'll send my preliminary report. The final will be pending tox screens."

"Thank you." Bree ended the call. "There are the bullets we needed. Let's hope they're in good enough shape for a ballistics match."

When a bullet was fired from a gun, marks were left on the bullet and casing. Those marks could be used like fingerprints to match a bullet to the specific gun that fired it, unless the bullet itself was too damaged for a comparison.

Matt cracked his knuckles. "I'd like to search Peter's home and office to see if he has any unregistered guns."

"We don't have enough evidence against him for a general search warrant." Bree was crossing her fingers the judge would grant her a limited warrant for his registered weapon. So much of the law fell into expansive gray areas.

She drove back to the station and headed for her office. "Let's regroup in the conference room in ten."

She hadn't even lowered her butt into her chair when Zucco's voice over the radio caught Bree's attention. "12-65."

A suspicious person.

Bree always had one ear tuned to the radio. Over the years she'd developed the ability to filter out most of the chatter and notice only important calls. She turned up the volume to hear Zucco give the Masons' address and add the radio code 12-69.

Zucco had spotted a suspicious person trespassing at the crime scene.

CHAPTER TEN

Renata's heart stuttered. She couldn't see the features behind the sun's reflection on the glass. But she knew it was a male from the size and general build. He disappeared, leaving the curtain swinging. The intruder had seen her!

Renata bolted from her patrol car and raced for the Masons' house. As she ran, she slapped her lapel mic. "Officer in pursuit of a trespasser at the crime scene."

"Ten-four," dispatch responded.

Renata rounded the side of the house. She stopped at the corner and peered around the corner of the building in time to see a tall figure run out of the patio door, right though a broken section of yellow crime scene tape.

"Stop! Police—sheriff's department!" Renata corrected herself.

The man wore black pants and a dark-blue long-sleeve shirt. A black baseball cap was pulled low on his forehead, and he'd tied a bandana around his face. Both hands were covered with black leather-type gloves. He didn't pause or turn to look at her but ran for the trees.

Renata gave chase, her black athletic shoes thudding on the lush grass of the Masons' backyard. The initial sprint winded her, but in a dozen strides, her lungs got with the program, and she settled into a steady pace. But still, he drew away.

She cursed her short legs, short everything. Why couldn't she have been born six feet tall with legs for miles? No, she was *petite*, which in her opinion was a euphemism for *child-size*.

The intruder was tall and lean, with a stride significantly longer than hers. But then, almost everyone's legs were longer than hers. *Damn it.*

He disappeared into the trees. Dead leaves and pine needles crunched under Renata's shoes. She shoved aside branches as she ran. Not knowing which way to go, she slowed and scanned the ground. Nothing. The earth was too dry and hard-packed for him to leave footprints. Beyond the artificial greenness of the Masons' rear yard, the weeds underfoot were mostly dead, with plenty of bare patches of dried dirt, as hard as concrete in places.

She stopped and listened for movement. With the forest so dry, it was nearly impossible to move through the trees without making crunching sounds. She might as well be running on Bubble Wrap.

A twig snapped, and fabric swished ahead. Following the sound, she ducked through a stand of small pines. A needled bough sprang back and slapped her in the face. She caught a glimpse of dark-blue fabric and drew her gun. "Stop right there! Sheriff's department!"

The figure stopped. His head cocked sideways until he was in profile to her, as if he were listening over his shoulder.

She breathed. "Let me see your hands!"

The cap and bandana still concealed his face. He slowly raised his gloved hands. His left hand was closest to her. He began to turn slowly, then whirled, sinking to one knee as he spun. His right hand swung around, and a shot rang out.

Renata dropped to the ground as the bullet struck a tree two feet away. Bits of bark exploded, pieces raining down on her back. Another shot shattered the air. A small cloud of dirt puffed four feet ahead of her face.

She covered her head with one arm and spoke into her mic. "Shots fired!" She rolled behind a tree and sat up, pressing her back to the trunk as cover. "Suspect is male, Caucasian, six two, one eighty, black pants, dark-blue T-shirt, black ball cap, black bandana over his face. He's headed north into the woods."

She closed her mouth, turned down the mic on her radio, and listened.

The woods were quiet. No birds chirped. She should be hearing him run away. But the forest was silent except for the rush of a dry breeze through the brittle foliage and the roar of her own pulse in her head. Her heartbeat echoed like a jackhammer in the Holland Tunnel.

Had he gotten away?

Gun in hand, Renata twisted to peer around the tree. A dark-blue shape crept forward through the underbrush, closer.

He was coming *toward* her.

Light glinted on the gun in his hand. Renata's heartbeat went staccato.

He wasn't running. He was backtracking and stalking her. Most criminals tried to escape the cops. But not this guy.

He was hunting her down.

Renata shifted to one knee and took aim. Something crunched under her knee. The man flinched at the sound, his face turning toward her. She pulled the trigger. Her gun bucked in her hand, the sound cracking through the dry air. A small animal burst from a shrub nearby and zigzagged away. The man ducked behind a fallen tree. His gun swung into the light. Renata pulled back behind the tree as his shot rang out. She leaned around and fired back at him again.

Yippee-ki-yay, motherfucker. I'm not running either.

A bullet struck the tree at her back. Renata turned and squeezed off another shot. "I have plenty of bullets, asshole!" She saw a dark-blue flash and fired twice more. "You're under arrest. Put down the gun and show me your hands!"

Footfalls and the sound of something large crashing through underbrush moved away from her. The sound faded.

Guess he didn't like return fire.

She swiveled, scanned the forest, but saw nothing.

Where did he go?

She briefly considered following him, then thought better of it. In the heat of the moment, she wanted to pursue. But that would be foolish. She had no backup. She didn't know these woods. Hell, she didn't know any woods. She would have been more comfortable chasing him through dark alleys.

Renata thought of the Masons, helpless in their own bed, their bodies ripped apart by bullets. He'd left a bloody mess for their teenage daughter to find. Just another criminal, preying on the vulnerable, unwilling to take on someone who could defend themselves.

Coward.

The thin wail of sirens approached.

Renata stood and brushed dirt and leaves from her uniform, but she vowed she would find him. He'd made this personal.

Chapter Eleven

Bree spotted patrol units at the curb ahead, lights flashing. She slid into the spot behind Todd's vehicle, slammed the gearshift into park, and bolted out of her vehicle.

Matt jumped out of the passenger seat and joined her on the sidewalk. "Zucco is OK."

"I know." But gunfire had been exchanged.

Zucco had reported that the suspect got away, but Bree would not relax until she saw her in person. Sometimes being sheriff felt like parenthood. She felt responsible for every deputy under her command.

Together, she and Matt rushed around the side of the house.

Zucco walked out of the woods and stopped in front of them. Bree scanned her deputy for bloody holes, but all she saw were twigs, leaves, and dirt stuck to her uniform. "Are you hurt?"

"No." Zucco's eyes flashed with fire, not fear. "But he got away!"

"What happened?" Bree kept her voice low, but she recognized that her deputy was processing a surge of adrenaline. On a good day, Zucco was a firecracker. After being shot at, she was a bundle of dynamite.

Zucco paced in a circle as she recounted the foot chase and gunfire exchange. Her hands flew around as she punctuated her rage with gestures.

"Let's check out the scene." Bree motioned toward the woods.

Zucco led the way. She stopped and turned in a circle. "I took cover behind this tree."

"Let's find those bullets." Bree wanted to know if the same person who'd shot at Zucco had also killed the Masons.

Matt and Todd began searching the ground. Zucco pointed to a hole in the tree trunk. "Here's one."

Barely a foot from her head.

Bree breathed. She could have lost a deputy today. Having Juarez shot earlier that summer had been bad enough.

Todd photographed and videoed the area. Then he dug the bullet out of the tree trunk and bagged it as evidence.

"I've found another," Matt said.

Todd walked to where the shooter had stood. Todd squatted and brushed dead leaves with a gloved hand. "And a shell casing."

An hour later, they'd recovered three bullets fired from the suspect's gun and a few that probably belonged to Zucco. She'd given the shooter a good fight. Good enough that he'd retreated.

For that Bree was grateful. "Take the rest of the day off," she said to Zucco. "Tomorrow, you're on desk duty with Juarez until we've investigated."

All officer-involved shootings required mandatory decompression time. Since no one had been injured today, Zucco's downtime would depend on her reaction and the investigation of the incident. If Zucco's body camera corroborated her story, she should be back on duty quickly. The shooter had broken the law by crossing the crime scene barrier. Zucco's pursuit was completely justified. He'd also fired the first shots, and Zucco had returned fire in self-defense. Zucco hadn't endangered any bystanders. Her actions had been appropriate. The only person she might have endangered was herself.

"Yes, ma'am." Zucco looked regretful. She was one of the more aggressive deputies. Bree knew Zucco didn't regret chasing a man into the woods alone. She was unhappy because she was being pulled from patrol duty.

"You should have waited for backup before chasing him at all."

Zucco grumbled. "Yeah. Probably."

Bree raised her brows.

Zucco sighed. "You're right. Sorry. I won't do it again."

But she didn't look sorry, and they both knew she probably would do it again. While they'd all like to be as careful as possible, sometimes it wasn't possible. Cops were caught alone all the time. When she'd worked patrol in the city, Bree had always had a partner, but out here, deputies rode solo. The fact was that they didn't have the budget or manpower to make sure backup was available all the time.

As much as she wanted to protect them, Bree couldn't guarantee her deputies' safety. But she wouldn't allow them to take unnecessary risks either. She would keep an eye on her newest deputy. Courage was commendable, but impulsiveness was a liability.

After Bree had taken over the sheriff's department, she'd cleaned out corrupt, misogynistic deputies, updated procedures, and modernized the actual building. There hadn't even been a locker room for female officers—but then, the previous sheriff hadn't hired any female deputies. Her latest addition—inspired by her own recent foray into therapy—was greater access to mental health care services.

Todd pointed to the woods. "I'll take a deputy and see if we can follow his tracks." He headed for the trees.

Bree and Matt returned to the Mason house. On the back patio, Bree studied the doors. "If it's the same person, he went in the same way he did when he killed Shelly and Josh."

"Why not?" Matt asked. "It worked the first time."

"Kind of dicey to go back the day after the murder. Forensics finished up a few hours ago. Why take the risk?"

"Maybe he didn't find what he was looking for last night."

"Then why did he kill the Masons so fast?" Bree asked. "If he was looking for something specific, why didn't he make them talk first? Why not threaten to kill Claire if they didn't?"

"All good questions," Matt agreed. "And why did he leave before he found what he'd gone there for? If Claire interrupted him, he could have killed her. He'd already murdered two people. He's obviously not squeamish, though like we discussed before, maybe he couldn't kill a kid."

Todd returned. He opened the map app on his phone. The neighborhood of McMansions backed to woods. Most of the area behind it was empty. "A trail of broken underbrush leads to Backwater Creek Road." He tapped on a green section of the screen with a blue line running through it. "There's a walking trail by the creek. He could have left a vehicle here and walked through the woods. It isn't far. There's enough foliage to screen his vehicle from the road."

"Tire tracks?" Bree asked.

Todd shook his head. "The parking area is gravel."

Bree turned back toward the house. "We need to search the house again."

"I'm in." Matt fell into step beside her.

Forensics had finished with the house, so they didn't bother with gloves. Bree stood in the kitchen and pivoted in a circle. "We need to look beyond a normal forensics evidence search."

"We don't know what we're looking for." Matt frowned. "Could be as small as a safe-deposit box key."

"Let's get started in the home office." Bree turned into the corridor.

They paused in the doorway, taking in the whole room. Matt went to the bookshelves and ran his hands over the frame and molding. Then he began pulling books and shaking them.

Bree pulled back the area rug and checked the floorboards underneath. She inspected the underside of the rug. Like Matt had said, a safe-deposit box key would be very easy to hide. They finished the office and repeated the in-depth inspection for the rest of the downstairs.

In the garage, they looked in every storage box and inside both vehicles.

They found nothing else of interest and moved to the second floor. Hours later, they stood in the primary bedroom. The bedding had been removed. Obviously, the mattress had been protected by a waterproof cover, because it looked oddly pristine. Squares of bloodstained carpet had been cut out and taken away as evidence by forensics. But the room still looked like a scene from a horror movie with the remaining bloodstained carpet and spatters on the headboard.

"We'll have to cover all of this before we bring Claire in here," Bree said.

"Yes. A couple of sheets will do it." Matt lifted the mattress and checked its seams. While it was raised, Bree examined the box springs, and then Matt pulled the headboard away from the wall and she checked behind it.

Bree turned toward the closet. "I feel like we're missing something."

"It's possible we're wrong about why he came back here. Maybe he's a sick fuck who wants to relive the murders."

Bree shuddered. "Could go either way. Except the murders don't feel like the actions of a random killer looking for thrills. They feel . . . purposeful."

"They do," Matt agreed.

They went into the walk-in closet. Matt started with the carpet, pulling it away from the wall. Bree moved clothing and looked for holes in the wall. They opened every box, inspected every pocket, and checked inside every shoe.

Then Bree looked up, where a rectangular attic access panel was framed in the ceiling. No dangling rope indicating there was a built-in pull-down ladder. "Was there a stepladder in the garage?"

"Yes. I'll get it." Matt left the room, returning in a few minutes with a four-step ladder, which he set up below the attic access. He climbed up, pushed on the panel, and slid it to the side. He stuck his head and shoulders into the hole. "There's something up here, but there aren't any floorboards. I might be too heavy to walk across." He descended the ladder.

"I'll go." Bree went up the rungs and hoisted herself through the opening. Placing her feet on the two-by-fours framing the access hatch, she pulled her flashlight from her duty belt.

"Be careful." Matt climbed the ladder as she started across the attic.

She shined her light into the space. The beam highlighted a large object in the far corner under a rafter. "There's something up here. I need to get closer."

Matt poked his head and shoulders through the opening. "Don't fall through the floor."

"I'll try not to." Stepping from joist to joist, she carefully picked her way across the space. When she got closer, she recognized a tarp. Lifting the blue woven nylon, she uncovered three backpacks. She relayed the finding to Matt.

"What's inside them?"

She crouched and smacked her head on a rafter. Dust rained down, and she sneezed. "There's no room up here. I'll bring them down. Give me some light."

Matt shined his flashlight into the space so Bree could return hers to her duty belt. Then she took photos of the backpacks from different angles.

"Ready," she called over her shoulder.

Matt lowered his beam to illuminate the joists. Bree donned gloves, slung a backpack over each shoulder, and carried the third by the straps. With the added weight of the bags, her return trip across the unfloored attic was more precarious. A joist creaked and she wobbled. She paused to catch her balance, then continued to pick her way from joist to joist. As soon as she reached the hatch, Matt took the bags from her with a gloved hand and descended the ladder.

She climbed down.

He carried the bags outside the closet and set them down on a clear spot of carpet. "Not much dust, but they were covered, so who knows how long they've been up there."

One bag was black, another was dark gray, and the last was navy blue. Matt drew open the zipper of the black bag. Bree did the same with the gray one. She pulled her flashlight off her belt and shined it inside the bag. "I see some clothes." She shifted them aside. Underneath sat an opaque brick. A sliver of excitement raced through her, as if her instincts knew the block would be important. "What is this?"

She reached into the bag and lifted one out and peeled away a few layers of plastic wrap. A twenty-dollar bill stared back at her. "It's money. Lots of it." Each block consisted of four or five banded stacks of bills a half-inch thick. She fanned the top of a stack to see bills ranging from fives to hundreds. She rechecked the bag and spotted another block. "There are plastic-wrapped blocks of money under the clothes. What did you find?"

"The same in the main compartment." Matt opened a second zippered compartment. "Protein bars, an empty bottle, water purification tables, a prepaid phone, and a sizable bottle of blood pressure medication."

Bree's bag was similarly equipped. She went to a smaller front compartment and removed a Canadian driver's license. The photo was Claire but the name read *Clara Zahn*. There was a Canadian passport in the same name. "I found Canadian documents for Claire under a fake name."

"And this one has Canadian identification with Shelly Mason's photo and the name Shannon Zahn."

Bree checked the third backpack. The contents were the same. "Josh Mason's other name is Jake Zahn."

"If these are fake, they're damned good ones."

"Those would be very expensive."

"Money didn't seem to be an issue for the Masons." Matt weighed a block of cash in his hand. "How much cash do you think is in each brick?"

"They're mixed bills. No way to know for sure except count it. We'll drop them at forensics. They can count the money and make sure it's not counterfeit. Everything needs to be swabbed and dusted for fingerprints anyway." Bree reassessed the bags. "Alternate IDs, cash, changes of clothes, food, water, essential medication. These are go-bags."

"Yep. Who keeps those besides spies and criminals, and why would a pair of lawyers need them?" Matt asked.

Bree's gaze found the blood spatters on the headboard. "Probably the same reason they're both dead."

CHAPTER TWELVE

Matt stretched a tight shoulder in the passenger seat of Bree's SUV while she drove toward the farm. "You'll be home in time for Kayla's bedtime."

"I don't like missing dinner with the kids." Bree made a right at a stop sign. "But bedtime is somehow worse. I don't know how long Kayla will still want me to read to her. I hate to miss a single night."

"I love a good bedtime story too." Occasionally, Kayla asked Matt to read to her. It always felt like an honor.

They'd dropped the go-bags with forensics and picked up Claire's phone. Forensics had downloaded the contents, but since Claire didn't share an account with her parents, Matt wasn't sure if the information would be very useful. He wanted Josh and Shelly Mason's digital information.

Bree planned to return the phone to the teen in the morning.

Matt's phone beeped with a voicemail from Cady. Something about the forensics lab gave the building poor cell reception. Calls didn't always go through.

Matt stabbed the "Play" button.

Cady's voice sounded strained. "I need your help with something. Could you stop by when you have a chance?"

He tried to call her back, but the call went to her voicemail. He tapped the phone on his leg.

"Everything OK?" Bree asked.

"I don't know. Cady asked for help, but I can't get through to her." He slid the phone into his pocket. "Do you think the kids would mind if *I* miss bedtime?"

"They'll understand. They love Cady. Go see her. You won't be able to relax until you do."

"Thanks."

A few turns later, she stopped at the farm. He kissed her, climbed into his Suburban, and headed for his sister's place a short drive away.

He parked in front of the kennels of the house he'd built after the shooting had ended his career as a deputy. The property was huge, with kennels, a pond, and plenty of acres for working dogs. He'd intended to train K-9s as a second career. Except his sister had filled the kennels with rescues before he could even get started.

The family had played musical houses over the past months. Cady had lived with her four rescue dogs in her own little home, but now that Matt was living with Bree, it made sense for his sister to move into his larger property and be on-site with the kennels. Recently, Todd had rented out his place and moved here with her.

Matt stepped out of his Suburban into the fading twilight. The kennels erupted into a frenzy of barking.

His sister emerged, one hand on her back. Athletic and nearly six feet tall in her socks, Cady carried pregnancy well.

Matt kissed her on the cheek. "You look great."

Cady smiled. "Thanks."

"Did you get the results back?" Matt almost kicked himself for asking. What if they weren't all right and she didn't want to talk about it?

"Yeah. Everything is good."

"Fantastic!" Relief bubbled up in Matt's chest.

Cady rubbed her stomach, which looked like she'd swallowed a volleyball. "I'll be glad when this is all over."

"I know." He patted her shoulder. "Now, what can I help you with?"

"It's two things." She turned and walked toward a small shed, leaving the din of the kennel behind. "Todd converted this into a quarantine kennel. We needed to make changes with that new canine respiratory disease going around."

"Good idea."

"Now we keep all newcomers here until they're vetted. We built three separate enclosures and use an air filter. It's the best we can do, considering we don't even know how the disease spreads." She rolled the sliding door, exposing a four-by-four vestibule with three interior doors. Cady opened the first door and stepped aside. "Take a look."

Matt poked his head in the doorway. A furry gray lump slept on a bed raised off the concrete floor. As he entered, the lump raised its head. "A puppy?"

"Look closer."

Matt crouched. The puppy stood, stretched, and fell out of its bed. From the gangly limbs, he estimated it was about three or four months old. Matt watched it sort out its feet. Its eyes were yellow gold. "That's not a dog."

"Nope," Cady said.

The pup sniffed the air but did not run toward him.

"That's a wolf. Where did you get a wolf puppy?" Matt assessed the pup. It was thin, with scraggly fur. "Whoever had this animal didn't know how to care for it."

"Some guy had it on a leash when I was picking up an owner surrender. I knew it wasn't a dog right away."

"Did the guy know?"

"First, he tried to hide it, then he said it was a Siberian husky puppy." Cady rolled her eyes, making it clear what she thought of that story.

"Bullshit." Matt sighed. "Do you have his information?"

"He wouldn't give it, but he let me take the pup." His sister excelled at de-escalating situations and talking people into relinquishing animals they couldn't care for properly.

"So, he knew it was illegal." Wolves were endangered. It was illegal to keep one without a special permit. Even wolf-hybrid dogs were illegal in New York State.

"That's what I thought," Cady agreed. "It felt like a precarious situation, so I didn't push and was glad to get the pup away from him."

Matt hoped the guy didn't have additional wolf puppies or other illegal animals. Unfortunately, the exotic pet trade was booming. "Can you describe the guy?"

Cady nodded. "He was in his early thirties. Six one or two, wiry, shaved head. Dressed in a muscle shirt, ripped jeans, and biker boots." She tapped her forearm with the opposite hand. "He had a tattoo of a sword with roses wrapped around it."

"Where was this?"

Cady checked her phone and read off an address.

Matt wrote it down, recalling a meth lab Bree had busted near there a couple of months before. "Not the best area."

"I know." Cady nodded. "I didn't go alone."

Matt held his tongue. He could be overprotective. Cady was a smart woman. She didn't take foolish chances. He had to trust her, not treat her like she was a child. Even though, to him, she would always be his baby sister.

"I brought the pup here," she said. "I don't even know who to call. I've never had this happen before."

"I'll contact the zoo." Matt and Bree had encountered illegal exotic animals the previous winter, including venomous snakes. The memory gave him a phantom ache in his leg where he'd been bitten. "Can you hold on to him until tomorrow?" Matt pulled the door closed, leaving the skinny animal in peace.

"Sure." Cady rested her hands on her rounded belly. "He's probably better off here than at the animal shelter. At least I'll keep him isolated. I gave him water and puppy food. I hope that's OK."

"Best you can do for now. It's possible it's a hybrid. The zoo will figure it out and hopefully find it a home," Matt said as they left the shed. "You had something else you needed?"

"Yes. A normal thing."

"Good." Matt followed her into the din of the kennel. As always, it was full of dogs. Some wagged at their doors, desperate for attention. Others slunk to the back of their enclosure, wary of people. Matt's heart ached at them all, but he knew his sister worked tirelessly to place every dog in a good home.

Cady stopped in front of one of the larger cages. Inside, a tall, lean dog leaped at its kennel door.

"That's a Belgian Malinois. How did you get him?"

"He was an owner surrender. The guy saw a movie with a Belgian Malinois military dog star and had to have one. You know how that goes."

"Usually, not well."

"Nope. The owner couldn't control him at all. When I went to pick him up, he ran straight up a wall onto a first-story roof, which summarized why the owner needed to rehome him."

"How did you get him down?"

"I taunted him with a rope toy." Cady patted her belly. "I surely wasn't going up after him."

"He looks serious." Matt and the dog assessed each other. Matt blinked first. The dog practically vibrated with energy. "Does he have a name?"

"Not yet." Cady's mouth thinned. "I don't think he's going to make anyone a good pet, Matt."

"Probably not. This is not a couch potato. It's a working dog."

"Like Greta," Cady said.

Greta had a similar story. Matt had recognized her potential and pulled her from the rescue.

A Labrador mix in the next cage lunged onto the chain-link divider, the dog's tail wagging like a helicopter blade. The Malinois exploded into a fury of barking and growling. The other dog backed down and whined.

OK. Not dog friendly. "Is he aggressive toward people?"

"He hasn't tried to bite anyone, but he's wired for action. He has a lot of energy. Todd's going to take him running and see how he does."

"Exercise will help, but this kind of dog needs mental stimulation," Matt said. "Let Todd run with him, and I'll start working with him too. We'll see what he's got. He's the right breed. Looks intelligent. Definitely not timid. All good qualities in a working K-9."

"Thank you."

"No worries. If he works out, it's a win-win. K-9s from specialty breeders are expensive. We have nothing to lose here." He kissed her on the cheek. "Love you."

"Love you back."

He drove home. Kayla was asleep, but Matt stopped in Luke's room to say good night. He changed his clothes and went down to the home office.

Bree was at her desk, drinking tea and staring at her laptop.

He filled her in on his trip to the kennel.

"I have three thoughts." Bree smiled. "One, I'm so glad Cady is doing well. Two, I would love another K-9, but I'll have to work on the board of supervisors. We'll need money for training and equipment. Hopefully, they see how valuable Greta is and get on board."

"The public has been supportive."

"This is true," Bree said. "Our K-9 fundraisers have been successful, and Greta has improved the department's public image overall. People love dogs."

"And three?"

She frowned. "Your wolf pup reminds me that I responded to a call about an alligator in Grey Lake last night. It was right before Claire's 911 call came in, so I forgot about it."

"An alligator?"

"Yep. The caller had been drinking, so I wasn't convinced he actually saw one at the time."

"And now?"

"Now I'm wondering if I should have taken the call more seriously." She lifted a shoulder. "It seemed so impossible. Still does."

"I thought I'd seen everything, but this is my first illegal wolf puppy," Matt said. "Who needs a wolf as a pet?"

"People are weird." Bree shook her head.

"People are also stupid, and stupid is dangerous."

Chapter Thirteen

Claire set off down the sidewalk, leaving the foster home behind as fast as she could. She was practically running, heading for the playground a few blocks away. There wasn't anywhere else within walking distance.

The morning air felt surprisingly hot on her face, considering it was still early, and sweat broke out beneath her T-shirt. She slowed her steps. She had only one clean set of clothes. Probably wasn't smart to get this one all gross.

She shoved her phone deep in the back pocket of the shorts the foster mom—Janice—had bought her. The T-shirt and canvas sneakers were new too. There'd been no time to wash them last night, and the fabric felt stiff and scratchy. Everything about this house was uncomfortable.

She needed a minute. Just a damned minute. Since Monday night, she'd felt as if she'd been stuck in a nightmare. No, a horror movie. The other kids at the home never stopped yelling, even when they were happy. They'd screamed and screeched off and on all night. Janice apologized and offered Claire earplugs. She said the kids had some *issues*.

Don't we all?

If the kids' lives were perfect, they wouldn't be here, would they?

Yeah, the rest of the fosters were little. The oldest was seven. But they all had one thing in common: they had nowhere else to go.

Do you want to go out to breakfast? Janice's husband had asked her.

With those other kids? The screamers?

Hell no.

She needed to sort through the past day and a half. No. She didn't want to think about that at all. She wanted to think about dumb work, getting ready for a new school year, worrying about AP Spanish and college applications. She was supposed to be a senior this year. But everything had changed.

She breathed.

Her life had been ripped out from under her. A bright speck of anger warmed inside her. Tears burned the corners of her eyes. It wasn't fair. She hadn't done anything to deserve what had happened to her.

Claire rounded a bend in the road and crossed the street. She looked over her shoulder. She couldn't see the house, but she wasn't that far away. A couple of blocks maybe, not that she'd been counting, but Janice had made her promise not to leave the neighborhood. Where would she go? She didn't have a car, and the house was like, seven miles from town. She could walk, she guessed. But walking to Grey's Hollow wouldn't solve anything.

The playground appeared ahead. It was a small one, with swings and a climbing structure for little kids. She stepped over the curb, sat on a swing, and turned it around and around. The chain twisted tighter and tighter, raising the seat higher, until she pulled her feet off the ground and let it spin back.

When it finally jerked back into position, Claire planted her feet on the ground. The dizziness matched her emotions, swirling out of control, leaving her with a vague sense of nausea.

She stared down at the cheap sneakers, bought in a late-night, desperate shopping trip to Walmart. Claire hadn't been thinking straight, but Janice had known what to buy. She had a list in her phone: two outfits, sneakers, pajamas, toothbrush, one pack each underwear and socks. How many times had Janice made this late-night run? How many kids had she supplied and housed at the last minute?

How many of those kids ever got to go home again?

Claire could never go home. She wasn't even sure she could step into that house to get her stuff. Not after what she'd seen there, what had been done there. She closed her eyes, as if that would block out the mental images. Nope. Still there.

If she had a vehicle, she would have driven away last night, gone as far away as possible.

Put a thousand miles between her, the house, and the terrible memories.

Instead, she'd spent the night in a strange bed with its own horror movie soundtrack playing in the next room that no earplugs could fully block, not even with the pillow smushed over her head.

She took a deep breath and dug her toe into the dirt under the swing. She needed to work through some next steps. But much of her future was out of her control—at least for the moment. Janice told her not to think ahead, at least not for the next couple of days. There were too many variables at play to make any sort of plan.

Claire would be eighteen in nine months. She'd be a legal adult who could make her own decisions. But this morning, there wasn't a single aspect of her life that didn't seem bleak. There were no good options to pick from, even if the decisions were hers to make.

The weight of the situation crushed her chest until she could barely breathe. Sweat moistened her palms, and she rubbed them on the shorts.

The sound of an engine startled her, her senses fine-tuned from stress. The sun felt hotter. She didn't have her phone. How long had she been here? She'd lost track of time. A car door slammed. Her foot stopped digging. Her head snapped up, like a deer smelling a predator on the wind. A man stood beside a dark SUV. His focus on her was so intense it nearly burned.

Claire stood and backed away from the swing, her heart thumping. He started toward her. Her sneaker caught in a patch of weeds, and she almost went down. But she regained her balance with a hand on the ground. Straightening, she looked up.

He was headed straight for her. A ball cap shadowed his eyes, but she could feel his gaze riveted on her. She should run. A voice inside her head screamed *Go!*

Chapter Fourteen

Bree drained her coffee mug as she parked in front of Claire's foster home. She and Matt had spent hours writing and reviewing reports the night before. Meticulous paperwork was a boring but essential part of a successful investigation.

Matt climbed out of the passenger seat and joined her at the base of the long driveway. The neighborhood was quiet and typically suburban. Modest older houses and SUVs lined the street. Mature trees and shrubs decorated generously sized lots. A minivan sat in front of the two-story house Claire was assigned to. A basketball net stood at the curb, and childish chalk drawings decorated the sidewalk. Bree listened for high-pitched voices but heard none.

A fortyish-year-old woman with a brown ponytail emerged from the front door. "Hi. I'm Janice."

Bree introduced herself and Matt. "We need to speak to Claire."

"She went for a walk," Janice said. "I thought it would be OK if she promised to stay in the neighborhood." Janice twisted her hands. "It is OK, right? She's seventeen."

Bree held up a hand to ease the woman's anxiety. "It's fine. She's almost an adult. Which way did she go?"

Janice pointed down the street. "That way, toward the playground. I feel so bad for her. She seems overwhelmed."

Bree glanced back at the chalk art, which suggested younger children were in residence. "Where are the other kids?"

"My husband took them out for breakfast," Janice said. "Claire didn't want to go. She's barely eaten anything since she got here. I tried to cook her breakfast, but she said she wasn't hungry. She needed some space."

"That's understandable." Bree didn't know how the girl was coping at all with what she'd experienced. Lindsay needed to look into therapy for Claire. She was going to need help processing her trauma. Even though she was nearly an adult, Bree still didn't like the girl being out on her own. Claire might want some alone time, but that didn't mean it was safe.

Matt scanned the street, as if he weren't comfortable with Claire being without supervision either.

"I've never fostered a teenager this old before." A frown line bisected Janice's forehead. "Mostly, we get younger kids. We're a little unsure how to help Claire, but we're trying."

A scream pierced the morning air. Bree whirled to see Claire emerge from behind a huge clump of shrubs on the corner two blocks away. She was coming at them in a flat-out run. Bree started toward her. Matt was already gone, sprinting like a decathlete. A figure rounded the corner behind Claire, clearly in pursuit. He was male, tall and thin, dressed in black and wearing a black baseball cap. He was too far away for Bree to see any additional details. As soon as he spotted Matt, he came to a sliding stop, whirled, and raced away in the other direction.

Claire and Matt passed each other. The girl paused as she reached Bree. Breathless, she wheezed out a few words. "The man . . . grabbed me . . . chased me . . ." Gasping for air, she waved down the block.

Bree gestured toward Janice. "Go inside, lock up!"

She glanced over her shoulder to see Janice herd Claire into the house and slam the door. Then she ran after Matt. With one hand on her lapel mic, she reported the incident and requested backup. The first ETA came in at seven minutes.

Too far away. This would be over long before a patrol deputy arrived.

Matt surged ahead. They ran several times a week together. While she couldn't match pace with his much longer legs, she was quick on her feet. But the man they were pursuing was also fast, and he had almost a two-block lead on them.

Bree pictured the neighborhood map from her GPS. Ahead, the road curved to the playground. She skidded into a sharp right turn, along the next short block, and veered left. Now she was running parallel to Matt, but her route was on the inside of the curve. With her shortcut, she'd gained a bit of ground on the suspect. Lungs screaming, thighs burning, she pushed harder. She spotted the playground on the next corner—a swing set, with a little fort and suspension bridge.

At the next intersection, motion in her peripheral vision caught her attention. She swiveled her head. The man in black raced across the bisecting street and passed the playground. Matt was fifty yards behind him, still moving at full speed, like a running back with the ball and the end zone in sight. But Bree's shortcut had paid off. She was closer. She veered across the grass, heading straight for the suspect.

The playground backed to a strip of evergreens, but over them, Bree could see the tops of houses on the other side. Another housing development. She wanted to catch him before he made it to the trees. She inhaled and gave him a warning: "Stop. Sheriff!"

He didn't even glance her way, and she saved her breath for sucking in oxygen. She was within a hundred feet now, and gaining on him. The suspect appeared to be flagging, his strides less even, less sure—more desperate. Swerving around a climbing apparatus, he stumbled in the thick layer of wood chips beneath the equipment.

Bree gained another few feet. She might not be as fast off the line, but she had endurance to spare. Her strides lengthened, anger fueling her. This man had tried to grab and chased a teenage girl. Possibly he'd killed her parents and shot at Zucco.

I'm going to get you now, you bastard.

Remembering Zucco's shooting, Bree drew her weapon. But she couldn't fire at his back. She didn't know if he was armed, and he was still too far away for an accurate shot. The houses beyond the strip of trees were close, and she wouldn't risk a neighborhood kid catching a stray bullet.

He swung an arm around. Bree caught the glint of metal. She dropped to the ground as the shot went off. The bullet struck the pretend bridge, splintering the wood. A woman screamed. He fired again. The shot whizzed over her head. Bree rolled behind the mini fort. Built of four-by-fours, it should block a bullet. With her back to the structure, she scanned the area for the screamer—and for Matt. He was on the sidewalk next to a woman with a toddler and a baby stroller. Matt gathered them behind the engine block of a Jeep parked at the curb. Then he crouched over them, also shielding them with his body. Bree returned her attention to the shooter. She peered around the wooden post and leveled her gun in the shooter's direction, but he was nowhere in sight.

The sound of an engine starting carried on the breeze. Tires squealed on pavement. The engine roared, then faded.

Fuck!

He was getting away.

She scrambled out from behind the play structure and ran toward the trees. With the threat gone, Matt left the woman and children and caught up with Bree. Together, they raced through thirty feet of buffer foliage. They burst onto the suburban street on the other side just in time to see the rear end of a black SUV in the distance. It turned out of the development and disappeared down the road.

Bree used her lapel mic to update dispatch. But her deputies on patrol weren't close enough to catch the shooter.

Matt paced in frustration. "We should have known he would shoot at us. That's exactly what he did when Zucco chased him. He could have hit that mother or one of her kids." He circled like an irritated big cat in a cage.

Bree let him walk off his adrenaline while she focused on bringing down her heart rate and catching her breath. "And what could we have done differently? Not chased him at all?"

"No," he said in a sulky voice. He wasn't even breathing hard. He pointed to an intersection more than a hundred yards away. "Did you get a plate number on the SUV?"

Bree shook her head. "Too far away. I couldn't even testify as to the make or model. It appeared to be the size of a Ford Explorer, definitely black."

Matt's jaw shifted in frustration. He continued to pace the asphalt, both hands on his head, cursing. Bree let him vent. He didn't get visibly angry often. They'd both seen too much in their law enforcement careers. But when the vulnerable were attacked, and he couldn't catch the scumbags responsible . . .

Yeah, she gave him a minute.

He stopped pacing. "I'll get the witness's contact information and a statement."

While Matt walked back to the mother and her kids, Bree updated dispatch, calling for responding patrol units to be on the lookout as they approached. But all they knew about the suspect was that he was a tall, thin man dressed in black and driving a black SUV, potentially a Ford Explorer. It wasn't enough information to issue an official BOLO.

Bree located the bullet buried in the wood of the play structure. She photographed it, then after donning gloves, dug it out of wood. She walked to the area where the shooter had stood when he fired at her and also located the shell casing. With the bagged-and-tagged evidence in her pocket, she walked through the evergreens and scanned the neighboring housing development.

A moment later, Matt joined her. "The ground is too dry for footprints."

Bree nodded toward the four houses facing them. "Let's knock on those doors. Maybe we'll get lucky and someone saw our shooter or has a doorbell or security camera that caught the SUV."

But they did not get lucky.

They retreated to the foster home, and Janice let them inside. In the kitchen, Claire sat at the table, hugging herself, crying silently. She was dressed in denim shorts and a T-shirt instead of Zucco's gym clothes. A chair was pulled next to Claire's, as if Janice had been sitting close, trying to comfort her.

Bree sat at the table across from Claire and pulled out her notepad.

Claire's face was pale and streaked with tears. She looked like she'd lost weight since the day before. She plucked a tissue from a box on the table in front of her and wiped her eyes and nose. "I'm sorry."

Matt stepped away, leaning on the wall like a sentinel.

Bree took the empty seat next to the girl. "Are you OK?"

Claire nodded. "I didn't cry until it was all over. Now, I can't stop."

"It's the adrenaline," Bree assured her. "It'll pass." She scanned the girl again. "You weren't hurt?"

"No." Claire sniffed.

She hunched over her folded arms. Janice set a glass of ice water on the table at Claire's elbow.

"Can you tell me what happened?" Bree asked.

Claire drew in a long, trembling breath. "The little kids were loud when they got up, and I needed some quiet, some space, you know? I went for a walk."

Janice hovered, her movements disrupting Claire's concentration.

Bree redirected her back to the story. "Where did you go, Claire?"

"The playground. It was empty. I sat on a swing. I used to love the swings when I was little." Claire paused and clenched her hands together.

Bree's heart cracked as she pictured the girl, sitting on the swing, seeking comfort from a childhood memory.

Claire continued. "I was there for maybe ten minutes? Then an SUV parked. I got this creepy feeling, like the driver was staring at me." She shivered. A tear rolled down her cheek, and she swiped it away with a fingertip. After a deep breath, she continued. "A few minutes later, he came walking toward me." She hesitated, her gaze turning inward as she remembered. "He was so focused on me, it was scary. And the way he headed right toward me freaked me out. At first, I felt dumb, like he was probably going to ask me a question and I was overreacting because of what happened to my parents. But I couldn't help myself. I had to get away from him." Her eyes widened. "I got up and started walking away. He followed me. I ran. He chased me." Claire's breaths sped up. "He caught me before I even got to the sidewalk." She rubbed her wrist, where a red mark indicated a bruise would develop. "He pulled me toward him. He was too strong. I couldn't pull away." Her breathing was choppy and frantic.

"You're safe now, Claire," Bree said. "No one is going to hurt you."

Claire nodded, but she was close to hyperventilating.

Bree turned to Janice. "Do you have a paper bag?"

Janice opened a drawer and produced a paper lunch bag.

Bree opened it and handed it to Claire. "Breathe into this. Deep and slow."

Claire did, and her breathing evened out in a few minutes. She lowered the bag. "I let him pull me closer. Then I kicked as hard as I could. I got him in the thigh. He released me and went down on his knees."

She'd probably caught him in the balls. *Good girl.*

Claire gulped. "Then I ran as fast as I could. I heard him behind me. When I turned the corner onto this street, he was still behind me. But he stopped chasing me when he saw you." Her eyes lifted to meet Bree's. "He was after me. I know it. I could *feel* it. But why?" As she asked the questions, her eyes fell to her wrist and the reddening marks around it.

Resolve hardened Bree's heart. "I don't know, but we won't let him near you again."

Claire didn't look convinced.

Bree didn't blame her. They hadn't considered that Claire could be a target, but then, they didn't know what had motivated the murders either. "Can you describe him?" Claire had been much closer than Bree or Matt. She wanted Claire's impressions, free of contamination by her own and Matt's recollections.

"I don't know," Claire sobbed. "It's all a blur."

Bree motioned toward Matt. "Was he shorter or taller than Investigator Flynn?"

Claire squinted at him. "A little shorter but skinnier."

"How old do you think he was? Twenty? Fifty?"

Claire tilted her head. "I'm not sure. He was wearing a baseball cap, a black one, pulled down so the brim shadowed the top half of his face. But from his body shape and the way he moved, I *think* he was older than me but not real old."

Bree agreed silently and made notes. "What was he wearing?"

"Jeans. Black T-shirt. Sneakers." Claire brightened. "He had tattoos. One was big. It looked like a tiger." She pointed to her left bicep. "I remember that!" Pride lifted her voice.

Bree wrote it all down. "The tattoo is a great detail, Claire. How about his hair?"

"Not sure." Claire brushed a hand over her scalp. "Because of the baseball cap. It must have been short, though, because I didn't see any hair sticking out."

"Good observation," Bree said.

Matt touched his own short beard. "What about facial hair?"

Claire shook her head. "I don't think so. If he did, it was only some scruff."

Matt asked, "Did he wear any jewelry? An earring, watch, or chain?"

"I don't know." Claire closed her eyes for a few seconds, as if trying to picture her assailant. "That's all I can remember."

"You did great, Claire." Bree tapped her notepad. "This is all good information." Bree skimmed her notes. "An adult man, not old, tall and thin with short hair. Tattoos, including a big tiger on one arm. He was wearing jeans, a black T-shirt, and sneakers. We saw him drive away in a black SUV."

Claire's chin lifted for a second. "I remembered a lot."

Bree nodded toward the girl's wrist. "Do you need some ice for that?"

Claire shook her head. "It's just a bruise."

"Let me know if it hurts more, OK?"

"OK."

"Now, excuse us for a few minutes." Bree motioned to Matt. "I want to get this description out to my parole deputies." And every other law enforcement officer in the area.

Bree and Matt stepped out of the house.

"She's not safe here." Matt's eyes searched the street.

"No," Bree agreed. "I'll call her social worker. She needs to be moved. For now, we're going to take her back to the station."

A patrol car parked at the curb.

"I'll have the deputy run the bullet and shell casing to forensics." Bree had another idea. "Remember when Adam drew a tattoo for us?"

Matt nodded. "You're thinking maybe he can do that again?"

"Maybe. The tattoo she described sounded specific. I'd rather have it drawn from her memory than bombard her with a thousand photos of tiger tattoos."

"True. That might confuse her."

Bree sent her brother a text. "Zucco's at the station. Claire seemed to like her. Maybe she can get her to eat something. The girl looks ragged."

"It's no wonder." Matt took Bree's notepad. "I'll put out a BOLO."

Bree returned to the kitchen and explained the situation to Claire and Janice.

Janice seemed relieved. "I'll get you a bag for your things." She left the room.

"You have things?" Bree asked.

Claire straightened. "Janice bought me some clothes, and a toothbrush and stuff. It was nice, but I'd rather have my own things. Can I go back to my house and pack a bag?"

"I can't let you into the house yet, but if you give me a list, I'll get your things." Bree was not ready to release the crime scene. Nor did she want Claire to see the place before it had been thoroughly cleaned.

"OK. Thank you." Claire's eyes misted, but she blinked away her unshed tears and straightened her spine.

"OK, then. Here's your phone back." Bree handed it to Claire.

"Thanks. I didn't think about how not having it made me feel more alone."

"Now you can talk to your friends," Bree said. *And call for help if she's chased* . . .

Claire looked away. "Yeah."

Did the girl *have* close friends? They hadn't uncovered any friends of the Masons so far. *Did they raise Claire to be a loner?* People with go-bags in their attic didn't trust easily or get too close to people. They could have passed that sentiment along to Claire subconsciously, if not intentionally.

"Are you OK leaving here?" Bree asked.

"Yeah. I mean, Janice is nice and all, but the little kids are a lot. I couldn't get a minute alone." She looked around. "Plus, I think I'd be scared here now. Who was that person? Did he kill my parents?"

"I don't know, but Lindsay will find you a new place to stay." But Bree also wondered how the man in the black SUV had found Claire.

Janice called Claire to the back of the house. Bree stepped outside to call Lindsay and update her.

"I don't know where to put her today," Lindsay said. "Let me make some calls. I'll get back to you."

"I'll take her to the station. She'll definitely be safe there until you find a placement."

When Claire reemerged with a trash bag full of clothes, Matt took the bag and carried it to the SUV. "The media is here."

"Already?" Bree asked.

Matt blocked their view of Claire with his body as she slid into the back seat of the SUV.

Bree drove to the sheriff's station. When they arrived in the parking lot, Claire glanced up from the phone she'd been staring at for the entire drive. She looked lost.

Pity swelled in Bree's chest. Solving the Masons' murders was the best way to keep Claire safe.

Chapter Fifteen

Matt scanned the sheriff's station lot. It was empty except for patrol cars.

Inside the back door, Bree called for Zucco, who was working at a cubicle in the squad room. "Settle Claire in an interview room." Stepping away from Claire, she lowered her voice. "Do not let her see inside the conference room."

"Yes, ma'am." Zucco gestured for Claire to follow her. "Are you hungry?"

They disappeared down the hallway.

"Conference room in ten minutes," Bree said, walking toward her office.

Matt grabbed coffee in the break room, then called the director of the zoo, who promised to send someone to pick up the wolf pup. They'd assess it and do their best to place it. Matt thanked him, called Cady, and updated her.

He carried his coffee into the conference room a few minutes later. Bree arrived, clutching her own steaming mug. She closed the door firmly behind her.

Todd was studying his laptop.

"Where are we?" Bree asked, plopping into a chair and holding her coffee with both hands.

Todd scrolled through his notes. "Phone and financial records for the Masons are in. I'll start reviewing those today. We're almost done with the neighborhood canvass. There are still a couple homes where residents weren't home."

"Any luck discovering the name of the housecleaning company?" Matt asked.

"No," Todd said. "And so far, no one except for Mrs. Haverford saw anything remarkable. We ran the plate number she wrote down." He pulled a printed photo from the file at his elbow. "The vehicle she photographed was a Ford Explorer in a dark color. The lighting isn't optimal, but it seems to be dark blue or black. The body style, grille, and headlights match the models built between 2011 and 2019. The license plate she gave us belongs to a gray 2020 Ford Explorer registered to Gloria Klein from Scarlet Falls."

"Gray and black could be confused if the gray is a darker shade. How different are the models?" Bree asked.

Todd spun his computer to show photos of two vehicles side by side.

Matt compared them to the photograph Mrs. Haverford had taken. "The shape of the grille of the vehicle parked in front of the Masons' home definitely seems to be a model from the 2011 to 2019 body style."

"We'll have to drive over and talk to her." Matt preferred to see the owner, vehicle, and license plate with his own eyes anyway. It was too easy to lie over the phone.

He wrote a note next to the pinned photo: *License plate discrepancy?*

Bree set down her mug with a *thunk.* "Claire said the man who chased her was driving an SUV, but she didn't know what kind."

They all went silent for a few seconds.

"Gloria Klein is seventy-four years old," Todd said.

Another few heartbeats of silence ticked by.

Matt had trouble picturing a seventy-four-year-old woman committing a brutal double murder, but he'd seen stranger things. "Doesn't take strength to pull a trigger."

Bree stood. "Someone else could have used her car. A neighbor, a son or grandson . . ."

Matt underlined the words *dark-colored Ford Explorer*. He capped the dry-erase marker and set it on the ledge. "Let's go find out if Gloria Klein is or knows our killer."

On the way out of the station, Bree stopped to speak with Zucco. "Pull photos of the crime scene. If Claire is OK, have her look through them to see if anything is missing from the house. Make sure none of the pictures include the bodies or blood. I won't subject Claire to the sight of her dead parents again. It'll be bad enough if the case eventually goes to trial. She'll have to relive the whole trauma."

"Yes, ma'am," Zucco said.

"Also, my brother is coming over to help her recall the tattoo she saw on the man who chased her. If I'm not back, I'd like you to supervise."

Twenty minutes later, Matt was in the passenger seat of Bree's SUV, checking Gloria Klein's motor vehicle records. "Last year, Ms. Klein received two tickets for impeding the flow of traffic." He glanced at Bree. "She was driving twenty-two miles an hour on the highway."

"Oh, boy."

"Yeah. She has no other violations on her driving record and no criminal record. Her house is registered solely in her name. She's on Facebook but no other social media. No husband mentioned anywhere. She posts about her grandchildren, but the only photos on her profile are pics of her cat."

"Well, here we are. Let's ask her." Bree pulled into an over-fifty-five development of tiny cookie-cutter townhomes. The neighborhood looked well kept but wasn't fancy by any stretch of the imagination. Parking was in a communal lot. The numbered space in front of Ms. Klein's unit was empty.

Matt scanned the lampposts. "I don't see any security cameras."

Bree reported their location to dispatch and returned the radio mic to its holder. "Do you see a gray Ford Explorer?"

"No." He climbed out of the vehicle.

They walked to the front door of Ms. Klein's unit and knocked.

"No doorbell camera," Matt noted.

The door opened a crack. Through the four-inch gap allowed by the security chain, one rheumy eye took stock of them. "What do you want?"

"Gloria Klein?" Bree asked.

"Yeah." Ms. Klein sounded suspicious.

Bree introduced them. "We'd like to ask you a few questions."

"How do I know you are who you say you are?"

Bree presented her badge, stepped aside, and waved at the official SUV behind them.

From behind the door, Ms. Klein scoffed at the badge, then looked over Bree's shoulder. "I guess the SUV looks legit."

Bree turned up both palms.

The chain scraped on the other side of the door, and it opened.

"You can come in." Ms. Klein stepped back and waved them inside. She was a tall, thin woman with white hair scraped back in a tight ponytail. Despite the blistering heat, she wore a sweater—and an eye patch. Her one good eye squinted at them. A tabby cat the size of a potbellied pig ignored them from a bed on the windowsill.

Expecting air-conditioning, Matt was disappointed that the house was approximately ninety degrees inside.

"Sorry about the suspicion. I read a news report about burglars pretending to be the police. Can't be too careful." Ms. Klein led them back to a tiny kitchen. "There's tea."

"No, ma'am, but thank you for the offer." Bree stepped aside so Matt could enter the room.

"Please sit down." Ms. Klein sat at a tiny round glass table. "I had cataract surgery yesterday, and I'm still a little tired."

Bree and Matt dropped obediently into chairs.

Ms. Klein wrapped her hands around a mug. A tea bag string and tag dangled along the side of the cup. "Now, what brings the sheriff to my door?"

"You own a gray Ford Explorer?" Bree asked.

"Yes." Ms. Klein nodded.

Bree folded her hands. "Where is the vehicle currently?"

"Why?" Ms. Klein asked.

"We have reason to believe the vehicle could have been at a crime scene Monday night."

Ms. Klein shook her head. "Well, that's not possible."

"If you haven't driven it, is there someone else who might have?" Bree asked.

"No. It's at the shop. I backed into a mailbox." She flushed with embarrassment, then tapped her temple next to her eye patch and shook her head. "This cataract got bad really fast."

"How long has the vehicle been in the shop?" Bree asked.

Ms. Klein reached for a paper calendar. "I dropped it off last Thursday."

Bree frowned. "Do you have a receipt?"

"I have an estimate. It's dated." Ms. Klein reached behind her and opened a drawer. She pulled out a folded piece of paper and handed it to Bree.

Matt looked over Bree's shoulder to read the estimate for body repair on a Ford Explorer.

"May I take a picture of this?" Bree asked.

"You can make a copy if you want." Ms. Klein pointed to the doorway. "There's a printer in my home office. Help yourself."

Matt took the paper to a cramped home office and made a copy on the printer/scanner/copier.

He heard Bree's voice from across the hall. "Do you have a photo of the vehicle?"

"I have dozens of photos and a video," Ms. Klein said. "The body shop recorded the damage thoroughly before they gave me an estimate."

Matt returned to the kitchen. Bree and Ms. Klein were bent over the woman's phone. Bree looked up. "Would you email me one of those photos?" She set her business card on the table.

"Of course." Ms. Klein tapped her phone screen with her thumbs with the speed of a teenager. "Done. Whoever said they saw my vehicle clearly got it wrong."

Bree said, "Thank you for your time."

They left the stifling town house. Matt pulled at the collar of his polo shirt, letting the fresh air hit his sweaty skin. "Body shop next?"

"Yes. We can swing by on our way back." Bree started the engine. "Would you compare the photos of Ms. Klein's Explorer to the one Mrs. Haverford took on the Masons' street? Is it the same vehicle?"

"Hard to say. Maybe. The color of Ms. Klein's vehicle is a dark gray metallic. The lighting in Mrs. Haverford's photo isn't great, so the color and details are hard to see."

Matt plugged the address from the auto body receipt into the GPS. They drove down a long country road and passed the turnoff for the Grey Lake public boat ramp and park. A mile later, Bree turned onto Bolton Road. They passed an orchard and farm that looked abandoned, then drove another mile to Like New Auto Body Repair. They went into the office. An employee in navy-blue coveralls approached the counter—Calvin, according to his name tag—and eyed Bree's uniform. He was in his late twenties, skinny, with the pale, pale skin of someone who never went outside. Sweat broke out on his pasty forehead.

Suspicion rippled along the back of Matt's neck.

Bree introduced them and asked for the manager. Calvin wasted no time rushing into the back. When the manager emerged, Matt noted Calvin was not with him.

The manager was a heavyset man in his fifties. "I'm Stan Padilla. Can I help you?"

"We're looking for a vehicle." Bree gave him the details.

"Yes." He nodded. "Ms. Klein's Explorer. We pulled a few dents for her and replaced a taillight lens."

"You've fixed it already?" Bree asked.

Stan shrugged. "We didn't even need to repaint. We're waiting for Ms. Klein to pick up her vehicle. Can I ask what the problem is?"

"We're following up on a case," Bree said in a casual voice. "I like to cross all my t's."

Matt wandered to the window and glanced outside. Calvin was getting into an old white Ford Fusion. He'd removed his coveralls. Matt tried to get a look at his biceps, but Calvin slipped into the car too quickly. Matt couldn't see his left arm. He made a note of the license plate as the guy drove out of the parking lot. When Matt turned around, Bree was asking Stan when the work on Ms. Klein's Explorer had been finished.

"Friday." Stan shrugged. "Like I said, it didn't take long. The damage was minor."

"We'd like to see the vehicle," Bree said.

"OK." Stan used an *I don't have time for this* tone. "It's out back." He led them down a narrow hallway and out the back door. Eight-feet-tall chain-link fencing surrounded a small parking area. A dark-gray metallic Ford Explorer was parked at the back. Bree photographed the vehicle. Matt walked a circle around it. Both license plates were attached.

"Do you have security cameras on this lot?" Bree asked.

"Normally, we do." Stan pointed to a camera mounted on the back of the building. "But we're having issues with the battery. The company is coming to install a solar charger tomorrow."

Bree stared up at it. "Do you have feed for the past weekend?"

Stan shook his head. "No. Sorry. We keep the gate locked." He motioned toward a large double gate secured by a thick chain and heavy-duty padlock. "I've worked here for eleven years, and we've never had a problem with theft or vandalism."

"Thank you for your time." Bree turned and led the way back through the office to the front door. "Where did Calvin go?"

Stan frowned. "Lunch."

"Little early, isn't it?" Matt asked.

"He was hungry." Stan didn't blink.

Matt and Bree left the office. Back in the vehicle, she turned to Matt. "Did you get Calvin's plate?"

"You know it." Matt used the dashboard computer. "Stan Padilla has no criminal record and nothing more than a parking ticket on his license."

"What about Calvin?"

"Calvin Wakefield is twenty-seven years old. Six years ago, he did three months in the county jail for petit larceny and vandalism."

"That's it?" Bree asked.

"Yes."

"Hm. He would have been twenty-one." She stared out the window for a second. "Should we talk to him?"

"Can't hurt. Without surveillance video, we don't know if the vehicle and/or its license were actually at the shop Monday night." Matt sensed Calvin wasn't coming back while they were parked in the lot. He pulled out his phone and opened his map app. "The only food nearby is a Burger King a mile down the road. It's the same direction Calvin drove off."

Bree backed out of the space and drove toward the Burger King. "Let's see if he's there."

Two minutes later, Matt scanned the parking lot and spotted Calvin's Fusion near the door. "There's his car."

Bree parked behind a van, where Calvin wouldn't see the sheriff's vehicle. Then they went inside. Calvin sat in a booth, scrolling on his phone. The sleeves of his T-shirt clearly showed his tattoo-free biceps. The tray in front of him held an empty food wrapper. He tapped on his phone, then stood.

"Hey, Calvin." Matt slid into the booth next to Calvin, forcing him to scoot over.

"Hey!" Calvin protested, his butt dropping back to the vinyl bench.

Bree took the spot across from him. "We wanted to ask you a couple more questions."

Calvin looked like he was going to barf up his meal as he turned his phone face down.

"Did Stan text you to tell you we left?" Matt guessed.

Calvin paled. "What do you want?" He was making a clear effort to calm himself, but his voice was a little too high.

"Was Ms. Klein's car at the shop Monday night?" Matt rested one elbow on the table and twisted sideways to face him.

"Yeah." Calvin cleared his throat. "I mean, yes."

Bree leaned both forearms on the table. "What about the license plates from her vehicle? Were they at the shop Monday night?"

Calvin's brows furrowed. "Uh, yeah?"

"Are you sure?" Matt pressed.

Calvin looked confused. "I don't understand what you're asking."

"We know about your record," Bree said.

He went from pale to ashen. "Whatever you think I did, I didn't do it."

"Why did you go to jail for three months for petit larceny and vandalism?" Matt asked.

Calvin's eyes went moist. "I stole a pig."

"A pig?" Bree repeated, as if she hadn't heard him correctly.

"Yeah." Calvin sighed hard. "It was a stupid prank. Me and my buddy were drinking beer one night. Eddy was bitching about his stepdad. Guy's a total douche." His gaze darted to Bree. "Sorry."

Bree nodded in acceptance of the apology and rolled a hand in the air, signaling for him to continue.

"He had this old Camaro he was restoring. Eddy accidentally scratched it walking through the garage, and his stepdad kicked him out of the house. We thought it would be funny to put a pig in the garage with the Camaro."

A true *hold my beer* moment.

Calvin continued. "But the pig did a bunch of damage to the garage and the car, and Eddy's stepdad pressed charges." His gaze locked on Bree's. "Eddy's stepdad was a deputy."

Bree sat back. "Did he send Eddy to jail too?"

Calvin nodded.

"What's Eddy's stepdad's name?" Bree asked.

Calvin reared back. "No. I don't want to get him involved. I can't get into trouble again. The lawyer said in a couple of years, I can get this record sealed if I don't get in any more trouble." His eyes went wild. A vein in his neck throbbed. "I won't go back to jail. Not ever. I'll kill myself first."

Matt didn't want to think about what had happened to Calvin in jail.

"OK." Bree held up both hands, palms out. "It's OK. I understand. I wasn't sheriff then. I wasn't involved."

Calvin exhaled, but he still looked like he was going to lose his lunch.

Matt thought about Stan, clearly looking out for Calvin. "Stan knows about it?"

"Yeah. He's my uncle," Calvin admitted. "He paid the lawyer, but he couldn't keep me out of jail. Eddy's stepdad wanted to make us pay."

Dick.

"I'm glad you have someone on your side." Bree stood. "Thanks for talking to us."

They slid out of the booth. Calvin dumped his trash and hurried out of the restaurant.

"Well, I feel shitty in a hundred ways," Bree said.

"Same." Matt held the door for her.

In the SUV, he dug deeper into Calvin's record. "Looks like the arresting deputy was Schneider. I knew him. Calvin's right. He was a total ass."

"He left the department when I was appointed sheriff." Bree headed for the station.

"Knowing Schneider, he didn't want to work for a female sheriff. He wanted to stay in the good-old-boy club."

Bree gave him a Look. "Good riddance to him then. I assumed I was better off without anyone who quit because I was appointed to the job."

Matt snorted. "You would have fired his ass within a month."

Bree earned the respect she had garnered with her deputies. She did the job with honesty and compassion, but she also didn't take any shit from anyone. People often confused kindness with weakness, which was foolish. In her job, it could be easier to not care. Being kind often took more effort.

"Now what?" Matt asked.

Bree stepped on the gas. "I'm not ruling Calvin out completely. He had access to the vehicle. He could have borrowed it or simply used the license plates. But the auto shop has other employees too. For that matter, anyone could have scaled that fence and borrowed those plates. Or Mrs. Haverford wrote down the numbers wrong. We should continue to look for another connection between Calvin or the auto body shop and the Masons."

"Calvin doesn't have a tattoo. He isn't the man who chased Claire and shot at us."

"Agreed, but he's still on the list as a potential accomplice, but he'll go at the bottom of the list."

"We have two dead people, and it seems our teenage witness could be the next target."

CHAPTER SIXTEEN

With photos of the interior of the Masons' house in hand, Renata studied the murder board in the conference room. Usually, she was out on patrol and didn't get a chance to help with investigations, except for peripheral activities like knocking on doors, running background checks, and making phone calls. Even in the NYPD, she'd been out on the street most of the time. She scanned the pinned photos, the hand-drawn arrows and circles, the lists of bullet point notes on the case.

Cool.

Renata left the room, closing the door behind her. She didn't want Claire to accidentally see anything in there. Then she carried the photos down the hall to the interview room where Claire waited.

She sat across from the girl and set the stack of pictures in front of her, face down. "Are you OK to look through these?"

Claire nodded, but her eyes looked unsure. "I want to help catch whoever killed my parents." She shoved some hair behind her ear. "If I help, it feels like I'll be taking back some control, control that was taken from me." She closed her eyes and drew in a single shuddering breath before meeting Renata's gaze once again. "My whole life is gone."

"I know, and I'm sorry that happened to you." Renata understood the need to actively participate. It was one of the reasons she'd become a cop. She couldn't sit back and watch. She had to *do*. She tapped the stack of photos. "Look for things that are missing or anything that doesn't look right."

For the next twenty minutes, Claire silently shuffled through pictures. Each one brought a new expression to her face: pain, fear, longing, sadness, anger. She covered the gamut.

She settled on two photos, and placed her fingertip on the picture of her dad's nightstand. Her father's dead body had been just out of sight. "Dad's watch is always on his nightstand. Mom bought it for him for Christmas two years ago. I went with her to pick it up. It was expensive."

"How expensive?"

"Over eight thousand dollars."

"Do you know what kind of watch it was?" Renata snagged a notepad and pen from the center of the table.

"A Tag something."

"Tag Heuer?"

"That's it."

"Can you describe it?" Renata asked.

Claire stroked the photo almost lovingly. "It was silver and black, bulky looking, with three little round faces on the big face, if you know what I mean."

"I do." Renata took notes.

Claire squinted at the photo again. "His money clip isn't there either."

"Did he usually carry a lot of cash?" Renata asked.

"I don't think it was a lot, but there was always some in it."

Renata wrote *unknown amount of cash and money clip*.

"Is there anything else that stands out as not there?"

Claire moved to a photo of her mother's jewelry drawer. "I don't see Mom's tennis bracelet."

"Do you have any idea what it was worth?"

"No. She had it before me. I think it was a present for their first anniversary."

"Diamonds?" Renata asked.

"I think," Claire said. "She kept it in a Tiffany box. The bracelet was her favorite. She wore it all the time. Wait. Sometimes she left it on her nightstand if she was going to wear it again the next day." She went back to another photo. "I still don't see it."

Mrs. Mason looked like a Tiffany kind of woman.

Claire suddenly pushed the pictures away. "That's all."

"OK. You did well, Claire. This information will be helpful."

Claire nodded and looked away, as if she couldn't stand the sight of the photos one more second. Renata gathered them and placed them out of sight in a folder. "Is there anything I can do for you?"

Claire shook her head.

"Do you want me to give you a minute?"

"Could you?"

"Yeah, sure." Renata stood. "Why don't I get us some lunch?"

"I'm not hungry."

"How about a Coke or something?"

"OK." Claire's response was toneless.

Renata scooped up the folder of pictures and left the room. As she closed the door behind her, she saw Claire prop her elbows on the table and rest her face in her hands. *She must be exhausted.*

Renata stopped at Marge's desk. "I need to feed Claire, but she says she's not hungry."

"Leave it to me," Marge said, and picked up the phone.

If there was ever a more efficient woman, Renata hadn't met her.

She got two Cokes and some pretzels from the vending machines in the break room. The girl needed a minute, but Renata had promised to babysit her. She wouldn't neglect her duty. She knocked lightly before entering.

When Claire lifted her head, her eyes were clearer. Renata set down the snack. Claire opened the Coke but ignored the pretzels. Renata dropped into a chair and opened her own Coke.

A minute later, Marge walked in. In her wake was a tall, rangy man in paint-splattered jeans and a T-shirt. Even his sneakers were speckled with color. Superficially, Renata admired the way his waistband hung low on lean hips, and the tousled hair that hung over his forehead. He carried a sketchpad and a box of colored pencils.

Fuck. Why did she like the wrong types? Why wasn't she attracted to clean-cut, successful businessmen? Nooooo. Always the bad boys for her. She'd once had a friend set her up with a banker. Good-looking, gainfully employed, nice personality.

Zero sparks.

Instead, she'd hooked up with the lead guitarist from a band. The sex had been off the charts, but had he contributed to the rent? Nope. Paid for meals? No again. He'd mooched off her for six months before she'd finally kicked him to the curb after coming home from the grave-yard shift and finding his friends passed out all over her apartment. They'd been snorting coke in her kitchen while she was on patrol. Someone had vomited in her kitchen sink. She never could decide if he'd been ballsy or stupid. Probably a little of both. Band groupies had convinced him he was the universe's gift to women.

Before the guitarist, she'd dated an aspiring actor. That had been a sparkler of a relationship. It had burned at a thousand degrees—for approximately forty-five seconds.

Maybe she needed one of those TV matchmakers because she had the worst taste in men.

She ripped her gaze upward, which didn't help because holy hell . . . those eyes.

She needed to get out more. When was the last time she'd been on a date? Not since she'd moved here. She'd been too busy working and taking care of her mom. If she wasn't paying bills, she was worrying about paying them.

Marge gestured. "Deputy Zucco, this is the sheriff's brother, Adam Taggert."

"Hey." He tucked his sketchpad under his arm and extended a hand.

Her boss's brother? *Get a grip, girl.* He was off limits. So far off. Practically on another planet.

"Adam is an artist. He's helped with witness recollections before."

Adam shook his head. "Bree thought I might help someone remember a tattoo."

"Yes," Renata said. An artist? Yeah. Perfect. Just once, she'd like to think a guy with steady employment was hot. This was why she used dating apps, for screening purposes, to make sure every man she dated had a real job. No more starving-artist types for her. She gestured toward Claire and introduced her.

Claire gave him a shy wave.

He sat down next to Renata, across from Claire, and set the pencils on the table. He leaned back, crossed his legs, and balanced his sketchpad on his knee.

"I ordered sandwiches. They should be delivered in a minute." Marge looked from Renata to Adam.

"Thanks, Marge," Renata said.

Marge walked out, closing the door behind her.

Renata's foot tapped under the table.

Adam selected a black pencil from the box.

"What do I do?" Claire asked.

He leaned back and lifted the sketchpad so she couldn't see the page. "Tell me what you remember. Where was the tattoo?"

"On his arm." Claire flexed her bicep and pointed.

"How big was his arm?" Adam asked.

"I don't know." Claire clasped and unclasped her fingers on the table.

Adam lifted and flexed his own arm. For a lean man, he had nice biceps. "Bigger or smaller than mine?"

"About the same," Claire said. "I think."

Adam cocked his head and waited. His hazel eyes seemed to shift color while Renata stared. Amber or green? Hazel. *Be cool. Stop staring.*

"Try closing your eyes," Adam suggested. "And breathe. There's no downside to trying this. The worst that can happen is we don't come up with anything, and I get a free lunch. No loss."

Renata sighed. *He needs a free meal.*

"OK." Claire shut her eyes.

"Where were you?" His voice went soft.

"On the playground."

"Walking?"

"No. I was sitting on a swing. He parked at the curb, got out, and walked toward me."

"When did you notice the tattoo?"

"Right then. Because after that, I ran, and so did he."

Adam didn't respond for a few seconds. Then he cleared his throat. "Can you picture it without the memory being too scary?"

"Yeah."

"OK, then. Back up. You're on the swing. He's walking toward you. Stop right there, like you're pausing a video. Think about the smells, the sounds, the feel of the ground beneath your . . ."

"Sneakers," Claire supplied. She breathed in and out. "There was a tiger in the center. One paw raised like it was going to lash out. It was snarling." She described the tattoo in greater detail, then stopped. "There was another tattoo below it." She lifted her arm and pointed to a spot above her elbow. "This one was a symbol or something. One long vertical line and others in V shapes, almost like arms propped on hips." She drew marks in the air.

Adam's pencil scratched on the paper. He mostly listened. Occasionally, he asked a question about a detail, a direction, or size.

Renata wanted to look at the sketchpad so badly she could barely sit still.

Finally, Claire slumped back into her seat and gulped some Coke. "That's it. I can't think anymore."

"OK." Adam turned the sketchpad. "Tell me what needs to be fixed."

Marge came in with a cardboard tray of sandwiches and three small liquid containers. "Chicken soup and turkey sandwiches," she whispered to Renata, obviously trying not to disturb Adam and Claire. She left the food and slipped out of the room.

Adam absently reached for a sandwich. Without saying a word, he passed a soup container and a wrapped sandwich to Claire. She took both, opening the soup and eating some while she assessed his work.

"Um. That's pretty good, but the tiger's face was narrower, and its raised paw was bigger." She moved her finger on the pad and gave him a few more corrections to the tiger and the symbol.

He frowned, pulled an eraser out of his pocket, and corrected something as Claire watched and gave direction. She set aside the half-empty soup container. She'd been so distracted, she'd eaten. "That's them. That's really them."

"Great." Adam removed the drawing at the perforation and handed it to Renata.

The hairs on her neck stood up as she stared at the image.

Adam opened a soup container while Claire started on a sandwich, still distracted.

"Could you always draw?" she asked.

"Yeah, but I practiced a lot." He picked up a plastic spoon.

Claire asked more questions, and Renata suspected Adam was intentionally eating slowly to pace his meal with Claire's, as if he knew she needed the diversion. So, he was both a talented artist and a decent human being.

Damn it. She didn't want to *like* him. Pure physical attraction was easier to ignore.

They finished lunch, and Adam stood. "It was nice to meet both of you."

"Thanks for your help." Renata walked him out of the interview room and down the hall.

"Take my number in case you need anything else." He read off the digits.

Renata entered them into her phone. Then she sent him a quick text. His phone chimed, but he didn't take it out of his pocket.

The sheriff and Matt were walking toward them. "How did it go?" The sheriff gave her brother a one-armed hug. He hugged her back, and Renata could see the family resemblance between them. Same lean features. Same hazel eyes. Same worried look.

Renata said, "We have a drawing of the tattoos."

"Excellent," said the sheriff. "I owe you, Adam."

He snorted. "You don't, but you're welcome."

After he left, they went into the conference room. Renata filled the sheriff in on Claire's recollections of the missing items from her parents' bedroom.

Sheriff Taggert frowned. "So, we have two expensive items missing and possibly some cash."

"Yes," Renata confirmed.

"Personal electronics were also taken," Matt said.

"So theft *could* have been the motive?" The sheriff didn't sound convinced.

Matt pursed his lips. "The killer still would have needed to know the layout of the house and the Masons' typical schedule, and if they were going to take the time to search the house, why ignore other small, valuable items?"

"Addicts looking for quick cash is always a possibility," Sheriff Taggert said. "Call forensics and see when we can expect a report."

"Yes, ma'am." Renata headed to the squad room and sat at a workstation.

Juarez was at the cubicle across the aisle, shoving a sandwich into his face. "How did it go with the boss's brother?"

"He made a sketch."

"I heard he's good."

"As an artist? The drawing is good." But what had impressed Renata was Adam's patience and the way he'd *listened* to Claire. He hadn't just heard her. He'd paid attention. "Hard to judge his professional ability on a pencil sketch. What does he do for a living?"

"He paints."

"Houses?"

"No. Paintings, you know, art."

Renata connected the dots. "So, he's unemployed."

"Adam Taggert, unemployed?" Juarez snorted and shoved a fry into his mouth. "Google him."

"Why? Is he a murderer or something?"

"Google him. I won't spoil the surprise for you."

Annoyed, Renata crumpled a sticky note and tossed it at Juarez's face. "I don't have time. Just tell me."

"Nope." He batted it back at her.

Renata liked him in a little-brother way, and he was just as irritating.

He dropped the remaining piece of his sandwich and sat bolt upright. "Holy shit."

Renata whirled. "Must be serious. You never swear." He was ridiculously polite, even a little naive at times.

"Yeah." He attacked the keyboard briefly, then got to his feet. "I have to talk to the sheriff."

Renata jerked a thumb. "She's in the conference room."

Juarez limped the first few steps. Despite claiming his bullet wound was mostly healed, he still walked gingerly enough that she suspected that claim was bullshit. He grabbed a paper off the printer and headed for the conference room. Renata picked up the phone to call forensics, but she kept one eye on Juarez as he disappeared through a doorway.

What had he found?

Whatever it was, it was big enough to elicit profanity from the department altar boy.

CHAPTER SEVENTEEN

In the conference room, Bree updated the whiteboard with the details about the license plate, Like New Auto Body Repair, and Calvin Wakefield. Stepping back and studying the board, she felt like she was running flat out on a treadmill, expending a ton of energy but not getting very far.

Matt dropped into a chair, opened a laptop, and started typing.

Someone rapped on the door, and it opened. Juarez poked his head in the gap. "Ma'am?"

"Come in," she said.

Juarez all but vibrated. "You'll never guess what I found."

"Close the door, please." Bree didn't want Claire to overhear. She was at the other end of the hall, but Bree would take no chances the girl was on her way to the restroom or something while they discussed her parents' murders.

Juarez obeyed, then spun around. His face shone with excitement. She sincerely hoped he did not play poker. He was incapable of playing it cool. Whatever he'd found, it was big.

Bree felt her brows creep up her forehead. She and Matt exchanged a look and a glimmer of hope.

Juarez didn't make them wait. "The Masons were not lawyers, at least not according to the New York State Bar Association."

It took Bree a minute to process the news. "What do you mean they weren't lawyers?"

"They weren't licensed lawyers," he said. "Neither one of them took the bar exam. Neither was a member of the New York State Bar Association. I found no record of either of them attending law school in New York, Pennsylvania, or New Jersey. I also checked the bar associations in those states, but nope."

"Fake lawyers?" Bree leaned a hip on the conference table. "I did not see that coming."

"Me either." Matt spun his chair to face the murder board. He studied the victims' photos with crossed arms. "How long have they been pretending to be attorneys?"

Juarez raised both hands. "Looks like a long time. We found seven years of tax returns. All reported income under the business code for other professional, scientific, and technical services instead of legal services."

"How did you learn this?" Bree asked.

"You said you wanted me to be thorough," Juarez said.

"I'm impressed." Bree shook her head.

Juarez flushed with pleasure.

"With Juarez or the Masons' fraudulent law firm?" Matt asked.

"Both," Bree said. "Nice work."

Matt turned to the board. "I've heard of people pretending to be doctors and performing surgery, but I have to admit, the thought of them getting away with this for years is still unbelievable."

Ballsy too.

"I found other information, if you're interested," Juarez said.

"Please." Bree rolled a hand in the air.

Juarez consulted his notes. "They bought their house twelve years ago. They have no mortgage. Real estate taxes are paid up. Before moving to Grey's Hollow, they lived in Stifleton, New York."

"That's about four hours from here," Bree said. "Any record of employment for either of them?"

Juarez shook his head. "Not that I've found. According to their birth certificates, Josh Mason was born in Rochester. Shelly Mason's maiden name was Franco. She was born in Pittsburgh."

The door opened again, and Todd walked in, a laptop under his arm. He glanced at Juarez and raised a brow. Bree motioned for the young deputy to fill in his chief deputy. Juarez had made the discovery. He deserved the credit.

Afterward, Todd ran a hand over his short hair. "That makes total sense, given what I discovered."

"What now?" Bree asked.

"I've been reviewing the Masons' phone and financial records." Todd paused. "They were running an email scam, a fake charity."

Bree slid into a chair. "Seriously?"

"Oh, yeah. They were raking in the money, funneling it all into their partnership account."

"What kind of charity?" she asked.

"They called it the Dreams Foundation and claimed to help homeless kids go to college." Todd set down the laptop and opened it. "They have a nice website." He stepped away so Bree and Matt could look at the screen.

Bree looked over Matt's shoulder. He scrolled through a home page filled with smiling teenagers and young adults. Testimonials praised the foundation for saving futures, giving hope, and fulfilling dreams of a better life.

"I have access to their email accounts as well," Todd said. "From what I could discern, they only did a small amount of very simple legal work, for which they charged hefty fees."

Bree thought of the interview with the angry real estate agent. "That's why Peter Vitale threatened to report them to the bar." She turned back to the board. "This changes everything. Instead of two lawyer victims, now we have two criminal victims."

"Did they take anyone for a significant amount of money?" Matt asked.

"So far, I found a ton of small transactions. Many of their donors seem to be senior citizens. Those small amounts add up, though. It was a nice source of income for them."

"Small amounts are less likely to be questioned." Bree tapped the dry-erase marker on her palm.

"Did someone discover their scam?" Matt asked. "Did they engage in other criminal activity?"

"Did the Masons' phone records indicate any personal relationships?" Bree asked.

"Hard to say." Todd took a seat and pulled his laptop toward him. "They primarily used email for business communication for the legal firm and the fake charity. The Masons weren't big texters. Plus, their cell service provider only keeps the content of text messages for ten days. In that period, they had very few texts, most of which were exchanged with each other and Claire. Normal messages about pickup times and grocery store stops. There were some delivery notifications and a dentist appointment reminder. Phone calls are also mundane so far. In fact, the most suspicious aspect is their nonuse of their cells."

"Given they were criminals, it wouldn't surprise me if they used burner phones," Matt said.

Bree's phone buzzed. She glanced at the screen. "An update came in from forensics. Trace evidence hasn't been analyzed yet, but nothing stands out so far." They'd found animal fur, carpet fibers, human hair, dust, et cetera, all of which would take time to evaluate. "This is interesting. There were traces of pine shavings on the bedroom carpet."

"Pine shavings?" Matt asked.

Todd typed on his computer. "Commonly used for landscaping, gardening, crafting, and as animal bedding."

"The Masons' back garden was very well kept," Matt said. "But I don't remember seeing bags of pine shavings anywhere."

Todd scrolled. "None in the garage."

Matt wrote *pine shavings* on the murder board. "Other evidence?"

"We have a general evidence log." Bree opened it and began scanning the list of items taken from the crime scene. It took several minutes to find what she was looking for. "There it is. A burner phone still in its sealed package was found in the glove compartment of the Audi Q7. No bag or receipt."

Matt stroked his beard. "If people go to the trouble of buying a burner phone when they already have a regular phone, they usually pay cash so that no one can track the phone to them."

"Otherwise, why not use your regular phone?" Bree agreed. "Anything else in the financials yet?"

"I'm still digging," Todd said. "Other loose ends . . . The judge signed the warrant to test Vitale's handgun."

"We need to pick that up," Bree said.

Todd continued to scroll. "Ballistics rushed the test on the bullets shot at Deputy Zucco. They were fired from the same gun as the one used to kill the Masons."

"OK." Bree picked up the tattoo drawing. She offered it to Juarez. "Make copies of this and distribute them among the deputies and update our description of the suspect."

He took the paper and left the room.

"I'll query NCIC and ViCAP," Todd volunteered.

The National Crime Information Center was a national clearinghouse for crime information. ViCAP was the FBI's violent crime database. Both systems allowed law enforcement to search for suspects, similar crimes, stolen property, missing persons, et cetera.

"I have to talk to Claire again." But first Bree needed a minute to gather her thoughts. She faced the Masons' photos. They didn't look like scam artists. They looked like normal professionals. "I don't want to upset her, but she might have information."

How much does she know?

Matt got up and stood beside her. "I doubt they told her they were frauds, but she might have other information she doesn't even realize she knows."

Side by side, they stared at the board.

"I can't put it off any longer." Bree pushed away from the table. "I'll question Claire again. Then we can pick up Vitale's gun and finish the neighborhood canvass." Bree was going to want some air to ease her guilt after the questions she needed to ask Claire.

"Want help?" Matt asked.

Bree considered the delicate nature of her questions. "I'm going to take Zucco in with me. She seems to have developed a rapport with Claire."

Bree stopped in the restroom to splash cold water on her face. Then she collected Zucco, and they went into the interview room. Claire was scrolling on her phone. She lowered it as they came in. Her gaze searched Bree's. Fear expanded the whites of her eyes.

Zucco sat next to her. "The sheriff has a few follow-up questions for you. Are you OK to answer them?"

"Sure." Claire set down her phone. "Is it about the tattoo?"

"No." Bree took the chair on the other side of the table, letting the girl have a bit of personal space. "You did a great job there. Claire, how much do you remember from your young childhood?"

"Are you talking about my life before the Masons adopted me?" Claire asked.

Bree exhaled in relief. *Claire knows she's adopted.* "Yes."

Claire shrugged. "Not much." She closed her eyes. "I don't see much. Maybe a flash of a face or a house if I think about it." Her eyes opened. "Nothing concrete. Nothing in detail."

Bree phrased her next question carefully. "Do you know how you came to be adopted?"

Claire nodded. "My biological parents died in an accident."

"Do you know their names?"

"No."

"How about where they lived?"

"No," Claire said. "I don't know anything about them. My parents—the Masons—didn't want to talk about it. Mom tried to have a baby but couldn't. She was sensitive about it."

"That's understandable," Bree said. "Do you know where either of your adoptive parents went to college or law school?"

Claire shook her head. "They didn't talk about college much, but they both went to law school at Syracuse."

"How about their families?"

Claire tilted her head. "They always said they didn't have any."

"Both of them?" Bree asked.

"Yes," Claire confirmed.

"You never met a grandparent, aunt, uncle, cousin? Did you get holiday cards? Go to any weddings?" Bree double-checked Claire's previous interview. Her answers were all consistent.

Claire shook her head.

"What do you know about your parents' histories?"

"I know Mom was from Pittsburgh, and Dad grew up in Rochester." Which matched their birth certificates.

"They've been married twenty-one years." Claire looked to the ceiling as she recalled facts. "They met in law school, got married in Vegas, then had their honeymoon in Mexico."

"You said they went to law school in Syracuse?"

"Yes." Claire looked confused. "Is something wrong?"

Bree was silent for a minute, deciding whether to tell Claire her parents weren't lawyers. But until she had more information, she wasn't going to destroy Claire's memory of her parents. What if Juarez was wrong? "We can't find some of their records."

"Oh." Claire shrugged. "I don't know where to tell you to look."

"That's OK," Bree assured her. "I'm going to get your things this afternoon."

"I made the list like you asked." Claire held up her phone. "Can I text it to you?"

"Sure." Bree read off her cell number.

"Do you know where I'll go tonight?"

"Not yet, but I will call for an update."

"Thank you," Claire said in a sad voice.

Marge poked her head into the conference room. "Sheriff? You have a call. It's Madeline Jager. She says she knows you're here. Do you want me to put her off?"

Madeline Jager was on the board of supervisors, and she was a nightmare, so much like a Disney villain that Matt had dubbed her "Cruella." Every time Bree left her phone unsupervised, he programmed the ringer to Cruella's song or changed Jager's contact name to "Cruella de Vil."

"No. I'll talk to her." *Give me strength.* Bree smoothed her face. "Excuse me, Claire."

Bree stopped to relay Claire's recollections to Juarez so he could investigate. As soon as she finished with Jager, she would also fill in the social worker. Maybe the Masons did have family somewhere, and they'd simply lied. Then Bree returned to her office and picked up the landline. "Sheriff Taggert."

"Sheriff," Madeline greeted, her tone stiff and formal as always. "I need to report something very strange."

"Go ahead."

"I saw an alligator in my backyard." Madeline huffed. "An alligator! And I heard you had a previous report on this monster and you did nothing! Why has the public not been informed?"

Bree rubbed her forehead. *Why? Why was this happening?* "Where do you live?"

"Grey Lake."

"A fisherman did report seeing an alligator, but he'd been drinking," Bree said. "His sighting seemed unlikely to be true. Are you sure it wasn't a hellbender, a snake, or a log?"

"I know what I saw," Jager insisted. "It was sunning itself on the bank, mouth open and all. I'm texting you the picture."

Bree's cell phone buzzed. She opened it—and found herself looking at a fucking alligator.

"Now do you believe me?" Jager snapped.

Bree remembered the previous winter and an encounter with illegally traded venomous snakes. Another thought occurred to her. "How big was it?"

"At least three feet long."

"A pet alligator would become unmanageable at three feet long. Maybe somebody dumped one." Bree had certainly experienced stranger things in her law enforcement career. And she'd arrested that illegal exotic reptile trader the previous winter. They'd confiscated baby alligators as well as the snakes, but how many alligators had he sold before they caught him? "I will look into that."

"You'd better find it before a child gets bitten or someone's Yorkshire terrier gets eaten. If that showed up on the news . . ."

Tourism and bad press were always first concerns of county politicians. A knee-jerk response hovered on Bree's lips, but she thought better of it. She took a single breath and let it out slowly. "I'll check it out."

"Personally?" Jager asked.

Bree had planned to send an animal control officer, but of course, Jager would want her issue to be handled by the sheriff. Politics would give Bree an ulcer. "Yes, I'll see to it personally."

Because why not toss an alligator at her while she was in the middle of investigating two murders?

Chapter Eighteen

Matt looked through the passenger window of Bree's SUV and sized up Peter Vitale's house. For a real estate agent, he was a poor judge of location. The house sat across the street from a junkyard, and the house next door sported unupholstered furniture and a discarded washing machine in the front yard.

"Claire said the man who chased her drove a black SUV." Matt pointed to the black Honda Pilot parked in the driveway. He checked the vehicle registration. "It's Vitale's."

"Put on your vest." Bree reached for the radio mic to report their arrival to dispatch.

But Matt was already reaching into the back seat. They'd been shot at enough times that it was his habit to wear body armor when serving any warrant, even one as seemingly mundane as this. He secured the straps and reached for the door handle. "Let's go."

Vitale kept his own small yard tidy enough. Next door, a chain rattled. A large dog barked and leaped into its collar.

Bree jumped, and Matt instinctively stepped between her and the dog. She'd worked hard to overcome her fear of dogs, and he would not allow a bad encounter to thwart her progress. The chain held, but Matt kept one eye on the property as they walked to Vitale's front porch.

They flanked the door, always cognizant of the possibility of bullets coming through it. Bree knocked. No one answered. She knocked again, then shouted, "Sheriff's department."

Footsteps approached. The door opened, and Vitale glared at them. "Yes?" He was dressed for work, in slacks and a long-sleeve dress shirt.

Bree handed him the warrant. "We're here to collect your handgun."

"Seriously?" He rolled his eyes. "Wait here." He closed the door in their faces.

They waited. Tension knotted Matt's shoulders as he watched the door and Vitale's SUV.

Five minutes later, the door opened. Instead of his irritated expression, Vitale looked harried. "It's gone."

"Gone?" Bree asked.

"Yeah." Vitale ran a hand over his head.

"When did you see it last?" Bree asked.

"I don't know," Vitale said.

A neighbor's door slammed. They all turned to see a man blatantly staring at them from across the street.

Vitale gave the neighbor a frown, then stepped back. "You may as well come in."

Their boots scuffed on the worn oak floor of the foyer.

Bree repeated her question. "When did you last see the gun?"

Vitale crossed his arms. "I took it to the gun range two weeks ago."

"Which range?" Matt asked.

Vitale gave the name, which Matt recognized. That part of his story could be checked out.

"Where do you keep it?" she asked.

"In my nightstand," he said.

"Show me." Her tone brooked no argument.

Vitale led them down a hall to a ground-floor bedroom.

"No gun safe?" Bree asked.

"I can't use it to protect myself if it's in a safe." Vitale opened the bottom drawer of his nightstand.

Matt glanced inside. A tangle of charging cables. Three books. Earbuds. No gun. "Can't use it to protect yourself if it's not here."

Vitale folded his arms across his chest. "I want to report a stolen gun."

"Did you have a break-in?" Matt asked.

Vitale threw both hands into the air. "I guess! I don't know what the hell else could have happened."

Bree crossed to the window and examined the frame. "Ground floor. No alarm system. A neighbor who clearly doesn't like you." She pointed at the man across the street, who was still staring at Vitale's house.

"All reasons I have a gun," Vitale smart-mouthed.

Matt winced. *Big mistake.*

"*Had* a gun," Bree corrected, then skewered the real estate agent with one of her signature no-bullshit glares. She had that look down cold. "Unless you're lying. It's awfully convenient that your gun is missing the day we come to collect it."

Vitale paled. "Why would I lie?"

Bree stepped closer. "To avoid going to prison for murdering Josh and Shelly Mason."

Vitale's mouth opened, then closed, then opened again. "If I was going to commit a murder with my gun, I would have reported it stolen weeks ago."

Bree didn't blink. "So, you've thought this through?"

If Vitale was smart, he'd shut the fuck up now. Clearly, he was not, because his jaw kept flapping. "No. Not until you came—I mean, I just realized it was missing."

"You're sure it's not elsewhere in the house?" Matt asked.

"I never keep it anywhere else. I take it to the gun range about once a month. I clean it, then it goes right back in the drawer." Vitale's voice weakened. He was probably processing how much trouble he was in.

"Would you mind rolling up your sleeves?" Matt asked.

Vitale gave him a side-eye. "Excuse me?"

"I'd like to see your biceps." Matt didn't explain why. He held his breath. He couldn't force Vitale to show them his arms, not without a warrant.

Vitale's expression was all *Fuck off,* but he slowly rolled up both sleeves and pushed them past his elbows. His left arm was clear.

But Matt saw blue ink on his right bicep. "You have a tattoo."

"Yes," Vitale said.

"Let's see the rest of it."

"What the fuck?" Indignation flushed Vitale's cheeks. "You want me to take off my shirt?"

Bree interceded. "We can't force you, but it is important."

Vitale looked to her and then met Matt's eyes again. "I should call my lawyer."

A beat of silence passed as none of them said *she's dead.* But Matt was fairly sure they were all thinking it.

"Fine." With jerky, angry movements, Vitale unbuttoned his shirt and pulled out the arm with the tattoo, revealing a small dragon on his upper arm.

Matt and Bree shared a disappointed look.

"Good enough?" Vitale's tone returned to smart-ass.

"Yes," Matt said. "Thank you."

While Vitale put his arm back into his sleeve and buttoned up, Bree took the report for the stolen firearm. Then Matt followed her to the SUV. Bree used her cell phone to call Todd. "We need to dig deeper into Peter Vitale's background. I want to know if he borrowed a crayon in preschool." She slid the mic back into its holder and started the engine.

Pulling away from the curb, she asked Matt, "Your thoughts on Vitale, now that we know he doesn't have a tiger tattoo on his bicep?"

"He's still on my list. He didn't notice his gun was missing? It's not like he kept it hidden away somewhere. How did he not look in his nightstand for two weeks?"

Bree raised a brow. "But he doesn't have a tiger tattoo."

Matt shrugged. "Maybe Claire got it wrong. She was under a great deal of stress. Adrenaline messes people up. Or we could be looking at two suspects."

"That's a lot of maybes."

"Yes," Matt admitted.

"And is he stupid enough to use his own gun to commit a murder?" Bree asked.

"We both know most criminals are not that smart. He might have considered ballistics too late, then disposed of the gun when he realized it could be linked to him."

"If he made a mistake that big, he made others." Bree pulled away from the curb. "If that's the case, we'll find them, and then we'll nail him for murder." Her phone buzzed on the console. "That's the social worker. Cross your fingers." She answered it on speaker. "This is Sheriff Taggert. Tell me you found a place for Claire."

"Well, yes," Lindsay said. "I have a space with another couple who were recently approved as foster parents. There are no other children in residence yet, and they have an alarm system. I've made them aware of the situation and am placing Claire under a false name. But that's not why I called." Her tone turned ominous.

A sliver of warning snaked up Matt's spine. Instinct told him the case was about to go sideways.

Lindsay continued. "I've been trying to dig into Claire's background, but when I tried to verify her adoption order, I couldn't. In fact, the judge who signed it doesn't exist—and has never existed in that county. If she was truly orphaned, then there should be a paper trail. If she had no family to take her in, she would likely have passed through the foster care system. But I haven't been able to find any records. The adoption order itself appears to be an excellent fake."

"If she wasn't adopted by the Masons, where did they get her?" Bree asked.

"Good question," Lindsay said.

Bree tapped a fist on the dashboard. "I'll continue to dig on my end."

"I'll do the same," Lindsay said. "Because Claire had to come from somewhere."

Bree ended the call. "Fuck."

"That about sums it up." Considering everything else about the Masons' life was fiction, Matt was not surprised with Lindsay's revelation. "So, now we have to figure out how and where the Masons got Claire?"

"Looks like."

"Claire said that Shelly couldn't have a baby of her own. How badly did she want a child? Was she desperate enough to not care where the child came from?"

Bree shrugged. "We can't depend on what Claire says. The Masons clearly lied to her."

"True." Matt considered all the sketchy aspects of the Masons' lives. "Most of her past seems to be a big, fat fabrication."

Bree drove to the Masons' house, and they got out of the car. They went upstairs into Claire's bedroom. Bree began opening drawers and consulting Claire's list of clothes and personal items. "We need a DNA sample for Claire to submit for rapid analysis. If the Masons didn't adopt her legitimately, that leaves illegitimate options. She could have been stolen, trafficked, sold . . . Who knows?"

"I'm on it." Matt found a carry-on wheelie bag in the top of the closet, exactly where Claire had said it would be. He also grabbed her backpack from the closet floor. School would be starting soon. But where would she go? His heart squeezed. Claire's entire life had been shattered. How would she cope with no one familiar to lean on? Matt gave silent thanks that Luke and Kayla had had Bree to help them pick up the pieces. She had made sure their home and school had remained consistent. She'd given up her job and life in Philadelphia, so the kids' day-to-day lives didn't have any more disruption. She'd put them first.

Then he resolved to keep the kids' world large, to be there for them, to make sure they had his parents and Cady—their own metaphorical village, enough people in their lives that there was always someone to have their backs no matter what the future brought. He cursed the Masons for not providing Claire with the same. Why had they even brought a child into their lives? Were they so self-centered that they couldn't imagine she could have a life without them?

He opened the suitcase on the bed, and Bree began filling it. Then Matt went into the bathroom, tugged on a glove, and pulled an evidence bag out of his pocket.

"What are you doing?" Bree walked in, opened the drawer, and took out a purple toiletry kit.

Matt lifted Claire's hairbrush. "Collecting Claire's DNA."

Bree agreed with a nod. "Take the toothbrush too."

Matt bagged and tagged the DNA sources while Bree packed Claire's bag and backpack. Then they locked everything in the SUV.

Matt consulted their list of neighbors who hadn't yet been interviewed and scanned the street. A car sat in the driveway of the house diagonal to the Masons', and the solid front door stood open. A cat looked out the glass storm door. "Looks like someone is finally home there."

They walked across the street and knocked on the door. Matt could hear the cat purring through the glass. "He could give your cat a few lessons on hospitality. Every other cat I encounter is friendly. Vader treats me like I'm the enemy."

"Not the enemy, an intruder. He's territorial. You're male."

"Luke is male, and Vader loves him."

"This is true." Bree smiled at him. "Look, Vader and I have been together a long time. He's temperamental, but I love him the way he is."

"I'm trying to love him too." Matt was an animal person, and most animals flocked to him as if he were Doctor Doolittle. Vader didn't seem to care.

"I know, and I appreciate it." Bree patted his arm in a way that said those efforts were also pointless.

A woman of about forty walked down the hallway. Shorts and a tank top revealed lean legs and defined arm muscles. She nudged the cat aside with a bare foot and opened the door. "Can I help you?"

"We'd like to ask you a few questions." Bree introduced herself and Matt.

"I'm Geneva Lawrence. Come in." Geneva opened the door wider. "I assume this is about the Masons? I heard what happened to them. It's awful."

"Yes, ma'am," Bree said.

The cat rubbed on Matt's boots and purred. He stooped to give it a scratch, and it flopped down and rolled onto its back. Matt rubbed its belly.

"We've been on vacation." Mrs. Lawrence led them to a huge, sunny kitchen. "I haven't been to the grocery store yet, so I can't offer you anything except water."

"We don't need anything, ma'am." Bree pulled out her notepad. "How well do you know the Masons?"

"We've been neighbors for twelve years, so I should know them well." Mrs. Lawrence adjusted her ponytail. "But I don't. Somehow, in more than a decade, we've never gotten beyond the waving-in-passing stage."

Matt went through the usual questions about the days leading up to the murder, suspicious people or vehicles, unusual behavior, et cetera, but Mrs. Lawrence had no information since they'd been in Costa Rica for the last two weeks.

"What can you tell us about the Masons?" Bree asked.

Mrs. Lawrence propped one foot on the opposite calf, standing like a stork. "Well, we don't have kids, so we don't have that in common. The Masons are lawyers. I believe they worked from home."

"What do you do, Mrs. Lawrence?"

"I sell makeup online." She smiled, revealing perfect teeth. "The income isn't much, but it's fun." She propped one fist on a hip and tapped her mouth with her forefinger.

"How often did you interact with the Masons?"

"I probably waved to them once a week. That's about it." Mrs. Lawrence snapped her fingers. "We share a house cleaner, but Amanda isn't a gossip. If she was, I wouldn't use her. Who wants their personal business leaked to the neighborhood?"

"No one," Matt said. "What's the name of her company?"

"A-Plus Cleaning. Her name is Amanda Ward." Mrs. Lawrence pulled out her phone and read off a number. "We've been using her for years. She's reliable and thorough. Works real hard when she's here. She's helped me decorate for parties and clean up after. One year, I broke my arm, and she put up my Christmas tree for me. I hate that I'm considering firing her."

Bree cocked her head. "Why?"

Mrs. Lawrence slid her phone back into the pocket of her shorts. "Because her son, Liam, recently got out of jail and is living with her."

"Do you know what he did?" Bree asked.

Mrs. Lawrence pressed a finger to her lower lip. "I don't remember. Nothing violent. Something to do with money. Theft, maybe?" She shrugged. "Amanda's always been great, but I don't know if I feel comfortable with her having access to my house anymore. Even if she doesn't give him our key and codes, he might get them from her. He's a criminal."

Good point.

But Matt didn't know the particulars of the case, so he didn't comment on it. He and Bree asked a few follow-up questions, but Mrs. Lawrence didn't have any more useful information.

Five minutes later, Matt followed Bree out of the Lawrences' house.

"We need to talk to the house cleaner and her son." Bree checked the time on her phone. "Tomorrow. Let's go home for dinner. We can regroup and review files tonight at home."

"Do you want to talk to the cleaner and her son at their place or bring them in?"

"Let's bring them in. He'll feel pressured by being in the station."

"Liam Ward, the son of the Masons' house cleaner, just got out of jail for a financial crime. The Masons were committing at least one financial crime. Is it possible they knew each other?"

"Who knows?" Bree asked. "Let's drop off Claire's bags at the station and take the DNA to forensics."

"Then home?" Matt hoped.

Bree sighed hard. "Yes, but first, we also have to stop at Madeline Jager's house on Grey Lake. I almost forgot. It's sad when an alligator sighting in upstate New York seems trivial compared to the rest of your day."

"Jager?" Matt did not want to see the county administrator. She was like a virus—or shingles—lying in wait to attack you when you were down. "I'd rather deal with murder suspects."

"Same," Bree agreed. "But I need to follow up on the gator personally. Jager will not get off my back unless I pay her a special visit. The political aspects of this job are almost worse than crime."

"In my opinion, there isn't that much difference between the two."

CHAPTER NINETEEN

Bree stepped out of her vehicle and scanned the gray clapboard home. A matching detached garage sat on the other side of the driveway. Considering Jager's loud personal style, the house was unexpectedly low-key. The county administrator lived at the ritzy, semi-isolated end of the lake, as opposed to the end where the public boat ramp and various campgrounds were located.

They walked to the door and knocked. Jager answered the door, teetering on pointy-toed, spike-heeled pumps. Poofy, unnaturally red hair sat atop a super skinny body, giving her a lollipop look. Her eyes widened. She almost looked surprised, but her eyebrows and forehead were Botoxed into full paralysis. "Sheriff, I'm surprised to see you here."

Jager gave Matt a more appreciative full-body scan. "Mr. Flynn."

"Ms. Jager," Matt said.

Everything about Jager rubbed Bree the wrong way, like petting a porcupine backward.

Be nice.

"I promised to come personally." Bree smiled, the expression feeling as brittle as spun sugar. "These creatures can be elusive. I'd like to see it for myself."

"I appreciate you attending to my call personally," Jager said. "Even though it took so long."

Bree pressed her lips together to hold back the retort. She was in the middle of a murder investigation. "Can you show me where you saw it?" she asked.

Jager conceded with a nod. She pushed the door farther open. "Come in. I'll change my shoes. I just got home."

Bree and Matt followed her down a hallway into a great room. Leather pub chairs faced a massive stone fireplace. The kitchen shone with the warm tones of butcher block, brick, and copper. The entire rear of the house was floor-to-ceiling windows looking out onto the lake.

Jager changed into a pair of boat shoes and led the way through a sliding door. The back of the house sported a two-tiered deck. "I was drinking my coffee out here this morning when I saw it." She pointed toward the dock, where a small sailboat bobbed on the quiet water. "There. Near the dock."

She led the way down a flight of wooden steps to the sunburned lawn. Grass crunched underfoot as they walked past two kayaks stacked on a rack.

Matt gestured toward a muddy sluice on the bank. "It made itself a little slide."

"What is that?" Jager sounded tired.

Matt walked forward and crouched. "The spot where it drags itself in and out of the water. There're claw marks here too."

Jager gave him an exasperated look.

Matt stood. "It means it's come up on the bank here more than a few times. Is your house empty all day? If it's truly a gator, they tend to be elusive and shy away from human activity."

"So I should make more noise?" Jager asked.

Matt shook his head. "No. It's good to know where it's living. We don't want it to move on. We want to catch it."

"I suppose it would be bad optics for me to shoot it," Jager said.

"Probably," Bree responded. "I'll call the zoo. They'll have an expert that can help us trap it."

Matt turned to Jager. "Do you have pets?"

"No."

"Good," he said.

Bree scanned the lake. No sign of a big-toothed, three-foot lizard. "Do you have security cameras out here?"

Jager shook her head. "Do we have to tell the public? I don't like negative news, though I guess we're at the end of the summer season." She was always obsessed with optics and tourism.

"Unfortunately, yes." Bree propped a hand on her duty belt. "But how do we keep the locals from having alligator-hunting parties?"

Matt pulled his shirt away from his chest, as if cooling himself. "We deal with more than enough *hold my beer* moments as it is."

"On that we agree." Jager nodded.

Bree imagined a flotilla of canoes full of locals armed with shotguns and flashlights. "Problem is, we can tell them a hundred times not to hunt the gator, but we all know some will anyway."

Jager stared at the muddy slide in the lake bank. "It's the last thing I want to do, but we should tell the public. Someone could get bitten." She shuddered.

"Let me talk to the zoo before we make an announcement," Bree said.

"Make sure that happens today, before this thing eats somebody's toy poodle. We don't need that kind of bad press." Jager turned back toward her house. "Thankfully, it's the end of the season. Otherwise, we'd risk losing our summer crowd."

Bree thought the gator-in-the-lake news would attract more people than it would repel, but she said, "I'll keep you updated on our plans." She turned to leave.

"You need to hold a press conference about that double homicide too!" Jager called to her back.

"I will." Bree waved a hand without turning around.

"Don't blow this off, Sheriff," Jager warned. "The public has a right to know."

In the SUV, Bree called the zoo director. "You're on speaker. Matt Flynn is also here." She explained about the alligator.

The director said, "That's two calls from your department in two days. First a wolf pup and now an alligator."

"How is that wolf pup?" Matt asked.

"Being treated for worms and malnutrition," the director said. "We'll keep him in quarantine until we're sure he's disease-free. Then we'll look for a permanent placement at a zoo or sanctuary, depending on what the DNA tests show."

"What do we do about the alligator?" Bree asked.

"You have a juvenile alligator on your hands. It was probably a pet that got too big for its enclosure, so the owner dumped it in the lake. Best course of action is to catch it. I'll send a handler out to assess the situation. We should be able to devise a trap."

"Is it likely to be dangerous to the public?" Bree asked.

"At three feet in length, the animal will primarily consume fish, frogs, snakes, turtles, maybe birds."

"Small dogs?" Matt asked.

"Possibly. In the wild, they're not likely to approach a human unless they feel threatened. They're shy, but if this one was a pet, it's been fed by humans. It might have no natural fear. We don't know how it will behave."

"OK." *Not good.*

"Best case is that we remove it from the lake," the director said.

"I agree, but what happens if we can't find it? It'll die over the winter, right?"

The director hesitated. "Not necessarily."

"Wait." Bree pressed both hands to the wheel. "I thought alligators couldn't survive winter."

"Theoretically, they can. In cold snaps, I've seen them in frozen swamps in the Carolinas. They put their snouts above the waterline and the water freezes around them. It's the freakiest-looking thing."

"So if we don't catch it, it hibernates and wakes up again next spring?" Bree did not need this on top of a double homicide investigation.

"Brumation is the form of hibernation used by alligators," the director corrected. "But we don't know what would happen. This wouldn't be a cold snap. A prolonged, harsh winter would make them vulnerable to all sorts of issues. That said, alligators haven't changed in eight million years. In fact, they didn't look much different thirty million years ago. They are survivors, practically dinosaurs."

Wonderful.

Bree didn't want the animal to suffer. It wasn't the alligator's fault some dumbass let it loose in a New York lake. But it did not belong here. She did not want to deal with this alligator next year. If it survived, it would grow larger. "I'd rather not test any theories."

The director laughed. "We'll do our best. You're sure it's only one?"

A few seconds of silence ticked by. Bree wasn't going there. "Can I give your name to the press? They're going to have questions once I issue a statement."

"Of course."

"Thank you." Bree connected him with animal control, instructing her officer to keep her in the loop. After ending the call, she dictated a statement for the press into her phone while she drove.

"You're not going to do a press conference about the alligator?" Matt asked.

"I don't have time for that."

"You're going to get nonstop calls from reporters."

"Yep, and every citizen that spots a floating log will be calling in." Bree had a headache already. "Let's hope we can catch it before everyone loses their mind."

Matt's frown said he doubted it.

She sighed in resignation. "I'll talk to the press tomorrow."

They stopped at the station to see Lindsay's car in the rear lot, where Bree had instructed her to park so Claire could be moved with the least exposure. Inside, Bree handed Claire her bag. Bree wrestled with keeping secrets from Claire. But what good would telling her about her parents' fake charity or lack of legal licenses do? The girl looked beaten down enough. Bree decided to hold off until she had some answers to go along with the bad news.

Marge stood in the back hall, clutching the strap of her shoulder bag. "The press has been calling nonstop."

"About the murders or the alligator?" Bree asked.

"Both," Marge said.

Matt gave Bree a Look.

"OK, OK. I'll do a press conference in the morning." Bree headed for the door. "Tonight, I need an hour to clear my head."

Matt led the way to the exit. "I want to work 24/7 until we catch this scumbag, but it's not possible. Hopefully, we'll be able to look at the case with fresher eyes after a little downtime."

She drove to the farm.

Dinner with the kids proved to be the best distraction. Afterward, Bree and Matt followed Luke out to the barn to feed the horses.

"I'll bring them in." Matt grabbed a lead rope and headed for the pasture.

Bree measured grain while Luke climbed into the loft and tossed down a bale of hay. He jumped off the ladder and pulled a pocketknife from his pocket to cut the baling twine. "I texted Claire Mason today, but she didn't answer me."

"It was nice of you to reach out. I'm sure she appreciates it, even if she can't respond."

Luke nodded, sorrow brimming from his eyes. "I thought I probably understand better than anyone what she's going through."

Bree dumped feed into Cowboy's bucket and met Luke in the aisle. "Are you OK? This must bring back bad memories."

"It does." He tossed hay over his horse's half door. "But it's not like I don't think about Mom most days anyway."

Bree put a hand on his shoulder. "I think about her all the time too."

Luke brushed a single tear from his face. "I try to think good thoughts about her—to remember all the fun we had—but I still get sad."

"Me too," Bree said.

"Sometimes, when I'm having fun or I haven't thought about her for a day or two, I feel guilty."

"She wouldn't want that." But Bree understood survivor's guilt very well.

"I know, but I can't help it."

"I understand. I feel guilty for not being here when your mom needed me." Had Bree ever admitted that to Luke before? Probably not. It hurt to think about it, let alone talk about it. But if she wanted him to process his emotions in a healthy way, she had to model that behavior, right?

Adulting—parenting—was fucking hard.

"You do?" He brightened.

"Yes. We feel what we feel, even when those emotions aren't always based in logic. If we suppress our feelings, they don't go away. They become more twisted."

Luke gave her a solemn nod, the look in his eyes far too wise for his years. "I wish I'd been older, so I could have protected her. That's not very logical."

"And I wish I'd been here, even though I couldn't have predicted or prevented her death." She squeezed his shoulder. "We know in our hearts that neither of us was responsible. But her being gone hurts so much, we want her back. We want the impossible, and knowing we can't have it hurts all over again."

"It's better now than it was last year."

"That's good. We will move forward. We have no choice but to live. You mom would have wanted you to have the best life." Pain speared Bree's heart as she thought of her own guilt over the happiness she'd found after her sister's murder. Erin's death had forced Bree to open her heart. She often felt as if she'd stolen Erin's life and happiness. Another emotion not based in logic but solidified in her heart just the same.

"Anyway, I'll leave Claire alone unless she wants to talk."

"That's probably a good plan." Bree released his shoulder. "And I'm glad you talked to me. You can always talk to me, OK?"

"You too," Luke said.

Their conversation was interrupted by Matt bringing his Percheron, Beast, down the aisle. Luke finished distributing hay and helped Matt bring in the rest of the horses. After Luke returned to the house, Matt leaned against the barn wall and scratched Beast's neck. "Everything OK with Luke?"

"Yeah. Sometimes I think he's more mature than I am." Bree did not always process her emotions in a healthy way. In her past, she'd done the very thing she'd warned Luke about. She'd suppressed everything—good and bad—and stuffed it into a deep, dark recess of her mind, where it thrived and grew like a mushroom.

And now, according to her therapist, because she'd never allowed herself to actually feel those emotions, she had to open the doors and windows and let in the light, to accept the good and bad memories, and experience her trauma all over again.

CHAPTER TWENTY

The next morning, Bree stood in the monitoring room and watched Amanda Ward on one screen. She was a thin forty-year-old in beat-up black sneakers, bleach-spotted black yoga pants, and a white T-shirt that read A-PLUS CLEANING. Clearly, she was in her work clothes. She sat at the table in one of the interview rooms, with one arm wrapped around her own waist, curled in on herself. She gnawed on a cuticle on the other hand. Her makeup caked on her dry skin, and the bottle-blond ponytail that emerged from the back of her black A-Plus Cleaning baseball cap looked brittle enough to snap.

"Did we bring them in via deputy and patrol car?" Matt asked.

"No. Zucco called them and asked them to come in to answer some questions about the Masons. What do we know about Amanda?"

He opened a file. "She has no criminal record, not even a traffic ticket. She's had her own cleaning business for thirteen years and lived at the same address for seventeen. Mrs. Lawrence had only good things to say about her work ethic."

"She looks tense. Because she did something? Or is she upset that we also asked to talk to her son, who was recently released from jail?" Bree could believe either one. She'd seen plenty of mothers cover for their criminal offspring.

"She hasn't asked for an attorney, nor has he," Matt said.

Bree shifted her attention to another monitor, where Amanda's son paced in a different interview room. He was tall and lean, dressed in jeans, a blue button-up shirt with the sleeves rolled partway up his forearms, and white Nikes. His hair was short on the sides, with slightly longer waves on top. It appeared freshly cut. "What about Liam Ward? Compared to his mom's clothes, his look expensive. So does that haircut."

Matt flipped pages. "Liam is a different story. Three weeks ago, he was released from jail, where he did six months for running a gift-card scam. Lucky for him, he only stole small amounts, and it was his first offense."

"His record is clean before that?"

"Yes."

"How old is he?" Bree asked.

Matt glanced at his paperwork. "He's twenty-three."

"So, Amanda was seventeen when she had him. Is she married?"

"No," Matt said.

"We'll let him sweat awhile longer. I want to question her first." Bree sized up Amanda again. She looked scared, like a rabbit who smelled a fox. Would she shut down if frightened more? "I'll go in alone. If I need you, I'll let you know." Bree stood. "You watch her from here and observe her body language." Matt was very good at reading the physical cues that didn't match or went beyond verbal answers. The body often told the truth even when the lips lied.

In the interview room, Bree sat next to Amanda.

"Hey, Amanda." Bree turned toward her. When possible, Bree preferred to interview subjects without a physical barrier. She wanted full view of all Amanda's body language.

As Bree faced her, Amanda shrank, as if terrified.

"Thanks for coming in today," Bree said. "This interview is being recorded. That way, everything that is said here is clear, and there are no misunderstandings."

Amanda nodded. Her eyes were red-rimmed and puffy, as if she'd been crying. "I can't believe they're dead. I was there that morning." Disbelief filled her voice.

"It's terrible," Bree agreed. "What time did you clean their house?"

"I'm there every other Monday from eight to eleven."

"Were you there alone?"

Amanda shook her head. "No. My assistant, Janelle, was with me."

"Janelle's full name?"

"Patterson," Amanda said. "You want her number?"

"Yes, please." Bree wrote it down on a notepad. "Were the Masons home while you cleaned?"

"No."

"Is that normal?" Bree asked.

"Yeah. Most people go out."

"Did they say where they were going?"

"No. They weren't home when I got there." Amanda unwrapped her arm from around her waist and dropped her hands into her lap, as if she were relaxing with the mundane nature of the questions.

"Were they ever?"

"Sometimes, but they'd leave within a couple of minutes," Amanda said.

"How did you get in?"

"I have the code to the garage door."

"Do you have the alarm code too?"

"No," Amanda said. "It was never on."

Bree wrote on her notepad. Access didn't matter that much. The house had been entered through the patio door, but she wanted some ordinary-sounding questions to form a rapport with Amanda. Frankly, if Amanda had wanted to steal from the Masons, she had plenty of opportunity that didn't involve cutting the glass in the patio door. Maybe she had thought direct theft would be too easily traced to her. Maybe she'd cut the glass to make it *appear* like an outside job.

"Do you keep a record of the entry codes?"

Amanda nodded. "On a folder in my phone."

Which her son could have accessed if he was sneaky enough. The fact that he'd served time for running a gift-card scam told Bree he was, in fact, the sneaky type.

Bree asked, "While you were in the house on Monday, did you see anything unusual?"

"No."

"Did you see anything odd in the neighborhood?"

"No. Everything seemed to be the same as usual."

"Did the Masons pay on time? Were they difficult clients?" Bree asked.

"They paid in cash every time I cleaned, and they were one of my easier cleans. Neat with their stuff. Not particular about anything. Never had parties." She touched a knuckle to her lower lip. "The only even slightly strange thing was they didn't let me clean the office. The door was always locked."

"Did they say why?"

Amanda lifted a shoulder. "Shelly said there was sensitive client information in there, and they needed to maintain their clients' privacy. It made sense, but Shelly was, I don't know, a little weird about it."

"Your son got out of jail a few weeks ago," Bree said.

Amanda's face went white, and her arm snaked around her waist again. "Yeah."

"Has he been to the Masons' house?"

Amanda blinked. "He dropped me there, at the curb. He didn't go inside."

"So he knew where they lived."

"Yes," Amanda admitted. "He needed to borrow my car that day for a job interview."

"He had an interview on Monday?"

"Yes," Amanda nearly whispered.

So, Liam had been outside the Masons' house the day they'd been murdered.

"Did Liam ever meet the Masons? You cleaned for them for years."

"I don't remember." Amanda stared at her lap.

"Did Liam ever go into their house with you?"

"I don't remember. I have a lot of clients. Sometimes I confuse them." Amanda lifted her chin, but Bree could see the lie in her eyes.

"But Liam has met some of your clients?"

"Yeah." Amanda's jaw shifted back and forth, as if she were wrestling with a decision. "He's filled in for my assistant a few times."

"Since he got out of jail?"

"No!" Amanda stiffened. "Before."

Bree waited. She sensed Amanda was going to say more.

Amanda's face was full of worry with a dash of indignation. "I've already lost three clients because of it."

"*It* being Liam's conviction?" Bree asked.

"Yeah." Amanda swallowed, her face miserable, but she didn't elaborate.

"Is the Masons' house one of the ones Liam helped clean in the past?" Bree tried again, changing up the phrasing slightly. She was always surprised how often people forgot how they already answered a question.

Amanda's jaw set. "I already told you. I don't remember." She met Bree's gaze for the first time in the interview. Amanda's expression was determined. She was not giving up anything on Liam. So, she was a frightened rabbit for herself but a bear for her son.

Bree backtracked. "You raised Liam by yourself?"

Amanda nodded.

"What about his dad?"

"Useless." Amanda practically spit out the word. "When I told him I was pregnant, he told me that was my problem."

"You didn't sue him for child support?" Bree asked.

"Waste of time." Amanda's voice turned bitter. "He dropped out of high school, sold drugs for a while. He's been in and out of jail so many times, he has friends there. It's like a revolving door for him."

"Does he have a relationship with Liam?"

"He sees him once in a while, when he's not in jail. That's it."

"So Liam knows about his father's criminal activity?"

"Yes," Amanda said. "And so did the judge in charge of Liam's case."

"He was harsh?"

Amanda's spine straightened. Her arms folded across her chest. "It was Liam's first offense. He shouldn't have gone to jail."

"He had a lawyer?"

"We couldn't afford a good one. The one they gave him was always juggling a hundred other clients. He couldn't even remember Liam's name without checking the file folder. Liam was trying to help me. I got pneumonia and couldn't work for a couple of weeks. I don't have health insurance. A couple of doctor visits and the cost of the medicine drained my savings. I got behind on a few bills . . ." Amanda studied the table for a few seconds. "Liam was young. He made a mistake, but he was trying to help me. Sending him to jail made everything worse." Her chin lifted again, and Bree knew she would get nowhere interrogating her.

"Where were you Monday night?" Bree asked.

"I went out with a friend for tacos and margaritas. Her life has been even shittier than mine lately." Amanda gave Bree the friend's number and the name of the Mexican restaurant. But Bree already knew the alibi would check out. The same way she knew Amanda blamed herself for her son's crime.

"OK." Bree stood. "Thanks for cooperating. I'll let you know if I have any follow-up questions."

"That's it?"

Bree nodded. "Yep. You're free to go."

She rose slowly, as if not trusting what Bree had said. "What about Liam?"

"I'm talking to him next," Bree said. "If you need to get to work, I can have a deputy take him home afterward."

Amanda thought about it for a few seconds. Then she picked up a shabby purse and clutched it by its torn strap. "No. I'll wait for him."

"Suit yourself." Bree motioned toward the door. "I'll have someone show you to the lobby." She summoned a deputy for the task and returned to the monitoring room.

Matt was watching Liam. "She lied about Liam going to the Masons' house. He'd been there."

"She didn't technically lie. Amanda said she didn't remember. She didn't deny he'd been there."

Matt gave her a Look.

Bree shrugged. "How can we prove he was in the house?"

"We could show his picture to Claire," Matt suggested. "Maybe she'll remember him."

"Maybe."

"How do you want to handle him?" Matt asked.

Bree thought about it. Amanda didn't act like a tough mom. She was protective but not a disciplinarian. She seemed more passive, even permissive. But they didn't know how Liam would respond to a male authority figure. "We'll tag-team him and see who he responds best to."

Matt was a masterful interviewer, with the ability to shift personas like a chameleon to best suit the circumstances. Bree wondered if Liam would respond better to a male authority figure, something his own upbringing had likely lacked.

They filed into the interview room. Liam stopped pacing, freezing momentarily. With his shoulders hunched, he looked like a coyote caught in the beam of a flashlight. His entire persona was a contradiction. His posture and demeanor were defensive and insecure, but his clothing and hairstyle screamed *frat boy*, as if he wanted to be part of the rich, privileged world and was trying to project that confident image with his personal style.

Bree introduced them. As she talked, Liam's gaze kept straying to Matt. She gestured toward the table. "Have a seat."

Liam eased himself into a chair, his posture remaining wary. He pressed his hands flat to the table, and she could see the cuticles of his fingernails had been ravaged. His fingertips trembled, and he dropped them to his lap.

Bree let Matt take the seat next to Liam. She sat opposite as she gave him the same spiel about the video camera. She didn't dance around the topic. "You went to jail."

"I did my time." Despite the words, his voice quivered. He cleared his throat and swallowed before continuing with a more level tone. No doubt jail had been brutal. "I wouldn't take any risk of going back in there."

"I understand," Matt said. "Six months can seem like a very long time."

"Forever," Liam muttered.

Matt commiserated, "Seems like a bogus amount of time for the stupid scam you were running. If you were some rich dude's son, you would've gotten away with a slap on the wrist."

"Yeah." Anger colored Liam's cheeks. "I couldn't believe it. Seemed like they were trying to make an example out of me. Nothing I could do about it, not with that lazy-ass public defender. He didn't give a shit about me at all. Barely talked to me. Kept calling me Ian."

Matt shook his head, capitalizing on the younger man's obvious grievance. "That sucks."

Liam raised his chin, like his mother. "It wasn't fair."

"Not at all." Matt huffed. "Look, we're talking to everyone who was near the Masons' home around the time of the murder. We know you dropped off your mom. What time was that?"

"Around eight."

"Where did you go?"

"I had a job interview." Liam shook his bangs off his face.

"Where?" Bree asked.

"Electronics Depot," he said to Matt, barely sparing Bree a glance.

Did he think an electronics store would hire someone who had done time for theft or fraud? Who would trust expensive, easily transported merchandise and customer financial information to an ex-con? She wanted to laugh out loud at his audacity. He was going to have to accept reality. His employment options would be limited. "The one on the interstate?"

He nodded but continued to fix his gaze on Matt. Bree had called it. Liam sought male approval. Matt had played this game before. He had the physique of a professional athlete, with an air of authority he didn't have to work to exercise. It hovered around him like an aura made of testosterone.

"How did that go?" Matt asked.

Liam's mouth tightened. "They don't hire anyone with a criminal record."

No kidding?

"That's a shame," Matt said, his voice sympathetic but with an edge, as if he were angry for Liam. His straight face never wavered. Damn, he was good. "You'll keep trying, though, right?"

"Of course." Liam looked at Matt like a puppy trying to please.

"So you dropped off your mom, then went to the interview, then what?" Matt asked in a casual tone.

"I went to the grocery store. I wanted to help Mom. She works hard. It took a while because she uses coupons for everything." He sighed.

"Which store?" Matt asked.

"The one near the interstate. Mom follows the sales, and that's where the best specials were this week."

"Sounds like your mom knows how to stretch a dollar," Bree said.

Liam's mouth turned down. "I guess."

"You don't approve?" Bree asked.

"She shouldn't have to chase discounted ground beef," he snapped.

"There's no shame in being frugal," Bree said. "Only fools waste hard-earned money."

Liam looked away, his expression unrepentant.

Matt asked, "So, what were you doing before you ran the gift-card scam?"

"I worked in the marketing department at Henderson Sports Chalet. The pay wasn't that great." Liam's eyes went small and angry. "Mom needed medicine, and that costs money. I wanted to help her. We should live in a nice house instead of a crappy little dump. But my only option was community college because Mom wouldn't cosign a student loan." He sneered. "I could have done better."

"Sounds like your mom didn't want you to go into debt," Bree said.

"She's satisfied if she can pay this month's bills. I want more." His tone suggested he was entitled to more.

"She runs her own business," Bree said.

"She cleans other people's toilets." Liam turned a glare on Bree, the first time he'd made full eye contact with her. His eyes were boiling over with resentment and indignation.

Bree resisted the urge to smack the disrespectful little shit. His mom was cleaning houses to put food on the table and a roof over his obnoxious head. She even sent his spoiled butt to community college, and he had the nerve to not appreciate it at all?

She knew Matt felt the same, but he held his line.

He used a commiserating tone. "It's hard starting out with a disadvantage like that, and I respect that you wanted to give back to your mom. Sounds like you want better for her."

"Yeah." Liam stared down at his torn fingernails. "It didn't work out the way I planned, though. I thought I'd supplement our income a little. I kept the numbers small. I didn't really hurt anyone."

"Did you ever meet Josh Mason?" Matt tossed the question in all casual-like.

But Liam saw it coming. Where his mother had been defensive, Liam was cunning. His eyes narrowed. "I don't recall." Did he sit around watching congressional hearings on C-SPAN? Or was that a phrase his lawyer had coached him to use to avoid lying under oath?

"How about Shelly?" Matt asked.

Liam didn't meet Matt's gaze, but curled his hand in front of himself and talked to his fingernails. "Not that I remember."

"Were you ever in their house?" Matt pressed. "You've helped your mom clean, right?"

Liam was ready. His worship of Matt's testosterone evaporated like fog on a sunny morning. "Yeah, but that was a long time ago. I don't remember which houses."

"What were you doing Monday night?"

"Why do you want to know?" Liam asked. "Is that when the Masons were killed?"

"It is," Bree said.

"Do you have any tattoos?" Matt asked.

Liam folded his arms across his chest. "I'm not answering any more questions without a lawyer."

Bree guessed he didn't have an alibi.

"OK." Matt lifted his hands in mock surrender.

Liam glared at him, like Matt had betrayed him. "Am I free to go?"

"You are." Bree stood, crossed the room, and opened the door. She summoned a deputy to escort Liam to the exit. "Your mom is waiting in the lobby. Thanks for coming in."

Liam said nothing as he left.

"Well, that was interesting." Matt said. "He's a smart one."

"Cagey," Bree specified. "I'm sure his time in jail made him even more so."

"No one comes out of jail more innocent than when they went in."

"Nope, but it's interesting that his attitude is so different than Calvin Wakefield's."

"Calvin Wakefield had a one-time lapse in judgment. Liam planned to steal from people."

"True," Bree agreed.

Matt stroked his beard. "If Amanda wanted something from the Masons' house, she had plenty of time alone to search. She had no need to break in or kill anyone."

"Unless she was trying to make it look like someone broke in," Bree said. "What about Liam?"

"*If* he's been inside the Masons' house—and from his answers, I'll bet he has . . ." Matt paused. "Then he knew they had a few valuables he could swipe. He isn't dumb enough to use the garage code provided to his mother, and he's already shown that he's willing to steal."

"But murder? That would be a whole new level up for him as a criminal."

Matt frowned. "Like I said before, no one becomes more innocent in jail. But would he break in while they were home? We've established he isn't completely stupid."

"He got caught running that gift-card scam," Bree pointed out. "So, he isn't a master criminal either."

"Definitely not," Matt said.

"We keep him on our list, but without evidence, all we have is a theory."

CHAPTER
TWENTY-ONE

Facing the murder board, Matt leaned against the conference table. Behind him, Todd and Bree pored over reports and photos.

Matt waved his sandwich at the suspect column. "Could be worse. At least we *have* suspects."

"Three of them." Bree picked at her salad. "But our list is driven by motive. We're sadly lacking in actual evidence."

She flipped a page. "Let's start with Peter Vitale. Where do we stand?"

Todd lifted his fingers from his keyboard. "He had a beef with Shelly Mason's legal advice. He threatened her. He also has a gun, which we can't use for a ballistics match because it's missing. He claims it was stolen. According to him, the gun was last used at the range two weeks ago. This part we confirmed with the gun range."

Bree leaned back and studied the board. "He has no alibi that can be verified. He has a tattoo on his bicep, but it's a dragon, not a tiger." She looked down at the paper in front of her. "His gun is a 9mm. The bullets used to kill the Masons and the bullets fired at Zucco and us were all 9mm, but that's a very common caliber. So, by itself, that fact doesn't prove anything. We don't have a ballistics report on the bullets fired at us at the playground yet, but I'm willing to bet it's going to match the others."

"Do we have any evidence suggesting more than one suspect?" Todd asked.

"No," Bree said. "But we can't rule it out."

"We've established Vitale had motive and opportunity," Matt said. "But without his gun, we have no physical evidence that ties him to the murder scene. We have a partial shoe print, but we need something more to establish probable cause and obtain a warrant to search his house and check his shoe treads for a match."

"Him having the wrong tattoo will not help get a warrant," Todd said.

Bree agreed with a nod. "Let's ask Vitale where he was Tuesday afternoon around lunchtime. So far, he's been cooperative. Let's hope he doesn't lawyer up."

Matt made a note on the board under Vitale's name. "Next?"

Todd tapped on his keyboard. "Calvin Wakefield."

Bree shuffled her papers. "Have we found a connection between Wakefield and the Masons?"

"Not yet," Todd said. "Wakefield has a criminal record and had access to the vehicle that was seen outside the house the night of the murder."

"That's not enough," Bree said. "Opportunity isn't enough. We have no motive or evidence."

Matt underlined the words *no tattoo* under Calvin's name. "He doesn't have a tattoo at all."

Bree frowned. "We'll keep him on the list as a potential accomplice, but not as our primary focus unless we establish a firm connection between him and the Masons. Next?"

Matt tapped the board. "Liam Ward. To me, he's the strongest suspect. His mother works for the Masons. He and his mother both refused to say whether or not he knew Josh and Shelly. They also wouldn't say whether or not Liam had ever been in the Masons' house. Liam has a record for running a financial scam. The Masons also ran a financial scam. He dropped his mother at the Masons' house the day of the murders."

"Does he have a tattoo?" Bree asked.

"He was wearing sleeves when we interviewed him," Matt said.

"We need to find out, but he won't talk to us without a lawyer." She pursed her lips, studying the board. "We can stake out Liam's house and try to get a photo of him with his biceps exposed."

"If he doesn't have a tattoo?" Todd asked.

"Then we'll start interviewing local tattoo artists and showing them Adam's drawing. I have a connection there that might be able to help," Bree said. "But let's start with step one and work from there."

"Yes, ma'am." Todd left the room briefly to give the order.

When he returned a couple of minutes later, Bree continued. "Now, let's go back to the Masons. Have you found any emails that relate to a threat or complaints about their fake charity or illegal legal services?"

"Not in recent emails. I'm going further back, but they kept their fraud low-key. They even provided fake receipts for tax deductions. I suspect the reason they weren't caught is the low dollar amounts of each donation. We have the email addresses of thousands of donors, and we're working our way through the list. But it's going to take time."

"No partners or business associates that you could find?" Bree asked.

"Not yet," Todd said. "But we're still digging. The Masons used shell companies to filter the money from the fake charity. It'll take time to get warrants, receive financial records, and dig into everything."

It could be weeks before they received all the information. Financial institutions were generally cooperative, but only after every legal requirement had been met. Their clients—rich people—had the resources to initiate lawsuits. Matt understood—law enforcement also needed detailed paperwork to ensure all evidence was admissible in the event of an eventual trial. But in the middle of a double homicide investigation, the time delay was frustrating. The suspect had already shot at them twice. They needed information sooner, not later.

Someone rapped on the door, and it opened. Marge walked into the conference room and closed the door behind her. "Sorry to interrupt, Sheriff. But Madeline Jager is here. She wants to speak with you. She knows you're here."

"It's fine." Bree exhaled hard. "I'll be out in a minute to talk with her."

"I'll get her some coffee." Marge withdrew.

Bree's phone buzzed. She picked it up and read the screen. "It's Rory. Let's hope forensics has something for us. We need a lead like nobody's business." She pressed the phone against her ear. "Sheriff Taggert. Can I put you on speaker, Rory?"

"Sure," Rory said.

Bree set down the phone and tapped the screen. "Go ahead. Matt Flynn and Todd Harvey are here with me."

"So the rapid DNA results came back." Rory hesitated. "The results are shocking—but then again, they're not."

"Tell us," Bree prompted.

"Claire Mason is a missing child," Rory said. "Her DNA matches that of Blaire Sawyer, who disappeared twelve years ago in Chandler, New York. Blaire was five at the time."

Stunned, it took a few seconds for Matt to process what he'd heard. Then he checked the map on his phone. "Chandler is only an hour north of here."

"That fits the timeline of her fake adoption by the Masons," Bree said. "You're right. It's shocking, but then again, not. Thanks for rushing this."

Matt reassessed. They already knew the Masons were criminals. Being involved in one more crime shouldn't be surprising. But they'd been clever to keep their secret this long.

She ended the call and turned to Todd, who was already attacking the keyboard of his laptop. "I want to know everything about Blaire Sawyer, her biological family members, and how she went missing."

CHAPTER

TWENTY-TWO

Bree spotted Jager in the break room stirring a steaming mug with a wooden stick. Surprise visits from the county administrator were never good news. Bree braced herself and entered. "You need to speak with me?"

Jager looked up, her eyes suspiciously deadpan. "Yes."

What is she up to?

The room smelled of fresh brew, so Bree poured herself a mug. "Let's go into my office." She led Jager through the squad room and closed her office door behind them.

Jager settled herself in a guest chair, crossing one bony leg over the other.

Bree perched on the edge of her desk. "Did you see the alligator again?"

"No. The man from the zoo came out and set up a camera. But that's not why I'm here." Jager held her coffee in both hands, glaring over the rim. "The media reported on a shooting at a playground yesterday. What. Were. You. Thinking?" She enunciated each word as if it were its own sentence. "And why wasn't I informed?" she asked as if she were Bree's boss. She wasn't.

"Excuse me?"

"They interviewed a mother with a toddler and an infant in a baby stroller. The woman was in tears, talking about how terrified she was when she heard gunshots while on her way to the playground. They played the clip over and over. It's going fucking viral. So, I'll repeat my question: What were you thinking, exchanging gunfire with an armed suspect in a residential neighborhood?"

"We did not engage with an armed suspect. We chased a man who tried to abduct Claire Mason. He opened fire on us, and we did not fire back because of the location." Bree's head throbbed. "What would you have us do? Not chase him at all?"

Unmoved, Jager speared Bree with her gaze. "Did you catch him?"

Bree paused for a nanosecond, then spit out, "No."

"Then what was the point of pursuing him?" Jager snapped.

Bree counted to three. "This was not a planned event. We didn't know he was armed or that he would fire on us. All we knew was that he was chasing our victim, a teenage girl who has already lost both her parents to murder."

Jager didn't comment, but there was no give on her face or in her tone. Was she capable of understanding someone else's point of view? "Are you any closer to making an arrest?"

"We're working on several leads and have a person of interest."

"Who?"

"I cannot give out his name at this time," Bree said. She would not let Jager sabotage the case, even unintentionally.

Jager was not impressed. "You need to arrest someone for those murders."

Of course they needed to find the killer, but crimes were not solved by sheer willpower. This time, Bree couldn't hold back the retort. "Will anyone do? Or should I continue solving the case?" She regretted the words the second they left her lips.

Damn it! You let her get to you. Again.

"I see you're in no mood to be reasonable." With a spine rigid with indignation, Jager set her coffee on the desk and stood. "We discussed a press conference to address the issue, and you didn't get back to me with a time. So, I set one up for this evening. You're welcome to attend or not. Up to you."

Bree didn't respond for a few seconds, swallowing her first few instinctive replies and settling on, "I'll be there."

"Six o'clock sharp. Have an update ready. If I were you, I'd make it sound like I made some progress." Jager walked out.

Bree's mind spun. *How dare she?* Stupid response. Jager had no shame. This wasn't the first time she'd forced Bree's hand to the detriment of an investigation. Jager wouldn't pass up any opportunity to get in front of the press and elevate her own position. Bree had no time to play politics. She had actual work to do. Juggling work and family time was already like walking a tightrope over the Grand Canyon. Now, there would be no dinner or bedtime with the kids, all because Madeline Jager wanted her face on the news.

Bree was still silently fuming when Matt knocked on her doorframe and poked his head in ten minutes later. "Everything OK?"

Bree leaned back in her chair and stared at her ceiling for a few seconds. "Politics will be the death of me."

"Jager?"

Bree shifted forward. "Yep. She's called a press conference for this evening."

Matt dropped into a chair. "Ugh."

"I want to be a cop. I want to protect the residents, solve crimes, and put away the bad guys. I don't have time to juggle politicians' egos." Bree scrubbed her hands down her face. "That woman brings out the absolute worst in me." Mentally, she smacked herself for snapping back. *Stupid, stupid, stupid.* She'd allowed Jager to draw her into *her* narrative.

"She would drive a nun to drink. She is not an easy person."

"It's my fault. *I* should have scheduled a press conference. Then I could be in control. I procrastinated, and this is what happened. Lack of action meets consequence."

"You didn't procrastinate. You were working the case—and being shot at."

Bree shrugged. It didn't matter. "Let's not waste any more time on Jager."

"The detective who worked Claire/Blaire's case is available for a call in five."

"That was fast." Bree pressed both palms on her desk and pushed to her feet.

"We got lucky. She answered my email immediately." Matt led the way back to the conference room. "She's eager to talk to us."

Todd spun his computer so Bree could see the screen. A photo of a young child dominated Bree's attention. Despite the years that had passed, she recognized Claire immediately. The Masons had had a few framed snapshots around the house from Claire's younger years. She was a tiny thing, with wispy long blond hair and big eyes, sitting in a pile of fall leaves.

"Can't argue with DNA." Bree eased into a chair. "And that's definitely her."

Matt placed his phone on the table and made the call.

A woman answered, "Detective Shillings."

Matt leaned closer. "This is Investigator Matt Flynn, Sheriff Bree Taggert, and Chief Deputy Todd Harvey."

"You found Blaire Sawyer?" Shillings sounded incredulous.

Matt gave her a quick synopsis from the Masons' murders to the fake adoption papers and rapid DNA request. "The Masons changed her name to Claire."

Shillings's sigh reverberated. "They picked a name close to her real one. Maybe to make it easier for her to learn and respond to the change.

Five-year-olds are adaptable. She would have believed what she was told."

Which she did.

"What can you tell us about the case?" Matt asked. "How did she go missing?"

"Her father, Dallas Sawyer, crashed his car into a ditch during a snowstorm. By the time a passing motorist reported the accident, Mr. Sawyer was dead and cold. The state troopers that responded didn't even know there had been a child in the car until they went to do the death notification and the mother started screaming, 'Where's my daughter?'" Shillings paused for a breath and maybe to collect herself. "The child safety seat in the rear of the vehicle was empty, with no sign that a child had been in it during the accident. No blood, et cetera."

"I can't imagine," Bree said, and meant it. She pictured Kayla out with Matt, a state trooper knocking on the door . . . *No.* Her experiences in law enforcement always took her to the worst-case scenario, but that kind of doomsday thinking would not serve her today. Shaking her head, she banished the image. For now. She knew it would probably come back in her nightmares, when she could not control her imagination.

"Yeah," Shillings continued. "That's when I was called in. Between the medical examiner and Mr. Sawyer's personal timeline, we determined he'd been dead for approximately six hours."

"Did you try and track her?" Matt asked. "If she wandered from the vehicle, she had six hours to get lost."

"We did," Shillings said. "It was January. The temperature had dropped to single digits that night, and three inches of snow had fallen since the accident happened. If there were tracks, the snow had filled them in. We called in dogs. Even in a coat and boots, a five-year-old couldn't have gotten far in those conditions. Frostbite can occur in minutes at that temp. We searched that night, the next day—when the storm had passed—and again after the snow melted. We put out alerts. We checked hospitals and put her photo on TV, in case a passing motorist had found her. But we never had a lead on the child. Not a single one. She vanished into thin air, without a trace, poof. All the clichés applied."

"Is her mother still living?" Bree asked.

"Yes." Despite the positive response, Shillings's tone was sad. "About a year after the accident, she tried to drown herself in pills and vodka. Thankfully, she survived, but she's never recovered from losing her daughter. I touch base with her once a year. She suffers from debilitating depression and substance abuse. Some years, she's sober. Others, not. I understand her reaction, but she also had—has—a son, Denver. He's twenty-two now."

"How do you think she'll take the news?" Bree asked.

"I don't know. I assume she'll be happy her daughter is alive, but she's lost twelve years . . ." Shillings paused. "I'll drive out there now and let you know when we can set up a meet. I assume she'll want to see her daughter ASAP."

"Yes, and we have to tell Claire," Bree said.

"She doesn't know?" Shillings asked.

"The Masons told her that they adopted her after her parents died in a car accident."

"That's clearly not what happened," Shillings said. "And we need to find out what did."

"Absolutely," Bree agreed. "Let's do the meetup between Claire—sorry, Blaire—and her biological mother tomorrow. Blaire can have the night to digest the news. Then we should put our heads and case notes together."

"Sounds good. I'll get back to you." Shillings ended the call.

The conference room fell silent for a few heartbeats. Then Bree said, "Do we bring Claire into the station or go see her at the new foster home? I've never had to tell a victim their entire life is a lie before. What's the protocol?"

Matt shook his head. "There are no good options."

"No." Bree called Lindsay and summed up the situation.

"Better take her to the station," Lindsay said. "Her new foster mother called me a while ago and said Claire was being difficult. They weren't sure how they'd manage her. So, I'm not sure that situation is going to work out."

"Claire is traumatized, not *difficult*." Bree swallowed her very personal—and angry—response. That was the exact same argument her grandparents had used when they'd taken the younger Taggert orphans and rejected Bree. At the age of eight, she'd had the most difficulty processing the trauma. Thankfully, a cousin in Philadelphia had stepped up. But the Taggert kids should have been kept together. Separating them had created a whole new trauma Bree and Adam were still working to overcome.

"I know, but she needs to be with someone who also understands that. I'll work on finding a new place, but it isn't going to be easy. We're overflowing with kids in need of placement. I'm trying to get her in to see a child psychiatrist as well, but there's a waiting list. The sooner she gets help processing all this, the better." Lindsay ended the call.

Bree stood, crossed to the door, and called into the squad room for Zucco.

Zucco hurried into the conference room, her face hopeful. "Ma'am? Am I back on full duty?"

"Tomorrow. For now, I have a special task for you." Bree updated Zucco on Claire's status as a missing child.

"Holy shit." Zucco blinked. "I can't believe it. How is Claire going to take the news?"

"It's going to be a shock," Bree said.

Because the news was going to traumatize her all over again, just like Bree and her siblings had been damaged a second time by the adult response to their situation. Frustration surged through Bree. She could see Claire's emotional situation escalating, but Bree felt powerless to stop it. Claire's past life was unraveling, and her present was nothing but crisis upon crisis.

How could she possibly recover after having her life literally stolen?

CHAPTER

TWENTY-THREE

An hour later, guilt squeezed Bree's heart as she faced Claire over the interview room table. Zucco sat next to Claire. Matt occupied a chair at the other end of the table.

Shillings had called back to say that Mrs. Sawyer was heading to Grey's Hollow immediately. She wanted to see her daughter when she arrived. If the girl wasn't at the sheriff's station, she would call her lawyer. Bree understood her haste. She couldn't imagine thinking her child was dead for twelve years. She wouldn't want to wait a single extra minute before laying eyes on them.

But Claire had arrived at the station pale and teary eyed. Did she sense more news was coming? Was it residual stress and grief from the Masons' murders—from discovering the violent and bloody scene? Or something else . . . ? Was this what the foster mother had meant when she'd said Claire was being difficult? On the other hand, maybe there was friction at the new home that caused Claire to react. If the family couldn't empathize with a teenager in distress, they had no business being foster parents. Most of the kids who would come to them would be traumatized. Bree knew some great foster parents, but she also knew others were in it for the money. Some simply didn't have any idea what they were getting into.

Normally, Bree didn't procrastinate when delivering bad news. When you were standing on someone's doorstep at two in the morning, they already knew you were there to tell them someone died. But this was different. There was no way Claire was ready for this news. No one would be. It was a blindside with a capital *B*.

Bree began with a single *brace yourself* statement. "There's no good way to give you this news."

Claire, already paper white, went paler. "How much worse can it get? My parents were murdered."

Bree took a deep breath. "Your parents said they adopted you after your biological parents died in a car accident?"

Claire nodded, her eyes wary.

"That was only partially true. Your father died in an accident. You were in the car with him, and you disappeared from the scene."

Claire's brows dropped. "I don't understand."

"Your given name is Blaire Sawyer. You went missing twelve years ago. Your mother is still alive, and you have an older brother, Denver, who is twenty-two."

Claire stared, her face frozen with disbelief.

Bree continued. "Your mother lives about an hour north of here."

Claire shook her head slowly, her chin raised, unwilling to even consider the information as true. "No. That can't be right. Both of my parents died in that crash, and the Masons adopted me." But her words rang hollow, as if she already knew Bree was telling the truth but Claire wasn't willing to accept it.

Bree continued in a gentle but firm tone. "We ran your DNA through our databases and hit a match. You were reported missing by your mother, Pamela Sawyer." Bree slid a family photo, supplied by Shillings via email, across the table. The background in the picture—a generic-looking Christmas tree—looked like those offered at the mall during the holidays. The four Sawyers, dressed in matching red sweaters and jeans, smiled for the camera. The family looked average and completely normal. There was no sign their entire world would implode a few weeks after this picture had been taken. Dallas had the beginnings of a paunch and a slightly receding hairline. Pam's blond hair was cut in a smooth, chin-length bob. Five-year-old Blaire grinned widely, but her older brother sported the awkward smile typical for a ten-year-old.

Kayla was constantly losing teeth and had recently become self-conscious about the gaps in photos.

Claire ignored the picture for a good five seconds, but curiosity drew her gaze like a mosquito to a porch light. She shook her head, her lips mashed flat, her chin jutted in defiance of what she couldn't process. "I don't know these people."

Bree tapped the little girl in the photo. "That's you." In the few framed photos they'd found in the Masons' home from Claire's young childhood, her hair had been cut short. Despite the change in hairstyle, it was clearly the same child.

A single tear tracked down Claire's cheek. She reached for the photo, picking it up by the edges with both hands. Lifting it, she studied it with an expression that twisted awe and terror. Recognition slowly dawned in her eyes. "Why? Why did they do this?"

"We don't know," Bree said.

"How did they even get me?" Claire asked the question with trepidation, as if afraid of the answer.

"We don't know that either." Bree took a breath. "There's more, Claire."

"More?" Claire's voice rose in near panic. She looked to be one breath away from shattering.

Zucco moved closer, as if offering silent support.

Bree said what needed to be said. "The Masons weren't lawyers. They made their money running a fake online charity."

"They were scammers?" Claire asked, wide-eyed.

Bree nodded.

Claire's gaze fell back to the family photo. "If they stole money from people, did they steal *me?*"

Probably? Bree couldn't think of a better explanation. The Masons could have stumbled upon Claire the night of the accident and simply kept her. Or they could have adopted her from a less-than-reputable agency that acquired the child through those means. Had Shelly Mason been so desperate to have a child that she hadn't cared how she got one?

"We're going to work with the police in Chandler. That's where you went missing." Bree tapped on the boy's face in the photo. "If there's a bright side in all this, it's that you have a mother and a brother. You aren't alone."

Claire lifted the photo closer to her face. She touched her brother's face with a forefinger. "I think he used to push me on the swing in our backyard." She looked away. "Am I making that up? How can I suddenly remember him after all these years of having no real memories at all?"

The mind suppresses memories it can't handle. Bree knew this firsthand. She'd only recently begun having memories of her own mother. "Your mother can't wait to see you."

Claire dropped the photo like it burned her fingers. "When?" Panic edged her voice.

She's been waiting for twelve years. But Bree didn't say that. She didn't want to create any more pressure for Claire than was necessary.

"She's on her way here now." And there wasn't anything Bree could do about that, and it was killing her that she couldn't protect Claire from being forced into the meeting before she was ready.

Claire's fingers trembled. "Do I have to go with her? I don't even know her."

"No," Bree said. "You do not have to go with her today. There is no right or wrong response to what you're feeling. You have a lot to process, and you have every right to ask for some time to do that."

Technically, a seventeen-year-old could petition the court for the right to make her own legal decisions. But how would a judge respond? Would they rule that she was mature enough? Or that she'd suffered so many tragedies that she wasn't in the right frame of mind? How could anyone make that call? If Claire wanted to make her own decisions, where would she go? The Masons' illegally obtained money wouldn't be available to her. Life insurance usually paid out within a couple of months, but how would that be affected by Claire's change in identity or the Masons' crimes? Without her biological mother and brother, Claire had no home and no support.

"Will they make me go with her in the end? Even if I don't like her?" Claire whispered the question.

"I can't say for sure. But you're almost an adult. The judge will talk to you and consider your feelings." But Bree made no promises.

A knock preceded Marge opening the door and sticking her head through the opening. "Detective Shillings is here with the Sawyers."

Bree met Claire's eyes. "Ready?"

Claire chewed on a cuticle but nodded. "Not really, but I don't have a choice, do I?"

Marge withdrew.

Matt got up. "This room is too crowded. I think maybe only the sheriff should stay."

Zucco took the hint. She gave Claire a supportive pat on the shoulder. "I'll be in the squad room if you want to talk afterward."

Matt and Zucco left the room. Through the open door, Bree spotted three people approaching. Though he'd grown up, Denver Sawyer was recognizable from the Christmas photo. But his mother didn't look like the same person at all. She'd aged twenty-five years in twelve. Her hair was frizzy, unkempt, and streaked with gray. Her skin was sallow, and yellow tinged the whites of her eyes. She'd lost thirty pounds at least, and was almost skeletal. Loose skin hung on prominent bones.

Her son followed, his steps dragging with reluctance. The woman behind them was in her midforties, with no-fuss short brown hair. She was dressed like a cop, in a white shirt and black slacks with a badge on one hip and a firearm on the other. Detective Shillings, Bree assumed.

Mrs. Sawyer came through the door on shaky legs. Bree suspected this week hadn't been a sober one. Her son stuck close, but he looked like he'd rather be anywhere else. His face was locked in a sullen expression. Though his sister had been stolen, his life had also been ruined. Shillings introduced herself, Mrs. Sawyer, and Denver.

Before Bree could respond in kind, Mrs. Sawyer stopped a few feet shy of Claire and whispered, "Blaire?"

Denver's gaze found his sister. He nudged Shillings. "You're sure about that DNA, right? Because we've been through this before when those other girls said they were Blaire."

How many times has this grieving family been victimized by fake Blaires? Anger surged through Bree that people would prey on the desperate relatives of missing children.

Shillings nodded. "We're sure. The DNA matched, as do childhood photos and the general timeline."

"Blaire." Mrs. Sawyer spoke the name again, this time with reverence as she reached for Claire, her thin fingers bent like talons.

Claire shrank away.

Bree stepped in, offering her hand and diverting Mrs. Sawyer's attention. "I'm Sheriff Taggert."

Mrs. Sawyer reluctantly tore her gaze off her daughter. "Thank you for finding my girl."

"Remember what I said, Pam?" Shillings asked in a gentle voice. "Blaire's going to need some time."

But Mrs. Sawyer only had eyes for her daughter. Bree's heart broke for all of them. Claire, who barely had snatches of memories of her prior life, and for Mrs. Sawyer and Denver. But they had experienced every agonizing second of the past twelve years thinking Blaire was dead—or worse.

Mrs. Sawyer stepped closer.

Shillings blocked her with an arm. "Let's not crowd Blaire, OK? She just found out who she really is. Having all this sprung on her must be overwhelming."

"I want to hug my own fucking daughter!" Red-faced, Mrs. Sawyer shoved Shillings's arm away.

Claire leaped to her feet, sending her chair backward. It toppled, hitting the ground with a metallic rattle. Shaking, the girl sidled along the wall, keeping the table between her and Mrs. Sawyer.

"Blaire!" Mrs. Sawyer begged. "Don't you remember me?"

"My name is Claire." She took another step sideways.

"Your name is Blaire," Mrs. Sawyer corrected, her words sloppy and edged with temper. "And you're *my* daughter."

Booze or pills?

Claire seemed to shrink.

The mother's slurring speech brought Bree's father to mind. She placed herself between mother and daughter. "I think Claire has had enough for today."

"I'll decide what's best for my daughter." Mrs. Sawyer tried to reach around her.

But Bree didn't budge. Claire's eyes were wide, her face paper white.

Shillings caught Mrs. Sawyer by the arm. "That's enough."

All the anger seemed to bleed out of Mrs. Sawyer. Her eyes brimmed, then tears streamed down her face. "I want my baby back."

"I know," Shillings soothed, then spoke in a soft voice. "But Blaire isn't a baby anymore."

"Maybe we should take a break," Bree suggested. She felt pity for Mrs. Sawyer, but Claire was Bree's primary concern. "Everyone has had shocking news today. Good news, but still shocking."

Denver shouldered his way into the mix. "Come on, Mom. You're scaring Blaire. Remember, she was always afraid of new stuff when she was little. Give her a break. Let's get some food. You were too anxious to eat before."

Mrs. Sawyer's eyes softened when she looked at her son. "What would I do without you? You're the only one who cares about me. You're the only one who understands."

"Let's get some air." He tugged her toward the door, and she relented. As he herded her out of the room, he glanced back at Claire. "She wasn't always like this. Just since . . . you know. I'll work on her. Maybe you and I could talk?"

Claire's gaze skittered away from his. She stared at the carpet. Her head bowed in one small nod.

"I'll get her your number," Shillings said, as if anxious for Mrs. Sawyer to keep moving.

Matt appeared as soon as the Sawyers stepped through the doorway. He must have been waiting in the hall. "I'll walk you out." He led Mrs. Sawyer and Denver away.

Shillings blew her bangs out of her eyes. "Sorry about that. Never know where her mood's going to go. She's at the point where she needs a couple of shots to function, you know? Maybe finding Blaire will be the motivation she needs to detox." She gave Claire a sympathetic look. "Are you OK, Claire?"

Claire didn't respond.

Shillings said, "I'll talk to her, and Denver will help. She needs to see things from your perspective. But I'd also like you to think about what she's experienced. Losing her husband was awful, but having her child disappear—having no answers—not having any idea what happened to you, not knowing if you were hungry or cold, alive or dead— that broke her." Shillings moved toward the door. "I'm not saying you have to be all huggy. All I'm asking is that you be kind to each other.

Give each other the time needed to absorb all that's happened. It's a lot. Neither one of you should be expected to roll with this kind of chaos."

Bree bristled. "Claire is the child here, and time is exactly what *she's* asked for."

"Yeah." Shillings's shoulders slumped. "I know. It's funny. This is the best this situation could possibly turn out, and it's still shit. I mean, Claire is healthy and whole. Usually, that's not how long-term missing persons cases resolve." She stopped short of saying the rest out loud.

It's more common for DNA to be matched with remains, not a living person.

But Bree understood the irony. She escorted Shillings out the door. In the hallway, she spotted Zucco lingering and motioned for the deputy to go in with Claire. Then Bree fell into step beside Shillings. "I have a press con this evening. I'll do what I can to protect the family's anonymity, but we both know it won't be long before the media uncovers that Claire is Blaire."

"I know," Shillings said. "There were reporters in the parking lot when we came in. But I have more information for you on Dallas Sawyer. Let me escort the Sawyers to their vehicle and grab the file from my trunk. I'll be back in a few."

Bree gestured toward the conference room. "We'll be in there when you're done."

The Masons' case was so spectacularly twisted, Bree wouldn't even guess what information Shillings could have about Sawyer.

CHAPTER TWENTY-FOUR

How do I live with all the lies?

Claire reeled as her bio mom left the room. That's not what she'd expected. It couldn't be true. She couldn't be that woman's daughter.

But her denial felt as empty as her heart.

For the very first time, it hit her. She had no one. She was completely alone. She didn't remember Pam Sawyer. Claire had zero memories of her. Why not? How could she have been raised by this woman for the first five years of her life and retain no recollection of her? It seemed impossible.

But was it?

A sickening sense of déjà vu flooded her. The Sawyers *had* felt familiar in a way she couldn't fully understand.

Maybe she didn't want to.

After the sheriff had told her that her biological mother was still alive, she hadn't had time to imagine what her bio mom was like. She'd had a couple of minutes to think, *Maybe I'm not alone.*

Because the reality of her situation since *it* happened was that she had no one. No one to attend her high school graduation or drive her to college for her first semester. No one to walk her down the aisle if she ever wanted to get married.

So maybe, in the middle of the shock, she'd had a little glimmer of hope. After the last few days, she wanted to feel normal, to belong somewhere. She didn't want to be related to that woman. Drunk or high, it didn't matter. Living with her would be a nightmare.

She did not want to belong to Pam Sawyer. She was repulsive.

This was not how things were supposed to turn out.

What was she going to do?

Fear burst through her like an electric shock. After it passed, its absence left her limp and exhausted. She hadn't slept. Had barely eaten. Wasn't hungry. Her head spun. Her bones hurt. Emotions she was too tired to identify crushed together inside her, like too many people in a subway car. She could barely breathe.

Overwhelmed, she put her head on her crossed arms and closed her eyes. She couldn't even cry. The people she'd believed were her parents weren't. They hadn't been anything like they'd said. They'd been crooks. They hadn't bothered to make sure she was taken care of. They'd left her with no one.

They hadn't loved her.

What was she supposed to do?

The reality that hit her, one more person squeezed into that subway car, was that she couldn't do anything. She was trapped. The sheriff seemed to care, but what could she do?

Was Claire's future one foster home after another until she turned eighteen? Crowded houses, sometimes with foster parents who cared, sometimes not. How many creepers would she have to fend off? And what would she do when she turned eighteen?

Claire had one other option. But using it wouldn't be easy.

Did she have the guts?

CHAPTER
TWENTY-FIVE

Bree stared at the murder board while she waited for Shillings.

How could the Masons' murders and Dallas Sawyer's accident possibly be related? Then again, how could they not? Was it a coincidence that three deaths circled around one girl? Bree's head spun with the possibilities. But there was no point in speculating. The investigation had uncovered one bizarre turn after another.

Matt entered the conference room. Shillings joined them a few minutes later, eyed the murder board, and slapped a thick folder on the table. "Dallas Sawyer's death was ruled an accident by the medical examiner, but when we discovered a child was missing and we never found any sign of her, I had my doubts. How does a kid disappear without leaving as much as a mitten behind? Anyway, I unofficially kept his case open in my mind even as it was declared cold by the powers that be. Those doubts were reinforced when we discovered an open FBI investigation into Dallas Sawyer."

"FBI?" Bree asked.

Shilling nodded. "Dallas Sawyer was one of the partners in a start-up tech company called Wall Digital Technology. The FBI suspected the company was a front for a ransomware-scareware scam.

They'd target seniors with pop-up messages on their computers alerting them to fake viruses that could only be removed with their software, Safety Sweep. You'd be surprised how many people fall for that. But the FBI could never prove he was behind it. People are reluctant to report these kinds of scams because they either don't know they were scammed or don't want to admit it. When you factor in spoofing, anonymous email servers, and a jumble of shell companies, it's hard to prove who is doing what." She paused for a breath. "Right after Dallas died, the tech company headquarters burned to the ground. Every piece of hardware was destroyed in the fire, including the backup servers. After that, the case went nowhere. The FBI suspected Sawyer's partners were foreign and took the operation completely overseas."

"Must have been a hell of a fire to conveniently destroy all potential evidence," Bree said. Most modern buildings had fire-suppression systems and alarms.

"Right?" Shillings asked. "Fire department response was rapid, but the place fucking melted like wax. Not surprisingly, an accelerant was found, and the fire was ruled arson. The owners blamed a competitor, but no one was ever charged."

Matt asked, "But you never tied Claire's disappearance to the FBI investigation?"

"No," Shilling said.

"What was Sawyer's cause of death?" Bree asked.

"He bled to death. He had a chunk of glass lodged in his neck. There was a broken bottle of green juice shattered in the vehicle. The ME theorized he was lifting the bottle when the accident occurred, and the airbag propelled it into him. Shards sliced his face and neck in the accident. His carotid was severed." She opened her file and pulled out accident photos. She tapped on one showing the interior of the vehicle. "You can see the extra shards here." Below the collapsed airbag, glass shards and blood covered the seat. "And the fatal piece here." She pointed to an autopsy photo showing the piece of glass sticking out of the victim's neck. "This is what having a glass bottle between you and an airbag inflating at two hundred miles per hour can do."

Airbags saved countless lives, but they weren't perfect. The force with which they deployed could break ribs, facial bones, even an arm if the driver's hand was resting on top of the wheel. Anything between the airbag and driver was a potential projectile.

Shillings continued. "The missing person case went cold almost immediately. Actually, it started cold and stayed that way. One of the most frustrating cases of my career. I'm due to retire next year. I'm thrilled that Blaire was found, but I want to know how she ended up with Josh and Shelly Mason. Every cop has that one case they'd sacrifice a body part to solve. This is mine."

"We'd also like to know how the Masons were involved," Bree said. "And if it somehow ties to their murders."

"We need to start by looking for connections between the Masons and Dallas Sawyer," Shillings agreed. "I'll show pictures of the Masons to Mrs. Sawyer. Maybe we'll get lucky and she'll recognize them. I'm also going to reach out to the FBI agent who handled the Dallas Sawyer case. I've spoken with him before about the case. I'll include you in any communication and keep you updated." She gestured toward her folder. "I'll email you copies of everything."

"We appreciate that," Bree said. "We'll keep working the Masons' murder case. I'll update you if we find any link between Dallas Sawyer and the Masons, but so far, Claire is the only connection."

"If these cases aren't connected, it'll be stranger than if they are," Shilling said on her way out the door.

"I agree." Matt added the information they'd received about Dallas Sawyer's death to the side of the murder board. "I'll make this a sidebar, since we don't know how or if it's related to the Masons' murders."

"If it's a coincidence, it's a big, fat one." Bree was not a big believer in coincidences, especially not in murder cases. "I'm going to ask Dr. Jones to have a look at Dallas's autopsy."

"You think he was murdered?"

"I don't know," Bree said. "But the cause of death is unusual."

"The accident could have been caused by someone. It's not that hard to run a vehicle off the road. Maybe they didn't even want to kill him, just give him a warning. Given Dallas's suspected criminal activity, it isn't a stretch to think someone could have wanted to threaten or kill him."

"But did the same person kill Josh and the Masons?"

"We need more information from the FBI to find a link between them, but that is a possibility. Considering the Masons had the Sawyers' daughter, it's also possible that they killed Dallas."

CHAPTER TWENTY-SIX

Feeling useless, Renata watched Claire melt down. She couldn't imagine finding out her entire life was fabricated, that she was a whole other person. Then, the first time she saw her biological family, her mother lost her shit on a bender.

She pulled the sheriff aside. "How about I take Claire to visit her cat instead of sitting around the station? She can have dinner with me and my mom. It might make her feel normal for a few hours."

"Are you sure you want to give up your evening?" Sheriff Taggert asked. "You're about to go off duty, and tomorrow is your day off."

"Yeah. It's fine. I didn't have any plans except some yard work." Renata never had plans. "My mom will enjoy the company, and she's good with teenagers."

"OK, then," the sheriff said. "Check in with me later. Don't say anything to Claire, but she might not be going back to the same place."

"All right." Renata sent her mom a quick text. Then she waved to Claire. "Wanna get out of here for a while?"

"Yes!" Claire jumped to her feet.

"Let's go." Renata led the way to the rear of the station. She and Claire climbed into her Jeep. As Renata drove out of the employee lot, she spotted two news vans driving into the front parking lot. "Keep your head down. Press."

Claire ducked sideways.

Renata kept one eye on the rearview mirror until the sheriff's station was out of sight. "You can sit up."

Claire turned to look through the rear window. "Thanks. Where are we going?"

"My house. I thought maybe you'd like to see Chunk."

Claire smiled. "I would love that."

"I am not the best cook in the world, and I'm hungry. What kind of fast food do you like?"

"Could we have pizza?"

"Of course! I have a place on speed dial. What do you want on it?"

"Veggies?"

"My favorite." Renata ordered the grilled vegetable pie. She added a quart of chicken pastina soup and garlic knots to the order in case her mom couldn't stomach pizza today.

"Can I put down the window?" Claire asked. "I could use some air."

"Sure. Good idea." Renata turned off the AC and lowered her own window. She turned on the radio. "Put on whatever you like."

Claire fiddled with the stations for a few minutes, then settled on a Taylor Swift song. Renata wasn't a die-hard Swiftie, but "Shake It Off" felt appropriate. She rested her elbow on the doorframe. The hot wind whipped her hair and reminded her of summer day trips to the beach.

Claire leaned back, sang along, and tapped out the rhythm on the armrest. It was the first time Renata had seen the girl almost relaxed. She turned down a side street toward the pizza parlor. A dark SUV made the turn behind them. Renata made a few additional, unnecessary turns, circling a block. The SUV disappeared.

Coincidence? Lots of people drove dark SUVs. Renata leaned toward cautious and took Claire into the restaurant with her when they picked up the order. Then she kept watch all the way back to her mom's house.

The drive was short, and Renata pulled into her driveway ten minutes later. She shifted into park, then paused. "My mom is sick. Cancer. They caught it early. Chances are she's going to be OK, but the treatment is hard."

"I'm sorry."

"Thanks. I didn't want you to be shocked because she looks . . . well, sick, but it's not contagious."

Claire nodded. "OK. I appreciate that."

"Then let's go inside so you can hug your cat." Renata climbed out of the vehicle.

Claire helped her carry the food into the house.

Renata called, "Mom?"

"In the sunroom," her mom answered.

Renata led Claire through the house. They set the pizza box and take-out bag on the counter in the kitchen, where her mom had set the table for three. Her mom and the cat were in almost the same position they'd been when Renata had left that morning. "Have either of you even moved today?"

Her mom laughed. "Yes, we did. But it's so nice out here, even though my garden is in terrible shape."

Chunk agreed, purring, stretching out, and flexing his murder mittens.

Renata introduced Claire. "This is my mom, Teresa Zucco."

"Hi, Mrs. Zucco."

Renata's mom scoffed. "Teresa, please."

Chunk spotted Claire, heaved himself to his feet, and ambled over to say hi. Claire was all smiles as she scooped him onto her lap and hugged him close. The cat purred louder.

"He missed you," Teresa said.

"Maybe," Claire said into Chunk's fur. "But he likes everyone. Thanks for taking care of him."

"You're very welcome. I've enjoyed his company. But now I'm starving." Renata's mom held out a hand. "Little help."

Renata pulled her to her feet. "Then let's eat." Renata retreated to her room to change into shorts and an oversize T-shirt. She considered her gun safe, but instead opted to switch her weapon to a holster that nestled the gun at the small of her back, the most comfortable and discreet on-body carry she'd found for her petite frame. She tugged the hem of her shirt over the gun.

When she returned to the kitchen, her mom and Claire were dispensing pizza and chatting as if they'd known each other for years. Chunk begged like a dog at Claire's feet. The girl tore off a tiny piece of pizza, and the cat ate it with gusto. Her mom enjoyed the company so much she ate an entire slice of pizza, and Renata vowed to make sure they socialized more regularly. After dinner, her mom and Claire attacked a puzzle on the dining room table while Renata cleaned up. Chunk climbed onto the table and stretched out on top of half the pieces. Laughing, Claire moved him.

But Renata's mom quickly tired. "I'm sorry, Claire. I need to rest for a bit. We'll do more of the puzzle later, OK?"

"Yeah. OK." Claire sipped her Coke.

After her mom left the room, Renata sat down at the table and squinted at the puzzle box. "A thousand pieces?"

"It's a hard one too." Claire pulled edge pieces from the box.

"I can see that." Renata started collecting pieces that seemed to be the same shade of green. "Thanks for distracting my mom. She needed that."

"So did I." Claire's mouth flattened, tiny lines fanning out that had no business forming on a teenager.

"Want to talk about it?"

Without looking up, Claire asked, "Do I have to go back to that foster home?"

Suspicion crawled up the back of Renata's neck. She fought to keep her voice neutral. "Why do you ask?"

"I don't like *him*."

"Him?"

"The foster dad." Claire shuddered.

"Is there a specific reason?"

Claire paused. "I just don't like the way he looks at me. It makes me uncomfortable. I can't explain it. He didn't *do* anything."

Renata bristled. "How about I call the sheriff and see what your options are?"

Claire's shoulders curled forward, and her voice went meek. "OK."

How terrible would it be to have this little control over your life?

"Give me a couple of minutes. There's ice cream in the freezer. Help yourself." Renata picked up her cell phone and walked out the back door into the yard. Weeds crowded the raised herb and vegetable garden. Her mom hand-watered her plants, but she didn't have the energy to pick weeds, and she refused to use chemicals. Renata made a mental note to work on the beds when she had a day off.

A black fake wrought-iron fence surrounded a yard the size of a baseball diamond. This was her mom's haven. Before cancer, she had done almost all the maintenance herself. Despite the fact that the yard behind them was empty, Renata appreciated the ornamental trees and shrubs along the fence that provided privacy. In front of the shrubs, flower beds were usually full of annual blooms, but this year the beds sat empty and forlorn. The grass should be lush and soft, but the drought had killed it. They'd have to resod the whole lawn in the spring.

Renata wandered across the crunchy dead grass and scrolled on her phone for the sheriff's number, hoping to catch her boss before she left for the press conference.

A door opened and closed. "Renata, is that you?"

"Over here, Mom."

Her mom walked across the grass. "It's still hot out here."

"It's ridiculous," Renata said. "But the weather has to break soon. It's almost September."

Her mom faced her. "I overheard what Claire said about the foster home. She can't go back there. Kids have good instincts."

"I know." Renata lifted her phone. "I'm calling the sheriff now."

"She could stay here."

"Here?"

"Yes, here."

"Someone might be after Claire," Renata explained. "She's been pursued."

"All the more reason for her to be somewhere safe." Her mom didn't blink. "I still have my Glock and the license to carry. I might be sick, but I'm not useless." As a retired cop, her mom could carry concealed as long as she maintained her certification, which she did.

"I know you're not. I don't like you taking risks."

Her mom gave her a Look. "I served the NYPD for twenty-five years. I know what risk is, and I'm willing to take it on to protect that child. She needs someone to look after her, in more ways than keeping her physically safe."

"And you are the perfect person to do that." Renata sighed. Teresa Zucco had raised Renata as a single mom after her husband had bailed on them when Renata was a baby. There weren't many problems her mom couldn't—or wouldn't—tackle.

"Yes, I am."

"OK," Renata relented. "But it isn't up to me. I have to call the sheriff. Then she'll set all the balls rolling. You'll probably have to talk to the judge to get an emergency approval."

"I know how the system works. You'd better get on that."

"Yes, ma'am." Renata dialed her boss. Even though her mom had volunteered to put herself in danger, the knot of anxiety in Renata's belly loosened. Her mom went back inside while Renata made her call. The sheriff sounded relieved after Renata explained the situation. As she ended the call, a twig snapped beyond the fence line. In the yard next door, the neighbor's ninety-pound pit bull, Baby, burst into a barking frenzy.

Renata dropped into a crouch, her hand automatically reaching for her weapon. Her heart burst into a sprint. Baby's dog tags jingled as he paced the fence. Renata parted the branches of a towering rhododendron. She spotted the dog. Baby snuffled and snorted along the bottom of the fence separating his yard from the one where the noise had originated.

He spotted Renata and trotted over, but one ear remained cocked at the adjoining property. Renata followed the dog's focus. She stepped behind the bush and sidled along the fence. When she reached the corner, she ducked behind the narrow trunk of a dogwood tree and peered through its branches. She saw nothing but weeds in the empty lot. She looked back at the dog. Baby sat, his posture relaxed, his skinny tail thumping on the ground. The threat was likely gone.

Renata walked along the entire rear fence line, stopping at an area where the weeds had been trampled flat. Empty beer bottles and cigarette butts littered the ground. Teenagers? Renata examined the ground more closely. The weeds were flattened all the way to the base of her fence. She spotted something small and black waving in the breeze. A single black thread was caught in a screw in the fence. Someone had stood, leaning on the fence, maybe facing her yard. Renata lined her own body up with the prints and assessed the view. Through the branches of the dogwood and above the trimmed azaleas, she could see directly into the dining room, where Claire was at the table, working on the puzzle.

It was clear that people—likely teens in this neighborhood—had been using the empty lot to hang out and drink beer. Everyone in the neighborhood knew Baby, and the dog was usually quiet. Despite the likelihood that the intruder hadn't been a true threat, Renata couldn't shake her uneasiness.

She was about to turn away when she spotted a black item in the shadows of an oak tree. Renata hopped the four-foot fence. Her heart stuttered as she identified a baseball cap with the words A-Plus Cleaning on the front.

CHAPTER TWENTY-SEVEN

Matt scanned the crowd gathered for the press con, looking for trou-blemakers, but all he saw were the usual news crews. At the front of the room, Madeline Jager settled behind the podium. Bree stood at her side. Her features were locked in a serious-polite expression, but Matt recognized the lines bracketing her mouth. This was not where she wanted to be.

Jager assumed control. "Thank you all for coming. We're here to address the shocking double homicide that rocked our community this week. As you know from previous statements, Josh and Shelly Mason were viciously murdered in their very own bed. Our sheriff's department has been working tirelessly to solve this brutal crime, and I'm told they are currently investigating several persons of interest. Before I turn the mic over to our esteemed Sheriff Taggert, I'd like to add that Randolph County will be offering a five-thousand-dollar reward to anyone who provides information that leads to the arrest of a suspect in the murders of Josh and Shelly Mason."

Matt groaned silently. *Why? Why do politicians love tip lines and rewards?* They usually led to a ton of useless, unrelated calls that took time away from the actual investigation. They rarely provided any real leads.

Clearly, Bree wasn't happy either. Exasperation flashed across her face for three seconds before she wrestled her features under control. Her eyes briefly met Matt's—a moment of silent commiseration—before she turned her attention back to the crowd.

Reporters began yelling questions.

"Can you tell us the name of the suspect?"

"Who are you investigating?"

Jager turned to Bree. "I'll let Sheriff Taggert give you those details."

Bree stepped up to the podium. "At this moment, I cannot divulge the names of those under investigation. When we have enough evidence to make an arrest, I will let you know."

"Is the Masons' killer a threat to the public?" a reporter asked. "Should people be worried?"

Bree leaned over the mic. "Our initial investigation leads us to believe the Masons' murders were personal in nature."

"What about the playground shooting?" another man yelled. "Is it true that a suspect you were pursuing opened fire in a residential neighborhood and then got away?"

"Yes. That was the unfortunate outcome of our decision not to return fire and risk civilian lives." Bree framed her answer with care.

A woman called out, "But the killer is still on the loose!"

Bree ignored the comment and pointed at another reporter with a raised hand.

"Pam Sawyer claims the Masons' daughter is her own daughter, Blaire, who went missing twelve years ago. She says your department is keeping her from her child." A silver-haired man in the front row extended his mic toward Bree.

Damn it! Pam did this? So much for guarding the family's privacy. Anger burst through Matt. He tamped it down. Bree would do what she could to protect Claire, but he wished the girl's biological mother had the same instincts.

Excitement spread through the crowd.

Matt gave Bree credit. Pam going to the press was an unexpected move. But Bree didn't blink as she explained how the discovery had come to light through DNA testing.

"Why won't you let Mrs. Sawyer have her own daughter?" Heads nodded at the question.

"Blaire Sawyer is now seventeen. As happy as we all are that she has been found alive and well, the situation is complicated. Imagine what Blaire is going through this week. I'm going to ask you to respect her privacy and her need to process the recent upheaval of her whole world."

"Did the Masons steal her?" a reporter shouted.

"We don't yet know how she came to be with the Masons, but we do know that the Masons were involved in other criminal activity." Bree detailed their illegal legal services and fake charity, giving what seemed to him like purposefully mundane details.

Matt scanned the crowd. The financial aspects of the case seemed to bore everyone in the room and quell their initial excitement over Claire's real identity. Who said Bree wasn't good at politics?

A few seconds of silence passed.

Then Bree leaned forward. "For our next order of business, an alligator has been discovered living in Grey Lake."

Excited murmurs spread through the room as everyone reanimated, and Matt applauded her use of the distraction.

Bree continued. "We've fielded two calls regarding alligator sightings and have confirmed the animal's presence with a photograph. I'll have my office release a copy of that image for your use." Reporters shot out rapid-fire questions at the same time. Bree held up a hand. "The animal is estimated to be three feet in length. At this size, it is not expected to pose a significant threat to the community. In an abundance of caution, we suggest keeping your pets on leashes and away from the water's edge. We also advise staying out of the lake until we've caught the alligator. We've enlisted the help of a reptile expert from the zoo." Bree gave his name, his credentials, and the contact number of the zoo.

Someone yelled, "Where did it come from?"

"We don't know for certain, but the most likely explanation is that the animal was a pet that outgrew its enclosure and was released." Bree paused for effect. "Please don't do this."

A quick burst of quiet chuckling rippled through the crowd at her dry tone.

But the questions didn't stop. Reporters yelled over top of one another. They repeated themselves and hammered at Bree for every detail about the gator's activity. Bree answered a few questions, then silenced the group by simply holding up a hand. Pride surged in Matt at the way she commanded the room.

"We are doing everything in our power to capture the animal. We do not want anyone going after it on their own." She leaned closer to the mic and enunciated very clearly. "I will not tolerate hunting parties. Alligators tend to shy away from human activity, but if this one was raised and fed by humans, it might not. You might lose a body part you're attached to, and civilian interference will disturb the animal, drive it deeper into the wilderness, and hamper our efforts to capture it. We'd like to accomplish this without harming the animal, if possible. It's not the gator's fault it's in the wrong place."

Her gaze panned the room, and Matt knew she was making eye contact with cameras, letting the public know she was serious. Because he'd lived in this town his entire life, he also knew at least a dozen alligator hunting parties would be planned by morning.

She looked down and checked her phone, then ceded the mic back to Jager, leaving the politician to wrap up. She turned from the crowd and caught Matt's eyes. The gleam of her own hunting instincts shone

Melinda Leigh

in her gaze. Something was up with the investigation. He fell into step with her as they strode from the room.

"What's going on?" Matt asked in the corridor.

She shook her head and didn't answer until they were in the middle of the parking lot. "I told you Zucco's mom volunteered as an emergency foster for Claire?" She unlocked the SUV.

"Yes." Matt climbed into the passenger seat.

She closed her vehicle door and started the engine. "Someone was watching the house. Zucco found a baseball cap bearing the logo for A-Plus Cleaning in the vacant lot behind her place."

"You want to talk to Liam?"

"I do," Bree said. "We'll knock on his door and request an interview. If he sends us away and wants to meet us at the station in the morning with his attorney, that'll do."

"We can get a look at his biceps anyway."

"That's the thought." Bree drove to an older neighborhood. Mature oak trees lined the street, their roots pushing up entire blocks of sidewalk. Small houses crowded compact lots. Bree parked in front of Amanda Ward's house. Liam's description of a "crappy little dump" had been overly harsh. Sure, the homes were small. If you stood in the side yard, you could touch their house and the one next door at the same time. But most of the houses appeared well kept, and Amanda's bungalow was cottage-cute. She'd put clear effort into making it cozy. Flowerpots adorned her porch, and the door was freshly painted in a bright french blue. *Liam should appreciate his mother.*

A black Ford Explorer was parked at the curb. As they walked past the SUV, Matt touched the hood. "Still warm." Someone had driven it recently.

Bree led the way up the front walk. The sun had set, and twilight was rapidly fading.

Matt thought of Liam and his attitude and veered to the side. "I'll go around back, make sure he doesn't skip."

198

"Good plan."

"Give me two minutes." Matt crouched as he jogged through the side yard, discreetly looking into the windows on his way past. No sign of Liam. Matt emerged into a backyard the size of two parking spaces. He took a position at the corner of the house, out of sight but with a view of the back door.

The house was tiny, so he heard the front door open and Bree ask to speak with Liam.

"He isn't here, and he isn't talking to you without a lawyer," Amanda said. "I already called one. He says you can call him if you want to talk to Liam."

"His name?" Bree asked.

Amanda gave it. Having seen no sign of Liam, Matt returned to the sidewalk through the other side of the house. On the way, he might have peered into a few rooms. But he didn't see Liam in any of these rooms either.

Bree was on the sidewalk, staring down the street. A man stood on the porch of the house across the street, smoking a cigar.

Matt fell into step beside Bree as they approached him. "Good evening." She introduced them both.

The man smiled. "I know you, Sheriff. Are you looking for Liam?"

"We are."

The man snorted. "What did the little shit do?"

"You don't like him?" Matt asked.

"I don't like the way he treats his mama. She does everything to raise him right, and he's always looking to score easy cash. Too lazy to work hard." The neighbor crossed his arms.

"We want to talk to him," Bree said in a neutral voice. "Have you seen him?"

The man nodded. "Yesterday. Not today."

"Does Liam have a tattoo?" Matt asked.

The man puffed on his cigar. "He does. A big-ass tiger." The man patted his own bicep.

"Thank you very much." Bree took his contact information, and they walked back to the SUV. "Based on the tattoo and cap, we're going to request a search warrant for Liam's house. I'll call his attorney and arrange for him to come in for questioning. Hopefully, we can search his house while he's at the station."

Matt couldn't wait to arrest the man who'd chased Claire and shot a firearm in a residential neighborhood. "So back to the station?"

"Unfortunately." Bree drove in silence. On the way, she called home and they talked to the kids. Then they listened to the radio chatter for the rest of the trip.

They weren't in the conference room for more than three minutes before someone knocked on the door.

Juarez poked his head through the opening. "Sheriff? Some dude just walked in and confessed to killing the Masons."

CHAPTER TWENTY-EIGHT

Random confession? Matt was too jaded to think the case could be solved that easily.

He set down the dry-erase marker. "Who is he?"

Juarez checked his notes. "His name is Simon Osborne."

"Osborne . . ." Matt searched his memory. "Why does that name sound familiar?"

Bree shuffled some papers.

Juarez said, "We interviewed his mother, Elaine Osborne, in the neighborhood canvass."

"Found it." Bree lifted a paper from a folder. "Elaine Osborne lives on the same street as the Masons, six houses away."

"Is Simon her husband?"

Juarez shrugged. "Dunno. Want me to put him in an interview room?"

"Yes." Bree stood and started toward the door.

Matt followed her. "Why do I have a feeling this is going to get even weirder?"

"Seems to be the vibe for this case," Bree said.

"Yeah." Matt opened the door to the interview room as Juarez brought a bony, hairy man down the hall. He was about six feet tall, but scrawny in a malnourished way. His face was pale, his shaggy hair unwashed, and the scruff on his chin patchy.

"Aren't you going to handcuff me?" Simon asked Matt in a cheerful voice.

Bree turned to Juarez. "Did you check him for weapons?"

"Yes, ma'am." Juarez steered Simon into the room. "He's clean."

"Then we'll hold off on the handcuffs for the moment." Bree pointed to the monitoring room.

Juarez nodded.

Bree addressed Simon. "I'm Sheriff Taggert. This is Investigator Flynn."

Simon gave Matt a disappointed look. "She's your *boss*?"

"She is." Matt kept his voice neutral.

Simon shook his head.

After two seconds of silent communication with Bree, Matt took the lead. They both recognized Simon's not-so-subtle misogyny. While Matt would like nothing more than to school the dude, they'd get more information out of him by playing along with his prejudices.

Matt gestured toward a chair for Simon and took the seat next to him.

Bree sat on the opposite side of the table. "This interview is being recorded." She read his Miranda rights and asked him to sign the acknowledgment.

Simon scrawled his name with a flourish, in huge loopy letters, like he was signing the Declaration of Independence.

"So, Simon, what brings you to the sheriff's station today?" Matt set one elbow on the table, taking up some space.

Simon sat bolt upright, with both of his arms at his sides. He didn't lean or shuffle or cross his legs or arms. His posture was robotic. "I killed the Masons."

Bree collected the paper and set it aside. "How?"

"What do you mean, how?" Simon sounded annoyed. "I shot them?"

"Are you asking us or telling us?" Bree asked.

Simon rolled his eyes. "I'm telling you and wondering why you're asking."

Oh, boy.

Simon leaned forward. "I shot them in their bedroom. Made a real mess."

"Let's back up." Matt shifted forward, testing Simon's personal space requirements.

But Simon seemed oblivious. Most people shifted backward to reestablish their personal space boundary. Simon's posture didn't change an inch.

Matt switched the direction of his questioning. "How do you know the Masons?"

"I live down the street. Well, my mom does," Simon corrected himself. "I've been staying with her temporarily."

"For how long?" Bree asked.

"Four years." Simon shifted in his chair, as if the admission made him uncomfortable.

"Is your dad still living?" Matt guessed his dad had died or left.

"No." Something flashed in Simon's eyes, but he blinked it away. "He died."

"I'm sorry," Matt said.

Simon's sadness seemed low-key. "It was a long time ago, but thanks."

"Where is your mom right now?" Matt asked.

"She's at work." Simon seemed oddly disconnected. Some aspects of his demeanor were almost childish.

"So," Bree said. "Back to the Masons. Did you know them well?"

"I never even talked to her." Simon shook his head. "But I saw *him* every day." He pronounced *him* like *devil*.

"Him?" Bree asked.

"Josh." Simon hissed out the name.

"Did you like him?" Bree pressed.

"No." Simon was sure about this. "I know what kind of person he was."

Matt waited for him to elaborate, but he just sat there blinking back at them. Finally, Matt asked, "What kind?"

"The kind that poisons dogs," Simon said in a *duh* tone.

"Why do you say that?" Matt asked.

Simon's shoulders dropped with exasperation. "Because Josh Mason poisoned my mom's dog."

"Did you see him give the poison to the dog?" Bree asked.

"I don't need proof." Simon tapped his temple. "I know."

Matt's head ached. This was like trying to connect the dots without a pencil—or dots. He took a cleansing breath, then dived back in. "Why do you think Josh Mason poisoned your mom's dog?"

"He jogs past our house every day. Daisy jumps at the fence and barks at him. He doesn't like it." Simon's eyes narrowed. "I saw him throw a stick at her two weeks ago. A few days later, she got sick. She's OK, but the vet said she must've eaten something she shouldn't have." Simon sat back, as if this statement were enough.

"Dogs eat things," Bree said. "My own dog eats plenty of random objects: acorns, socks—"

"He did it!" Simon's face reddened. Then he sat back, muttering to himself. *"They don't know. Don't get mad. They don't know."*

The conversation was a hamster wheel.

Matt said, "So, you suspect—I'm sorry—you *know* that Josh poisoned Daisy, so you killed both Josh *and* Shelly."

Simon nodded, then held up a hand. "I only wanted to kill Josh. But Shelly was there, so . . ." He looked confused for a second but shook it off.

Matt watched his eyes go vague. "Are you sure?"

"Mostly." Simon seemed less sure now. "I blacked out that night. It happens, and when I wake up, I don't remember anything."

"Do you remember shooting the Masons?" Matt asked.

Simon's head tilted, like a crow's, but he didn't respond.

Matt tried another direction. "What about Claire? What do you have against her?"

Simon's head cocked in the other direction, like a bobblehead. "Nothing. Why?"

Matt didn't say anything about Claire being chased. "You killed her parents."

Simon shrugged, but his gaze shifted downward. He looked furtive in a Gollum-like way.

"Do you know Claire?" Matt asked.

Simon glanced away. "Sometimes, she jogs with Josh. She wears these tight running pants . . ." Simon blushed.

Oh, yes. He's seen Claire.

Bree clearly noticed it too. "Are you attracted to Claire?"

Simon didn't answer.

"She's a pretty girl." Matt whistled.

But Simon wouldn't even look at him, let alone answer.

Matt exhaled and stared at his shoes for a good thirty seconds. *I'm getting nowhere.* He didn't know if he should take Simon seriously. His attitude was almost cavalier—when it wasn't creepy. "If you blacked out, then how do you know you killed them?"

Simon leaned a few inches closer. "Because I wished it to happen."

Bree flattened both hands on the table. "You wished it?"

"Yes, I wished he was dead. I don't remember anything about that night. But in the morning, he was gone." Simon lowered his voice. "The same thing happened to my father. I wished he was dead, and then he was."

Matt wanted to look at Bree, but he didn't feel comfortable taking his attention off Simon, not even for a second.

"OK." Bree rose. "Well, I'm going to have Deputy Juarez put you in a cell while we check out your story."

"You're arresting me." Simon's eyes gleamed with excitement.

"We're going to hold you while we check out your statement," Bree said.

"You don't believe me?" Simon froze. A strange light shone in his eyes. "I blew them to pieces. Don't you care?"

"Of course we care," Bree assured him. "We're taking this very seriously."

"We have to verify what you've told us first," Matt said. "I'm sure you understand."

"Understand?" Simon's eyebrow rose. Other than the brow, nothing moved. He sat eerily still, like a mannequin. Only his eyeballs moved, like he was doing a complex math problem in his head. Then he exploded. Hissing like a movie vampire, Simon launched himself at Matt. Fingers bent like claws aimed straight at Matt's face. A nail scraped across Matt's skin, burning as it tore through flesh. Matt reacted instinctively, all the years of being used as his older brother's Jiu Jitsu practice dummy sending him into an automatic response. He tossed Simon sideways, the thin body twisting, flipping, and hitting the floor flat on his back with the heavy thud of a thrown sandbag. The air whooshed from his lungs.

Matt reached for the handcuffs on his belt and moved forward to restrain Simon.

Most people would have been down, gasping for oxygen like a trout on dry land. But not this dude. Didn't he need to breathe? Before Matt could wrestle Simon's arms behind his back, he rolled and attacked Matt again in a heartbeat. Simon's movements were frenzied, powered by rage, with zero finesse. It was like trying to subdue a giant, furious feral cat.

Or an octopus-cat hybrid with claws at the ends of all its tentacles.

Matt grabbed a wrist, maneuvered Simon's body, and put him in an arm bar. But the guy clearly didn't feel the pain of hyperextension. He thrashed wildly. Either he didn't realize Matt could break his elbow, or he didn't care. But Matt didn't have the heart to do it. The guy clearly had a mental illness or was on drugs, or both. Unwilling to seriously hurt the man, Matt finally lay on top of him, using his much greater body weight to pin him to the floor.

Simon was much stronger than he appeared. He bucked, creating enough space to turn his head, bare his teeth, and sink them into Matt's forearm.

"Fuck." Matt jerked his arm away, then forced Simon's cheek to the floor.

"I've got him. Shift over." Bree was at his side, cuffs in hand.

Matt carefully moved, keeping Simon's head pinned as the guy writhed under him. The cuffs snapped closed, but restraint didn't stop Simon. He spit at Matt as his head swiveled around as if he were possessed by demons.

The door opened. Juarez and Todd charged in. Someone brought a bite mask. It took both Todd and Juarez to secure it into place around Simon's head. Another deputy supplied leg shackles. When Simon was finally trussed up, he looked like Hannibal Lecter. Normally, Matt didn't like restraints, but they had no other option, not with a biting, spitting, clearly ill suspect. Simon was a threat to himself and others, and safety had to be the priority.

Every cop in the room was breathing hard and sweating as they stood in a circle around Simon, whose body had finally gone limp. Except his eyes. His gaze still jerked wildly around the room.

"Holy . . ." Matt was dumbfounded. He wiped spittle from his cheek. "Wow."

"Yeah. Wow," Bree agreed.

"I feel like Steve Irwin after he wrestled a twelve-foot croc." Matt's chest heaved. Warm blood dribbled down his face and dripped from his arm.

"What do we do with him?" Juarez asked.

"He's going to the hospital for drug testing and a psych eval," Bree said.

"Should I put him in a cell?" Juarez gaze the suspect a wary look.

"Yes, but I want him under constant, close surveillance. That's eyes on him every second. Make sure he's breathing and as comfortable as possible given the circumstances. We don't know if he took drugs before he came in here."

"You want me to transport him?" Juarez stared down, his eyes full of doubt.

Bree shook her head. "He might hurt himself in the back of a patrol car. Call for an ambulance and let them know what happened so they come prepared."

"Yes, ma'am." But Juarez didn't look entirely comfortable as he stepped to Simon's side.

"I'll help." Todd took the prisoner's other arm. "Let's get your feet under you, Simon."

Bree led Matt to the break room.

He leaned on the counter. His face and arm stung, and his heart was racing. For a skinny guy, Simon had been strong. "I can't believe I let him catch me flat-footed."

"I didn't expect that either." Bree scrutinized his face. "I'll get the first aid kit. You should probably go to the ER. Human bites are nasty."

"I'll call my dad. We can stop by their house on the way home." His father was a mostly retired physician who kept up his medical license. Matt tried not to flinch as Bree cleaned the bite wound with antiseptic and wrapped gauze around his arm.

"At least the scratch on your face is shallow. Your beard protected your skin somewhat." She doused a cotton ball and dabbed it on his cheek.

He suppressed the hiss at the sting.

Todd appeared in the doorway. "He's in the holding cell. Seems quiet for now. Juarez is watching him, and the ambulance is on the way."

"I'll be glad when they take custody," Bree said. "He's too unpredictable."

"That was something," Matt agreed.

"You think he did it?" Todd asked.

"I don't know what to think," Bree said. "He doesn't have a tattoo, and the details he knew about the crimes were all on the news." Her lips pursed. "Get a full background check and a search warrant for his house. Maybe we'll get a match on his shoe treads or fingerprints."

"Find out how his father died," Matt added.

Bree nodded. "We'll talk to his mother." She checked the time. "Do the warrant paperwork and assign a deputy to run a full background check. Then go home and get some sleep."

"I'm on it." Todd left.

"You think there's anything to Simon's story?" Matt stood.

"There's a lot of baggage to unpack here." Bree closed the first aid kit, slid it into the cabinet, and tossed the wrappers.

"So much," Matt agreed.

Could it be that simple? Matt wanted to prove Simon killed the Masons. They wouldn't have to worry about Claire anymore. But in his experience, nothing was that easy.

CHAPTER TWENTY-NINE

Bree rolled over the next morning straight into a giant wet dog nose. Ladybug stared directly into her eyes, the dog's square face about an inch from Bree's. "Good morning."

The dog's tail stub wagged hard.

"Any chance you could bring me a double shot of espresso?" Bree asked her.

Ladybug pawed at the blanket with strong feet.

"OK, OK. I'm getting up. Geez." She tossed back the blanket and swung her feet off the edge of the mattress.

With her job done, the dog leaped from the bed. Bree heard her heavy steps going as she descended the steps as gracefully as a buffalo.

Tempted, Bree glanced back at her pillow, but the sounds of people moving about the kitchen downstairs stopped her. She'd missed dinner and bedtime the night before. She would have breakfast with the kids if she had to crawl down the steps. Matt's side of the bed was empty, and from the sound of water running, he was in the shower.

They hadn't gotten home until after midnight, and she'd slept fitfully. She stretched a kink in her back and stood, her spine cracking.

Feeling old and stiff, she shuffled to the bathroom. Matt opened the sliding glass door and leaned out. "Want to join me?"

She eyed the lack of steam. "That water is cold, right?"

"Yes. It's bracing and good for inflammation."

She shuddered at the thought. "Then no. To be more specific, no way in hell."

But he reached out, snagged her with a wet arm around her waist, and dragged her in. The cold water sluiced over her body and soaked her pajamas. Shock raised goose bumps everywhere.

Laughing, she shivered, and her teeth chattered. "I'm going to get so even. Let me go."

"Nope." He pulled her close and blocked the spray. Reaching behind him, he adjusted the faucet. A minute later, the water warmed.

Bree melted into him. "I don't know how or why you tolerate cold showers." She turned, splaying her hands on his impressive chest. "I heard the kids downstairs."

He kissed her. "Nope. That's Dana. The kids aren't awake yet."

"They'll be up any minute." But she raised her arms as he pulled her sopping tank top over her head and dropped it in the corner of the shower.

He lifted his mouth from the curve of her neck and stared down at her. "Unless we have to get to work—"

Bree cut him off with a finger on his lips. "No. No work talk. We need—and deserve—a normal morning to ourselves." If there was one thing she'd learned since moving back to Grey's Hollow, it was that they needed more to their lives than crime. "But I do want to have breakfast with the kids."

"As much as I prefer to linger, I can work fast when it's required." Matt trailed a kiss down her jaw to her collarbone.

Bree laughed. "Not too fast, I hope."

"Don't worry. I'm thorough."

And he was.

Twenty minutes later, Bree dried herself on the bath mat. Matt stepped out of the shower and wrapped a towel around his waist. "I hope that was better than espresso."

She waggled a hand from side to side. His face fell.

Bree couldn't keep a straight face. She laughed out loud and snapped the towel at him. "That's what you get for dragging me into a cold shower."

He grinned and kissed her again. "Go get your precious coffee."

"I will." She sauntered into the bedroom, dressed in her uniform, and jogged downstairs.

She took a cappuccino out onto the back porch. She sat and watched the horses graze for ten minutes. The door opened and Kayla came out, carrying a glass of milk. She took the seat next to Bree.

"I missed you last night," Bree said. "What did you have for dinner?"

"We made pizza. I got to stretch my own dough."

"Sounds great." Bree sipped. "Do you have plans for the day?"

Kayla nodded. "Shannon is having a pool party."

"Fun." Bree didn't have to ask about safety. She knew Shannon's mom would watch them like the Secret Service on the president. "Last hurrah before school starts."

"I can't wait for school!" Kayla drank her milk and wiped her upper lip with the back of her hand. "I love it."

"How are we even related?" Bree teased, satisfied that Kayla, despite the trauma and grief she'd already experienced, was a happy child. By leaving her career in Philadelphia, Bree had allowed Kayla and Luke to retain their own home, their school, their friends. She'd given them the gift of stability. And she received far more in return than she could ever quantify.

Kayla grinned. "I'm hungry."

They went inside, where Luke and Matt were already chowing down on Dana's french toast. They took their time eating, listening to Kayla's happy chatter.

After eating a ridiculous amount of food, Luke pushed back his plate. "Can I borrow Cowboy tomorrow? I want to take a friend on a trail ride."

"A friend?" Bree asked. "Can she ride?"

Luke blushed. "Her name is Maya, and I don't know."

"Is Maaaaa-ya your girlfriend?" Kayla asked in a teasing, singsong voice.

Luke rolled his eyes. "She's a friend."

But his red cheeks suggested he'd like her to be more than that. "You can borrow Cowboy, but if she hasn't ridden before and she's small enough, Pumpkin might be a better option, if it's OK with Kayla."

Kayla's sturdy little Haflinger should be sainted.

"She's very small. Is that OK with you?" Luke asked his sister.

"Sure. Pumpkin likes girls." Kayla bobbed her head. "And he's a very good boy."

"Plan to go early," Bree said. "Before it gets too hot, but I don't have to tell you any of this. You know horses better than I do." And because it was required now that she was a parent, she added, "Be careful."

"Thanks." Unbelievably, he forked yet another slice of french toast onto his plate. He'd become an eating and growing machine. She was grateful for shorts so she didn't need to buy him pants every eight weeks.

Thirty minutes later, Bree drove to the station in a much better mood. "I feel like a new person. It's amazing what an hour or two of normal will do."

"Truly." Matt stepped out of the vehicle. They entered through the back door. Matt veered toward the conference room while Bree headed straight for her office. She set her stainless-steel thermos full of cappuccino on the desk and booted up her computer.

Marge appeared in the doorway. "You look like you're in a good mood."

"Breakfast with the kids."

"Well, hold on to that feeling." Foreboding filled Marge's voice.

"Please don't burst my bubble, Marge."

Marge sighed. "Jager is here."

"Already?" Bree kept her tone even, but inside she was whining. Her positive mood deflated like a released balloon. It was too early to deal with politics. "There should be a rule prohibiting early-morning visits from bureaucrats."

"Sorry." Marge nodded toward Bree's travel mug. "Do you need more coffee?"

Bree lifted her cappuccino. "No. I'm good. Dana put extra shots in this. Bring her in."

"Your poor heart." Marge shook her head and walked away.

Bree took a bracing sip as Jager strode in. Her face was expressionless, as usual, but Bree detected the vague signs of concern bracketing Jager's mouth. Today's suit was an eye-popping fuchsia that not many people could have pulled off. Jager managed the color with flair.

She closed the door behind her, never a good sign. "We need to talk." She planted herself in one of the chairs facing Bree's desk.

"What happened?"

"Two things." She held up a perfectly manicured finger. Her polish matched her suit. "One, Pamela Sawyer and her attorney held their own press conference late last night."

Bree sagged back into her chair. She couldn't suppress the *ugh* that slipped from her lips.

"Exactly," Jager said. "They doubled down on all that BS about you keeping her daughter away from her. Is it true that Claire is staying with one of your deputies?"

"How the hell did they get that information?"

214

Jager shrugged off the question, as if it didn't matter. "What were you thinking?"

"Claire likes my deputy, who lives with her mother, who is retired NYPD. It seemed like a good solution since we suspect Claire could be in danger."

"Stop calling her Claire. Her name is Blaire, and she has a family that wants her back."

Bree pushed her mug away, the coffee souring in her gut. "Claire isn't ready. She was in tears. Was Pam sober for the press con? Because she sure as hell wasn't when she came to meet her daughter."

Jager cocked her head. If frowning were possible, she probably would have. "Hard to say. Sober enough. I mean, she looked like hell, but in this instance, that worked for her in generating sympathy. Her attorney did most of the talking. Sawyer mostly cried and looked sad."

"I don't understand why she would do this to Claire. Why not give the kid a day or two?"

The look Jager gave Bree was full of *my sweet summer child* vibes. "*You* wouldn't understand. *You* aren't a political animal. *You* don't have an alternate agenda. You have empathy and standards and ethics." She rolled a hand as if those things were superfluous.

Is Jager trying to be helpful? She understood politics and alternative agendas. That was for sure. Bree rocked forward, her chair squeaking. "And you think Pam Sawyer has an agenda?"

Jager's eyes narrowed. "Definitely."

"What do you think she wants?"

"What does everyone want?" Jager stated in a matter-of-fact voice. "Money."

"Her daughter returned after being missing for twelve years. That doesn't happen very often. She could have a book deal tomorrow."

"Did she strike you as a memoir writer?"

"It's her story. She doesn't have to write it. She could do interviews and podcasts. The ways to monetize the situation are endless, though most people would want to focus on getting to know their long-lost child, at least for the immediate future."

Jager's half smile was indulgent. "You're kind of amazing. After all the shitty things you must have seen people do in your career, after your own personal tragedies, you're still an optimist. You still think most people are good at heart."

A memory floated into Bree's mind. The worn farmhouse kitchen of her childhood. Bree sat at the table, copying spelling words. Her mother handed her a wooden spoon dripping with batter. The taste of vanilla and sugar flooded Bree's mouth. Masculine laughter sounded so real; it almost made her turn her head to look for the source. Her father walked into view. He wrapped his arms around his wife and nuzzled the back of her neck.

The image burst like a bubble from a child's wand. Bree nearly gasped at the flood of emotions. She covered her reaction with a cough. *Where did that come from?*

Jager shifted forward, resting her clasped hands on the edge of Bree's desk. "How many horrible acts do parents commit against their children?"

Still reeling from the memory, Bree didn't respond. She hoped the question had been rhetorical because her throat was locked tight.

Jager continued. "People hurt the ones they love every day."

Was she referring to acts Bree had witnessed in law enforcement? Or her parents' violent history? Her father had been obsessed with the wife he viewed as his possession. He'd been determined to keep her forever, even if that meant he had to take her to the grave with him. His love had been as real as his rage.

"People sell their kids for drugs," Jager said. "Kids are molested and murdered by their own parents. Using your kid's disappearance to make a few bucks seems tame in comparison." She paused, her attention riveted on Bree. "Are you all right?"

"Yes." Bree's answer felt hoarse. To clear her throat, she sipped her now-tasteless cappuccino. "How do you think Pam will try to use the situation to make money?"

"Maybe she'll sue the county. Maybe she'll sue you personally, though that would probably be extra. Pam's a hot mess, but her attorney looked sharp. He'll know the big bucks come from the government."

"What would she sue us for?"

Jager threw up her hands. "Who knows? If she has enough public support, she'll get a settlement. Right or wrong won't matter. The county will only assess which is cheaper, paying her off or going to court."

Bree rubbed her forehead.

"I know politics give you a headache," Jager said, her voice ringing with sympathy that sounded genuine. "I also know you and I don't see eye to eye on many issues. But politics is my jam, as the kids say. This is one time you should probably take my advice."

Bree's hand dropped to her lap. "Which is?"

"You have a couple of options. One, hold another press conference. Say how upset Claire is, et cetera. Fight fire with fire, to be cliché." Jager unclasped her fingers and tapped one on the desk. "Or you can hand the kid over and say she needed a little space to process the shock. People will buy that. You'll look good."

"It's not up to me. This is a decision for Claire, social services, and a judge."

"That's not how it appears."

"And that's all that's important."

Jager tossed up a palm. "Now, issue number two."

There's more? Fuck.

"The Wards' attorney has also been busy. They're filing a harassment suit against you and the county."

"Harassment? Liam is a murder suspect. I'm not convinced that Simon Osborne is guilty."

"Osborne confessed." Jager enunciated the words clearly. "You don't understand optics, do you? You're investigating Liam for the murders of Josh and Shelly Mason while you simultaneously already have a suspect in custody for those murders."

The good news? Bree didn't need any more caffeine. Her blood was pumping with anger.

"Simon hasn't been charged with murder. He's in custody because he attacked—and bit—Matt."

Jager lifted a *whatever* shoulder. "I know you're mad. If I were in your shoes, I would be too. But don't be mad at me. I'm just the messenger here. It's hard for you to believe, but I'm trying to help you." Her tone softened. "I know I haven't always had your back. When the governor appointed you, I didn't think you were a good choice for sheriff. You didn't—and still don't—have a sufficiently cold heart for politics. But I've come to learn that you are one hell of a cop. You're smart. You're ballsy as all hell. You're a certifiable badass—which is marketable, by the way. But most importantly, you put the community first. You risk your life to keep people safe." The corner of Jager's mouth tipped upward. "And by doing those things, you've become very popular. The public has taken note of your heroic qualities. Who would have thought taking the high road could pay off."

Bree was truly speechless for several seconds. "I don't know what to say. Thank you?"

"You're welcome. But will you take my advice?"

"I make no promises. It's a lot to process."

"Of course you would never make a promise you weren't certain you could keep." Jager breathed. "I'll sum it up. One, get Claire back to her family. Two, lay off on Liam Ward until you know if Osborne is guilty."

"I'll take your suggestions under advisement."

Jager grinned. "Now that was an excellent political response." She stood and smoothed her skirt. "Please keep me in the loop. I mean it. I can help you interpret this politics/optics nonsense you abhor."

"I appreciate the offer." Bree remained neutral. While Jager had been softening toward her lately, their relationship didn't exactly feel like teamwork. More like frenemies? But she did have to admit that Jager excelled in the political arena.

"I am available if you need more advice." Jager left Bree's office.

Bree stared at the empty doorway, feeling like she'd just survived a natural disaster, something sudden and unpredictable, like a tornado.

Marge appeared. "I didn't see any steam coming out of her ears. What happened?"

"Some bad things, but Jager was . . ." Bree was still uncertain. "Helpful?"

"That's . . ." Marge paused, clearly searching for the right word. "Disconcerting. Will you take her advice?"

"I don't know yet. I have some work to do." Bree went to the conference room. Matt paced in front of the murder board. Todd was typing reports.

Todd looked up from his laptop. "I have good news and bad news."

"I could use some good news. Start there." Bree dropped into a chair.

"The search warrant for Simon's place came through."

"And the bad news?"

"The one for Liam's was denied." Todd frowned.

"I was afraid that would happen." Bree summed up her conversation with Jager.

Matt pivoted. "It's understandable. The logic is sound from a legal perspective."

Bree agreed. "Simon has backed us into a corner. We have no choice but to focus on him, but I was hoping to also keep pursuing Liam as a suspect. I guess we're following Jager's advice on this one. We determine the validity of Simon's confession and work from there. Let's start with his mother."

CHAPTER THIRTY

A half hour later, Matt leaned on the kitchen counter and studied Mrs. Osborne. Still dressed in blue work scrubs, she sat in stunned silence across her kitchen table from Bree. Mrs. Osborne was a tall woman, with broad shoulders and strong hands. Her hair, more salt than pepper, was pulled back in a simple ponytail. She seemed capable, intelligent, and utterly exhausted.

Bree unfolded the warrant. "We need to search the house."

Mrs. Osborne waved a cooperative hand. "Simon spends most of his time in his computer room. It's upstairs, across the hall from his bedroom." She hadn't seemed surprised or angry when they showed up on the doorstep with the news about Simon's confession.

Bree motioned to Todd, who started up the steps with two deputies in tow.

A white pit bull—Matt assumed this was Daisy, the dog Simon claimed Josh Mason had poisoned—barked and scratched on the other side of the glass patio door.

"She's friendly, but she'll get in your way." Mrs. Osborne stood, crossed to the fridge, and took a rubber KONG toy out of the freezer. She opened the patio door and handed the KONG to the wiggling, wagging dog. "That's a good girl." She closed the door. The dog lay on the patio with the toy between her front paws. "She loves frozen peanut butter." She returned to her chair. "Do you mind if I make some coffee?

I've been up all night, and it doesn't seem like I'm going to get any sleep anytime soon."

"That's fine, ma'am," Bree said.

Mrs. Osborne moved around the bright kitchen. Morning sunlight poured through the window over the sink. The furniture was a bit worn, but the house was clean and pleasant with rustic farmhouse decor. "The biggest surprise to me is that Simon confessed. He likes to get away with things. Then again, he also likes to prove he's smarter than everyone else, and if he doesn't tell anyone, who would know? But there's one thing I'm sure about. He hated Josh Mason."

"Why?" Matt asked.

Mrs. Osborne put a pod into the machine and placed a mug under the spout. She pressed a button, and the machine gurgled to life. "He thinks Josh poisoned Daisy, but I don't think he did. Daisy is always eating something she shouldn't. Last month, she puked up a golf ball. The month before, the neighbor's kid left a box of crayons outside. Daisy was pooping rainbows for days." She looked away, the corners of her mouth dragging down. "Josh would run past this house every morning. Simon likes to sit on the porch and watch the neighborhood. He expects people to stop and talk to him. Most people don't want to do that. They're busy, and frankly, he can be unsettling. Still, most folks are polite. They wave and say hi, make an excuse, like 'Hi, Simon, gotta get to work. Have a great day.' But Josh ran on by. He completely ignored Simon, and that made him mad." She took a breath and studied her clasped hands for a moment. "Simon fixates on things, and everything makes him angry when he's in that mood. I've tried to get him help, but he won't go. I can't make him. I don't know what to do. My only option is to kick him out. But how will that help? He'd be homeless." Her eyes were sad, but almost relieved. She flattened a palm at the base of her throat. "I've been living with the fear that he'd hurt someone for years. I haven't slept since the Masons were killed."

"Do you think he killed them?" Bree asked.

"I don't know what to think. I hope not." The coffee finished brewing, and she lifted the mug. "Coffee?" Bree shook her head. Mrs. Osborne added a drop of cream and a teaspoon of sugar to her coffee and stirred. "I need to get him an attorney."

"If he can't afford a lawyer, one will be appointed for him," Bree said.

"Does Simon have money?" Matt couldn't imagine Simon holding down a job.

"No, but I have a little rainy-day fund from his father's life insurance. A private attorney would be best, right?" Mrs. Osborne dropped back into her chair at the table and wiped a tear from her eye.

"Public defenders can be good," Bree said in a neutral tone.

They were hit-or-miss in Matt's opinion.

Mrs. Osborne's chest heaved with an exhausted sigh. "You must think I'm a horrible mother. I probably shouldn't be cooperating with you. It's not that I don't want him to be innocent. I don't want him to have hurt anyone. But I need to know the truth before I can help him."

Matt's heart bled for her. "You're in a terrible situation."

She eyed Matt's bandaged arm. "When you arrived, you said he'd confessed to murder but that he was arrested for assaulting a law enforcement officer. Was that you?"

"Yes, ma'am." Matt didn't mention that his father had given him an antibiotic shot and a ten-day course of medicine. Apparently, the bacteria in a human mouth were worse than a dog's. Matt was grateful humans had blunt teeth instead of big pointy ones.

"I'm sorry." She lifted her mug with both hands and sipped her coffee, the movements mechanical.

Matt nodded. It wasn't Simon's fault, and Matt bore him no ill will, but he also didn't want Simon to hurt anyone else. He didn't want that uncontrolled rage turned on a defenseless person. The person—or Simon—could be severely injured.

Or killed, if Simon was telling the truth.

"Simon says he blacked out the night the Masons were shot," Bree said. "Were you home that night?"

Mrs. Osborne shook her head. "I'm a nurse at the hospital. I was on night shift. Seven to seven, like last night." She flushed, not a healthy burst of color, but two bright spots on an otherwise pale face, as if she had spiked a fever. "I give Simon a sleeping pill crushed in his dinner. I'm not proud of it, but I don't know what else to do. He gets agitated as soon as the sun goes down. I'm afraid to go to work or close my eyes."

"Did you give him one last tonight?" Bree asked. "Because he came into the station late in the evening."

"I did." Mrs. Osborne frowned. "Maybe he didn't eat his dinner." Her face fell into her hands. She lifted her chin, her eyes bleary and bleak. "He must suspect what I've been doing."

Which meant if Simon came home, his mother would never sleep again. Did that also mean he'd be angry with her? Was she not safe?

"Are you afraid of him?" Matt asked.

She tilted her head. "I worry about other people. I don't think he'd hurt me."

Think?

The bite on Matt's arm and the scratch on his face burned. He had fifty pounds of muscle on Simon, and he'd barely been able to defend himself. Simon had superhuman strength. "Do you have a gun in the house?"

"No!" she answered. "I would never take the risk. There's no lock or safe he wouldn't be able to crack. For all Simon's issues, he can be brilliant."

Bree's voice gentled. "How did your husband die?"

"He had a heart attack." Mrs. Osborne looked puzzled. "Why?"

"Simon suggested he was responsible," Matt said.

Mrs. Osborne's brows dropped. "I don't see how. The doctor called it a *widow-maker*. Phil had hereditary heart disease, and he ate bacon every single day, no matter how much I begged him to stop. His arteries were so blocked, they could have been filled with glue."

"Simon said he wished his father dead, and then it happened," Bree explained.

"Simon also says he can control the weather with his mind, so take what he says with a grain." Mrs. Osborne lifted a palm. "My husband was a good man, but he refused to believe Simon was mentally ill. He thought he could use normal discipline to change Simon. He used to say, 'We have to be firm and consistent. He'll come around.' But sending him to his room, grounding him, or taking away his electronics made things worse, not better. We had a time-out chair when he was little. My husband would send him to the chair if he misbehaved to think about what he'd done and why it had been wrong. On the surface, he was a little boy sitting silently the way he'd been told. But I could see from his eyes that he wasn't sorry. He was seething."

The word *plotting* jumped into Matt's mind. Goose bumps rippled up his arms. Simon sounded like that little kid from *The Omen*.

"He's gotten worse over the years. He's paranoid. He has delusions. He believes every conspiracy theory on the internet. You don't know how many times I've disconnected our router or canceled our Wi-Fi service to try and keep him off the internet. The problem is, Simon is smarter than I am. To him, it's a game, and he wins every time."

"Ma'am?" Todd called from the hallway. "You need to see this."

Matt and Bree followed him up the stairs. In the hallway, Todd gestured toward a dark room, where a gloved deputy rummaged through a dresser drawer. "That's Simon's bedroom. We didn't find much in there, but . . ." He stopped at the opposite doorway. "This is Simon's computer room."

Compared to the pleasant space downstairs, Simon's room felt like a cave. The walls were painted flat black. The blinds were closed tightly, and strips of duct tape sealed the edges where sunlight might peer through. A huge desk with multiple wide-screen monitors dominated the space. The setup reminded Matt of a mall security office—or the bridge of the *Enterprise*.

Todd gestured toward one of the screens. On it, what appeared to be a dead body lay in the middle of a dark street. Cops clustered around the corpse. Except, the scene wasn't quite authentic . . . Some parts seemed blurry or pixelated.

Todd waved toward the computer tower under the desk. "This is quite a setup. I'd like to get Rory in here. But this was on the screen when we woke the computer. There's a whole file of pictures like these. Hundreds of them."

Matt crouched to get a better view of the screen. *Wait . . .* He recognized a TV actor from a popular detective series. The picture *wasn't* a real crime scene. "Is this a screenshot from one of the *CSI* shows?"

"We think so," Todd said. "He has multiple streaming services set up on his computer. Most of his favorites seem to be crime shows."

"They have to be TV scenes." Bree rapped a knuckle on an image of a woman in designer slacks and a leather jacket. "I don't know any real female detectives that wear four-inch heels to a crime scene. Can you imagine stepping on roaches, rat droppings, or blood in those?"

Matt glanced down at Bree's sturdy boots.

Bree looked away from the screen. "OK. Simon was fixated on TV detective shows. That isn't a crime. *CSI* is one of the most popular shows ever, isn't it?"

"It's not just a screenshot." Todd pointed to the body on the screen. "Look closer."

Bree and Matt both leaned in.

Matt squinted. "The face looks . . . wrong?"

"Yes." Todd zoomed in.

And Matt saw it. "Oh."

Bree gasped. "That's Josh."

Todd nodded. "Josh Mason's face has been photo edited onto the corpse." He clicked the mouse, moving through more images of TV corpses, all bearing Josh's face. He'd been hung, decapitated, buried alive, shot, stabbed, and suffocated, and that was only in the images they'd opened.

"You said there are hundreds of these?" Bree stepped back.

"Yep," said Todd. "On this computer, Josh has been killed over and over, in every way imaginable. And TV is quite creative."

"And yet Simon simply chose a gun as his murder weapon," Bree mused.

"We need to find out where he got the gun." Matt straightened and tore his eyes off the screen. The images confirmed Mrs. Osborne's statement. Simon hated Josh Mason.

CHAPTER THIRTY-ONE

By afternoon, Bree was back in the station. Her deputies were completing the search of Simon's house. Rory had collected the computer equipment and personal electronic devices. Simon's shoes had been taken for comparison to the partial footprint outside the Masons' house. Fibers, hair, dust, and DNA had been collected to compare to trace evidence found at the crime scene. Unfortunately, all this would take time.

If Simon had invented his story for attention, time would work against them and could potentially allow the real killer to get away with murder.

Matt brought two sandwiches into the conference room. "Chicken or turkey?"

"Chicken." Bree unwrapped it, then set it down. "We found a lot of evidence that Simon had been obsessing about killing Josh Mason. Why do I not like him for the murders? Do I have a problem with moving on if that's where the evidence leads?"

"We've been fixated on Liam. Ideas like that take hold. But our stubbornness doesn't mean we're right."

"What about the tattoo?" Bree asked. "Did we put too much emphasis on *it* as well?"

Matt bit into his turkey sub and chewed thoughtfully. After he washed the food down with Coke, he said, "Maybe the mistake we made was assuming that the murderer was the same person who's chasing Claire."

Bree lifted her sandwich and took a mechanical bite. "Why would anyone else be after her?"

"Most crimes are about money. The Masons were grifters. Did anyone else know about their financial scheme? Maybe Liam? Takes one to know one, right?" Matt ate the rest of his sub in a few more bites.

Bree opened her sandwich and ate a pickle. "If Liam figured out what the Masons were up to, maybe he wanted a piece."

"Maybe he thinks Claire has information or a way to access more money."

"She's a kid," Bree said.

"Liam was running scams when he was young," Matt pointed out. "People project their own desires onto others. Liam likes scams. He thinks he's entitled to money that isn't his. He probably assumes everyone thinks that way. If Liam's mom was running a grift, Liam would want in on it. So he might assume Claire has knowledge of her parents' scam."

"Ironically, Amanda seems honest."

"And Liam seems to see that as a weakness."

"Liam had burner phones when he was arrested on the other charges." Bree shoved the food aside and reached for her laptop. She scrolled through reports. "Yes. The police suspected Liam of selling burner phones for illegal activity, but they couldn't prove it. Josh Mason had a burner phone in his vehicle, and there were three prepaid phones in the go-bags."

Matt shook his head. "Common brands, sold at convenience stores everywhere. There's no way to tie them to Liam. Every good criminal knows about burners."

"That's the problem with this case: too many criminals, including the victims." Disappointed, Bree returned to her sandwich.

"Everyone is up to no good," Matt agreed. "But it's a big leap from Liam's gift-card scam to killing two people. The Masons were executed. That was not a spur-of-the-moment decision."

"So, you think Liam is innocent?"

"Innocent in general, maybe not, but we haven't proven he's guilty of murder."

"You're right." Bree stood and stretched. Her phone vibrated. "This is the hospital. I'm waiting for a call from the doctor." As sheriff, Bree was responsible for the jail and all its prisoners, including those in the hospital. She answered the call. "Sheriff Taggert."

"This is Dr. Ingram. I'm the psychiatrist who's treating Simon Osborne."

"What do you think so far?" Bree asked.

The doctor answered, "It's too early to say."

"Is he going to jail or are you keeping him?"

"He's currently on a seventy-two-hour psych hold." The doctor hesitated. "Obviously, we need to do more testing before we can reach an accurate diagnosis, but schizophrenia is one possibility."

"Can we question him?" Bree asked.

"No. There's no point, and I won't risk the fragile stability we've achieved overnight. He's sedated and relatively calm today. What he says doesn't mean much anyway. He's delusional. He has hallucinations. He is having a severe psychiatric episode—a crisis."

"Are schizophrenics typically dangerous?"

"In general, mentally ill people are more likely to be victims of crime than perpetrators. It's more common to see suicide than murder," the doctor said. "That said, Simon does have violent outbursts, so I can't say no for sure."

"Why would he confess to a crime he didn't commit?"

"He might actually think he did it. He doesn't know what's real and what isn't."

"What do you think will happen after your seventy-two hours are up?" Bree asked.

"I think it's likely we'll seek a court order to keep him longer. We used to think disorders like schizophrenia were hopeless, but we have good treatment options now. It's possible for Mr. Osborne to make a significant recovery with a combination of medication and cognitive behavioral therapy. But it's complicated. Let us get through the next few days, and we'll touch base again."

Bree ended the call. "Talking to Simon is pointless." Her phone vibrated. "It's Rory." She answered the call. "You're on speaker. Matt is also here."

"First of all, I prioritized comparing Simon's shoes, as you asked. They do not match the partial shoe print found in the Masons' back garden. Because the print was only a partial, we were unable to determine the exact shoe size, but it's between a men's nine and eleven. Simon wears a ten and a half. So, even though we didn't find the matching shoe, Simon does wear the correct size."

"He could have disposed of the shoes he wore to commit the crime," Matt said.

Disappointment filled Bree. She wanted something solid, not wishy-washy possibilities. "What else?"

"We've analyzed the trace evidence from the original scene. There's one thing that's a little unusual." Rory paused. "We originally found gray animal fur. Since the Masons owned a gray cat, I didn't think much about this at first. But the fur isn't from a domestic cat. It's from a mountain lion."

"Did you say *mountain lion*?" Matt spun.

"Yes," Rory said in a cheerful voice. "I supply the results. Thankfully, it's up to you to decide if they're meaningful and if so, how."

Bree thanked him and ended the call.

Matt shrugged. "We all know people pick up weird trace evidence. The shooter could work at the zoo. Or possibly one of the Masons had recently been to the zoo. If someone walked through the cat house, they could potentially pick up a bit of cougar fur."

"I'll find out if anyone in the Mason household had visited the zoo recently." Bree made a note to call Claire and to have Juarez check the Masons' credit card statements for any recent charges at a zoo.

"Or." Matt tapped his marker on his opposite palm. "What if the same person who tracked cougar fur into the Masons' house also sold the illegal wolf pup my sister confiscated."

"And the alligator in Grey Lake?" Bree asked.

Matt paced. "That could have come from the guy we arrested last winter. We know he sold baby alligators." He whirled, gesturing with the marker. "But we're receiving reports of an increase in exotic pet trading. Maybe we're dealing with one of those. It can't be a coincidence that Cady found a wolf pup, and a few days later, we run across cougar fur at a crime scene."

"Does your sister know where the wolf came from?"

"I have the general location and a description of the guy who had the pup."

"Then we should take a drive." Bree needed air anyway. The conference room, murder board, and lack of progress on the case were making her antsy.

"Let me call Cady and get as much information as I can."

"I'll check in with Marge while you do that." Bree returned to her office, checked her messages, then touched base with her administrator.

By the time she was done, Matt was ready. They left via the rear door. The GPS led them to an old neighborhood of skinny houses on weedy lots. There was barely enough room between the buildings to run a lawn mower. Not that it appeared that had been needed recently. The small lawns were scorched to dirt in places.

Matt pointed to a faded blue house with a front porch made of cracked concrete. The entire structure listed to the left, like the foundation was compromised. "That's the house where Cady picked up a dog. She said the guy with the wolf pup was hanging out on the corner."

"No one is there now." Bree scanned the block.

"Do we knock on doors or stake out the place?"

Bree reached for her door handle. "Let's talk to people. A stakeout will take hours, and we'd have to get another vehicle. Plus, we busted a meth lab on the next street recently. The neighbors were grateful to be rid of it. Let's go talk to them."

She drove around the corner and parked at the curb in front of the boarded-up meth house. Bree led the way to the house next door, where a man in his fifties answered her knock.

"Sheriff Taggert!" He stepped out onto the porch. "What can I do for you?"

Bree introduced Matt. "We're looking for someone. Early thirties, six one or two, shaved head. Has a tattoo of a sword and roses on his forearm."

"I know a guy who looks like that," the man said. "His name is Shawn. He lives in the gray house on Fourth Street. I don't know the number. But he drives one of those monster trucks. It's black with purple flames on the sides." He rolled his eyes. "You can't miss it."

"Thank you for the information." Bree shook his hand.

"Well, I sure appreciated you getting rid of the drug house." He jerked a thumb at the neighboring lot. "The county is trying to get the place condemned and knocked down. I'm sure it'll take a while, but in the meantime, at least no one is going to blow up the block."

Bree eyed the vacant house. Graffiti already covered the plywood nailed over the windows. "If you see anything concerning, you call us." She made a mental note to have a patrol car check on the property frequently. The last thing the neighborhood needed was squatters.

"Will do," he said.

They got back into their vehicle. Bree cruised to Fourth Street, two blocks away. The black-and-purple monster truck was, indeed, unmistakable. She parked on the street.

Matt turned the mobile computer terminal toward him and typed. "The house belongs to Shawn O'Boyle. Taxes are paid. Has a couple of speeding tickets."

"OK, then." Bree led the way up a cracked concrete driveway. Two giant rottweilers barked and paced behind the chain-link fence. The hairs on Bree's arms stood straight up. A warning from her instincts about the house? Or in response to the big dogs?

Thanks to Matt—and Ladybug—she'd mostly overcome her fear of dogs. But a large canine with an aggressive bark or growl still had the potential to put her in panic mode. She breathed to slow her heart rate, but she couldn't stop the clammy sweating of her palms.

Matt scanned the yard with a critical eye as he followed her onto the stoop. They flanked the door, and Bree knocked. A curtain shifted in the window. Matt and Bree instantly went on even higher alert. She wiped her hands on her thighs. Slippery fingers wouldn't have a good grip on her weapon, if it became necessary to draw it.

The door opened, and a man who fit Cady's description stared out at them. "What do you want?"

"Mr. O'Boyle?" Bree asked.

At his wary nod, Bree introduced herself and Matt. "We'd like to ask you a few questions."

"About what?" O'Boyle's eyes narrowed to suspicious slits.

"The wolf puppy you had in your possession a few days ago," she said.

"I didn't know what it was." He shifted back, his shoulder and arm behind the door.

"Let me see your hands!" Bree pulled her weapon and leveled it at him.

"OK, OK." O'Brien lifted both hands in front of him, palms out. "Fucking cops."

"Step outside." Bree backed up. "Slowly."

He moved onto the stoop. Bree covered while Matt patted him down.

"He's clean," Matt said.

Bree holstered her gun.

"You don't have any right to come onto my property and drag me out of my house," O'Brien crossed his arms over his chest. "I didn't do anything."

"Except have possession of an endangered species," Bree pointed out. "It's illegal to own a wolf in New York State."

"Government overreach at its finest," O'Boyle yelled. "Fucking fascist government! How dare they tell me what kind of animal I can keep on my own property."

Bree ignored his outburst. "Where did you get the pup?"

He frowned. "I don't have to answer your questions."

Bree reached for her cuffs. She'd come prepared to simply take his information and give him a pass. But if he was going to be difficult, then she'd use whatever leverage she could.

He raised his hands again. "Fine. Whatever. I don't know the dude's name. I found him through a Facebook group. He calls himself the Wildlife Whisperer."

Bree pulled her notepad from her uniform shirt pocket and wrote down the details.

Matt already had his phone out and opened to the Facebook app. He tapped on his screen, then turned the phone to face O'Boyle. "Is this the profile?"

O'Boyle peered at the screen. "Yeah."

Matt showed Bree the profile. The Wildlife Whisperer didn't use a photo of himself. His profile pic was a snarling tiger.

"Where did you meet him?" Bree asked.

"The parking lot of the old Shop 'N' Fresh."

Matt returned his phone to his pocket. "The pup you had wasn't in very good condition."

"I know it. I was pissed. Made him reduce his price." O'Boyle seemed proud.

"How many pups did he have?" Bree asked.

"Three more." O'Boyle scratched his bald head.

Matt swore. "Can you describe him?"

O'Boyle shrugged. "I dunno. About my size and age."

"Hair or eye color? Distinctive features?"

"He was wearing a hat, and I didn't notice his eyes." O'Boyle rolled his own eyes.

"What was he wearing?" Bree asked.

"A ball gown," O'Boyle sneered. "I don't remember. I don't pay attention to what other dudes are wearing."

Bree sighed. "When was your meeting?"

"Last Friday night at seven o'clock." O'Boyle sounded bored.

Bree shoved her notepad back into her pocket. "You don't have plans to obtain another exotic animal, do you?"

"No." O'Boyle mashed his teeth. "My dogs didn't like the pup, and they like everybody and everything." He gestured to the dogs, who were now sitting at the fence and whining. "They look badass, but they're a couple of babies. But the wolf . . ." He shook his head. "They knew it wasn't a dog, and they weren't happy to have it in the house."

"Do your dogs have water and shade back there?" Matt asked.

O'Boyle waved both hands. "They have a frigging baby pool and a dog door. I take good care of my boys."

Matt conceded with a nod. "Good to hear."

"Thank you for your help." Bree backed away.

"So, I'm not in trouble?" O'Boyle gave her a side-eye.

"Not at this time." Bree remained noncommittal. "Don't buy any more exotic pets."

"No worries," O'Boyle said. "That one cost me a thousand bucks." He made a *poof* noise. "All gone. Don't know how I let that bitch talk me into giving her the wolf." He sounded disgusted with himself. "I could have sold it myself."

Matt made a low-key, growly noise.

Bree said, "She *saved* you money. The fine for engaging in illegal trade of endangered animals could cost you a lot more than that."

"How much can it be?" O'Boyle scoffed.

"As much as twenty-five thousand per violation."

He paled, and Bree left him with that thought, hoping he had learned his lesson.

CHAPTER
THIRTY-TWO

In the SUV, Matt scrolled through the Wildlife Whisperer's profile, looking for any personal information or anything that might indicate his location.

Bree turned to Matt. "You didn't punch him for calling Cady a bitch."

"Trust me. I wanted to." He exhaled hard. "But he didn't know her name and we gave him mine. If he knows she's my sister, he could find her." His sister's privacy and safety was more important than giving a jerk who insulted her a black eye. Cady would have laughed off the insult anyway. He could hear her in his head: *Who cares if he's mad? I got the pup.* And she would be right. She was good at her job and had very few issues because she didn't let her ego get in the way of her common sense. She de-escalated confrontations. Her only goal was to successfully remove animals from bad situations.

"Good thinking." Bree started the engine, then rested her hands on the wheel. "His dogs looked healthy, right?"

"They looked fine." Matt glanced back at the fence. O'Boyle and his dogs had disappeared from the yard. Matt channeled his sister's attitude. "Except for the insulting comment about Cady and the fact that he bought a wolf pup, O'Boyle didn't seem like a terrible person. If he takes good care of his pets, I can overlook one incidence of dumbassery."

Bree snorted. "Same. You can tell a lot about a person's character by how they treat animals and kids."

"You know it."

She put the vehicle into gear. "Let's get the account information from Facebook."

"Already on it." Matt scrolled on his phone. Rory specialized in digital media. Matt swiped at his screen and sent a message. "Rory will need a subpoena, and then Facebook will need time to gather the info, so we won't have instant data on the profile."

"I don't expect he'll find any information that's real or useful." Bree turned toward the station. "Most criminals know all the loopholes, and exotic animals are big business these days."

"It's Friday. We going to the empty lot tonight?"

Bree nodded. "Hopefully, that's when and where he conducts his business."

Matt continued to scroll through posts and pictures on the Wildlife Whisperer's profile. "I see the wolf pups. Before them, he posted about capybara pups, a chimp, two bear cubs." He paused, his stomach simmering with anger. "And a cougar."

"So, there's a good chance that the Wildlife Whisperer is our killer."

Matt continued to skim through posts, scrutinizing the backgrounds for clues to the animals' location. The cougar had a sizable cage. Behind it were rough wooden walls. The wolf pups were in a large dog crate. "Some of these animals are bedded in what looks like wood shavings. They could be in a shed or barn."

"Pine shavings were found at the crime scene."

"But how is the Wildlife Whisperer connected to the Masons? Their only pet was a house cat."

"Exotic pets are an illegal scheme. Maybe Josh and Shelly were somehow involved." Bree's phone vibrated with a text. "Dr. Jones wants us to stop by her office."

"So, she wants to tell us something she doesn't want to put in an email or report."

"Well"—Bree turned the vehicle toward the medical examiner's office—"she did agree to look over the autopsy as a favor."

The ME's office was in the municipal complex. They checked in at the counter and were escorted back to Dr. Jones's office. There were no bodies in sight in the office wing, but Matt could still smell death in the hallway.

Dr. Jones sat behind her desk. She wore clean purple scrubs. She woke her computer. "I've reviewed Dallas Sawyer's autopsy, as you asked."

"Thank you," Bree said.

Dr. Jones nodded. "You're welcome, but you won't love my findings."

"Was he murdered?" Bree asked.

"It's plausible," said Dr. Jones. "But my official opinion would be inconclusive."

"What makes it inconclusive as opposed to accidental?"

Dr. Jones took a thoughtful breath. "I don't want to second-guess a colleague. He had no reason to believe this was anything but a vehicle accident, with the fatality being somewhat of a fluke. We all see some strange things in this line of work, and this does initially present as an accidental death." She paused to shuffle the photos. "But I have a few questions." She slid a photo of the still-dressed body forward. "What do you see on the victim's clothes?"

Bree studied the photo. "Blood. A lot of blood."

"Glass," Matt added.

Dr. Jones slid a second photo next to the first, a close-up of the label from the broken bottle of juice. "And in the vehicle?"

"Same," Bree said. "Blood and glass."

"What do you not see?" she asked.

Matt spotted it, or rather the lack of it. "Green juice. Todd drinks that brand. It's hard-core green with bits of green."

Dr. Jones flattened a palm over the file. "Although it's possible that he was on the last sip. We don't know exactly what time he left his house. His wife wasn't home at the time. But the vehicle was found about three miles from his address. Did he drink a sixteen-ounce bottle that fast?"

"I mean, I can drink coffee that fast." Sometimes Bree drank her coffee like a frat boy with a beer bong. "But that stuff? I'd have to choke that down while holding my nose. It's *thick*."

"The bottle could have been empty," Matt suggested. "But an empty bottle would probably be in the cup holder, which is not between the airbag and the occupant's face."

Dr. Jones nodded. "Like I said, it's just a question. Alone, it isn't as meaningful."

"So there's more?" Bree asked.

Dr. Jones slid a close-up of the fatal wound out of the pile. "The wound itself is larger than the piece of glass, and the outer edges of the wound are very clean, no jagged edges, more like a knife slice than a cut made by a broken piece of glass. The cut also has a distinct beginning and end. The start of an incised wound is deeper and becomes shallower toward the tail. This cut was made in this direction." She moved the tip of her finger from under the rear of the jaw to beneath the chin. "So, not only should the wound not have a direction if the glass was pushed straight forward"—she flipped to another picture of the glass protruding from the victim's neck—"but it's backward."

Bree froze. "If the glass shard originated in front of his face, the direction of the cut should move from the front of the neck to the back, not from the rear to the front."

"Yes." The ME straightened and folded her hands. "I'm not saying the original ME was definitely wrong. But I did have these questions."

"The side window of the vehicle was shattered in the accident. If you're right, then someone approached the vehicle, reached in through the broken window, and cut his neck, and then shoved a piece of glass bottle into the wound, hoping the cut would be attributed to the accident. How would you plan that?"

"Do we know if the bottle was definitely his?" Dr. Jones asked. "Or did someone bring it to the accident site?"

Bree lifted a hand. "His wife wasn't sure, but he was an athlete and particular about his diet."

Matt frowned. "There must have been some improvising at the scene, but if someone ran him off the road, they'd be on hand to finish the job."

"And they'd be on hand to take Claire from the vehicle," Bree said.

"Do we know why Mr. Sawyer was out that night?" Matt asked.

Bree nodded. "An issue with a false alarm at the tech company's building."

"Where was Mrs. Sawyer?" Dr. Jones asked.

Bree said, "At a school event with their son. Her presence there was confirmed by multiple witnesses."

"That's a wild theory," Dr. Jones said. "I don't know how you'd prove it. The ME who performed the autopsy didn't doubt the glass shard killed him, and that doctor has since passed away. We can't ask him any questions."

Bree could guess what had happened. The ME had missed it because the cause of death seemed obvious. He'd made assumptions and issued a report that confirmed those preconceived ideas. Detectives sometimes made the same mistake. They let their own interpretations lead the investigation instead of following the evidence.

"No one is perfect. He missed it. Doctors misdiagnose illnesses. People make mistakes." Matt waved a hand over the photos. "We're looking for a possible murder, so we're looking deeper."

But Matt knew Dr. Jones wouldn't have missed the inconsistency with the wound. He looked over the photos again. Something nagged at him.

"Something wrong?" Bree glanced sideways.

"I don't know. I feel like I'm missing something." But he couldn't place it. "I'll remember when I stop trying to."

Dr. Jones collected the photos. "I'm sorry I can't give you a more definite answer."

"You've been very helpful." Bree stood. "I know you're busy. I appreciate you taking the time."

"You're welcome."

Matt held the door as they left the ME's office. "Do we have time to stop at the station?"

Bree lifted her phone and checked the screen. "If you're quick. I want to get into position in the vacant grocery store parking lot well before seven."

They returned to the SUV and drove to the station. Bree stopped in the squad room. Matt headed directly to the conference room, where Todd was typing on a laptop.

"May I?" Matt gestured toward the computer.

"Sure." Todd turned it to face Matt.

He accessed the crime scene photos from the Masons' murders and began scrolling through them.

"What are you looking for?" Todd asked.

"I don't know." But Matt would know it when he saw it.

Bree entered. "Juarez checked the Masons' credit card statements. No charges at any zoos for the past month. He also checked the trace evidence list. No weird animal fur was found on any of the Masons' shoes. The only traces were found on the carpet in front of the Masons' bed and on the stairs."

"So, it's likely the killer brought it with him," Todd said.

Matt froze, his gaze locked on a photo of the Masons' refrigerator. "I remember what was nagging at me." He pointed to the computer screen. In the Masons' fridge were three bottles of cold-pressed green juice.

Bree pursed her lips. "Josh Mason was a runner. Dallas Sawyer was a cyclist. Both watched their diets. It could be a coincidence."

"Plenty of people drink green juice," Todd said. "I do."

"But it's one more coincidence," Bree said. "At the bottom of a coincidence dogpile."

Her phone rang. She looked at the screen. "Shillings." She answered the call. "Taggert here. You're on speaker."

"I spoke with the FBI agent," Shillings said. "Guess who was an employee of Dallas Sawyer's company, Wall Digital Technology?" She paused for a beat. "Josh Mason. Winner winner chicken dinner?"

Bree snorted. "That's about right. It's seeming more and more likely that Josh Mason killed Dallas Sawyer for some reason we haven't yet discovered."

CHAPTER
THIRTY-THREE

Claire looked up from weeding and read the text. I'M COMING FOR YOU.

Despite the heat from the sun on her bare arms, goose bumps rippled across her skin. She was tired of running. Tired of not belonging anywhere. Tired of crying.

For twelve years, she'd answered to Claire Mason. Her name had been the first word she remembered learning to write. It was the name on her passport and her driver's license. It was the only name she responded to when called.

And it wasn't hers.

How could her parents—no, they weren't her parents—how could the Masons have done this to her? If she was honest with herself, Josh and Shelly hadn't been good parents. She'd never been allowed to bring friends home. They discouraged her from joining teams or clubs. *If you let people get close to you, you're vulnerable. They'll use you every time.* More advice from Josh that made a whole bunch of sense in hindsight. Claire had been actively discouraged from making friends. Acquaintances were fine if she didn't confide in anyone or provide them with any leverage to use against her. According to Josh, that's what friends did.

You can't trust anybody.

In the end, Josh had proven his own words to be true.

Now that Claire knew the truth, she understood what had driven them to isolate her.

Fear.

If people got close, eventually someone might discover their secret. Make that *secrets*.

Claire glanced over her shoulder at Deputy Zucco—Renata, as she'd said to call her. Deep in her gut Claire knew that she could trust Renata and her mother. Something about them made her confident that they wouldn't betray her. For one, they didn't make promises. They were up front about the shittiness of her situation, and that they didn't have the power to prevent even more suckage from happening. Claire was at the mercy of the legal system.

The Zuccos were probably the nicest people she'd ever met. Claire sensed that they cared about her. Or *were* they trying to play her? No. Josh had been wrong. He'd been a criminal. *He* hadn't trusted anyone because *he* hadn't been trustworthy. His whole being was seeped in betrayal.

But none of that changed her current circumstances. Claire couldn't let the Zuccos get hurt.

He was going to catch her sooner or later. He wouldn't stop. She knew this from the persistence of his pursuit. He'd already killed the Masons. The memories flashed into her mind. The shocking red of the saturated sheets. Josh's wide-open eyes. The sticky wetness of blood on Claire's palms. Shelly's ruined face. She would have been horrified to see the damage he'd done. Claire never smelled death before, but now she would recognize its stench anywhere.

He would kill Renata and her mother too, just as viciously and without hesitation. He might even enjoy it. She glanced at her phone again.

I'M COMING FOR YOU.

What could she do?

CHAPTER

THIRTY-FOUR

Renata plucked another weed from the flower bed. Why had she let the yard fall into this state? Sweat trickled down her back, but she didn't remove the loose shirt she wore over her tank. It concealed her gun, which Claire didn't need to know she was carrying. Simon Osborne might be on a psych hold, but the sheriff wasn't convinced he was the one who was after Claire. He didn't have a single tattoo. While Claire might have been wrong about the details, Renata couldn't see her imagining the existence of a tat.

So, she would keep her sidearm handy.

Across the patio, Claire knelt on a cushion, pulling weeds from the herb garden. "Is this an herb or a weed?" Claire pointed to a plant that looked like the branch from a miniature Christmas tree.

"That's rosemary. It's an herb. Pull off a little piece and smell it."

Claire pinched a few needles and brought them to her face. She smiled. "Smells good."

"We can use some of those herbs with dinner," Renata suggested.

"Really?"

"Sure. There's basil and oregano. We can make a nice pasta sauce." Renata wasn't the best cook, but she could manage the basics. "We used to have fresh vegetables too. Maybe next year we'll do it again, when Mom's feeling better. She had the green thumb—and she's an amazing cook."

"You said she's gonna be OK, right?" Claire's voice trembled.

"Her prognosis is very good." Renata tried to sound certain. Claire needed the reassurance. They all did.

"I've never done much cooking," Claire said. "My mom—I mean, Shelly Mason—preferred ordering instead of cooking. And Da—Josh—practically lived on smoothies. He was obsessed with his macros."

"Macros?"

"The percentage of his diet that came from protein, carbs, and fats. He tracked every bite he ate."

"That sounds . . . hard." Renata was going to say *unhealthy*, but who was she to judge? She was so addicted to Thin Mints, she bought two dozen boxes every February, froze them, and rationed them out the rest of the year.

Behind them, a door opened and closed. Her mom approached, carrying two tall plastic cups. "I brought you some iced tea."

"Oh, great!" Renata tugged off her gardening gloves and tossed them onto the patio. She took the cup and chugged. The icy liquid cooled her parched throat. "Thanks! I needed this."

"Me too." Claire sipped her drink. Her cheeks were flushed with heat.

Her mom rocked back on her heels and looked over the garden. "You've done a great job." She propped a fist on her hip and got that look on her face, the one that meant she was planning—and Renata had more days of gardening work ahead of her.

"I know that look," Renata teased.

"I was thinking. We could still have some fall vegetables, not from seeds, of course. We'd have to buy actual plants. Maybe some kale and cabbage. It's still warm enough for lettuce."

A smile pulled at Renata's mouth. "Whatever you want. We can run by the nursery tomorrow."

"We'll do it," her mom decided. "Clip some of those herbs for dinner tonight."

"Already planned on it."

Her mom shielded her eyes from the evening sun, then stepped into the shadow of an oak tree. "I wish I could help."

"You do the planning." Renata gestured toward Claire. "We'll do the grunt work."

"I'm afraid I need a nap." Her mom turned back toward the house. "But first, I'll check the freezer and see if we have some of that good ravioli left." Still talking to herself, she headed back into the house.

Renata said, "That's the first she's shown interest in anything in months. She likes you, and I think she's enjoying having you here."

Claire pointed to a plant. "Herb or weed?"

"Weed."

Claire ripped it out by the roots with more violence than necessary. Dirt cascaded from the roots as she tossed it into a bucket. Her voice was barely audible. "I like her too."

Renata's heart ached for her. Claire had lost everything she loved. She must be afraid to allow herself to care about anyone.

A pinging sound startled Claire. She reached into her pocket and pulled out her phone. Glancing at the screen, she paled.

"Is something wrong?" Renata asked.

"Nothing. Just Denver trying to connect. I'm not sure I'm ready." She lowered the phone to her lap.

Renata didn't want to pry, but she also sensed Claire needed someone to talk to. "Can you tell him you need more time?"

Claire lifted the phone and typed with both thumbs. "I'll try. But he's worried about *his* mom." She glanced back at the house, at the door Renata's mom had entered. "The same way you're worried about yours."

Clearly Claire wasn't ready to see Pam Sawyer as her own mother yet. Would she ever? There was no way to go back and undo the damage done twelve years ago, and Pam's substance abuse wouldn't help. Not that Renata blamed Pam. How did one cope with losing a husband and having a child go missing? The thought was unfathomable. Renata wasn't going to condemn the woman. But the fact remained that her addition was going to be one more obstacle for the family to overcome in a situation that was already unthinkable.

A twig snapped in the vacant lot, and Renata froze, listening. The tawny bodies of three deer wandered through the trees.

"Claire," she whispered and pointed.

Claire's eyes opened wide, and she mouthed, "They're beautiful."

They watched in silence until the deer moved on. The back of Renata's neck itched. Sweat or nerves? Whatever. The deer had put Renata on high alert. "It's late, and I'm getting hungry, you?"

Claire stood and peeled off her gloves. "Yes. Which herbs do you want?"

Renata reached for a small pair of scissors in her mom's gardening tote on the patio next to her. She handed them to Claire and pointed out the basil, oregano, and rosemary. "Snip some thyme too. That's the one with the tiny leaves."

They took the herbs into the kitchen.

"How can I help?" Claire asked. "I need to keep busy."

"I'm going to grab a quick shower. Would you wash the herbs and lay them out on a towel to dry?" Renata pointed to the freezer. "One of the neighbors gave us a loaf of french bread last week. We froze half. Would you see if you can find it in the freezer?"

"OK." Claire turned toward the sink.

While the girl was occupied, Renata took a tour around the house, checking locks and looking out all the windows. The street was clear. She cleaned up and dressed in clean shorts, a tank, and a loose short-sleeve shirt over her weapon.

When she returned to the kitchen, the bread was thawing on the counter next to the drying herbs laid out on a towel. Claire sat on the floor, petting her cat. Chunk purred and rolled onto his back for a belly rub.

Renata laughed. "He looks ridiculous with his feet in the air."

"He doesn't care." Claire looked up. "Are you done in the bathroom?"

"All yours," Renata said.

"Would it be OK if I took a bath?"

"Sure. Take your time. My mom is still napping. I'm going to chop the herbs and attempt to make my mom's pound cake." Renata reached for the box on the counter. No recipe app for her mom. She had a box of recipes handwritten on index cards. "No promises. I am not the baker that she is, and I'm not sure we have all the ingredients. I've never made this before, but it's always been one of my favorites."

"I don't need cake," Claire said. Then she smiled. "But it would be nice."

"Then wish me luck."

Claire retreated down the hallway. Renata heard footsteps, then the bathroom door closed and the fan turned on. She imagined Claire soaking in the tub, getting some alone time, maybe crying. She'd been talking about the people she still thought of as her parents. Then the bio brother had texted. All that had to elicit some devastating emotions. The girl needed to decompress.

Renata opened the box and flipped through the well-organized cards. Under the DESSERTS tab, she found alphabetized recipes and quickly located the pound cake recipe card. Didn't look too hard. *Wow. That's a lot of butter.*

Normally, she'd play music when she cooked or cleaned, but she wanted to be able to hear if her mom or Claire needed her, so she opted for silence. The faint sound of water rushing into the bathtub floated down the hall. The cat watched as she assembled the ingredients and broke out the mixer. She poured the mixture into a loaf pan and checked the preheating oven to see it wasn't to temperature yet.

Her phone pinged, and she glanced at the screen, surprised to see a text from Adam Taggert. love 2 meet 4 a coffee

She stared at the message. Adam Taggert wanted to have coffee. Was that because he couldn't afford to buy food? *Don't be a bitch.* He was nice with Claire, more than nice. He was empathetic, considerate, and helpful. She remembered what Juarez had said: *google him.*

A few links took her to a gallery in New York that showcased his paintings. Her eyes popped at the price tags. She nearly dropped her phone. He'd sold one painting for more than she made in five years.

Holy. Shit.

Her mom appeared in the doorway. "Did something happen?"

"No." Renata shook her head. She explained about Adam. "The thing is, I liked him, but I completely judged him based on him being an artist."

"You've had *bad* experiences with those."

"Now I'm thinking of meeting him for coffee. What does that make me? A gold digger? I wasn't interested when I thought he was broke. Now that I know he's not, suddenly he's fine to date. Does that make me shallow?"

"Would you have dated him if he was a gainfully employed electrician?"

"Yes."

"Then you're not shallow." Her mom chuckled. "You don't want to date unemployed men who are using you for free room and board."

Renata winced. That was exactly what had happened to her in the past.

Her mom continued. "That makes you mature and responsible. There is nothing wrong with wanting the same in a potential partner. Maybe you were a little judgy, but you've been burned. It's understandable."

Renata frowned.

"Meet the man for coffee," her mom said.

"Maybe I will."

"Where's Claire?" her mom asked.

"Taking a bath." Renata glanced at the preheating oven. Not to temperature yet.

"I just passed the bathroom. It's awfully quiet in there."

Worry bloomed in Renata's gut. "It hasn't been that long, but I'll check on her."

She wiped her hands and headed down the hall. She pressed an ear to the bathroom door. Nothing. No splashing. No crying.

Renata knocked on the door. "Claire? How much longer are you going to be. I'm about to start dinner."

No answer sounded from the other side of the door. Stomach knotting, she rapped again. "Claire, are you OK?"

When no one answered, she tried the doorknob. Locked.

Her mom stood at the end of the hallway. "The key's on the top of the doorframe."

Rising onto her tiptoes, Renata stretched and swept her fingertips over the top of the doorjamb. She pulled down the interior door key and used it to unlock the door. "Claire, I'm coming in."

She pushed open the door. Fresh sweat broke out on her lower back, and her heart kicked up a gear. The tub was full of water. A breeze blew through the open window over the toilet, and the room was empty.

"What is it?" her mom asked.

"Claire's gone." Renata crossed to the toilet. The organizer tray from the top of the tank that held spare TP and a spray bottle of air freshener had been moved to the vanity. *So Claire could climb out.* Renata looked out the window. The sun had dropped below the trees, casting the street in long, reaching shadows. She saw no sign of Claire.

Renata backed out of the room and headed for the front door. "I was focused on keeping the people out. I didn't realize I needed to keep Claire in."

"She seemed content here." Her mom trailed along behind her. "How long has she been gone?"

Renata checked the time on her phone. "No more than twenty-five minutes."

"What can I do?"

"I don't know. I'm calling the sheriff." Renata reached for her phone in her pocket and went into her bedroom to change into a pair of cargo pants and sneakers. "We'll probably put out a BOLO. I'll drive around. See if I spot her."

"I'll check with the neighbors. Maybe someone saw her." But her mom headed toward her own room. She emerged a minute later, looping a belt around her waist. The belt held a holster and her own handgun. "Just in case."

"I'm not arguing. I want you armed."

They separated at the front door.

"Please stay close to home," Renata said. "I know you want to help, but you're physically not up to a foot search. I can't worry about both of you."

Her mom gave her a reluctant nod and lifted her phone. "I'll call the neighbors instead. Go find her. If she's on foot, she can't have gotten far."

Renata wasn't sure about Claire being on foot. She had a phone, maybe an Uber or Lyft account. She could have called a friend to pick her up. Claire had been gone for thirty minutes now, and darkness would fall fast. If she got a ride, she could be miles away.

CHAPTER THIRTY-FIVE

Bree crouched in the weeds behind the vacant supermarket, waiting for the Wildlife Whisperer to make an appearance. The setting sun fired the sky in bright orange. A gnat buzzed by her face. She waved it away.

Next to her, Matt rose onto his knees and looked over the low cinder block wall that defined the former receiving area. He used the scope on his rifle to sweep the area. He might not be able to qualify with a handgun, but his aim with a long gun was excellent. Todd and another deputy were on the opposite side of the building. Empty fields stretched out behind the vacant store. The surrounding landscape was too open to take cover anywhere else.

"Who thought building a store out here was a good idea?" Matt asked, lowering the rifle. "It's too far from town."

"It's too far from anything."

"I see a vehicle approaching," Matt said.

"Right on time." She lifted a pair of binoculars and peered over the wall. "Light-colored minivan." The sun blazed into her eyes.

"If our killer drives a black SUV, then maybe that's the buyer," Matt said.

"Here comes another vehicle." She waited for it to come into focus. "I can't see the details." She looked away from the binoculars, blinked, then tried again. "Looks like a dark-colored SUV."

"Bingo," Matt said. "I'll bet that's our man. Can you read the plate?"

Bree adjusted the focus on the binoculars, but it didn't help. "No. We'll give them a few minutes to get out of their vehicles." She touched her earbud and relayed the situation to Todd.

The two vehicles parked a few yards apart. Doors opened. Two people got out of the minivan. A man stepped out of the SUV. They met behind the SUV.

"It's go time," she said into the mic. "Stick to the plan."

She and Matt returned to her SUV, hidden behind the building. There was no way to creep up on the meeting. The fastest way to cut them off was by vehicle. She started the engine. She'd parked the SUV facing the direction of the lot. Now she eased forward, then stomped on the gas pedal and whipped the steering wheel left. The vehicle shot around the corner of the building. They roared forward. The three men froze for a few seconds, then sprinted for their rides. But they didn't have a chance.

Bree used the vehicle speaker. "Put your hands up."

All three men, clearly seeing that escape was not possible, froze. Their hands shot up to the sky.

Bree stomped on the brake. Her tires slid on the sandy asphalt before coming to a stop behind the dark SUV. Todd's cruiser blocked the minivan. Bree flung open her door and leveled her weapon at the men. Matt sprang out of the passenger seat, rifle in hand. Todd and the deputy jumped out of their cruiser and took aim at the three suspects.

"Don't move. Sheriff's department," Bree commanded.

"Please don't shoot!" One man cringed, his hands as high as he could lift them.

Todd and the deputy moved in, patted down the men, and cuffed them.

Matt went to the minivan. He glanced inside the rear hatch and shook his head. "Just an empty animal crate."

Bree approached the SUV, a dark-blue Mazda. She saw a cardboard box with holes poked in the top in the cargo area. She shouted at the three men, "What's in the box?"

"Nothing," a bald man answered.

She reached inside and flipped off the lid. "Confirmed. Empty."

No animals. Disappointment crashed down on Bree. None of these men were the Wildlife Whisperer. They were all his potential customers.

Todd walked to Bree and handed her three wallets. Taking them, Bree approached the men. All three were middle-aged. None looked fit enough to be the man she and Matt had chased. She read the names on the driver's licenses, then matched the photos to their faces.

"Check for outstanding warrants," she instructed the deputy.

"Yes, ma'am." He retreated to the patrol vehicle.

She pointed to a bald man. "Paul, is this your Mazda?"

He nodded.

"Why are you here?" she asked.

Paul frowned. "I don't have to answer your questions. I haven't done anything wrong." He rattled his cuffed hands. "You have no right to detain me."

Bree stared him down. "We're looking for a murderer."

Paul went pale and sputtered.

Bree repeated, "Why are you here?"

Paul's jaw tightened but he didn't answer.

Bree turned to the other two men, who had arrived together in the minivan. "How about you two?"

The bearded one, Jake, said, "We came to meet someone."

"Who?" Bree asked.

"I don't know his name," Jake said. "He goes by the Wildlife Whisperer on Facebook."

His friend tried to elbow him. "Dude. Shut up."

Jake was clearly the weak link.

Bree focused on him. "Why were you meeting?"

"Don't say anything," the companion warned.

Jake shrugged. "She thinks we're here to make a drug deal or something. We're not." He faced Bree. "We're buying a monkey. Nothing wrong with that."

"Do you have a permit?" Bree asked.

"Why would I need a permit?"

"Because it's illegal to keep a monkey as a pet in the state of New York."

"Huh." Jake's face creased. "I did not know that."

She speared Paul with a glare. "What were you going to buy?"

His shoulders drooped. "I haven't bought anything."

Yet.

Paul shuffled his feet. "Hypothetically, I might have been interested in a chimpanzee."

Bree rubbed her forehead. *Why? Why did people want to own weird animals?*

"You were going to put a chimpanzee in a cardboard box?" Matt yelled. "Have you even seen a chimpanzee? What the—" He stepped away to collect himself.

Bree spoke to Paul. "Exotic animals are illegal to buy and own. Most of them come from horrific situations. Many are poached and their parents slaughtered. A good number die en route. If they do survive, there's a good chance they aren't healthy, and they'll be even harder to keep. You could catch a disease from them. Chimpanzees are known to bite. They are strong animals and can be dangerous unless kept by a professional."

"This was supposed to be a baby," Paul said to his shoes.

"They grow!" Matt shouted from twenty feet away. He muttered. Bree heard the word *stupid* multiple times. He was usually a very controlled and calm person, but when animals or kids were at risk, he could lose his temper.

Jake and his companion had the decency to look ashamed. "I didn't know any of that. I won't buy anything. I promise."

His companion nodded like a bobblehead.

But Paul didn't look sorry. His glared at Bree in silence.

The deputy returned. "No outstanding warrants. No criminal records. Paul has a few speeding tickets, all paid."

She stepped closer, addressing all three men. "We are taking your names and information. We will be watching you."

She motioned for her deputy to remove their handcuffs. She had no option. She couldn't arrest them for wanting to commit a crime.

Matt joined her, and she said, "We're no closer to finding him."

"Was he tipped off?" She scanned the area.

"I don't see how," Matt said. "We weren't visible from the road. We were in position thirty minutes early, and we didn't see anyone around."

But Bree wondered. "Then why didn't he show?"

Matt lifted a palm.

Bree's phone buzzed. She pulled it from its belt holder. *Zucco.* She answered, "Taggert."

"Claire is missing." Zucco explained in a few sentences. "I didn't expect her to run."

"I'm on my way." Bree lowered the phone and relayed the news to Matt as she headed for the SUV. "I'm afraid that might be why he isn't here."

Matt finished her thought. "Because he was busy going after Claire?"

◆ ◆ ◆

Bree called for backup. She also put out a BOLO on Claire as she and Matt raced for Zucco's house. Her deputy met them in the driveway. One look at Zucco's face told Bree she was devastated.

"I can't believe I lost her," Zucco said.

"What happened before she left?" Bree asked.

Zucco recounted a very normal afternoon and evening. "She seemed excited to help make dinner. I was hoping I could get her to eat an actual meal."

Bree closed her eyes and thought. "Did she seem upset?"

"She's been upset since I met her."

"Good point."

"I checked the doors and windows before she took her bath. Everything was locked up tightly. I kept an eye on the street all day. No unusual cars. It was a very ordinary day." Zucco piled both hands on top of her head. "She seemed good, considering."

Another patrol vehicle—the K-9 team—pulled up to the curb. In the back, Greta barked. Collins unloaded the black shepherd and outfitted her in her tracking harness. Greta began to dance, excited to work.

Zucco pointed out the window where Claire had climbed out of the house. "Claire took her backpack with her. We don't have an item of hers."

"That's OK," Collins said. "She'll pick up the scent from beneath the window."

Greta was a long, lean dog with energy to spare, but Bree was grateful the sun and temperature had dropped. The fading light meant nothing to the dog, but excessive heat would make her job more difficult. Collins walked her beneath the window, gave her a command, and let her sniff the grass. The dog's nose hit the ground, then lifted to scent the air. She circled a few times, then charged forward, leaning into the harness. Collins let out some leash and broke into a jog to keep up. The dog stayed on the scent like it was a line marked with powdered chalk.

Bree, Matt, and Zucco stayed well behind the K-9 team. They jogged two blocks, then the dog abruptly stopped on the side of the road. She sniffed in a circle several times, alternating between scenting the ground and air before looking back at her handler and whining.

259

"She's lost the scent. We'll try to pick it up again." Collins led her in a spiral pattern. The dog lunged sideways, then sat next to the storm sewer grate and whined. Collins watched her dog. "She found something."

Matt approached the grate and crouched. "It's a cell phone." He pulled a glove out of his pocket and picked up the phone by the edges. The case was bejeweled and purple, with a cardholder attached to the back.

Collins pulled a stuffed hedgehog out of her pants cargo pocket and tossed it to the dog. "That's a good girl. You did it."

Greta leaped and snatched the toy from the air. Wagging her tail, she squeaked the stuffed animal over and over.

"That's Claire's phone!" Zucco said.

Bree looked over Matt's shoulder. The phone screen was a spider-web of cracks. "That's a newer model. It should be fairly durable. I drop mine all the time. It doesn't shatter that easily."

Matt agreed with a nod. "It didn't drop out of Claire's pocket. It was intentionally smashed."

Collins rubbed Greta's head. "If she lost the scent, Claire was probably picked up in a vehicle."

Bree pointed to the four closest houses on both sides of the street. "Let's see who has doorbell or security cameras."

They split up. Bree jogged up the driveway facing the sewer grate. She spotted a camera mounted under the eaves over the driveway, pointed at an older-model Mercedes sedan. She knocked on the door. A fiftyish man in basketball shorts and a T-shirt answered the door. Bree explained what she needed in rushed words.

"Of course. I bought the driveway cam after my car window got busted a few months ago." He stepped onto the porch and pulled his phone from the pocket of his shorts. He tapped and swiped the screen. "Do you know what time the car stopped here?"

"Within the last hour," Bree said.

"OK." He lowered the phone so she could see the screen. With one finger, he fast-forwarded the video. Claire came into view.

"That's her," Bree said.

Claire was walking in a rushed pace, almost jogging, and looking over her shoulder. A dark SUV sped into view and stopped next to her. She tried to run away, but a man leaped out of the vehicle and caught her by the arm before she'd taken two strides. His back was to the camera. He wore shorts, a T-shirt, and a black baseball cap pulled down low. He whirled her around and got in Claire's face. She shook her head, pulling backward and trying to free her arm. But the man was too strong. He dragged her back to his SUV and shoved her into the back seat. He closed the door and drove away. Between the camera angle and the cap, his face was a mystery.

"Shit," said the homeowner. "Do you know who he is?"

"No." But he looked familiar to Bree. She was almost certain he was the man who'd shot at them at the playground. "Can you see the license plate number?"

The homeowner nodded. "I got you, Sheriff. Let me zoom in." He rewound until the plate was in view. Then he stopped the video and took a screenshot. Switching to his photo app, he selected the picture and zoomed in. "Bingo."

Bree wrote down the plate number. "Thank you. Would you please send me the video and photo?" She read off her cell phone number.

"You got it." He tapped a few more times. "Done."

"Thank you."

"Happy I could help."

Bree met her team back on the sidewalk. "I got the plate of the vehicle that took her." She ran for Zucco's house, using her shoulder mic to relay the plate to dispatch. She opened the door to her SUV and slid into the driver's seat. Before dispatch could respond, she'd plugged the license plate number into the computer.

Matt stood next to the open door of her vehicle, his hand propped on her seat. "Well?"

Bree stared at the result. "The SUV is registered to Denver Sawyer."

Matt leaned back. "Huh."

Dispatch repeated the information.

Bree tapped the steering wheel.

"Did she go with him willingly?" Matt asked. "Maybe he called her."

Zucco appeared behind him. "Then why did she sneak out the window? Why wouldn't she tell me she was meeting her brother?"

Bree opened the text from the homeowner and showed them the video.

He watched. His brow furrowed. "She didn't go willingly."

"No," Zucco said.

"Are you calling the Chandler PD to intercept them at his place?" Matt asked.

Bree pointed to the dashboard computer. "Denver doesn't live in Chandler. That's where their mother lives. Denver's address is in Grey's Hollow." She plugged the address into the map app.

Matt leaned closer. "That's near the Scarlet Falls township line. It's also very close to the auto shop where Gloria Klein's SUV was stored last weekend."

Bree digested that fact for a minute. "Did Denver Sawyer kill the Masons?"

Matt said, "It makes perfect sense if he found out that Josh Mason killed his dad and stole his sister."

"But did he have any connections with the Masons?" Bree agreed the motivation was solid, but how did he accomplish the murders?

"The logistics don't matter right now," Zucco said. "We have to go get Claire."

CHAPTER THIRTY-SIX

Pain slammed up Claire's arm as Denver dragged her out of his SUV by the duct tape that bound her wrists in front of her body. A porch light on the small house was the only light. No, wait. It wasn't a house exactly. It was a trailer. The rest of the lot was dark. Thick woods surrounded the property. Besides the trailer, the only other building was an old barn.

"Move it." Denver pulled harder.

Claire stumbled to keep up. He opened the barn door. The smell of animals hit her hard. Claire gagged as he yanked her through the door and rolled it closed. He flipped a switch on the wall. A bare bulb cast a cone of dim light in the center of the space.

The barn had a few doors at the back, indicating rooms of some sort, but the rest of the building was open, with metal fencing dividing the space into pens. It looked like large animals, maybe horses or cows, had once occupied the pens. But now the barn held zoo animals in cages.

Something screamed from the shadows.

Denver loosened his grip. "Don't you dare try to run again." His voice rang with disappointment. "That scene in the street was enough."

"I won't," she said in a small voice, because that's how she felt—as small and helpless as the little girl she must have been when Josh took her. Had she cried back then? Had she known what was happening? That her father was dead? Had she seen him die?

Maybe it was best she couldn't recall the trauma. Or maybe the trauma was the reason she couldn't recall the accident or her previous life. But either way, she grieved for the little girl she didn't remember being—and for the relationships with her parents and brother that were missing, as if someone had used an eraser on her brain.

"What was our dad like?" she asked.

Denver shook his head at her. "You really don't remember?"

"No."

"He was kind of a nerd. He loved baseball. He liked to gamble too much. He and Mom used to fight about that a lot."

"Was he a good father? Did I spend time with him?" She really wanted to know.

"Yeah." Denver's voice turned wistful. "He was a pretty good dad. There was this minor league team in our town, and he used to take us to games all the time. We'd get hot dogs and Cokes. I know it doesn't sound very exciting, but I really miss those days."

"I wish I remembered," Claire said.

"We can go to baseball games. Just you and me, like we did back then." He gestured around them. "I bought this place last summer, when I found out about Josh—and everything. I wanted to be close, to watch him—to watch you."

Claire shivered.

He continued. "There's nothing around. I found a good way to make some quick cash, and I needed the solitude. I had to get away from Mom. But we don't have to stay here. I put some cash aside. We can go somewhere else." He turned on another overhead bulb and stood her in front of one of the pens. He'd built a cage inside, and a mountain lion paced behind the bars. It crouched and emitted another earsplitting scream.

"I'm getting ten grand for him." Pride rang in his voice. He pulled her to the next pen, this one built from plywood. The door was closed. He pushed her forward. "Look inside."

Three capybara babies scrambled in three inches of wood shavings. "They go for five hundred each."

The next stall held two gray puppies in a dog crate. Next to the pups, several baby monkeys filled smaller, stacked cages.

"Wolf pups go for a thousand apiece." Denver spun her to face him. "I can provide for you. We can be a family. Just you and me. Mom doesn't have to be part of it. I know she scared you."

She scared me. She didn't kidnap me.

Claire tried to school her face into an expression of enthusiasm. But she couldn't. She couldn't even stop crying. The tears and sobs kept coming. She could barely get air into her lungs in between them. Her entire body was a heaving, snotty disaster.

She sucked in a deep breath and willed her voice to steady. "I don't want her to be my mother." Pam Sawyer had made Claire feel sick, like someone was twisting her insides. She couldn't—wouldn't—go live with her.

"I don't either." Denver stared at her, his eyes hard and mean. "Before Josh Mason killed Dad, before he took you, she was a good mom. But after . . ." He shook his head. "Then I didn't exist anymore. She could only think about *you*." He said *you* with venom.

She could feel his hatred on her skin like a sunburn. "It wasn't my fault."

"I know." His voice softened, but the hard look in his eyes remained. He blamed her all the same. "We don't need Mom. I can be enough for you." He said the words with conviction, as if he could make it true. He was never going to let her go. But what was he going to do with her?

He'd killed Josh and Shelly. Would he kill her too? They barely knew each other, but they were siblings. Could he kill his own sister?

She knew in her soul if she didn't live up to his expectations as the perfect sister, he could—and probably would. Another sob trembled through her. How could she have trusted him, even for a second?

"Fuck!" Denver yelled and shook her by the bicep. "Stop that, or I'll give you something to cry about." He gripped her arm tighter and pulled her to the post in front of the cougar's cage.

Claire stumbled, fell, and landed on her hands and knees. Her head struck the post. Stars swam in front of her eyes. The pain shocked her body out of crying mode. She sat up and cradled her skull with both hands.

Denver used a rope to tie her bound hands to the post. "You'll learn. We are going to be a family. I'm going to take care of you." His face softened. He reached out and cupped the side of her face. "I know you don't remember me, but you will. You'll learn to love me."

His touch made her want to recoil, but she forced herself to remain still. Instinctively, she knew rejecting him would make him angrier.

He stroked her cheek. "But until you do, I won't let you go. Everyone leaves me. I had no one to help me after Dad died. No one. You were gone. Dad was gone. Mom mentally checked out. She didn't even remember to feed me. *I* was the one making sure *she* ate. How fucked up was that? I was just a kid, and I was worse than alone. But that won't happen to you. I'll make sure of it. I'll live up to my responsibilities. I expect you to do the same. You might not love me yet, but you will in time."

She rose to her knees. The barn interior swam, and the floor felt as if it were tilting, like the fun house at the annual carnival. She curled her hands around the post to steady herself. Breathing through her nose, she willed her vision to clear.

"You can't escape." He gestured toward the cougar's cage. "If I can keep him, then you don't stand a chance at getting away."

Hopelessness swamped Claire until she was weak. What had she done? She should have told the sheriff and Renata everything after she'd received his text. But she'd wanted to keep him from hurting Renata and Teresa. If Claire hadn't left, then Denver would have come inside for her. Both Renata and her mom would have fought, but Claire couldn't let them die for her.

Denver wasn't the loving brother she'd wanted.

He was a monster.

"I saved you," he said.

"You're scaring me." Claire sniffed. "Let me go."

"Why? I'm your brother. It's time you accepted that. If you behave, I'll take care of you. All we have is each other. Mom can't manage. I'm sorry about that. But I was just a kid when she started drinking. I couldn't stop her."

"I want to go back." Claire felt the tears flow again. "Please take me back."

"Fucking stop crying!" A vein on the side of his temple pulsed and throbbed like an angry worm.

Claire sucked back a sob and willed her eyes to stop tearing, but it was no use. Her emotions were out of control. She trembled, and the pain in her head made her want to vomit.

"You could be in the trailer right now. I made you a bed and everything." Denver paced the barn.

The cougar screamed. Claire flinched. The animal's cries pierced her eardrums like a dental drill. "Please let me out. I promise not to run."

"I can't do that. You're lying. I know a lie, Blaire. I've lived with an alcoholic for twelve years. You *will* run, and you'll tell the sheriff about me. I can't trust you yet. No. You'll either adapt to your new life or you'll die."

Claire almost peed her pants when he pointed the gun at her face.

His mood shifted. His eyes went cold and dark. Whatever he was going to say, he meant it. "If I can't have you, no one can."

CHAPTER
THIRTY-SEVEN

In the passenger seat, Matt adjusted his earpiece. A half-moon glowed high in the clear night sky. Darkness had fallen in the time it had taken for warrants to be obtained and the team to gear up. Fueled by anticipation, adrenaline that had been trickling into Matt's bloodstream for the past several hours increased like a faucet had opened.

Behind the wheel, Bree pointed to the screen on the dashboard computer. They couldn't see the buildings from the road, but the map was on satellite mode, showing a clear picture of the property owned by Denver Sawyer. A clearing held a small house and a barn. The rest of the land was covered in trees. The property backed to Grey Lake.

"I don't see a dock," Matt noted.

Bree leaned over and squinted at the screen. "He could have a small boat tied on the bank, but I don't see where he could be hiding a significant vessel."

"The biggest thing he could have is a motorized inflatable."

Bree opened her vehicle door. Patrol cars parked behind them, with the K-9 unit at the back. She went to the rear hatch and opened it. Matt took the AR-15.

"Let's do this," Bree said as the team gathered. "Just like we planned. Radio silence unless absolutely necessary. We have no idea what or who we're going to find, but we want to sneak up on all of them."

They checked communications before heading in. They crept down the driveway. Tree branches blocked the moonlight. Matt's eyes adjusted to the dim, but he watched the shadows. The woods were thick enough to hide a man. He glanced back at Collins and Greta. No one could hide from the dog, which was why Matt loved having a K-9 team on board.

They approached the end of the driveway. The house turned out to be a trailer. Matt took a long breath, then listened. Branches rustled overhead as the wind ruffled the canopy. The team separated into three units, with the K-9 bringing up the rear. Matt and Bree circled around the trailer. The shades were drawn over the windows, but no light glowed inside.

Silently, Matt and Bree approached the front door of the trailer while Todd and Zucco circled around back. Across the yard, light shone from the windows high up on the barn walls. Matt pointed, and Bree nodded. She gestured toward the trailer, indicating she wanted to clear it first. She stepped up on the cinder block that served as a front step, then tried the doorknob. The door opened with no resistance. He glanced at Bree. Her face reflected his own surprise.

But then, the lock was so flimsy, why bother using it? Matt could have broken down the door with one kick. He stepped into the trailer. Bree came in behind him. She held her flashlight and used it sparingly, holding it low, shielding the light, and shining it into dark spaces. In the bedroom, a squawk startled Matt. His heart rate surged as he swung the AR-15 around. Bree's light illuminated two parrot-type birds in a cage.

Matt exhaled and lowered the rifle.

The trailer was small enough that they cleared it in less than a minute. Then they went out into the night, quietly pulling the door closed again.

With hand gestures, Bree indicated that the team was to move on to the barn search. They surrounded the building. Greta danced and emitted a soft whine. Collins quieted her with a whispered command but held her back.

The team surrounded the barn. An earsplitting scream pierced the hot, dry air. The sound reverberated in the humidity. Every hair on the back of Matt's neck stood straight up. There was no mistaking that distinct vocalization.

The cougar.

Matt and Bree approached the barn entrance. The rolling doors weren't completely closed, and a sliver of light sliced through the inch-wide gap. Matt put a shoulder to the door and peered through the opening. Claire stood under a bare light bulb. Her hands were bound and tied to the center post in the barn aisle. Behind her, Matt could see the cougar in a cage. The stressed animal crouched and cringed. Matt could sense its distress, and he couldn't imagine the other animals' primal response to having an apex predator housed right next to them. They all had to be terrified. Matt squinted into the shadows, trying to locate Denver. But his field of vision was limited. He needed to open the door.

The cougar's head swiveled. Its gaze locked with Matt's, and it screamed again. He went cold inside, like he'd just been hooked up to a chilled IV.

Denver stepped into view, his profile to Matt, a handgun aimed at Claire's head.

No! Matt wouldn't let her die. He lifted his AR-15 and nudged the door open wider. His finger curled around the trigger, but the angle, the shadows, and the dimness didn't give him the best targeting view. "Drop the gun!"

At his flank, Bree took aim. "Sheriff's department. Drop the weapon. Hands in the air."

"Fuck you!" Denver stepped sideways, putting Claire between him and the door and blocking any clear aim from either Matt or Bree.

I should have taken the shot from the doorway.

Denver moved forward and untied Claire's hands awkwardly with one hand. He dragged her back against his body, using her as a shield.

"Put it down, Denver." Bree moved to the right.

Matt shifted left. If they separated enough, one of them should be able to get a clear shot. He wouldn't make the same mistake again. He wouldn't hesitate to pull the trigger.

"Stop moving!" Denver shouted. "I'll shoot her."

"You don't want to kill her," Matt said. "She's your sister. She's your blood."

"She's ruined," Denver snapped. "She doesn't remember me. She's afraid of me."

"You're pointing a gun at her head," Matt said. "Of course she's afraid."

Bree moved ever so slightly farther to the right.

"Stop!" Denver's face reddened. He dragged Claire backward, toward the animals. He pulled her next to the cougar cage. Agitated, the animal swiped a huge paw at them, but the bars were too close together for it to make contact. The animal growled, mouth opening, teeth gleaming in the harsh light. Those teeth looked big enough to rip off a head.

In one move, Denver opened the cage and dived for the wall. The lights went out. Blackness fell over the barn.

And the cougar screamed.

CHAPTER THIRTY-EIGHT

Terror gripped Bree's insides like a huge fist. She put her back to Matt's. "Where's the cat?"

"No idea," Matt answered.

She'd largely put aside her fear of dogs, but an intense fear of loose cougars seemed reasonable.

Back to back, they spun in a slow circle. Bree stared into the dark corners. Something big moved on the left. Bree turned to face it, but she saw nothing. The monkeys shrieked. Other animals shifted restlessly, sensing danger. She couldn't sort the sounds. Her senses sharpened, her primal survival instinct awakened by the presence of an apex predator. She heard rustling, a low growl, and a throaty rumbling noise that made her go cold all over. The animal could be anywhere, sounded like it was everywhere. How high could a cougar jump? Could he get into the loft? Vader weighed fourteen pounds, and he could climb on top of the refrigerator. An eighty-pound cat must be able to jump high. Bree's gaze swept the darkness overhead.

"It'll probably run," Matt whispered. "They're elusive."

"Unless it's hungry. We don't know when he fed it last." She had no illusions regarding the cougar. In this scenario, humans were the prey. The big cat could land on one of them at any moment.

Bree listened hard, but there were too many animals in the barn to differentiate sounds and sources. "I can't see anything." She sidled toward the barn wall, toward the spot where Denver had flipped off the light switch. She could hear a big animal breathing. The cougar? Or one of the other animals? The breath sounded too deep to be a monkey or one of the capybaras.

"I'll bet the cougar can see us fine."

"Looking for the light." At the wall, Bree scraped her hand up and down the rough wood until her fingers encountered the switch. She flipped it. The bare bulb overhead turned on.

Just in time for her to see the long tawny tail of the cougar as it escaped out the barn door.

Fuck.

Matt ran after it.

She tapped her earpiece. "The cougar is loose! It ran out of the barn."

"I see it." Todd's voice sounded in her ear. "Aaand it's gone. The cat ran into the woods."

Now what?

Bree whirled, scanning the barn. "Where's Denver? And Claire? Does anyone see them?" Her gaze fell on a man-size door in the back of the barn. It was painted the same grayish-white as the interior of the barn. She hadn't noticed it before. She ran for it and grasped the handle. Unlocked. Leading with her weapon, she flung it open and swept her Glock from side to side.

No Denver. No Claire.

Where did that bastard take her? Claire must be . . . Bree couldn't even imagine the girl's emotional state. Her adoptive parents were murdered. She connected with her biological family only to be kidnapped by her brother for some reason Bree couldn't understand. Did

Claire know Denver had killed the Masons? Now he'd put Claire's life in danger—no! He'd actively threatened her life.

But she couldn't think about Claire's emotions—or Denver's motivation—right now. She needed a clear head to find the girl. She needed to save her life first, then she'd worry about the teen's trauma.

The girl could be hurt—or killed. Bree had seen plenty of dead people—all had been horrible—but more than a decade in law enforcement hardened a person.

Kids were different. You never got used to seeing a dead child. Images of Luke and Kayla flashed in Bree's mind. She had to save Claire.

She stepped out of the barn. The half-moon cast the weedy clearing in eerie gray light. Beyond, the woods were thick and dark. She scanned the tree line. Thirty feet away, a narrow trail disappeared into the forest.

"No sight of them on the west side," responded Todd for him and Zucco.

"The north side is clear," Collins said. "Checking the clearing. There's no one in front of the barn or around the trailer."

"There's a trail heading south, toward the lake." Bree walked toward it.

Matt's voice rang in her ear. "I'm right behind you."

He jogged across the open ground and took his place at her right flank, the rifle held comfortably across his body.

Bree shined her flashlight on the ground. "No footprints."

Matt crouched and pointed. "Broken underbrush. Looks like something went this way."

Bree updated the team. "Flynn and I are headed down the trail. Collins, I need you."

"On my way!" Collins responded.

Bree's earbud crackled, and Todd's voice sounded. "Zucco and I will try to cut off the suspect at the lake."

"Ten-four," Bree replied. She called in an update to dispatch and requested assistance from surrounding law enforcement officers. Given the location and distance from the interstate, it was unlikely that any state troopers were nearby. The neighboring town of Scarlet Falls was in her jurisdiction but also had its own PD. At minimum, surrounding LEOs could watch roads leading away from Grey's Hollow in case Denver managed to obtain a vehicle.

She heard motion behind her. Greta and Collins appeared. Bree and Matt stepped aside to let the K-9 team take the lead. Nose down, Greta sniffed in a circle, then picked up the fresh trail in a minute. Her head popped up, and she lunged forward, leaning into her harness with enthusiasm. The black shepherd loved the chase. Her job was a game to her.

The narrow trail forced them to move in single file. Bree jogged behind Collins. Matt brought up the rear.

"Do not forget there is a cougar on the loose," Bree reminded her team. She gripped her weapon in one hand and her flashlight in the other. With the beam pointed at the trail ahead of her feet, she headed into the darkness of the forest.

Where the cougar would be very comfortable. The cougar could have gone this way too.

Did Denver and Claire break the underbrush?

Or did the cougar?

Maybe it was all of the above.

An itch traveled up Bree's spine. Was the cat after Denver and Claire? As she followed the K-9 team into the darkness, she wondered who was hunting who.

CHAPTER
THIRTY-NINE

Matt jogged down the trail. Every ten steps or so, he checked behind them. A wild cougar shouldn't head toward three people and a K-9. They were making enough noise to startle any wild creature. But who knew this animal's history? Like the zoo director had theorized with the alligator, if it had been raised by humans, it might not fear them.

If this were a horror movie, the cat would totally be hunting the fuck out of the human who had imprisoned it.

If it ate Denver, Matt wasn't ashamed to admit that would bring a balance to the universe.

They kept up a fast pace, relying on the dog to guide them.

Denver had to know they'd give chase. There was no point in slowing down to sneak up on him. Five minutes later, the trail ended. They burst from the trees into the moonlight. Twenty feet of weedy, wet ground separated them from the bank of the lake.

Matt shined his light on the ground, which turned to muck at the lake's edge. He spotted footprints in the mud. "There."

Greta stopped and whined, then circled twice.

Matt looked out over the dark water, but saw nothing except the lake's flat, silvery surface. "He could have had a boat tied up under the trees." Matt crossed the grass to inspect the ground. He didn't see any sign that a boat had been dragged to the water.

"If he did, we're out of luck," Bree said. "We're always at the wrong end of the lake."

The sheriff's department had a dive boat, but it was docked at the other end of Grey Lake. The lake itself was miles long.

Greta sniffed along the edge of the lake.

"Maybe Denver thought walking in the water would hide his trail," Bree said.

But Matt had faith in the dog. Contrary to what people saw on TV, water did not impede the dog's ability to track. Scent clung to vegetation and debris in water. Cadaver dogs could even find bodies underwater. All walking through water did was waterlog your shoes.

Greta lifted her head and picked up speed.

"She's got the scent now," Collins called out, breaking into a jog again.

Todd spoke in the earpiece. "We see you. Coming out of the trees. No sign of the suspect or the cat."

The two figures of Todd and Deputy Zucco emerged from the forest and joined them.

Bree motioned for them to fall into place. The distance between the trees and the water narrowed, forcing the team to follow in single file.

Noise drifted from the lake, small splashes as paddles sliced through water. Matt spotted several lights and what appeared to be a double kayak. "Do you see those?"

"Yes," Todd said. "Kayaks or canoes, I think."

Voices and laughter drifted toward them. They walked another fifty yards. The boats drew closer. Three double kayaks and a canoe. A guy in the first kayak shined a portable spotlight ahead of his boat. The guy behind him held a large net. They slipped past with a polite wave.

"Gator hunters?" Todd asked.

"For fuck's sake." Bree sighed. "We don't have time for them. Let's hope they don't find it."

"With the amount of noise they're making, I wouldn't worry too much about them catching anything," Matt said.

Something splashed to his right. He whirled around, shining his light onto the water's surface. Ten yards away, at the edge of a patch of cattails, two red eyes glowed at him. *The alligator?* He blinked. Without making a sound, the creature disappeared below the surface.

Matt spoke into his earpiece. "Pretty sure I just saw the gator."

Ahead of him, Bree's stride faltered for a second, then evened out again, but she moved a little farther from the water's edge.

At three feet in length, the gator wasn't a threat to an adult human's life, but Matt swore he could feel the creature's eyes on his back.

CHAPTER FORTY

Claire stumbled, falling to her knees—again—in the shallow water. He'd made her run in six inches of water since they left the woods. To hide their trail, he'd said. She didn't think that would work, but she kept her opinion to herself. Denver didn't like to be told anything. He'd been clear about what he wanted from her. *Do what you're told and shut the fuck up.*

And he had a gun—so that's what she was doing.

Or at least trying to do. But her saturated sneakers were awkward and heavy, and the shore of the lake was alternately slippery and rocky. She didn't dare go barefoot. Her bound hands hit the lake and plunged to the slimy bottom. Water splashed into her eyes. Weeds and mud oozed between her fingers. She'd fallen three times and couldn't tell if the wetness on her face was water or tears.

"Get up!" Denver grabbed the back of her shirt and yanked. Instead of helping her regain her footing, the backward momentum threw her further off balance. She fell sideways, landing on her hip. Her butt struck a rock, and pain zinged through her hip and leg.

"I said get up, you stupid bitch!" Instead of any show of assistance, he lost it and kicked out at her.

His foot struck her side and knocked the air from her lungs. White-hot agony forced her body to curl. Her face went under for a second before she forced herself to her knees. "I'm trying." She spit out a mouthful of nasty lake water.

"Do you want to lie down and quit!" Denver grabbed the back of her neck. "Because I can make that happen." He thrust her head under. She wasn't prepared. Water flooded her mouth and nose, and her sinuses filled. She pushed against his grip, but he had leverage and strength on his side. Her lungs burned.

Panic bubbled in her throat. She clawed at the hand on the back of her neck, desperation making her sloppy. Her coordination flagged and her claws became slaps. Bubbles escaped from her mouth.

That was it, then.

I'm going to die.

Maybe I deserve it.

She couldn't hold her breath any longer. She was going to inhale. Her arms went limp. Her hands dropped into the water.

The pressure on the back of her neck released, and Denver hauled her up like a drowning puppy.

She gasped and fluttered. Her stomach clenched, and she vomited lake water. Over the sounds of her own retching, she could hear Denver laughing.

A tiny sliver of hate sliced through her anger. She was his only sister. His blood relative. Wasn't that what he'd told her? They were family. All they had was each other.

He'd lied to her. Just like everyone else.

Lies. Lies. Lies.

Her whole life was lies.

He jerked her arm. "Now get the fuck up and move or I'll drown you for real."

Claire rose to her feet and stumbled forward. She wouldn't be able to keep up this pace for long.

"It's not too much farther," he said, as if reading her mind. His hand hit the center of her back, shoving her forward. She barely stayed on her feet.

"Shut it." Denver yanked her sideways, hauling her behind a tree that leaned over the water. A few kayaks floated past. Men laughed and talked. A beer-can tab popped. Claire wanted to jump out, to swim toward them and yell for help. She drew in a breath, preparing herself.

Denver wrapped a hand over her mouth. "I'll kill them all."

She forced her body to relax. She may as well accept her fate. She was doomed. It was her own fault. She should accept that too.

The boats passed, and Denver pulled her out from behind the tree trunk.

"You have a plan?" She put a hand on her queasy stomach. A light shimmered on the lake. Not moonlight. Artificial light at the end of a dock.

"Of course I have a plan," he snapped, clearly insulted. He grabbed the back of her hair, turning her head.

A house sat on a rise—a big, expensive house with lots of glass overlooking the lake.

"We're here." He pulled her from the water, taking her hand in an almost-friendly grip. His moods shifted faster than she could keep up.

A few lights inside the house let them peer right into it.

"Looks like a fucking fishbowl," Denver said, dragging her up the back lawn. He ducked behind a planter and pulled her down to the grass with him. Then he glanced over his shoulder. The sheriff wouldn't be far behind. Claire knew they'd come after her. They wanted to save her. Wanted to help her. And all she did was make things worse.

Denver turned his attention to the house above them. Two decks, multiple sets of sliding doors, and lots of windows spanned the back of the house. A great room and big kitchen were visible through the clear glass. A slim redheaded woman in blue pajamas in the kitchen poured water from a kettle into a mug. The woman carried her mug out of the room, turning off the lights when she left. Another light turned on behind a different set of sliding doors on the upper deck. The blinds were closed, making Claire think the woman had gone into her bedroom. Denver tugged her toward the house. At the base of the wooden steps, he said, "Ditch the shoes. They're squeaking."

She toed them off, and he dragged her up the stairs.

Claire had left the Zuccos' house so they didn't get hurt. Now, Denver was going to hurt—or kill—this other innocent woman.

All my fault.

She'd been so stupid. Falling for his lies like a child.

We're going to be a family. I'll take care of you.

All bullshit.

But resisting was pointless. Denver was stronger than her, and he had a gun. He pulled Claire forward. He took the gun from his waistband and started across the deck. Instead of heading toward the woman, he steered Claire toward the sliding doors that led into the great room. The main lights had been turned off, but there were a few small night-lights plugged into outlets at knee height through the space. They emitted enough light for them to see through the glass from the darkness outside. The great room and kitchen were empty.

He shoved the gun into his pocket, then placed both hands flat on the glass and lifted the entire panel. To Claire's surprise, he lifted the whole glass door out of its track and slid it to one side.

She stood, stunned by how easily he'd broken into the house.

"Come on," he hissed.

She glanced back. She could jump off the deck. She wouldn't die, but she might break a leg. If she ran, would he shoot? Would he give himself away by firing at her? He could miss. It was dark. She'd be moving.

If I can't have you, no one can.

If she weren't a coward, she'd run and take her chances on his aim in the dark. The gunshots would warn this unsuspecting homeowner. Claire tensed, readying herself to lunge away. Before she could move, Denver grabbed a handful of her hair and pulled her into the house. Pain screeched through her scalp.

She'd waited too long. Again. She and the woman were doomed. Her cowardice would be the end of them both.

Claire's feet stumbled over one another as she tried to keep up with Denver. He used her hair to guide her movements, forcing her to march through the big room. They moved into the kitchen. She eyed the pots and pans hanging from a rack. They passed a full knife block, but she couldn't reach it.

Denver steered her toward a doorway that led into a short hall. Leaning close, he whispered "Shh" in her ear and gave her hair a tug for emphasis. Her scalp was beginning to go numb from the pain. His grip pulled her slightly off balance. They shuffled closer. Light glowed from a room at the end.

Just like the Masons' bedroom.

And Claire knew without a doubt that Denver was going to kill the woman in her bed.

CHAPTER FORTY-ONE

A light appeared ahead. Bree stopped and scanned the landscape. "Hold up!"

Ahead, Collins commanded the dog in German. Greta dropped to her belly, but she lay rigid as a Sphinx, her focus riveted on the house.

A back lawn sloped upward to a large house with a massive deck and big expanses of glass to take advantage of the views. A dock jutted out onto the lake like a pointed finger. At its base, a long metal trap held a raw chicken carcass.

The alligator trap set by the zoo's reptile guy.

"I know where we are." Bree studied the back of the house. A mosquito droned near her face. She waved it off as the mossy scent of lake water drifted to her.

Matt stepped up next to her. "Madeline Jager's place. I should have known we were close when I saw the gator."

"Now we have to worry about Claire *and* Jager." Bree studied the back of the house. "The great room looks dark, but there's a light at the other end of the house. Jager's bedroom?"

"Probably." Matt squinted into the night. "Looks like one of the deck sliders is open."

"Denver probably went inside." Bree's gaze swept the building again. "What's his goal?"

"He might be after a vehicle." Matt adjusted his grip on his rifle. "He already has a hostage."

"He doesn't need to keep Jager alive." Bree moved forward.

They crept closer. Through the glass on the back of the house, Bree saw two figures moving through the dark kitchen. She directed the team to split up. Collins and Greta would remain outside in case the suspect ran. Bree didn't want the dog alerting Denver inside the house before they had a clearer picture of what was happening or how many people were inside. Jager could have company. Todd and Zucco would move toward the front of the house, look for a way in, and block Denver in case he attempted to exit the front door to access the detached garage.

Bree and Matt headed for the deck steps—and the open sliding door.

The second tread squeaked. Bree froze. Matt's shoulder bumped hers. They waited. A cricket chirped. The cry of an owl carried over the water. When no sound or motion—or bullets—came from the house, Bree started to climb again, keeping to the side of the steps, where the treads had support. She transferred her weight carefully to each step. They reached the deck and crept across the boards to the open slider.

Bree glanced inside. Night-lights showed an empty room. With Matt at her flank, she swept her Glock into each shadow. They passed through the kitchen, dimly lit by another night-light in an outlet set in the backsplash. Sweat trickled down Bree's spine and gathered at the small of her back.

Voices murmured from a doorway. Bree continued toward them. A light shone at the end of a hall, but most of the room wasn't in her line of sight. With Matt behind her, they stole down the corridor. At the entrance to a room, she put her shoulder to the wall and pulled out her cell phone. Turning on the camera, she inched the lens on the device around the doorjamb. Better than risking her face. On the tiny screen,

Denver pointed a gun at a king-size bed. He held Claire by the hair with the other. Claire was between Bree and Denver. In the bed, Jager reclined against pillows, a book splayed on her lap. She was helpless, at Denver's mercy.

Like Josh and Shelly Mason, Bree realized with a sick feeling. An image of the bloody body on the white sheets flashed into her mind. She blinked it away.

"I know you're there," Denver said in a cool voice. "Come on in, or I'll blow her brains all over her wall. You know I will. I've done it before."

Bree withdrew her phone. She motioned for Matt to circle around to the glass slider or a window, where he'd hopefully have a clear shot at Denver. She stepped into the room, her gun pointed at Denver. "Put down the gun, Denver. You can't escape. The house is surrounded."

He waggled the gun pointed at Jager. "She has a car. I'm taking it and driving out of here."

Bree heard the team responding, reorganizing in her earpiece.

"I'll kill both of them." He must have pulled Claire's hair because she yelped. "You shouldn't worry about this one anyway." Denver paused for effect. "She's as guilty as I am."

Bree's heart thudded. "What do you mean?"

"She helped me." Denver's voice rose with glee. "How do you think I knew when the Masons would be in bed, that the security system would be off, the best way to get into the house? She wanted them dead too."

"I don't believe you." But in the back of Bree's mind, pieces of the case began snapping into place like LEGOs. Denver hadn't needed to know the Masons' routines. He didn't need to know the layout of the house or the time the Masons turned on their alarm system.

Because Claire did.

A second thought sent a chill into her marrow: *How much of the investigation was based on Claire's statements?*

"Why would Claire do that?" Bree needed to stall until Matt got into place.

"Because the Masons were shit." Denver's tone turned bitter. "Josh killed our dad. Then he stole Blaire and ruined my whole life. He wanted to do nasty things to her. Right, Blaire?"

Claire's legs sagged. Her head lolled forward for a few seconds. When she lifted it, her eyes were bleak with shame—utterly hopeless—as if she didn't want to draw another breath. But she didn't deny Denver's claim.

Even as Bree questioned how Denver had learned the truth, she knew he wasn't lying this time. Claire had helped him kill Josh Mason. What teenager could deal with learning her adoptive father had murdered her biological one? On top of all that, it sounded as if Josh had also made inappropriate advances on Claire. Bree hoped he hadn't succeeded.

Claire shook her head. She wasn't crying. She'd shut down. "I did it. I helped him kill them." She spoke in a monotone, her voice emotionless, dead.

Bree didn't waver. "Claire will face the consequences of whatever she's done, but I'm not going to let you take her anywhere."

"Oh, really?" Denver focused on Jager and straightened his arm. He was going to shoot her. His eyes gleamed with anticipation. He wanted to do it. Wanted to kill. Wanted to inflict pain on others to somehow compensate for his own. To make other people—anyone and everyone—pay for the damage he'd suffered.

Helplessness swamped Bree. She couldn't shoot him without risking Claire's life. Bree started forward, as if she could stop him—and his bullets—with her bare hands.

"No!" Claire spun and flailed at him. He shoved her away, pointed the gun at Jager, and pulled the trigger as Claire gathered a foot under her body and launched herself into the air. The gun went off, the sound echoing. Claire landed on the bench at the foot of the bed. A red stain bloomed on her shoulder.

No! Bree's heart stumbled. Whatever Claire had done, Bree couldn't let her die. But before she could save the girl, she had to eliminate the threat.

Movement flashed in Bree's peripheral vision: Jager rolling out of bed and taking cover.

With Claire out of the way, Bree fired at Denver, but he was already turning and shooting back at her. She dropped to the floor, squeezing off two more rounds as her knee smashed into the carpet. A quick flash of pain burst up her leg before adrenaline numbed it. A bullet whizzed by her head and stuck in the door. Bits of wood splintered and exploded into the air. She crawled behind the bed and took aim over the mattress.

The sliding glass door shattered. Glass pebbles rained across the floor like marbles. Matt stood on the other side, the butt of his rifle raised. He'd broken the door to get to them.

Someone groaned.

Claire.

The bloom of blood on her shirt was spreading quickly. Too quickly.

With Matt cutting off his escape path, Denver turned and raced for the bedroom door. On his way, he fired two shots toward Matt, who withdrew behind the doorframe.

Bree fired a shot at Denver as he disappeared down the hall toward the kitchen. Matt crouched in the doorway, rifle at the ready.

Bree waved him back toward the door. "He's headed toward the kitchen."

Matt went after him, charging through the room.

Bree had a choice. Stay and save Claire or chase Denver.

She headed for Claire, using her radio to update the team of Denver's retreat. Then she called for an ambulance. Regret already knotted her gut. She hated sending someone else—even her well-trained team—to do a dangerous job instead of doing it herself. It was the one type of delegation she couldn't accept. Yet she had no choice.

"I need a towel!" she yelled.

Jager shoved a thick white hand towel into her hands. It was folded in a fancy square, with a monogrammed *MJ* showing on the top. The bullet had pierced Claire's shoulder. Bree rolled the girl and checked for an exit wound. None. Settling her on her back, Bree placed the folded towel over the wound and pressed down.

Jager nudged Bree out of the way. "You go. I've got this."

"You're sure?"

Jager knelt. The blue silk of her pajama set soaked up blood as she used her stacked palms and body weight to apply pressure. "Yes. Go."

Bree scrambled to her feet. She could hear the team in her earpiece. Matt was in the lead. Bree headed for the door, sliding on a carpet of glass beads. Matt had gone through the house. Bree would try to cut off Denver outside.

Please. Don't. Die.

CHAPTER FORTY-TWO

Matt crept down the dark hallway toward the kitchen.

In case Denver had gone out the front door, Todd and Zucco had jogged off in that direction. Collins and Greta had the backyard covered. No sign of Denver by either team.

He's still in the house.

Matt breathed. He held the rifle close, ready to use it. Would Denver hide? Or would he run? He'd said he was going to take Jager's car. He'd need to go outside and cross the driveway to the detached garage. Denver didn't know the house. Matt was willing to bet he'd exit through the same door he entered rather than take time and potentially get trapped inside.

He slipped through the kitchen and emerged into the great room in time to see Denver dart out the open slider.

Matt raced toward the door. Denver ducked behind a huge potted plant and fired a shot at Matt. The bullet zinged past, striking the deck railing with a dull *thwack*.

Matt dropped to one knee and fired a single shot from his rifle. His bullet struck the side of the pot. Ceramic shards scattered. Denver was pinned down. There was no escape, unless he wanted to jump over the deck railing. But the ground was at least a fifteen-foot drop. If he went over the edge, he'd likely break an ankle. Matt shifted his position, trying to get a shot at Denver, but all he saw was an occasional flash of color.

"Come out!" Matt yelled. "You're surrounded. The only way you're getting out of this is to surrender. Toss your gun onto the deck and come out with your hands in the air."

Instead of answering, Denver fired another shot in Matt's direction. But he hadn't taken the risk of putting his head over the planter's edge. His shot had been a Hail Mary, fired without aiming. The bullet went wide.

How many bullets did he have left? Did he have extra ammunition?

Denver might be pinned, but he had good cover. No one could get close without risking a bullet.

A voice sounded in his earpiece. "K-9 coming in hot."

Nails scrambled on wood. The jet-black shepherd streaked onto the deck and leaped behind the planter. A high-pitched, terrified scream split the air. The dog's head jerked as she dragged him out by his lower leg.

Levered on one arm, Denver aimed his handgun at the dog's head, barely three feet from the gun's muzzle. At that range, he couldn't miss. Matt tried to take aim, but the dog's back-and-forth motions kept putting her in the way. Two shots rang out. Matt's heart clenched. *No!* He waited for the beautiful dog to go limp, but instead, Denver flopped onto the wood. The handgun clattered to the deck as he went still.

In Matt's chest, disbelief warred with shock. *How?*

He glanced back. Bree stood on the second deck, her arms outstretched over the railing, her weapon aimed straight at Denver from above.

Matt couldn't breathe for a full minute. Then relief surged through him like an electric current. When he started forward, his knees wobbled for the first two strides.

"Cover me." Matt jogged toward Denver. His gun lay on the wood a few inches from his hand. Matt kicked it away. "Get the dog!"

Collins rushed up the steps and commanded Greta to release. The dog's adrenaline was pumping, and Collins had to physically haul her off the man's body. Todd and Zucco came up the steps behind Collins.

Matt put two fingers to Denver's neck. A thin pulse thrummed. "He's alive. Call an ambulance." Matt cuffed him and patted him down for additional weapons before assessing his wounds. Bree's bullet had struck him dead center in the chest. "I need a first aid kit."

A miracle would be even more handy. Denver was leaking blood. A puddle was forming under his body. Matt had nothing to use as a pressure bandage. He carried a tourniquet, but that wouldn't help with a chest wound.

Todd sprinted off. The bedroom deck wasn't connected to the main one. Bree disappeared from sight only to reappear a minute later exiting the great room through the open slider. She said nothing as she approached, but Matt didn't see any regret on her face as she handed him a folded towel.

Matt pressed it to Denver's wound and applied pressure. Blood continued to pool on the wood. Not good.

Denver had presented a clear and present threat to everyone. He'd already shot a teenager—his own sister—just a few minutes before, and he'd murdered two other people earlier in the week. Bree had neutralized the threat, nothing more. Matt had no doubt the DA would agree the shooting had been justified.

"Ambulance is on the way." Bree nodded at Denver. "How is he?"

Matt shrugged. "Still alive." But Matt wouldn't put money on him staying that way. Pressure wasn't helping all that much. The folded hand towel was already soaked through. "Todd's getting the first aid kit. How's Claire?"

"Shoulder wound. Jager's with her."

"Jager stayed calm."

"She did," Bree agreed.

Todd returned, and Matt stepped aside to let him work. But there wasn't much to be done without a surgeon and an operating room.

"Ambulance and EMTs are three minutes away." Bree walked to Matt, right into his arms. So much for her usual policy of no PDAs on duty.

He wrapped his arms around her and pulled her close. "Once again, we didn't die."

"Yeah," she said to his chest. "Not dying is good."

Days of tension ebbed out of Matt's muscles. "I love you."

"Same."

CHAPTER
FORTY-THREE

Styrofoam cup in hand, Bree paced the hospital waiting room. Previous cups churned in her stomach.

Dozing in a plastic chair, Matt opened his eyes and rubbed the back of his neck. He rolled his head on his shoulders as if his neck ached. "How many of those have you had?" He nodded toward the cup.

She looked down at the coffee. "I have no idea."

Matt stood and stretched. "Any word on Claire?"

Bree had refused to leave until she could see Claire. Denver had been DOA at the hospital. "She's going to be OK. They're stitching her up. The bullet didn't hit anything vital."

"That's a relief."

Bree tossed back the contents of her cup. "It is." But she didn't feel relieved.

A nurse walked in. "Sheriff Taggert, you can see her now."

Bree and Matt followed her down the hall. They stopped outside a private room, where a deputy stood guard. Claire was handcuffed to the bed. A bandage peeked out from the neck of her hospital gown. Her face was hospital-sheet white.

Matt leaned on the wall.

Bree stepped up to the bed. "Hey, Claire."

Claire turned her face to the wall. "How could you want to see me?"

Bree said nothing, but she put one of her hands on top of Claire's and gave it a small squeeze. Despite Claire admitting to helping Denver, she was still a traumatized minor—and she was still alone and vulnerable.

A tear trickled down Claire's cheek. "I'm sorry. I'm sorry for everything."

"You don't have to talk right now," Bree said. "I just wanted to make sure you were all right."

"I want to. I want to get it out." Claire sniffed. "Denver contacted me a couple of months ago. He came into the store when I was working. At first, what he had to say freaked me out, but he kept coming. The store has a coffee shop. We started meeting before or after my shift. The more he talked, the more his story made sense. Josh had been . . ." Claire licked her lips. "His attitude changed toward me over the past couple of years. When I was little, he mostly ignored me. Shelly treated me like a doll. When I got bigger, she lost interest. But Josh *became* interested. He started accidentally walking in on me while I was in the shower and bumping into me in the hall. I could feel his . . . you know." Her face went red.

Bree watched her face. She looked sincere. But she'd lied so much, Bree wondered if any of this was true either. Josh might have made inappropriate advances. Then again, what if Claire had made it up to justify what she'd done?

"I wasn't allowed to have friends or join a sports team. Except for school and work, they kept me isolated. When Denver said he wanted to make them pay for killing our dad, I went along with it." Claire blinked away for a few seconds. "He said our dad had been a great guy. He said our family had been happy back then." A tear rolled down her pale cheek. "I wanted *that* family. I wanted a family that loved me. Josh and Shelly never did, not the way parents are supposed to."

But you can't go back. Bree knew this better than most.

"How did Denver find out that Josh killed Dallas Sawyer?" Bree asked.

"He was cleaning out his mother's attic and found an old file of his dad's. His dad—our dad—Dallas—worked for Josh. The company was a fraud, and Dallas was blackmailing him. He was pretty sure Josh had done it, but Denver wanted to make sure. So, he watched the Masons for a while. When he saw me, he knew who I was immediately—and that was his final proof. He confronted Josh a few weeks ago when Josh was out running. Josh laughed in his face and said he couldn't prove anything."

"Did Josh say why he took you?"

Claire shook her head. "Josh told Denver to fuck off."

Josh had been too smart to admit to a crime.

"Who chased you at the playground?" Bree asked.

"That was Denver. He wanted to throw off the investigation with misinformation. Liam already had a record. I'd seen him dropping off Amanda a couple of times. I knew what his tattoo looked like."

And she set up Liam with no remorse?

"What about Peter Vitale?" Bree asked. "Do you know him?"

Claire shook her head. "I never met him, but Shelly complained about his emails so many times, I knew you'd find those on your own."

But Claire had mentioned the angry client in her first interview to be sure Bree looked for him.

"Why did you leave the Zuccos' house tonight?" Bree asked.

"I like them." Claire picked at the edge of the tape holding her IV to her forearm. "Denver kept texting me. Half promises, half threats. I didn't want to go. Once I met my bio mom, I knew he'd been lying to me. All the times we met, he never mentioned she was an alcoholic—that she was so . . . awful. But if I had stayed, Denver would have come after me. He would have killed anyone who kept me away from him.

He acted like he owned me. They would try to protect me, and he'd hurt them. I couldn't let that happen."

Truth or lie?

"Do you know why Denver stole Josh's and Shelly's personal electronics?" Bree asked.

Claire stopped picking. "He wanted to break their codes and get access to their money. He was convinced they had offshore accounts."

They probably did.

"Get some rest." Bree released her hand. "We'll talk again." She didn't have a good read on Claire, but Bree was done. She needed sleep—and time to process everything Claire had told her.

"What's going to happen to me?" Claire picked harder at the tape.

Bree did the only thing she could. She was honest. "I don't know. It's not up to me."

Because Bree was taking a giant step back. With everyone safe, it was time to rest, recharge, and regroup. Bree had identified with Claire too well. She'd put herself—and her kids—in Claire's place. Bree hadn't maintained objectivity.

And that could have put the case—and her team—at risk.

"Do you think Renata would keep my cat?" Claire asked. "I don't want him to go to the shelter. He might be the only thing that ever loved me for me."

Truth. Heartbreaking truth.

"I'll ask her," Bree said.

"Thank you."

She and Matt left the room. Bree nodded to her deputy as she passed.

"What do you think?" she asked Matt once they were out of Claire's earshot. "We still don't know why Josh took her."

"Based on what Claire just said, Josh killed Dallas. The kid was in the car. She was a witness, so he had to kill her or take her. Shelly wanted a kid. Maybe that's all it was." He shrugged. "With Denver dead, all we have is Claire's word on everything, and Claire has lied extensively. So who knows?"

Bree agreed. "She lied smoothly. So why should we believe her now?" She waved a hand in the general direction of Claire's room. "She could have made all that up. How would we know?"

"Good point," Matt said.

"Well, fool me once and all that." Bree sighed. "I'll file my reports and leave the rest to the DA, the judge, a psychiatrist, et cetera. This will be one of those times when the system will have to sort out the mess."

"Claire is either a manipulated victim or a psychopath," Matt said.

"And I don't have the skill set to make that determination."

"But you have an opinion."

"I think not everything is black and white. She could be both of those things to some extent. But I am feeling a little manipulated." Or maybe she was uncomfortable with the way she had trusted Claire.

Why did I believe everything she said?

Matt nodded. "And yet you were still kind and compassionate." He turned Bree to face him. "Even though you felt like she was using you."

Bree's mouth turned in a wry half smile. "I know it makes me seem like a sucker, but at the end of the day, I have to live with myself. Experiencing trauma at a young age can affect you for your whole life."

Matt gave her a quick kiss. "That's why I love you. One of the reasons anyway. You don't let your ego get in the way of being a good cop—or doing the right thing." He drew back, studying her face. "You experienced childhood trauma, and you're not a killer."

She cocked her head. "And yet I'm not very upset that I killed a man tonight. I should be."

"It was justified."

"I believe so, but that doesn't mean it should be easy." Bree was more disturbed by her lack of remorse than the act itself. What did that mean?

"You're not a killer, Bree." He gave her biceps a gentle shake. "Denver made the choices that led to his death tonight."

"Either way, I'm the one who pulled the trigger."

Chapter Forty-Four

The next morning, Bree stared at her phone screen, where her therapist stared back.

"I blocked most of my childhood memories for decades," Bree said. "Why am I suddenly seeing and hearing my mother?"

"What kind of memories are you having?"

"Good ones." Bree tapped a finger on her steering wheel. "Until recently, I never had a good memory of my mother. All I saw were flashes of my father's rage—and detailed replays of the night he killed her. But now, I'm suddenly seeing other aspects of her. In my mind, she's becoming a whole person, not just his victim."

"She was a whole person, Bree, but you were hurting too much to see what you were missing."

"And now?"

"You're a different person. You've grown. You have emotional connections. You have a support system. You're secure enough to deal with the pain and grief. You can miss her now."

"Seems kind of late."

"Better late than never. How do the memories make you feel?"

Bree thought about that. "Not terrible. Sad, but it's nice to know she loved me."

Her childhood memories were jumbled inside her like Scrabble letters in a felt bag. Here she was taking them out, one by one, decades later, and trying to put them in some sort of order.

"Don't be afraid of the memories. Embrace them. Feel whatever they make you feel."

"But I don't want emotions to affect my work. The case we just finished . . ." Bree gave a quick summary of key aspects of the investigation. "I identified too well with Claire. Maybe because of my violent history, or because I projected my own or Luke's and Kayla's trauma onto her. Whatever the reason, I took what she told us at face value. I should have questioned more."

"You thought she was a victim."

"Yes, but I don't like that I wasn't objective. I don't like that my preconceived assessment of her affected how I conducted the investigation."

Her therapist lifted a hand. "Well, I'm sorry to say that you're an actual human, Bree. Unless you want to turn policing over to artificial intelligence, you can never completely remove the human element from your job."

A few minutes later, her session ended, and she frowned at her phone for a few minutes. Did she feel better or worse? She never knew.

The sessions left her tired, though.

Someday, she'd ask her therapist why she hadn't felt remorse after killing Denver Sawyer—and others. But today, she wasn't sure she wanted to know. She could process only so much self-revelation at one time.

She went back to her office. Todd and Matt were in the conference room, typing reports. She dropped into a chair. "Tell me we're tying neat bows on every thread."

"Maybe not every thread, but it's coming along," said Matt. "The zoo has taken charge of the animals in Denver's barn."

"Excellent," Bree said.

Todd pointed at his laptop. "One of Denver's shoes matched the partial footprint we found outside the Masons' house."

Matt said, "Here's something interesting. Claire had a key inside her phone case with the initials *SFCC* on it."

Bree's brain chugged at the initials. "Scarlet Falls Country Club?"

"Yep. Shelly Mason played tennis there. She had a locker."

"Do I want to know what was in the locker?"

Matt met her gaze. "Another go-bag. Money, fake IDs for Shelly and Claire."

Bree didn't know why she was surprised. "Shelly had her own escape hatch?"

"Maybe she didn't trust Josh," Todd suggested.

More LEGO bricks snapped into place in Bree's mind. "That's probably where Claire was headed when Denver grabbed her."

"That would be my guess," Matt agreed. "She was going to make a run for it."

Bree's phone vibrated. "It's Jager." Funny, she didn't dread answering like she usually did. "Taggert."

Jager said, "Did you see Pam Sawyer's press con?"

"She had a press con?" Bree stared at the phone. She couldn't have heard correctly. "Right after her son died and her daughter was shot?"

"Yep."

"That's cold."

"She tried to pin her family issues on you, but the press wasn't buying it. They asked her about her daughter's condition, and she couldn't answer. She hasn't even been to the hospital to see Claire, whom you saved."

"My team saved Claire," Bree said. "With your help."

"You and your team saved me too. Thank you." Jager's appreciation sounded genuine.

"What did Pam want?" Bree asked.

"Money, of course, but thankfully, the press framed her for exactly what she is, a lying, greedy psychopath."

"I should be glad?" Bree asked.

"Her lawsuit probably won't go anywhere, so yes. Be glad. About everything. Nice work. By the way, the alligator was in the trap this morning."

But the cougar had disappeared.

"Thank you." Bree ended the call. How did she feel about that conversation? Weird. Definitely weird.

A knock on the door interrupted them. Zucco peered into the conference room. "Any word on what's going to happen to Claire?"

"Nothing definite," Bree said. "She actively assisted in a double murder. She's going to be in custody for some time. She asked if you would keep the cat."

"Yeah. Sure. He's no trouble. Mom likes him."

Bree eyed her deputy's dark circles. Then scrutinized the other faces in the room. Her whole team had been working day and night on the case. They looked ragged. "Go home, Zucco. Take the rest of the day off."

"Yes, ma'am." Zucco ducked out.

Bree closed the files and addressed Todd and Matt. "You're both exhausted. Both of you take the rest of the day off as well. That's an order."

Todd and Matt closed their files.

Todd was already on his feet and headed for the door. "I'm taking Cady to lunch."

"How about you?" Bree poked Matt's impressive bicep.

"I have a date with a Belgian mal."

"I hope he works out," Bree said. "Last night highlighted the importance of having K-9s."

"Can't count the number of times a dog saved my ass."

"Our asses," Bree corrected. "I'll do whatever I have to do to raise the money."

Exhaustion washed over her. She'd barely slept for days, and the therapy session had left her wrung out. "I want to go home and take a nap."

Matt wrapped an arm around her shoulders. "Why don't you? I'll work with the mal for an hour or so. We could go for a ride afterward, maybe Luke and Kayla can come too. The heat finally broke."

"Luke had a riding date this morning. Might be fun to be there when they get back. I'd like to meet the girl." Bree thought about saddling up their horses. Sunlight dappling the trail. The smell of the countryside and animals in her nose. The rhythmic movement of the horse beneath her. Heaven. Absolute heaven. In her opinion, an afternoon with her family, horses, and dogs was the best therapy in the world.

She was incredibly lucky to have found peace after the tragedies that scarred her past. She silently repeated her new mantra: *I will not feel guilty for being happy.* If she kept saying it, someday she might believe it.

"Take the day, Bree," Matt said. "You deserve it."

Could she do that? Just leave, with work and messages still piled on her desk?

She leaned into Matt's arm. Yes, she could. Her job was just work. Her family and Matt were her life and heart.

Besides, she might as well enjoy some downtime before there was another murder.

ACKNOWLEDGMENTS

Special thanks to the writer friends who helped me develop this concept: Rayna Vause, Kendra Elliot, Leanne Sparks, Toni Anderson, Amy Gamet, and Loreth Anne White. Cheers, ladies! As always, credit goes to my agent, Jill Marsal, for her continued unwavering support and solid career advice. I'm also grateful for the entire team at Montlake, especially my acquiring editor, Anh Schluep, and my developmental editor, Charlotte Herscher. As far as teams go, I am lucky to have the best.

ABOUT THE AUTHOR

Photo © 2016 Jared Gruenwald Photography

Melinda Leigh is the #1 Amazon Charts and #1 *Wall Street Journal* bestselling author of *She Can Run*, an International Thriller Award nominee for Best First Novel, *She Can Tell, She Can Scream, She Can Hide*, and *She Can Kill* in the She Can series; *Midnight Exposure, Midnight Sacrifice, Midnight Betrayal*, and *Midnight Obsession* in the Midnight Novels; *Hour of Need, Minutes to Kill*, and *Seconds to Live* in the Scarlet Falls series; *Say You're Sorry, Her Last Goodbye, Bones Don't Lie, What I've Done, Secrets Never Die*, and *Save Your Breath* in the Morgan Dane series; and *Cross Her Heart, See Her Die, Drown Her Sorrows, Right Behind Her, Dead Against Her, Lie to Her, Catch Her Death, On Her Watch*, and the short story "Her Second Death" in the Bree Taggert series. Melinda has garnered numerous writing awards, including two RITA nominations; holds a second-degree black belt in Kenpo karate and has taught women's self-defense; and lives in a messy house with her family and a small herd of rescue pets. For more information, visit www.melindaleigh.com.